T0208920

Pawns in an endless war, scribes are feared and worshipped, valued and exploited, prized and hunted. But there is only one whose powers can determine the fate of the world . . .

Born into the ruins of Rzolka's brutal civil unrest, Anna has never known peace. Here, in her remote village—a wasteland smoldering in the shadows of outlying foreign armies—being imbued with the magic of the scribes has made her future all the more uncertain.

Through intricate carvings of the flesh, scribes can grant temporary invulnerability against enemies to those seeking protection. In an embattled world where child scribes are sold and traded to corrupt leaders, Anna is invaluable. Her scars never fade. The immunity she grants lasts forever.

Taken to a desert metropolis, Anna is promised a life of reverence, wealth, and fame—in exchange for her gifts. She believes she is helping to restore her homeland, creating gods and kings for an immortal army—until she witnesses the hordes slaughtering without reproach, sacking cities, and threatening everything she holds dear. Now, with the help of an enigmatic assassin, Anna must reclaim the power of her scars—before she becomes the unwitting architect of an apocalyptic war.

Visit us at www.kensingtonbooks.com

Scribes

The Scribe Cycle

James Wolanyk

REBEL BASE BOOKS
Kensington Publishing Corp.
www.kensingtonbooks.com

First Electronic Edition: February 2018
eISBN-13: 978-1-63573-020-3
eISBN-10: 1-63573-020-1

First Print Edition: February 2018
ISBN-13: 978-1-63573-023-4
ISBN-10: 1-63573-023-6

Printed in the United States of America

To those who show compassion, and to those who need it most.

Acknowledgements

Nothing occurs in a vacuum. A body is formed and sustained by chemical interactions, no different from stars that are molded by gravity, time, and countless other forces acting upon it. All things influence and cause one another, from missile strikes to the words we speak to one another, and with this fact in mind, this book is a product of everything that came before it. A product of my mother's enduring support, my father's kindness and guidance in life, my brother's humor, my teachers' patience, and my sense of hope, which the world has nurtured in me since birth.

Chapter 1

Their baying rose from the southern bogs, low and tortured, warning fieldmen to gather roaming sows and bleary eyed mothers to bolt their shutters. Then came the screeching that told caravan drivers to seek refuge behind earthworks and palisades.

But the targets of their hunt had no time to think of shelter.

Anna, First of Tomas, was too busy thinking of death. She wondered if it would be sudden and painless, numbing her exhaustion like bathing in winter streams. Perhaps death was agonizing, which explained the sobs of feverish men who—

Just two leagues, she reminded herself, even as her steps faltered among the oaks and saplings and lichen-choked stone, all looming monstrously in the fog. Even as her pulse drummed in her temples. *The lake is two leagues away.* But the air was humid and foul, too thick to breathe. Everything smelled of carcasses reclaimed by the mud.

Her predictions had placed the trackers at five leagues by dawn, yet beyond the latticework of branches, the skies were still a murky wash. Darkness hadn't yet been flushed from the horizon. No, it was impossible for them to make up this much ground before sunrise. They'd come earlier every year, ever since the village started to learn their tactics, but this was calculated.

Somebody told.

"What is it?" Julek winced. "You're hurting me."

Anna glanced down. She'd absently clamped onto her brother's wrist, turning his fingers a pallid blue. Her grip eased as she focused on the predawn stillness. Mother often told her that she had their kin's sharpest ears, but now she hated the honor. She heard the rustling of shrubs, the startled flight of a thousand birds, the slap of paws on damp reeds as huntsmen cut across the floodplains.

"Nothing," she said, hoping the boy was too young to understand. She was hardly an elder, but old enough to tell convincing lies. Old enough to make an eight-year-old feel that he wasn't being hunted, and that they'd spend their morning with toes dipped in crisp water, staring out at the dark pines across the lake. Weaving her fingers into the links of her silver necklace, Anna pulled Julek toward the ferns. "If we don't hurry, we'll spend all day out here."

"It isn't even sunup yet," Julek said. He frowned at the beasts' cries. "Anna, what's that?"

"Elk," she whispered.

Ahead lay the gloom of deeper woods, and behind them, a sprawl of waterlogged fields. She'd been forced to carry Julek through the bogs, and all the while she'd made him laugh by pretending she was his warhorse. Her new boots were ruined, and her linen leggings were soaked to the knee, but it hardly mattered. She wouldn't be returning.

"Come on, little bear," she said, waving a gnat away from her face. "Here, come on. I've got you."

He scrunched his brow, clenched his tongue between crooked teeth, and swung his right boot out. Pitching forward, he caught Anna's arm for balance. His left leg was more deformed, but the momentum pulled him into an awkward gait. "Anna, it isn't making me fast. Whatever you rubbed on my arm."

Anna stole a sniff of her free wrist, breathing deep for the twistroot's sap-like odor. In its place, she smelled only sweat and ancient wool, and realized the beasts hadn't latched onto a false scent. She'd mixed the salves incorrectly, perhaps forgetting the tallow to waterproof it on their skin. It was too late now, of course. They were closing in.

"Anna, please," Julek whined. "I need to sit down. That's all."

"When we reach the lake, we can sit down. Is that fair?"

"No," Julek said. "The lake is an hour away."

"Less than that, if we hurry. Isn't that right?"

"I can't hurry."

There was pain in his voice, and worse yet, sincerity. Back home, he could barely pace around the field or crawl onto his cot by himself, and he'd been excited by the idea of a secret trip to the lake without his riding pony. For once, he'd been trusted to keep pace on his own two feet.

Now it was an exercise in cruelty.

"Anna!"

"I know," she said softly. She blinked away prickling tears, wondering if they came from desperation or pity. When she saw another cluster of crows scatter from the treetops, she realized it was both. "Julek, we can't disturb these men. I need you to be quiet."

"Why?" he whimpered. "You're hurting me."

Anna bit into her lower lip, threatening to draw blood. She tried to soften her grip on him, but couldn't. Letting go meant death.

The boy jerked his arm back, twisting free of Anna's hold.

She rounded on him with clenched fists. "Julek!"

But he was already crumpled among ferns and overhanging thistle, his breathing hard and broken between whimpers. Thorns fixed his tunic in place, leaving his legs sprawled limply behind him.

"Julek, please," Anna whispered. She knelt beside him and reached out, but he recoiled, pinning his arm to his chest. His tunic sleeve ended above the elbow, exposing the lashes from the briar patches. Beneath the blood, mirrored across his face and neck and fragile ankles, his rounded sigil shifted in luminous white. The symbol was cryptic yet familiar in Anna's mind: the boy's essence, unique to him alone. To glimpse such a thing was a gift and burden known only to scribes. "I'm sorry."

Julek glanced away, wiping his nose with the back of his hand. "Just take me home, Anna. I don't like this. I want to go back."

"Fine," she said. Again she heard the trackers crashing through the underbrush. Panic put a burning flush in her cheeks. "Come on, Julek, we can go."

The boy looked up at her, tears streaking his freckles and trailing down his dusty cheeks. "You're lying to me."

Branches snapped, perhaps in the grove a pence-league away.

"Never," Anna said. She offered a hand to coax her brother's arm out of hiding.

He shook his head. "Something's wrong."

"No," she said in a broken whisper.

"You're crying," he said. "Anna, who are they? What's wrong?"

Out of sight, the beasts growled.

Anna snapped her focus to the expanse of dead brush behind them, scanning for any sign of disturbance among the thorns. But the morning was still a filthy gray, staining the forest in monochrome, and she couldn't discern anything beyond the dark slashes of trees and creeping fog. The scene only grew blurrier as her eyes watered.

She glanced back at Julek. "We're fine. I just cut myself." Anna held up her right hand and fought to ease the shaking. There was a smear of blood beneath her ring finger. "See? Just a small cut. I'll bandage it at home."

"You never cry." His next teardrop rolled until Anna wicked it away with a trembling thumb. "Are you scared?"

No, little bear, she wanted to say, even as the teardrop stung her skin, *everything is all right.* She opened her mouth, but the words vanished. Cracking twigs burned away her breaths.

It all seemed so foolish now. Even if she reached the raft, she didn't know where to go. The tanner's son never specified which direction she had to travel to reach Lojka, nor how far. And what good were her salt clusters if she conflated pinches and grabs, and had never asked how much to pay for anything? Some of the local boys even said that the northern cities didn't take salt as payment. Was she even going north? How far could they go without food?

The longer she stared into Julek's eyes, the less such things mattered.

"Give me your arm," she commanded. Julek obeyed with hesitation, and Anna took hold of his wrist with one hand and seized a wad of his tunic with the other, dragging the thin boy to his feet and bracing his body against hers. "Just like the fields, okay?" She dropped into a narrow squat and allowed him to lean forward, bearing his full weight across her back and meshing his hands beneath her chin. "I'll keep you safe, little bear."

On any other day, Julek would've been considered light. Most of his muscles were atrophied from years of housework and bed rest, and unlike the other boys—indeed, unlike Anna—his daily meal was a mug of boiled kasha. Their father could still lift him with a single arm.

But today it was all wrong.

Anna had been too nervous to eat for days. She'd traveled a league in total darkness, and another two in marshlands. Her feet were waterlogged and bleeding, her legs threatening to buckle with every step.

Lukewarm sweat beaded along her brow and stung her eyes. When she stopped listening to the wet pulse of her own heartbeats, she heard boots stomping through the brush behind her, quickening as they drew closer. With every exhale, her ribcage constricted. Stagnant air burned in her lungs as she emerged from withered grass and into the mire, hemmed in by drowning trees.

Her boots sank into the muck, squelching as she fought to move on. Flickers of memory, rusted trapper's teeth and bloody bear flesh and desperate animal thoughts, exploded into her awareness. *Escape.* But every step pulled her deeper, swallowed her boots to the ankle. Julek's weight damned them.

Anna worked to free her boot, her legs cramping with the effort, but it remained trapped. "Julek," she said, still pulling, "if I let you down now, could you walk?"

He made no response.

She repeated the question, tugging at the boy's trouser leg. "It's very important." The calm of her voice died with the crunching of nearby branches. She knew they were within sight, but she couldn't afford to look, especially with Julek clutching her. The boy's muffled prayers fed the dread in her gut. "Julek," she whispered to the shuffle of unbearably close steps. "I want you to stay beside me, no matter what. I know you can do that." Anna bent at the left knee, struggling to remain upright as Julek swung himself around and dangled freely. She reached down to pull his limp legs from the water, but the boy clutched her tighter. "Don't worry. Just hold onto me."

Her knees gave way, and she toppled to the left. But before she could feel the lukewarm water she collided with moss and termite-ravaged wood. Her pale arm slid into the notch between branches and exposed her own cuts, much deeper and brighter, running down leaf-littered skin from elbow to palm. But her flesh was bare, devoid of the sigils she saw on everybody else. A scribe carried no essence, they said. No protection against the bloodshed from which they spared others.

"It's okay," Anna whispered. Boots thumped nearby.

Julek stared up at her with wide, swollen eyes, his grip tightening around her neck. He was trying not to cry, trying to be like her. "Home, Anna. We need to go home."

Behind her the screeching that once seemed so distant was now deafening. It was a guttural moaning, no doubt muffled in some way, communicating starvation that only trackers could put into their beasts. Flesh wasn't enough to satisfy it now. It needed violence.

In spite of the blood, Anna's mouth went dry. She stared at Julek as her vision blurred, and the tips of her ears turned cold. Before long the crackle of leaves overtook her ragged breaths.

"You're quick," said a passionless voice, no more than ten paces away. "You must be exhausted. Set him down, rest against the tree. There's no need to hurry."

In Anna's mind it was a simple thing to retrieve the hunting blade tucked into her belt. But it seemed impossible to move her hands. When the beast growled behind her, close enough to rustle her trouser leggings with its hot breath, she lost her nerve.

"He won't bite," the tracker said. "Unless I take off his muzzle."

Anna shut her eyes, trying to ignore the beast's odor of spoiled lamb and urine. "You're making a mistake."

"Oh?" Yet the word held no curiosity.

Closer still, Julek's fragile pleas were wasted. "I want mum. Anna, bring her here. Please, Anna . . ."

She could hardly swallow. "I don't know who sent you, but—"

"If you didn't know, you would be sleeping right now."

Hearing the truth from a stranger chilled her. A week earlier, she'd heard mother and father speaking to one of the bogat's riders, negotiating for Julek, but their involvement had seemed tangential compared to the idea of losing her brother. Her nausea swelled with the tracker's reminder. Back at home, father would be rising soon, his rucksack laid out and ready to collect the boy's worth in salt.

Anna squared her shoulders.

"Easy, girl." The tracker clicked his tongue. "You don't want to introduce violence to our meeting. My companion has more claws than you, and he's already pulling for prey." He let out another bit of rope, filling the silence with the groan of fibers stretching and snapping taut. Claws raked the muck and stirred the cloudy water around Anna's ankles. "I'd hate to give him reason to feed."

Anna clamped her jaw to stop the trembling. "I'm going to set him down. Pull it back."

"It's out of reach."

But the breaths were impossibly close.

"Keep it where it is," Anna said. Reluctantly, she took hold of Julek's wrists and pried open his grip. After an initial wince the boy resigned, and Anna lowered him to the mud below, their hands joined in a trembling embrace. "Don't worry, little bear," she whispered, too softly to reach Julek's ears.

Creaking metal filled the air.

"Do you hear that?" asked the tracker. "Hazani iron. Strung with hemp, the cartel said. So far, hasn't missed a thing." There was a rustling of leather, then a delicate swish. "Right. You can turn around, girl."

Anna released Julek's hands, their combined sweat turning clammy on her palms, then glanced over her shoulder. Unable to see around the mossy bark of the oak tree, she wrenched her boot free and rotated her entire body.

Two paces away, the soglav strained against its handler's woven rope. When their gazes met, the creature went wild, surging forward and thrashing with gangly limbs. A rusted iron collar was the only thing separating the beast from its kill. Veins bulged beneath the shaved gray fur of its neck, and blood trickled from infected rings that spoke of razors within the collar. A leather muzzle, lashed to the broken stumps of its horns, enclosed its snout and teeth. Its eyes, black and beady and scarred by a practiced whip, widened with each tug against the handler's rope.

But that wasn't enough to protect her. Its claws tore at the muck and empty air in front of Anna, willing to trade agony for a meal.

Anna realized she wasn't breathing, and only then did she detect the stench of pus. She'd never been one to scream when frightened, but now, as with childhood coyote encounters, she surrendered to fear and froze.

Half-submerged in the bog, Julek held fast to her right leg and kept his eyes shut. He clutched tighter with each snap of the soglav.

Anna covered her brother's eyes. "Pull it back!" She could barely raise her voice above the snarling. Glancing beyond the beast, if only to calm herself, she saw the tracker waiting. "Please!"

Shrugging, the man yanked at the rope.

The beast sprawled backward and collapsed into muddy water, its arms and legs kicking as it struggled to stand. Its opportunity for a kill had evaporated, it seemed, as the soglav barely managed to lift its snout from the water and rise on its haunches. Its breathing was ragged, its muscles wobbling. Gnats swarmed over bloody flesh as they sensed the creature's surrender.

"Stay." His voice was cold. Though standing just ten paces from the soglav with the rope tethered to his belt, he showed no fear of the beast. He was likely an experienced tracker, and on the bogat's payroll. He wore a linked mail hauberk, the thick gloves of a falcon handler, and a simple iron helmet, outfitted for swamp crossing with a neck guard and burlap veil. Like his beast's eyes, his were his only window of expression. But he was neither starved nor enraged. He had the weary, drooping eyes of a dusk petal addict. And in his arms, aimed at Anna, was a crossbow with a black bolt. "He's the worst of the bunch, Grove knows. He ate three days ago. There's a difference between hunger and starvation." Holding his aim, the man wandered through the muck and kicked the soglav's underbelly. When the creature screeched and collapsed with a shudder, the tracker showed no distress.

"I'll pay you whatever he's worth," Anna said, with as much confidence as she could muster. She couldn't tear her gaze from the loaded bolt, or the fully wound hemp string that held it back. "I'll pay double."

"How old are you?" asked the tracker.

She narrowed her eyes. "I'm not a child."

"Right, then. Do you understand how payment works?"

"Of course," she whispered.

The tracker's gloved finger slid along the crossbow trigger as though stroking the feathers of a delicate bird. "So you know that not all men work for salt."

It crossed Anna's mind that the tracker might not have been Rzolkan at all. Sometimes, the northern traders—those from Hazan, mostly—carried bricks of metal or packed spices. Maybe that was his currency, she reasoned. Nobody in her village had ever paid with currency beyond salt or bartering, unless a saltless trader had been forced to pay his way through with a brick of other materials. Even then, the odd bricks were always sold to another caravan for salt. But this man's skin was too pale to be Hazani, and he spoke with the flawless tongue of someone from the eastern marshes.

Anna hardened her stare to hide her ignorance. "What do you want?"

"My cut." He gestured at Julek with the crossbow. "Tell me . . . what did you intend to pay with?"

She recalled the ribbon-wrapped bag of salt at her hip, which now felt heavy with the weight of its uselessness. "I'll pay whatever it takes. Please, keep this between us. You won't have to split your earnings with the others. I'll pay you everything."

"It was salt, wasn't it?"

Anna gripped Julek tighter.

"You couldn't buy a droba with all the salt in your stores, girl." He gave an amused growl. "And whatever you have in those little bags is worth far less than a rune. But your brother, according to my earnings in the contract—"

"I'll get you runes." She realized, in the ensuing silence, that she'd used her last maneuver. Her father had told her to stay mum about her gifts, to feign ignorance on the mere nature of inscribing, but now her father had forced her hand. The tracker's lack of retort gave her a hopeful flush, and she nodded, brimming with assurances before the man could refuse. "That's right. I can get you a rune. That's more than the bogat could offer, isn't it?"

The tracker's weary eyes shifted in thought. Violet wisps crawled over his irises, indicating the petal's haze. "It never looks good to break a contract," he said after a moment. "They marked the boy, not you."

Anna scowled. "His name is Julek."

"I don't care for names."

"It would be outside of your contract," Anna said with a dry throat. "I'll pay you, and you can tell them you never saw us. We wouldn't come back, and won't ever cause any trouble for you. I swear it."

"Your name isn't on the contract, *Anna, First of Tomas*." He made her name feel obscene. "I've no intention of dragging you before the court's scribes for this farce."

"We wouldn't need to use the courts," Anna said.

He cocked his head. "You know scribes, girl?"

"One or two."

"Playing coy," the tracker said. "It's only a matter of time until they're marked, anyway."

It was no achievement, in truth. According to Piter, the baker's son, there had only been two scribes born in the region since his family moved here, and that was ten years ago. And Anna knew firsthand the difficulty of hiding such gifts.

She knew the pain of it.

"It doesn't matter," Anna said. "I could get you a rune, some salt, and they would never know."

"It isn't enough."

"A droba, then." She hesitated to even say it, but if slavery was her only option, she would take it. There was always a way out, she'd found. Given enough time, she could escape. And even if he forced her to bed, she could—

"Do you think the bogat is a fool?" Another huff stirred his burlap veil, this one bearing a trace of indifference. The sort of indifference that only eunuchs or man lovers or people incapable of love could ever muster. "No need to answer, girl; everybody knows he is. But he loves his runes, and by the Grove is he a jealous lover. It would be remarkable if I reappeared in his court with a rune, and a sweet young droba, yet no sign of dear Julek, don't you think?"

Until that moment, Anna had never understood what elders meant when they spoke about hopelessness. In previous years, her father's smile had made the world feel less hateful.

Now her father was part of that hateful world, and she had only herself. With Julek's every squeeze on her leg she felt the tiny iron teeth of her father's traps. The silver necklace father had given her so long ago threatened to choke her.

"My service would last a lifetime," she whispered. "You'd never have to work for another bogat. You could live—"

"You're wasting my time." The tracker glanced sidelong, watching his broken soglav's ears flutter at the sound of distant movement. "They'll be here soon enough, girl. So I suggest you sweeten your offer."

The other trackers' graceless footfalls rang out, halting Anna. It was too gloomy for her to see the men or they her, but she knew the sun would appear soon. When it did, not even this tracker's silence could protect them. Her throat closed, and her fingers went numb.

Julek's small hands clasped around hers.

She inhaled. "I'll give you all of my salt, my oath, a rune, and—please. I know I have more salt near the fields. I hid it under a stump last autumn."

The tracker remained silent, letting the snap of branches fill the air. "That's not enough for retirement," he said finally. "I would need—"

"A scribe." Her eyes throbbed as she tried to hold back tears. Before the man could reply her composure shattered. "I could get you a personal scribe."

The crossbow shifted away from Anna, but the movement was so slight that it appeared accidental. "A scribe, for *him*?"

Anna nodded, shifting her hands to mingle her fingers with Julek.

"How would I get them?" His voice seemed more earnest than toying now, and that meant it was Anna's chance.

"I'm the scribe," she said, stunned by how foreign the phrase felt. It was true, but somehow it felt wrong, as if it were a dream or a ruse. They were words she'd been told to repress. But it was her mother and father who'd promised her security for her secrecy, and now their word meant nothing. She wanted to repeat the words out of spite. Those words tingled on her lips. *I'm the scribe, and I hate you.*

But the tracker's eyes remained inert. "Is that so?"

Anna nodded.

The tracker stepped closer, crossbow at the ready. The mist thinned between them, revealing a pale neck, thick and free of any runes.

He would die here.

Anna's hand broke away from Julek, creeping toward her blade. She'd never known the bogat's best men to work without a rune on their neck, placed by a knowledgeable scribe and written for their sigils alone.

I'm a scribe, and I'm going to kill you.

"Hands," the tracker said. He pointed with his crossbow. "Move the boy over here."

Showing no resistance, Anna placed her hand back on Julek's shoulder, well within the man's line of sight. She just had to play by the tracker's rules, and strike when the time arose.

"Julek," she said, gently clutching the boy's shoulder, "I want you to go and stand by this man. He won't hurt you, okay? I'll be right here."

The boy met Anna's gaze with a sniffle. He kept her gaze for a full moment, perhaps waiting for her to reconsider, then gave a nod.

"That's it," the tracker cooed. He glanced at the soglav, whose ears had stilled as the hunting party changed course and grew more distant. "I don't want this to be any more tedious than it is, so we're going to talk with some insurance. Fair, eh?"

Helping Julek to his feet, Anna frowned. "Yes." She pulled her brother close to her again, keeping her hands around his neck to avoid suspicion. It wouldn't be difficult to draw her blade when the time came, but crossing the distance between them, especially with a loaded crossbow, would be the real challenge. And the method to kill the man was not immediately clear either. He was covered in riveted mail, and surely much stronger than her. "What will you do with him?"

"Keep him out of our dealings," the tracker said. He whistled, and the soglav's ears perked up. Its eyes opened on the second call. "Send him over there, would you?"

She peered into Julek's eyes, trying to assure him with an even stare. She clenched both his shoulders this time, and guiding him backward, gestured for him to turn. Letting go of the boy's tunic churned the bile in her gut. Soon enough they'd be home free, and the *kupyek* would be dead at her feet. As Julek hobbled toward the soglav, Anna wondered how it would feel to take her first life.

Soldiers did it all the time. It couldn't be too difficult.

"You say you're a scribe," the tracker said as he traced Julek's walk with the crossbow. He clicked his tongue and the soglav dragged itself up from the muck, straining against its rope to sniff at Julek. Despite his veil, the tracker's amusement leaked out through hungry eyes, relishing the way Julek squirmed.

Anna forced herself to look at the tracker. "I am," she said. "If I go with you, you'll let him go."

"You're negotiating the deal now?" He laughed. "I appreciate the initiative."

"Yes or no?"

"Your story's already pushing it, girl. But if you're what you say you are," the tracker snarled, "how would I even know you'd be good company? You could run away, and I'd be more the fool because of it."

Anna frowned at him. "I have no reason to deceive you." She scanned the weaving on the tracker's burlap sack to determine if his jugular was prominent. It was. "You know where I live. You know where my family lives. If I slight you, you can go there."

"Same home you're fleeing, isn't it?"

The soglav's jaws snapped behind its muzzle. Anna shut her eyes, desperate to block out the spectacle. "Anybody in my village knows my face."

"Would they give you up?"

Anna opened her eyes. "For a bag of salt. But if you're out here, you need much more than that. You need a rune, at least."

The tracker's eyes wavered out of acknowledgment. Surely he knew about his own vulnerability; desperate men did desperate things. "What gave it away?"

"Your neck," Anna said. "Always the neck." Runes had been placed on other areas, according to the tales, but they existed for a fraction of the throat marking's lifespan. It made it easy enough to see the marked ones, if nothing else.

"It's too damned hot for a neck sleeve."

"You asked me how I knew."

The tracker huffed, but this time it was a cold, mocking sound. "The bogat will make your mother into a plaything for his warriors," he said. "The only thing he hates more than unlicensed runes is an unlicensed scribe."

Anna's face was stone. She'd been expected to crumble under the man's threat, but it was no use. Her parents deserved whatever fate they received. They had gotten her into this trap, and only she could get them out. "Do we have a deal?"

"You're persistent." His crossbow's trajectory never strayed from her stomach. "And clever, I'll admit. So let's say we have a deal for the time being. You'll give me a rune as a show of good faith, and we'll be off. Without him."

Anna spared a glance at Julek. She was prepared to see the tracker's blood spurting as if from a beheaded chicken, but she couldn't bear her brother's pain.

"And don't proceed with your ideas of murder," the tracker said. "There's a reason I take precautions."

Another hot wave of panic touched her cheeks. She realized that they *both* had collateral on the table. Even if her blade severed his jugular during the rune-scarring, the soglav would make a bloody mess of Julek. And there was no telling if the boy's screams would alert the others.

"Bleeding virgins, this is heavy," the tracker mumbled. He set his crossbow against a tree without releasing the tension. Even as he took hold of the soglav's tether on his belt, he stared at the weapon longingly. "Well made, but dense. I'll have to have it hollowed out." He spoke as though Anna had asked him about the device. Then he glanced up and flexed a gloved index finger, beckoning Anna forward. "Don't be shy."

She waded out of the muck, blade clenched in her right hand, her steps slow and deliberate. She handled the weapon as though it possessed her, keeping its edge well within the tracker's sight. Only in the shadow of his linked mail and rotting burlap did she understand his true size.

He had the jaundiced eyes of a man craving excess, and the smell of one too. Like the caravan workers, he gave off the odor of fermenting barley.

"Right here." The tracker lifted the tattered hem of his burlap mask. There was a pale and rubbery quality to his neck, revealing the dark lines of his jugular and windpipe.

It would be a simple thing to open his throat, Anna knew. It was no different than sawing through a chicken's neck. But the tracker had planned for her use of violence. She was brave enough to run or bargain or fight, but couldn't bear to see Julek torn apart, especially as a result of her arrogance.

And the tracker knew it.

Her trembling hand pressed the blade to his throat, and she studied his sigils. Her first lines were mechanical, mimicking the sides of a triangle, and blood only oozed when she mirrored the finer details of his essence. In her periphery, she watched the soglav hook its claws into Julek's tunic, pulling him into a hideous embrace. Her shaking hands squeezed the blade. Just over the tracker's windpipe she continued to carve the unique sigil that covered his body: an intricate, fifty-pronged blossom. Each prong was a quick, shallow cut, and she realized that any one of them could have been his death.

Working in silence, she kept her hand as steady as possible.

It seemed to last an eternity—two, three, four minutes—and all the while, she used her free hand to smear away the blood, never brave enough to look directly into the man's eyes. If she glanced up, it was only high enough to inspect her markings. She rarely needed to check. In her village, she'd secretly given runes to a handful of hunters tracking a brown bear. She was unlicensed, of course, but those who received her runes were unlikely to speak out. Hers were the best; they could last an entire hunt before fading.

Now she hated how well she could carve.

On the last few prongs Anna's hand wavered, and the man's neck muscles twitched excitedly. *For Julek,* she reminded herself. She swallowed her disdain, having already shed her pride, and resumed her work. When she was finished, she lowered her blade, and then her head. Even in the gloom she saw crimson splotches upon her hands and wrists.

Blood retreated into torn flesh. Skin pinched itself shut. Luminous hayat burned beneath the new rune.

"It's done," Anna said.

The tracker yanked up his crossbow and settled it into his arms. "I know." Red marks soaked through the burlap. "Let's move. He stays here."

Anna clenched her blade tighter. Until the tracker spoke those words, she hadn't considered the concept of leaving, of never seeing Julek again. She was abandoning him an hour from the river to Lojka, and with what? How far could a maimed boy walk on his own? When would the others find him?

"Don't tell me you've gone mute," the tracker said. He nodded toward the soglav. "This one is horrible traveling company as it is. I was hoping for some conversation on the road. You have a tender little voice."

"Not here."

"Eh?"

"You said he'd be spared," Anna said. "We need to take him to Lojka, at the very least."

"We're headed north. Lojka's not on the way." He sighed. "Don't pretend I've slighted you. The terms were clear, girl."

Anna stared at the tracker's still bloody burlap through the press of fresh tears, wondering if she could break the rune with enough force. She knew her own skill, but there had to be some escape from the bargain, some recourse against such a monster. Deeper yet, she hoped there was a loophole in her own guilt. The exact wording of their deal seemed so distant, so muddled by dread that Anna no longer remembered if she'd damned the boy.

The tracker beckoned her with a gloved finger. "Come along, then."

Julek had remained silent while in the soglav's grasp, but it was far from stoicism. He often shut down under duress. Most of his fearful moments—the autumn thunderstorms, or the midnight visits from drunken watchmen—were eased with Anna's company. When he hid under the bed, Anna would lure him out and hug him until he stopped shaking, and his voice would return.

But in that moment, it took all of Anna's strength to simply look him in the eye.

She'd sold him out, just like mother and father had.

Anna tore her gaze from the boy and set it on the tracker and his Hazani crossbow. She lunged forward. In a flash, she hooked her blade upward, straining to clear the hauberk's metal rings and pierce the burlap mask.

The tracker's attention was elsewhere, and he failed to raise his crossbow as Anna's blade bit into the burlap and glanced off bone, sawing through the soft flesh beneath his chin. He staggered back one step before halting.

It wasn't enough.

Anna forced the blade deeper until her hands pressed against moist burlap. She clutched the knife with pearl-white knuckles, her grip trembling, teeth gritted in exertion. No matter how hard she pushed, the blade had done its best, and could go no further.

Her rune held, slowly forcing the blade out of the tracker's flesh. Sinew snapped and rewound itself around the depths of the incision. Blood rushed back with a wet slurp, soon followed by the skin's closure, sounding all too similar to skinning fowl.

At each stage of reconstruction, Anna's hand moved farther from the gash in the burlap. Soon the blade's tip emerged from the burlap, hovering impotently over the evidence of her failure.

"Most would have tried that sooner," the tracker said. He used the crossbow's front edge to gently guide Anna back, and she complied in stunned silence. "You traded surprise for this?"

Anna couldn't breathe. The attack felt like déjà vu, a dream she'd often imagined but never experienced. Her hand, still holding out the blade for a second strike, shook as it dripped with fresh blood. There was no return. She knew what would happen next, but again it was all too dreamlike.

"I wish you hadn't done that," the tracker said.

He jerked on his beast's tether.

Before Anna could cry out the animal overshadowed Julek. The boy tensed, followed by a sickening *pop*. His hand jerked out of the soglav's hold for a moment, pale and thin and writhing, then dangled like a hangman's noose. There was no scream, no farewell, no immediate sense of death. Even the ravens sat expectantly on their branches, staring back at Anna.

"Let him go." She was too steeped in disbelief to care how childish it sounded. No matter how hard she tried, she couldn't look away from Julek's limp body, or the way the soglav slashed at it and rammed its muzzle against the bloody flesh. She tried to say more, but her words came as broken, rambling whimpers.

"I'll take the muzzle off," the tracker said. His crossbow nestled under his arm, he untied the tether at his belt, wandered up behind the soglav, and slid the twine loops over the creature's stumped horns. He stepped calmly back as the muzzle fell free, and the soglav tore into its kill. "He'll be busy for ten minutes or so. And he won't need to feed again, I think."

A single thought circled in Anna's mind. *I'm so sorry.*

The tears came quickly. She knew she should've looked away, or used the dagger she now held like a useless block of iron, but it was pointless. There was no sense in being brave now, or maintaining any illusions. Julek's body was still warm, but the sigils beneath his skin were gone, snuffed out when he was. Somehow, she felt she'd only known her brother through those markings. She'd known his essence in a way nobody else ever could.

The sigils were gone now, and they were a thousand leagues apart.

I'm sorry.

"North, right?" the tracker sighed. He shifted his grip to use both hands on the crossbow. "I think we decided on north."

Anna wanted to scream, but couldn't manage. "You—"

"Yes, I did."

"You killed him!"

The ravens fled into the canopy, squawking.

"What of it?" the tracker asked. "You broke the agreement."

The truth bit deepest. Alternatives played out in her mind—allowing the tracker to take her, leaving Julek to grow up and prosper on his own in Lojka—only for them to dissolve with her next scream. She buried her face in her hands.

"Chin up, girl," the tracker said. "In time, you'll be glad I did it. You'll see."

When Anna glanced through her fingers she saw the soglav continuing its grim work, raking its teeth across pale flesh and turning her brother's limbs into ragged strips of meat. Even then, she looked on. She needed to remember this.

"We haven't the time," he added. "Some respectable food will put the fire back in your eyes, I'm sure."

Branches cracked in the distance as the other trackers closed in. The skies were lightening, no longer dark enough to hide the grisly scene. Within moments company would arrive.

"You're too pretty to be found by them," the tracker said. He gestured to the northeast, where the clouds were a burning orange. "If you don't start walking, I'll have to carry you. I'm sure neither of us would like that."

She thought about running. If she was swift, she might even make it to the lake before they could catch her. But there was nothing to be found there. There'd once been a shadow of hope at the sandy shores, but it died with Julek. So Anna glared at the tracker, and stumbled toward him, dagger at her side. That night she would slit his throat.

Until then, she was his accomplice. And she hated herself. She hated that she stared at raw, bloody flesh.

"That's it," the tracker soothed her, paying no mind to the blade in her hands. "You and I are going to be very good associates, Anna." He lifted his head at the approach of the other trackers, still too far to identify them. "There's much to be gained in an honest partnership."

Chapter 2

By the time Anna spoke again, it was dusk. She didn't know how far they'd walked that day, or where they were, because every stretch of underbrush looked identical to her, and her eyes never found the courage to wander up or look back at the tracker. More to the point, she had no interest. There was thoughtless comfort in walking, and when she heard the tracker's steps slow to a crawl—a measured six paces behind her, as it had been since morning—she increased her pace.

"Slow down," the tracker said.

That was when she spoke. "No." Her throat was raw and cracked, but she couldn't bring herself to beg for water or take another rest. That would give her time to think.

"Have you ever seen a wolf's teeth up close? Nasty bites," he called out. "Some of them are starved in these parts."

Anna kept walking.

The tracker heaved a drawn-out sigh. "Do I need to threaten you with a bolt?"

She imagined the crossbow's thick rope clapping, the iron bolt tearing into her spine. She saw herself dying beneath the oaks. It was a more dignified death than Julek had been given, and less painful. Maybe she deserved it. If she just kept walking—

Wood creaked as the tracker wrenched back on the crossbow's arm, and once again, it halted Anna mid-step.

"That's it," the tracker said. "See? A bit of cooperation is healthy."

She turned, raising her head for the first time in hours. The tracker was a glob of shadow in the twilight, but beyond him, the skies were crimson. Soon enough the forest would become pitch-black. Finding her own way would be impossible. Back home, she knew the roads and trails three leagues in any direction.

Even if she could find her way back, she wouldn't go.

They sold him out, she told herself. *They sold us both out.*

Now the necklace felt tainted against her skin. She wanted to throw it deep into the woods, or bury it, or melt it. But it was more than jewelry now. Her parents would've recouped the cost of the gift with the salt they received for Julek's sale. No, it was far more than two palms of cast silver. It was the suffering of a frail boy.

"Did you see it yet?" asked the tracker. He fidgeted as he released the crossbow's tension and approached her, his silhouette swelling. "Look behind you."

Slowly, Anna glanced over her shoulder.

Something massive stood among the thinning trees. Wide and towering, jagged along its upper crest, immersed in shadow aside from the odd spot of sunset. Among the illuminated areas were weathered stones and scorch marks.

"What is it?" asked Anna, worried that the beast might awaken while she stared.

"Many things." The tracker stepped closer, crunching twigs beneath his boots. "But for tonight, it's a landmark, and a place to bed down."

A place to slit his throat. Anna looked at the tracker's darkened burlap mask, so exposed after he'd abandoned his helmet and neck guard. "A landmark to what?"

"Our destination."

She scowled. "Where is it?"

"You'll know when we arrive, won't you?" He stepped past her, carrying the odor of distilled sweat. "Come now. I'm a swift eater. You'll want a cut of the rations, I imagine."

Against her wishes, Anna's stomach growled. She followed the tracker into the ruins, confining her thoughts to the safe and reliable need for food.

The main courtyard was too shadowed to make out anything in detail, but it was as large as she'd imagined. In many ways, it was surreal. It was another place from her nightmares, in which she was so small she might be lost and never found again. She waited in the center of the expanse, her gaze following the tracker's movements with mindless interest.

He moved from doorway to doorway, altogether too confident in this new place. People had once lived here, and yet he moved through their property as though he owned it.

Eventually he emerged from a squat doorway. "Come along, girl."

* * * *

By the time it was full dark, Anna still hadn't finished her rations. The tracker had given her a crumbling portion of his hardtack disc, made from milled barley and rye, but the dryness of the hardtack had nothing to do with Anna's sluggish appetite. She'd always considered eating a waste of her time, having never considered it a priority when more pressing matters were at hand. *That's why you're bone-thin,* father had often told her. *That's why you haven't bled yet,* mother had said. But none of it mattered now. Surely her descent into cowardice would have stunned anybody back home, but it surprised her the most.

She rolled bits of the hardtack between her fingers until they crumbled, watching them slip through her fingers in the candlelight. It was the height of the summer, and the woods were still cool and fresh in the darkness, so the tracker hadn't bothered to build a fire. Back home—

Anna stopped herself.

You don't have a home. You had *a home.*

Across the chamber, resting against an empty stone archway that led into the courtyard, the tracker shifted on his seat of packed earth. He'd given up the chamber's only chair to Anna. In the candlelight his eyes twinkled with a bit more life, but the illusion was shattered by his burlap mask. "Generally we eat food, not plant it." He grinned. "And we drink water when it's offered to us. Or liquor, if it suits you better."

Anna glanced up from her work. The ceilings were low and close, and the chamber echoed with wind and its long-dead voices. At the floor near Anna's feet the tallow candle burned in an uneven, smoky cadence, its fumes pricking at her eyes. Their light washed over her ruined boots, which she'd set aside to dry, and so that she may give her blisters and open sores some reprieve.

"An old woman once told me to give my wife daughters, and daughters only," the tracker said. "She said I would never be in want of a story, or song. She said that daughters—women, you see—have the mind to remember songs."

For a moment the lure tugged at Anna. She opened her lips, ready to abandon her silence to ask why the tracker's wife couldn't sing for him, but thought better of it.

He noticed. "Do you know any songs, girl?"

"No."

"You had so much more to say earlier." The tracker reached for the heap of linked mail beside him. He shook the folds to flatten them out, candlelight shimmering over its rings. "You can use it as a headrest, if you like. Better than nothing."

Without the mail, he wore only a brown, sweat-stained tunic. As good as naked, for the purposes of murder. But there was no telling how long his rune would last. She'd carved it well, but most runes from Lojka's scribes never lasted more than six hours. Even if she'd never counted the exact duration of her own runes, she had no illusions about her talent: The tracker had to be vulnerable by midnight.

"What are you thinking about?" he asked.

Anna tore her attention from the hardtack. "I want to know where we're going."

"North isn't enough?"

In truth, Anna didn't know what she expected in his answer. Even if he told her their destination, and the roads and ferries and landmarks they'd encounter along the way, it meant nothing. Lojka was the closest town to Bylka, after all, and she'd never seen it with her own eyes. The larger cities were myths, for all she knew.

North was a vague direction, but it held all of her fear and ignorance about the world.

The tracker turned to the blackness outside. "I can guarantee that you haven't seen a keep this large in all your days." A longing drawl haunted his words. "Can you imagine how many people used to sleep here, work here, *fuck* here?"

"Stop," Anna said curtly. She dropped the remnants of the hardtack and glared at the tracker, searching for the lustful glimmer men held in their eyes. The same spark her father had beaten out of passing riders. But in the tracker's gaze she saw only the cloudy violet of dusk petals.

"Don't flatter yourself," the tracker said.

Anna's eyes never left the tracker. She waited, ready to draw the blade and carve his flesh. She wouldn't be able to kill him, of course, but she could at least put up a fight.

Or if all else failed, she could always cut her wrists to the bone.

That was what brave girls did, according to the songs. There was no place in the Grove-Beyond-Worlds for the girls who died as *rozbitsa konar*—broken branches.

"Have I stolen your hunger?" the tracker asked.

She grappled for a reply, hardly able to resist crying or grabbing for her weapon. He'd taken much more than her hunger. He'd taken a sweet boy, and a—

"Six hundred bodies used to live here," the tracker said, oblivious to her mind. "Not all within the walls, you understand. If you walk around the southern wall, you'll see where they put up the shacks and kitchens. That's where the tanners and bankers lived. There were kennels for hounds, and pens for sows, just down by the pond." He closed his eyes, and the burlap sack shifted with heavy exhales. "Alive. This place was alive, girl."

Anna took in a fresh view of the chamber, but was too tired to visualize any of it. Too numb to care for ruins or their glory days. Yet Julek had always told her stories of a keep in the bogs, a place they'd explore together someday.

"There's nothing to fight here," she said.

"There's a host of things to fight, girl. Soglavs, flesh peddlers, Laughing Men, azibahli from the north. . . ."

She tried to imagine the azibahli—massive, thinking spiders dwelling in caves and cities of webs, the focus of tales from mercenaries and caravan drivers alike. They were only myth, surely, but the thought chilled her.

"Even if it's quiet," the tracker said, "a keep isn't always for fighting. Sometimes it shows that you have something."

"Like salt."

"Like salt, yes," the tracker said, somewhat amused. "But stature is far rarer. Stature, and the sweat of a hundred men who would break their backs to see your banner raised. That's something you'd never see in Bylka. What stature does a glorified riding post have?"

Yesterday Anna might've snapped back at that. She might've thrown a punch, if he were one of the mouthy boys from the east side of the river. Her grandfather had practically built the town from his own pockets. But today it wasn't her home. It was another town she'd heard about from wanderers. "It probably has more stature than ruins."

"Perhaps," the tracker growled. "This was a Bala keep. Most of the landowners had foresight, you see. The moment they saw a Mosko standard in the wind, or a pack of riders, they opened their gates and hid their daughters."

"Maybe they should have surrendered," Anna said.

"Oh, they did. It's a fool's business to tear apart something you've been given." He inspected the vaulted ceiling, now crumbling and choked with gossamer threads, and shook his head. "The Moskos were always dense."

Clan names were a smudge in her mind. Her earliest memories were six years after the war had ended, and the only scar left in Bylka had been the river grove, where apple saplings sprouted from fields that had been put to the torch. She remembered the taste of those apples better than any of her father's excuses for silence, although she still wondered what made him wake and scream in the night.

"I'd imagine that the girls here looked just like you," the tracker told her. Anna clenched her fists.

"Long blond hair, slender—"

"You'll not look at me anymore," Anna snapped.

"Without a close watch, you might take off into the night. It's no place for young girls." The tracker picked up the bronze flask at his side, uncorked it, and drank. "Do you wish death on every man who has a kind word?"

"Only wicked men."

The tracker grunted. "Wicked. Do you know what *subjective* means, girl?"

Anna glowered. In truth, she'd never learned the term before, but she wasn't prepared to disarm herself so easily. Her father had operated a riding post, and his vocabulary rarely stretched past words of saddling and threshing. Mother had only given her words about weaving and mending. She'd learned an eternity's worth of curses from the boys who felted cloth by the river, but never words of substance.

She huffed at the tracker. "Do you know what *acquisition* means?"

"Mhm," the tracker said. "But it doesn't seem relevant, now does it? I'm not trying to make the daughter of a bucket hauler feel dim, you understand. I'm teaching you the power of words." He gave a wheeze. "More to the point, the power of an accusation. Calling somebody wicked without knowing its meaning—well, where we're going, they'll bloody your pretty face for it."

Outside, a pack of coyotes let off shrill howls. Anna sank lower in her chair, and for the first time that day, she longed for her bed. She longed for the crunch of wet gravel as the night watchmen patrolled the trails, for Julek and the way her blankets nestled against his in the common room, for the boy who made thought-catching snares out of roots and twine and old feathers, who brought Anna sweet dreams and restful nights. . . .

The tracker noticed. "Would you call them wicked, girl?"

"Who?" she asked faintly. Wind raked through the trees and over the broken battlements, giving Anna the sensation of gnats crawling across her neck.

"Why, the hounds," the tracker said. "Are they wicked?"

She shook her head.

"Yet they'd lick your bones, if you stepped outside." The tracker laughed as though he hadn't forced images of a charcoal-haired boy into Anna's mind, nor forced a lifetime of sleep-screaming onto her. "Some things lack a mind, girl. Some things are wicked because you have what they need, and they take it." He glanced out into the darkness. "To the sows you fatten and bleed, you're wicked."

"I don't care," Anna said. She watched the candle as it flickered, catching stray breezes from the courtyard and sputtering. Being thrown into darkness didn't seem so frightening anymore.

"Subjectivity." The tracker folded his hands over outstretched legs. "Remember it when you call a man wicked. Those who lived in this keep were probably honorable, until somebody else decided they weren't."

There was something cryptic in those words, and soon Anna understood: The man was sentimental about it. Underneath his mask, he was flesh—or something of the sort. "Who lived here?" she asked at last.

But the tracker's mind was elsewhere, and he closed his eyes. "It doesn't matter. None of them are here now, are they?"

"You seem to know about them."

"There isn't much to know anymore, girl." The tracker snorted. "Wars have a habit of changing things. Sometimes, they just make them disappear."

Another gust of wind raked the courtyard, moaning as it passed the open doorway and swept fallen leaves into the chamber. The candle flickered, painting the walls with a gloomy rust color, then regained its steady burn.

Anna wrapped her arms about herself and pulled her legs closer to the chair.

"Do you need a covering?" the tracker asked.

It surprised her, but she didn't let it show. She couldn't. He was a killer, not a savior, even if he wanted to appear that way. *Subjectivity,* she told herself. Instead, she loosened her arms, ignoring the onset of goose-flesh. "I don't want anything from you. I just want to sleep."

"There might still be a storeroom by the eastern wall, if—"

"I said no." Anna blinked to prevent the onset of any tears, which would undoubtedly sparkle in the candlelight.

"You'll be cold."

"What does it matter to you?" she asked with a crumbling voice. She immediately regretted asking. If he really cared for her, if he had some shred of—

"You're my investment," the tracker said flatly, severing her thoughts. "I need you alive, girl."

Anna pursed her lips. *Good. Make this easier for me.*

"Lower your hackles," the tracker said. "If you need a blanket, tell me now. I won't be waking from a dead sleep to search the stores."

She could hardly believe how quickly the warmth left his voice. There was no expectation of kindness, of course, but his lure of goodwill only made it worse. For a moment, she'd fallen for his ploy. And she hated herself for it.

"Well?" the tracker asked.

Anna stared back at the burlap sack and its darkened eye-holes. "The people who lived here got exactly what they deserved."

Wind screeched through the chamber without warning, snuffing out the candle's flame. Now there was only the distant yipping of coyotes, the rattle of branches against stonework, and the panicked breathing of one young girl.

But to Anna the chamber was far from blackness. The room's shape persisted in ghostly lines, carved into her vision like the etchings once made by Patrek on festival days.

She saw the one cut that could never be sealed by runes. She saw a wound ready to be torn open and infected until it festered. She saw her path to revenge.

She saw grief in the tracker's eyes.

Chapter 3

Anna woke so abruptly that she couldn't tell if she'd been sleeping at all. In an instant, she had both feet planted on the packed earth, her eyes wrenched open to the darkness, and her fingers tightened around the cold links of her necklace.

When she realized where she was, her stomach soured.

Outside the rain had thickened into a downpour, constant and deafening. She'd loved rain back home, where she could lie beneath a quilt's woven armor while father lit the candles. It was always warm inside, and the rain whispered and hummed on the roof and grass, never able to reach her. But here the rain shouted and the wind shrieked.

She pressed a hand to her forearm, finding the skin clammy and tender. Her throat was hoarse and her mouth dry, making swallowing nearly impossible. Somewhere in the darkness, she recalled, the tracker kept a skin full of water.

Him, she remembered suddenly. *I have to kill him.* The thought struck her while she stood, almost as intense as the hunger pangs and thirst and dizziness. Once she'd forced down her nausea she peered into the darkness.

One by one the chamber's murky curves emerged, until at last the familiar shape of a marching boot became visible.

I have to kill him.

Anna groped at her belt, scratching over linen and cracked leather as she searched for the hunting knife. At last her nails struck iron, still tacky with the tracker's blood. Another flash of sickness came over her as she seized the wooden tang and pulled the blade free. Her eyes had adjusted enough to see her target slumped against the wall. She lowered the blade to her hip, braced her thumb along the iron's upper ridge, and crept forward.

There was no time to think about what she would do after killing him. Fear put trembling in her fingers, but it had lost its power. Now it was a fever, constant and incurable.

Three steps, two steps, one, all the while breathing in his odors of decay, hearing his ragged breathing and grinding teeth.

A horse whinnied outside.

Anna froze in place, the blade shaking in her hands. *Put it through his eye.* But her arm was locked in place, as rigid as the keep's crumbling stone pillars. Voices rose in the blackness.

The first was deep and wounded, hardly audible over the storm. "Shut it up before I cut its stones off, *korpa.*"

"This is his first ranging," said a younger man.

They were lowlanders, surely. Men who carried their accent had often ridden through Bylka and stabled horses in father's barn, but Anna had never been allowed to speak with them. Men of Malchym, was all mother had said about them. That, and to never approach them.

Anna looked at the tracker's inert form, his unarmored chest rising and falling, and moved the blade closer. The iron tip snagged on his burlap. With a gentle hand, Anna lifted the sack's hem. The rune's faint glimmer of hayat energy remained on his flesh, luminous against the black wall. Her resolve fell away in tandem with her arm, leaving the blade shaking by her side. No matter how badly she wanted it, she couldn't bring herself to try—and fail—once again. Maybe they were right. Maybe *she* was right. She was a coward. And worse yet, she was complicit, and no better than—

"Check the east wing," the older man called from outside.

It occurred to her that the storm hadn't woken her up. It had only concealed their approach.

The knife still in her grasp, Anna stepped over the tracker and pressed herself flat against the cold, mossy stonework. Another hard wash of rain drowned out most of her hearing, but she was certain of a newfound silence, and the possibility that she was inside of the east wing. She sidled along the wall with an outstretched arm, her knuckles and iron blade catching on crevices. She came to a halt at the doorway, where her hand met the protruding frame.

Thunder bellowed from the gloom, sending the horses into fits and shaking the mud beneath Anna's bare feet.

"East!" screamed the older man, who now seemed farther away and on the left side of the doorway, perhaps near the stables. "We're not paid by the day, *korpa.*"

"They checked the tomesroom last week," said the younger man, much closer than Anna had anticipated.

"If they were as dense as you, they probably found everything *except* the ledgers," the older man growled. "Check the tomesroom, to the *east*. I don't care how many pints you burn, boy. Look over everything. Got it?"

There was a long pause, then, "*Tek*."

Anna heard the clopping of heavy boots moving away from the chamber, quickening, fading across the yard. She peered out from the doorway's edge.

A pool of lantern light outlined the younger man's form. He was already twenty paces away, jogging to escape the storm and reach the tomesroom across the yard. His lantern revealed flowing black garments upon his shoulders and a wide-brimmed hat, which sagged and fluttered in the downpour. Between the darkness and his eerie glow, the man was a monster. She'd seen enough monsters that day.

Anna glanced at the tracker's still form, then back at the yard, discerning little beyond flits of silver as moonlight met rainfall. And amid the downpour, almost invisible given its silence, a black horse circled the yard.

They hadn't tied the beast to a post or led it under an awning, which meant it was probably trained. And trained animals were ridden by trained men, if Anna's experience in the lodge had taught her anything. But trained for what? Julek had sometimes worked the stables with father, and might've noticed its mannerisms and the way it carried itself, whether it was meant for messaging or—

Might have, Anna thought. *Might.*

All she knew with certainty was that she couldn't mount, much less ride, a full grown horse.

She returned her attention to the riders. She hadn't seen a cudgel or blade on the younger man, but he was also cloaked in full garb, and didn't seem to expect trouble here. If they were good men, her salt could buy her passage to the next town.

Yes, that was it. She almost cried at the thought. Within hours she could be home again, or by a lodge's fire, and—

No, it was too early to think about who *wouldn't* be there. She tucked her blade away and set off running.

The rain was freezing on her skin, a far cry from dusk's warmth. Wind slashed across the yard. Before long, her hair was plastered to her face, her tunic soaked and frigid. Her feet barely found purchase in the mire, skidding and sinking, but the mud took the sting out of her sores. She was close, if the echoes of approaching masonry were accurate. When her feet touched solid stone, the rainfall stopped, leaving her dripping beneath the tomesroom's portico. She shivered and listened to her own breaths, now deafening in the small space. Warm air drifted past her like an invitation to the darkness. She raised her hands, wandering forward, brushing at nothingness until she felt the entryway's dry stone.

Bathed in the earthy rot of cheap paper, memories resurfaced. They came as vivid flashes of nights by the hearth, where she helped her mother sort missives and glyph scrolls on polished counters. She recalled the way her fingers felt against crisp sheets that had been continually rain-soaked and dried.

Metal crashed against stone with a hollow clap.

Anna flinched.

Somebody—the younger man, most likely—was stomping through the aisles. He walked with the reckless heft of a man who believed he was alone, making no effort to muffle his coughing or the thunderclaps of the scroll cases he tossed aside.

Anna crept forward, tracking the man by his haphazard throws. It was black as tar in the tomesroom, perhaps even worse without moonlight, but there had to be a light somewhere. She wandered forward, her right hand on the dusty shelving, and watched for the man's lantern.

At the end of the aisle, where her fingers curled around a mason's straight stone edge, a warm glow leaked across the floor.

Within the wash of light, far down the main aisle of scrolls, discarded strips of paper and crushed candle wax littered the floor like a crypt's bones. The man and his black covering blotted out a portion of the light, but the cone that projected before him bathed the walls and shimmered over brass cylinders, revealing the upper vaulting of the tomesroom. It was higher than Anna had expected, with its shelves melding into the ceiling's stonework.

She followed the man for a few paces. Her damp feet caught on a piece of paper, dragging it over stone, but the rain muffled most of the crinkling. As she shook her foot free, her toe struck brass. Pain shot up her leg, but the sensation was drowned out by bristling terror. The brass container spun down the aisle, scraping and clanking, before it came to rest just behind the man.

His silhouette spun, and the blinding light of his lantern, suspended by a hook, hovering at navel level, glared back at Anna like a pale eye.

"Milosz!" the man called. His light did not move. "Milosz!" he called again, this time far louder.

Anna raised a hand to shield her eyes from the light, but the glow was too intense to see anything. She stood in silence, trembling, hoping the man would soon realize her age and note her broken appearance, from a drenched tunic to mud-covered, bloodied feet. After a moment of waiting, she cleared her throat. "You have to help me."

The light jumped when she spoke. "Stay where you are," the man said between panicked huffs.

"I won't hurt you," said Anna. It was shocking that she even had to assure the man of such things. It also meant he was probably unarmed.

After a long pause, he risked a step forward. "What are you doing here?"

"It wasn't my choice," she said. She imagined the tracker waking and creeping behind her in the darkness, wrapping his rough hands around her throat. "I'm from Bylka."

"A riding post." Before Anna could reply, the man staggered back. "Milosz!" he yelled, the words bearing enough force to set Anna's ears to ringing. Tremors wracked his voice, the kind that young boys and girls developed when they began to fear death. "Keep your distance."

Suddenly Anna heard footfalls clopping through the mud outside, clapping over the portico's tiled floor, and finally clacking behind her. She glanced over her shoulder, but the darkness revealed only sprawling cobwebs on the shelving. The terror returned to her, but it was only another senseless emotion. Her body was simply drained of fright and dread. Instead she felt her heartbeat and its painful aches, and icy sweat forming on her neck like fresh rainfall.

If she were butchered right there, it would only prove that the day had been an awful nightmare, and nothing more.

For better or worse, she felt no blade. She just heard the wet boots slow and then come to a complete stop at her back, almost as close as the tracker had been that morning. The voice that followed fit her recollection of the older man.

"That's a strange looking ledger, Kaba," Milosz said. He hummed to himself then asked, with a bit more gravity, "Where did you find her?"

"She just appeared." Kaba set his lantern down on the floor.

"Appeared?"

"Yes," Kaba said. "What do we do with her?"

"I need to get away from here," Anna said suddenly. She stole a glance behind her, if only to show Milosz her face and youth. "I'm no harm to anybody. I was brought here against my will. Please, just help me."

Milosz grunted. "There are very few ways a girl ends up in this place." He spat on the tiles. "I suggest you speak quickly."

"Kidnapping," she said, turning to see the luminous sigils on Milosz's face and neck in the light's residual glow. He had a delicate, spiraling system that joined to form octagons. She studied the sigil carefully, forcing herself back to speech as she watched the symbols twist and turn. "One of the bogat's men did it."

"Which bogat?" Kaba asked.

Anna swallowed. She hadn't expected it to even be a question. "Radzym."

There was a lull in the exchange. Milosz seemed to be staring past Anna and toward his companion, grunting and shrugging his upper lip in discomfort. He had a hard look about him, as though he rarely experienced indecision. But this matter gnawed at him. His small, dark eyes narrowed, and he scratched at his beard, which glowed like silver thread in the light. Finally, Milosz folded his arms over his black cloak and nodded. "She isn't with them."

Kaba's reply was delayed. "How do you know?"

"Look at her," Milosz said as he inspected Anna. "Starved. And grains are about the only thing Nahora can get through our rivers."

"*Napawna*. She isn't on their rosters," Kaba said, "but they have sympathizers everywhere."

Milosz spat. "You've just come off the tit. What would you know about the wars, boy? What would you know about *sympathizers*?"

Although Anna's only indication of Kaba was his hovering light, she took his silence as an acceptance of defeat, or at least submission. Even Milosz let the quietness sink in to prove his point before continuing. But Anna struggled to focus, watching the runes contorting over Milosz's skin, warping and stretching.

"Where are you from?" Milosz asked.

"Bylka," she whispered. "My brother and I, we came from there."

"Where's your brother?"

"He's dead." The words were cold when they left her lips, but she felt less than expected. She'd seen young boys bury their fathers after they came back from fighting, and they didn't blink, much less weep, for three days, perhaps four. But after a certain point, they broke.

Anna hoped she would never reach the fifth day.

"What was his crime?" Kaba asked.

"*Cichbasz, korpa*," Milosz growled. The snap of his final curse filled the tomesroom. He spoke the grymjek, the clanspeak, better than Anna's own father. And there was a pointed brutality behind it. "What happened to him, girl?"

"The man who took me here," Anna said, trying not to let the tingling in her gut ferment into fear again. She hadn't wanted to discuss Julek; she hadn't meant to even bring him up. "He was a tracker. He did it over salt."

"A tracker wouldn't kill," Milosz replied. "We can't do a thing if you're on his writ."

"I wasn't," she said weakly. "He told me that my brother was the one that the bogat wanted. At first, he didn't want me. He didn't need me."

"Did Jan ever receive word back from Kowak?" Kaba asked, and Anna was grateful to return to comfortable silence.

"*Ne,*" Milosz said. Hardened leather plates rustled under his cloak. "Did the tracker tell you why he wanted your brother, *panna*?"

"No," Anna whispered.

Milosz said something to Kaba in full grymjek, and both men exchanged looks, somehow seeming insightful in the blackness. Milosz was the first to speak again. "Who gave Radzym the boy's name?"

My mother, my father. The words hung like cobwebs in her mouth, and she couldn't force them out. But that was all they needed, it seemed.

Milosz grunted. "Just like the others, then." He furrowed his brow. "Kaba, we'll have to send word from the next post. Tell Malchym that it's getting worse."

Despite the chill, she felt a surge of hot blood. "You knew they were taking people."

"It's beyond our influence, *panna*. But once we get word to Malchym—"

Anna whirled toward Milosz. "What is he doing to them?"

"This isn't a matter for you," Milosz said, his voice low but equally harsh. "Even if we knew ourselves." After a moment of quiet, letting the distant thunder break outside, Milosz bowed his head. "Fetch the gelding, Kaba. Add Radzym's name to the writ."

Add. There were others committing the same crime under Malchym's watch. The city of lights and luxury, of riders on purebred horses and gold-trim saddles, of soldiers sworn to clear-hearted oaths.

And they did nothing.

"*Panna,*" Milosz said soothingly, "why does he want you?"

"I don't know," Anna admitted. By now, she'd almost convinced herself that such a lie was true.

"Where is he?" Milosz asked, the question so chilling that not even Kaba ventured to interject. A lone peal of thunder broke over the tomesroom.

In their collective silence, Anna heard the patter of approaching steps. Heavy boots echoed from the doorway.

Without willing it, Anna shrank away from the beast. She skirted to the left and out of Kaba's wash of pale light, somehow winding up in a narrow aisle of scroll cases, but she felt far from hidden. Even in the darkness, hiding among the maze, the tracker could see her. She sensed it. He could peer through the blackness and rot, meeting her gaze directly. In the shelter of the shadows, she trembled.

"Milosz," hissed Kaba. He shook his light, the beam flickering across Milosz's back and illuminating folds of wine-dark fabric, tousled gray hair.

But the older man did not look back. Even with the light dancing and fidgeting, a victim to Kaba's shaking wrist, Anna discerned the slow, practiced withdrawal of a weapon. Polished metal reflected a mote of lantern light, then returned to shadow.

Anna stared at Kaba as her vision returned, the lingering flashes of white light fading by the second. Free of the lantern's glare, she could see most of the aisles again, and the horror on the young man's face.

His essence writhed like it had been left to roast over coals. It almost never grew so agitated. The only men with such violent sigils were on the cusp of death, and they knew it. The sigils knew it. Then at last the lantern in Kaba's hand became visible, starting with the brass hook from which it hung. An oval had been cut from the front of the cylinder, and the inner light—a lit candle, or perhaps a burning oil reservoir—spilled its light in a directed cone.

The tracker's voice jarred her. "I seem to have lost a girl."

"Is he armed?" Kaba asked. His light only managed to illuminate patches of the tracker.

"No," Milosz said. He lowered his blade's point to the stone floor, readying himself. "If he's wise, he'll listen very closely when I tell him to stand against the wall."

But the tracker did not move, and Anna didn't expect he would. She was the only one who could see the luminous snowflake beneath the burlap hem, the rune that she had carved almost an entire day earlier. Even now, in spite of its age, it pulsed like a white-hot furnace. She had never seen anybody's rune last so long, least of all her own.

And she had never seen them put to such murderous use.

"Ah," the tracker said, "so you met her?"

"Are you a tracker?" Milosz asked.

"By trade and pastime, yes."

"Where is the bogat's writ?" Milosz's stance hardened. "An agent of Malchym has the right to see such things."

"In another situation, I would be quick to show you it." The tracker took a step forward, forcing Milosz to raise his blade an inch, then sighed. "Unfortunately, this girl is worth a great deal to me, and I can't lose her. For all I know, you two are *mordyca*, out for the blood of innocents. After a while on these roads, such things aren't as shocking as you would expect."

The tracker glanced around the darkness, his hollow eye-slits giving him the appearance of a raven, or the spirits that mother chased away with her charms. "Why do you shelter her?"

"Shelter her from *what*?"

"Milosz, where is she?" Kaba swung his lantern from side to side, the brass hinges squealing with every pass. "Milosz, I can't see her anymore!"

Anna threw herself back against the stone shelving as the light rushed past, revealing the hordes of needle-legged spiders that made their home among the ruins. And then the light was gone, and she returned to the void. Her chest ached as she withheld her breaths, listening and waiting and screaming on the inside, feeling the legs of the spiders as they danced across her neck and forearms, spindly and prickling.

Callused fingers clamped around her neck. Before she could react, there was a grunt and a tug, and then she was rolling backward, pain exploding through her legs. Something on the floor bit at her, raking and slicing and tearing at the skin—the same sensation she had felt when the glassmaker's pane shattered—until she felt herself scrambling on the stones, still held round the neck by an unshakable force. The fingers squeezed, pinching her nerves and bruising the tender flesh.

Anna cried out.

"I have her," Kaba shouted from above her. He squeezed again, then dragged Anna to her feet, keeping her directly in front of himself. "Don't you move," he whispered. "Don't even *dare*."

Twenty paces away, Milosz continued to face the tracker. The two men were staring at one another, frozen, so detached that they could have been statues among the rubble. Kaba's brass cylinder, which rested just beside Anna's foot, framed the moment in pale light. Dust motes shifted and swirled as they crossed the illumined expanse.

"Kaba," Milosz said, never moving, "I want you to release her immediately."

"Good, we found her," the tracker said. "That's one less complication."

Anna tried to control her breaths, but Kaba's grip made it impossible. Every inhale, deep or shallow, reminded her of the pinched nerves around her airway. Her leggings clung to her skin, tacky where the glass shards had drawn blood and left their marks. But she had no time to feel *that* pain. With trembling hands, she combed along her sides—so softly that Kaba could not realize it—and felt for the blade.

"Once he stands against the wall, I'll release her," Kaba called.

Anna found the blade's coarse wooden tang. "Let go of me."

"Not another word," Kaba said as he squeezed harder.

But this time, she was not so quick to cry out. This time, she did not think of pain, or the deafening shouts beside her ear. She thought of the previous day, and how a man had fixed her in place with his crossbow, threatening death all the while.

"Now, Kaba," Milosz growled.

She wrapped her right hand around the blade, overcome with the same helplessness she'd felt in the path of the tracker's crossbow. Fed by the same wrath she'd tasted as the creature tore into Julek. "Release me."

"I will kill you," Kaba said. His breaths were overwhelming in her ears. He shifted his other arm, and Anna felt the cold, narrow press of iron against her neck. "Do you feel that? Shut up. Just shut *up*."

Anna snatched the blade from her belt, point down, and thrust backward. The iron tore through something soft, glanced off a harder substance, and then wriggled through the man's innards, its sinewy pull no different from venison. She forced her arm further back as Kaba began to scream.

Ahead, the tracker surged forward—seemingly unarmed—and charged into Milosz's rising blade. But the weapon did nothing beyond slow his pace. He walked onward as though consuming the iron, undaunted, and took hold of Milosz's neck.

Framed in the pale light, it appeared to Anna as a dance of spirits.

Something cold bit across her throat, followed by a more chilling sensation. She felt the tomesroom's decaying air slipping into her throat, but didn't dare take a breath. Liquid rushed free and soiled the neckline of her tunic, and suddenly her fingers and toes lost their warmth. Wetness spread over her chest and down across her stomach. She was faintly aware of the pitter-patter on the stone directly beneath her, and the little droplets that splashed back onto her bare feet.

This is what dying feels like, she realized. *This is how you felt.*

And in Kaba's ethereal light, the world fell away.

Chapter 4

In Bylka, the mourners did not wait for death to sing their songs. Two years ago, the thresher—Josep, second of Andrei—had been found coughing up blood in the fields. By sunset, he was sent to a small, lavender-smelling house on the far edge of town, so distant that even his hounds could not seek him out. And in that separate house, a group of ten children, boys and girls alike, sang songs in the grymjek. They sang without fail, even as the herbman covered the body in branches and called his kin to specify the death ceremony. They'd chosen the End of Teeth, likely because their storehouse's grains were low that year, and his hounds needed to eat *something*.

Anna had been one of those girls in the lavender house, and she had held her candle as wax burned her fingers. She remembered all the songs they sang to the dying man.

So when Anna slipped out of murky dreamscapes and into a world of pain and mellow humming, she thought she'd already died. She heard the voice whispering the old words into her ears, but she couldn't recognize the children who sang for her, or why they sounded more like a man than a boy.

Yet she knew she was alive, and somehow it disappointed her. Her body seemed reluctant to exist. No matter how hard she willed it, she couldn't swallow. Her throat burned, and her mouth tasted of stale saliva and blood.

"Easy," the tracker said.

Tears swelled at the corners of her eyes, and as she pinched her brows, she felt where older droplets had pooled and dried. She refused to make any noise—she never did—but the pain was unbearable. Without testing her theory, she was certain that she might never make a sound again.

She might never speak.

But as she opened her eyes, none of it seemed to matter. A ragged linen sheet was stretched out beneath her, barely covering the pile of straw and wool that served as her mattress. Above her and to the right there was a set of sealed, narrow shutters. Bars of light crept through the slats and across the nearby rug, offering glimpses into the woven pattern of spirals and hexagons. Fragrances that could only be termed *foreign* hung in the air, sweet and nostril-burning. Beneath that came the stench of rot, the earthiness of decomposing straw. And from outside, she heard horse hooves and the cries of merchants, beggars, flagellants, infants.

At the foot of the mattress, sunken low like a soglav on its haunches, the tracker stared at her.

"That's it." The tracker rested a hand on her ankle. A mixture of poultices and bandage wraps covered her from toe to knee. "Don't move too swiftly, girl. Otherwise you'll just tear it open."

Anna touched her throat with a shaking hand, ignoring the tracker's grunt of protest. Her fingers felt detached, gliding over the wound and the rigid, wax-coated zigzags where thread held her skin shut.

"Sedatives," the tracker explained. He shook his head. "Poor, poor girl. The Hazani probably gave you enough *nerkoya* to put down an ox. Not that you'd want to do without. Not right now, anyway."

Anna jerked her leg away from the tracker's touch. Her throat was too torn for speech, even as she strained to say *leave me* with parted lips.

"Like I said, you'll rip it," the tracker said. He gestured to his neck, where folds of burlap gathered like aging skin. "Do you feel it, girl? Probably not. But when the petals wear off, you'll feel the words stirring in there. Galipa said you were lucky. A touch deeper, and he might have severed the cords completely."

The tomesroom and their dusty blackness came over Anna, and she remembered that moment as though it had been last season, or before her life entirely. It seemed so far away, until she touched her neck again.

A heap of red-splotched rags, jars, and string sat on the floor beside the tracker. When he noticed Anna's gaze on the pile, he cleared his throat.

"It wasn't me," he said. "I can sew the flesh shut, but I'm no herbman, girl. That sort of thing is Galipa's work. Him, and his pale little boy." He shut his eyes, thinking. "Names were never my strength. They'll be up here soon." He produced a dark leather canteen shaped like a teardrop, then placed it beside Anna's leg. "Try to drink some of that. It should all go down."

Anna's vision fluttered in and out of focus as the tracker stood, examined her for an unusually long period of time, and finally exited through the doorway's hanging yellow curtain. The room lost its edges and melded together, and for once she could imagine she was nowhere at all. She let her head fall back onto the patchy linen and the comfort of the straw, her heartbeat and breaths so infrequent that death seemed possible. She closed her eyes, listening, entranced by the clamor of busy markets and flutes beyond the shutters. If she just held her breath for long enough, she might eventually slip away.

Then it came.

Visions of *light* screamed through her mind. Light, and hard, vicious angles that made her fingers curl for an ink quill. The lines arranged themselves and grew bolder, and she could do nothing to stop it. She was a vessel. Soon she felt the linen moving beneath her, her fingers wearing deep grooves into the fabric and underlying straw. The angles and light whispered to her in a foreign tongue. And she traced faster, with more resolve and confidence, until she burrowed too far and felt the cracked wood beneath the linen.

Blackness swallowed the visions, and there was nothing. Her heartbeats were beyond control, thumping so fiercely that it pained the stitching in her neck. She could hardly draw a breath without gasping.

Anna stopped tracing and opened her eyes.

Her finger slowed to a crawl inside the pattern's linen trenches. It was the symbol she'd seen in her mind, but now it was clarified: a jumble of octagons, all perfect in shape and size, linked by their inner points. It had been etched with such precision that Anna shuddered, pulled back her finger, and sheltered it in a tight fist.

Light.

The thought itself surprised her. Within the pattern's rigidity and flawless symmetry, she saw the glow of Kaba's lantern, how it had blinded her like the sun itself.

"Girl," called the tracker. She slid out of her focus, out of dreams and memory. His heavy boots clopped up the stairs, and the floorboards beyond the yellow curtain groaned. "I forgot something."

Anna had already brushed away the pattern and rolled over by the time the curtain moved, making sure that she kept her eyelids tucked—not pinched—shut. People could tell the difference.

The tracker moved to her straw mattress, filling the air with hints of stale sweat, and set something down near her back. It was hardtack, if the barley's vaguely rancid odor gave any indication.

She kept her eyes closed, even in the ensuing minutes of silence. Even when she was almost certain she was alone. Just before she ventured to look around, she felt a gentle hand on her shoulder, and something—not someone, as it was far too coarse to be skin—gave a soft touch to her hair, almost like a kiss. Anna's eyes shot open. She lay motionless for a moment, trembling, and sat up just as the curtain swung shut.

Then she pretended to rest again, and she did it so well that she actually slept.

* * * *

When she woke, the room was humid and dark. The air felt clogged, somehow suffocating, and it held the bitterness of smoking pork fat. She unfurled her hands, which had gathered clumps of linen during sleep, and tried to imagine Julek's face. Nausea set in when she realized she couldn't remember where all of his freckles were.

Anna rolled over, brushing against the tracker's ration of hardtack. It had been so long since she'd eaten that she no longer thought about food. Or perhaps, she thought as she sat up on the linen, the tracker had fed her while she was unconscious. It was revolting to think that he had kept her alive, caring for her and moving her and singing to her, all to keep his investment intact.

Maybe there's more to it, she told herself. *Maybe he does need a wife.*

But she felt as though she'd slept for days, and that would have given the tracker plenty of time to do whatever he wished. Her clothing had been changed from the ruined garments to a concealing brown dress, but she felt the same between her thighs. He hadn't touched her. With some relief, she shelved the notion.

Laughter and wet coughing echoed from downstairs.

She placed a hand on the wall behind her and rose to one knee, tucking her head to her chest when the dizziness set in. In the darkness everything felt loose and ethereal, but the *nerkoya* had faded. She managed to push herself up and hobble along the pitted wattle and daub, slowly learning to function in a body with no will to continue.

As Anna approached the doorway, she wondered if she could escape and survive on her own. She was out of the wilderness, out of—

The thought fled as she pushed aside the yellow curtain and slipped into the corridor.

It was a narrow, dimly lit space, lined with identical creamy curtains on both sides. Candlesticks hung from iron chains, illuminating only the rafters and the locked shutters at either end of the hall. Soft light spilled from the crevice of a larger central curtain.

She wandered closer and parted the folds carefully, revealing a wooden stairway and a square, coal-packed hearth at its landing. The thyme-laced aroma of boiling pork and trout hit her in the same instant as a gust of heat, and as she crouched for an unobstructed view, she saw the pots frothing above the embers.

The bitter smoke of flesh and fat wafted up past the beams, stirring Anna's hunger and forcing out belly growls.

She crept onto the stairway and ducked lower, trying to examine the common room beneath the rafters. The laughter was distant, likely in a partitioned room away from the pot. She craved escape from it all, even if it meant hobbling into the night, but not even her most urgent thoughts compared to hunger. She could plan after she ate. Until then she would think like a hound.

Two paces from the hearth and its pots sat something so outlandish that Anna couldn't term it a boy. It tipped back and forth in a dark rocking chair, staring into the coals as more laughter broke out nearby.

Can it even see? Anna wondered.

A loose-fitting tunic, knotted at the neck and sleeves with hemp braiding, covered most of its skin. Only the arms and hairless head remained exposed. And where the fabric left him bare, the flesh was unnaturally light, so pale that Anna swore she could see into his guts. She could see threads of clear fluid winding their way beneath his arms like roots on a sapling, and she watched the woven musculature of his jaw and forehead shift as he gritted his teeth. His eyes were blank pearls, formless and dazzling.

And for the first time, Anna saw how bright the sigils truly were. Despite the translucence of his flesh and the sickly pallor of his innards, she saw the sigils burning pure white. At times they seemed lost to the tangle of exposed veins and tendons, but Anna's mind never lost focus. She never lost complete awareness of what the sigil looked like: spiraling, jagged, and swirling in on itself until oblivion.

In the same instant, Anna *felt* the boy's flawless eyes turn on her.

Panic struck her. She stumbled backward, catching her foot on the edge of a step. Suddenly the sedatives and hunger and terror returned, blurring her vision as she collapsed on the stairs. The left side of her head ached, but the pain was a distant humming, much like her heartbeat and the kettle's spattering.

"Look, look," a young voice snapped. The sounds were pulses, always receding. "Look here, huh?"

Something warm cupped the back of her head, and an even warmer touch brushed the hair from her face. She opened her eyes and stared back at the pair of pearls, which seemed to gaze deeper than pupils ever could.

Up close, framed in her shifting vision, the boy wasn't so unsettling. His skin was smooth, like the polished stones Julek had skipped across the miller's pond. Bands of muscle fiber twitched as he narrowed his eyes and turned Anna's head from side to side. She liked that he was so clear, that she could stare into him and see his purity.

She tried to say something, anything, even to express agony, but could only push air through her throat in a hoarse whine.

"No," the boy frowned. "No talking. Talking makes the opening." He drew a finger across his translucent throat, mimicking a blade's cut.

Anna nodded, and the world resolved itself from a wash of colors and ringing in her ears. She looked past the boy's arm and stared at the kettle. Saliva flooded her mouth.

The boy trailed her gaze to the broth. "Oh." He straightened Anna's legs out over the steps and hurried to the bed of coals, then spooned broth into a clay bowl. After racing back up to her, he lowered the bowl to her waiting fingertips. "You drink."

She hardly needed his consent. Straining to keep her head upright, she pressed her lips to the clay's edge and drank. Pain tore across her tongue and lips and down her throat, but it was irrelevant compared to the comfort of a hot meal. When she finally leaned back and opened her eyes, she saw only remnants of viscous broth beaded along the rim of the bowl.

"Rest." The boy's voice muted the pain. He stepped around her and gingerly tucked his hand beneath her arm, lending support and beckoning her to stand.

Anna set the bowl down on a step and worked to push herself up. The boy was stronger than she'd imagined, wrenching her upright with little challenge. She swayed, but the boy, perhaps a palm or so taller than her, kept her balanced, and gave her the illusion of control. It was a lie, she knew, but he made her *feel* capable.

He made her feel strong.

And so she walked back to her quarters with the boy at her side, slipping in and out of wakefulness. Each time she lost consciousness, she saw the looming tree, Julek's missing freckles, the moss-covered shed behind her house, finally recognizing the row of shutters in her quarters. The hands settled her gently into straw and linen.

The boy knelt beside her mattress. A wash of moonlight framed the translucency of his skull and jaw, and his eyes glowed in the blackness. He didn't blink, didn't look away. "You haven't eat." Still staring, he picked up the chunk of hardtack and held it before Anna. "Why?"

Anybody who had spent appreciable time on the road knew why hardtack sat untouched. She opened her mouth to explain, or to say *I hate it*, but there was only a whistling of air.

The boy held up a lone finger, which appeared to Anna as a glowworm. He stood and left the room, but emerged several minutes later with something in his hands. "Look, look," he said, releasing his bundle on the rug with much clinking. It was difficult to see, but he'd brought several sheets of pressed paper, a set of quills, and an egg-shaped vial of ink. "You see this?"

Anna recognized the writing tools, but she'd never used them before. Her father had written most of the outgoing messages, and those had been written on vellum using riding glyphs—simple, quick, and practical. Most of the town had followed suit. But Arek, an older saltman with one working eye, had told Anna she was bright enough to one day learn true words.

"Write," the boy said. He placed a quill on the linen next to Anna, then uncorked the ink vial and set it on the floor.

She glanced down at the instruments, then shook her head. If it were anybody else before her, their smile less vibrant or hands less gentle, she would've strained to write *help me flee* with or without proper knowledge. Yet his presence settled her panic, and she could only gaze at the quill with longing.

"No write?" the boy asked.

Again Anna shook her head. She mouthed, "I can't."

"Why?"

She shook her head.

"So I teach," the boy said with a grin. "You want teach?"

After so many days of being discussed and discarded, such questions were unthinkable. She'd forgotten that only a select few knew about her gifts, and that to everybody else, she was simply a girl. She was somebody worth helping with no expectation of hayat's kiss. "Yes," her lips curled.

"I teach." He dipped his quill into the ink and scrawled something with flowing penmanship. "I Shem," he said, running his finger beneath the four symbols he'd written. As he came to each symbol, he paused and spoke. "S, H, E, M. Shem." Then the boy turned the quill's point on himself and smiled proudly. "Shem. And you?"

Anna stared into the boy's flesh and its soft glow. "Anna," she mouthed.

"Anna," Shem repeated with bold eyes. "Good. Now we write."

Chapter 5

In her sleep, Anna saw *light* as a monolith, dazzling and horrible. Each time she reached for its surface, it vanished and reformed as a luminous symbol in the sky, just as alluring as the pattern she'd traced on her linen sheet.

She saw it as joined hexagons burning against the clouds.

Light.

The tracker whistled from the doorway, jarring Anna from sleep. He stood with the curtain gathered in one hand, a tarnished silver pitcher in the other. His burlap sack looked brighter today, perhaps cleaner, but his eyes retained their violet murkiness. "Time to eat," he said, raising the pitcher higher. He sloshed its contents around. "Do you hear that, girl? Real milk. Don't be late." He slipped back through the curtains, his footsteps fading.

Anna sat up on the linen and rubbed at her eyes. The room was still dark, bathed in a cooling purple, but the city clamored beyond the shutters. Her throat was burning, as expected, but she felt surprisingly normal. No nausea, no panic, and no veil of sluggishness from the herbman's remedies. She felt over her sutures, rough and prickly, and winced as she wrapped a linen strip over the tender skin. Pain was a small price to pay if it meant staving off *nerkoya's* haziness. Yet even without the drugs, her world was distorted by the idea that the tracker had saved her, caring for her and protecting her during countless days on the road.

Remember what he is.

Remember that he has to die.

Gathering up the pleats of her brown dress, Anna rose and moved to the closest shutters. She realized, without the *nerkoya's* pall, that the lock was merely a hook behind the shutter doors. She could escape, once she learned the streets well enough. Killing the tracker would require time to recover, and potentially reinforcements, and in spite of its urgency, she delayed her dreams of slitting his throat. *Plan before you strike,* her father had once said of installing fence posts. Anna peered through the window's two slats at eye level, planning.

Directly below, wagons and horses ferried every manner of market good over cobblestones: silks, ingots, carrots, kiln-fired bowls, crushed dyes. Several giants, naked and hairless with wicker cargo loads lashed to their backs, hobbled through the crowds with pipe-playing handlers close behind. Even in the darkness before dawn, Anna recognized the distant blots of watchtowers and sprawling rooftops and fat-infused smoke smudging the air. Earthworks and timber walls formed cresting heights to her left, drawing the caravans into—

Malchym. The Western City.

Lost in its awe, watching fog tumble over its battlements and diffuse in the lowlands, Anna was slow to notice the branching alleys below, where maggot-stricken hound corpses lay among piss and creeping vines. Where roadside tenements bore jaggedly painted symbols and scorched wood and crooked nails, and old bloodstains endured on wattle and daub panels as dark dappling. Bronze-skinned children sat on porches and gazed at the passing procession, fixated on the salt-pouches of merchants and craftsmen. Wool-and-tin effigies of desert spirits stood watch upon chimneys, stirring in the breeze.

This is not the city, Anna realized. *These are its gutters.*

She examined the alleyways and their twisting paths, wondering if the chaotic layout might simplify her escape. Given proper planning, it surely would. But plans took time.

"Come along, girl," the tracker called from beyond the fabric.

* * * *

Most guests had already eaten and departed when she arrived with the tracker, wandering up to a long, cracked table littered with empty plates near the front door. The first hints of daylight spilled through the threshold, along with dust and flies and a trade caravan's foreign shouts.

Shem sat at the far end of the table with a starved, leather-skinned man to one side and a pale woman the other, eyeing his food curiously.

The woman was coughing into a handkerchief, her cheeks blushing in red and purple. Her eyes were red and watery, her black hair tied up in a copper wire. Triple-crowned spheres jerked beneath her skin as she stood and moved away, breathless. The leathery man had swollen, cloud-like sigils and tide-gem eyes, so blue that Anna couldn't resist staring. His emergent beard littered dark skin like snowflakes, and he had cropped white hair to match. His tunic was long and stained, unlike Shem's.

He smiled at Anna, and she forced herself to smile back.

Most others at the table didn't bother to raise their heads from the food, aside from a young woman with a shaved head and cinnamon-colored fabric gathered around her neck. She had a lean build and bronze skin, her eyes roaming among guests like a circling hawk. Her sigils were sharp, branching roots that wound their way into blossoms. She did not eat, nor did she place her hands upon the table. Beside her was a baggy-eyed mother with an infant clutching her breast, and to her right was a shirtless man with brown tattoos—henna, the messengers called it. A potbellied man without earlobes or eyebrows paced behind her, murmuring in a northern tongue to his blindfolded companion, *"Deguru yeftil, desh?"*

The tracker led Anna to an open spot at the far end of the bench, and waited for her to bunch up her dress and sit before he wandered away.

Before Anna could reach for her fork, a hand reached past her and provoked a flinch. Back home, she'd never spooked so easily. She spun, still calming herself, to find the sickly woman limping back toward the cooking hearth.

Her blue skirt danced in the doorway's breeze, just as mother's once had. The woman turned with red-ringed eyes, flashed an awkward smile, and slipped behind a set of curtains.

Only when Anna glanced back at the table did she notice that the woman had brought her a porridge-laden plate and fully filled mug.

"Shem, where is your mother?" The leather-skinned man was kneeling by one of the hearths, pulling iron bread molds away from the coals. His accent was rolling and unfamiliar. "Find her. Tell her to lay down, yes?"

Shem rose from his seat, collected a stack of porridge-streaked plates, and brought them to the hearth. He set them down gently beside a filled washtub. "Yes, *ba*." With a subtle bow, he, too, disappeared behind the curtains.

"Bread?" his father asked Anna. He pointed down at a blackened loaf near the coals. "Eat bread, ah?" Anna shook her head, and in turn, the man gestured to her throat. "How is it?"

She clutched the fabric around her neck.

"Eat," the tracker told her. He circled the table, crouched beside the hearth with a tin plate in hand, and used a cloth square to move a bread pan from the coals and turn the loaf over onto his plate. "You're right about her being rare. Stronger than most, I'll say. Not a trace of sick flesh." He locked eyes with Shem's father and gave a laugh like cracking ice. "Don't think I'm brushing over your miracles. Your salve did a lot, I'll say. But she survived five days in a cart. Five. Probably bled herself half-to-death by *Wicew*, but she made it." The tracker stared at Anna. "You don't find that every day." He paused. "Eat, girl."

Despite her nausea and their running conversation, which danced between northern pricing and how to disinfect a gut wound, Anna consumed more than she'd ever managed at home. She shoveled forkfuls of porridge up from her tin plate, pausing only to sip her weak beer or let the pain of swallowing subside. She chewed on dark bread and the innards of sweet, prickly fruit she'd never seen before, all under the press of their scrutiny.

"It needs to be dressed again, Anna," the tracker said. He studied her as he ate, stuffing cardamom seeds under his mask. Mentions of Anna's name drew her attention from a hovering forkful of porridge. "Galipa will make you another salve. How's the pain?"

Galipa, Anna thought as she moved the fork to her mouth. She stared at the northerner and wondered, distantly, if he'd done a good thing by saving her life. The tracker, too, had kept her breathing, but it hadn't been an act of mercy. Still, Galipa's smile, warm and inviting, despite the closed lips, showed his connection to Shem. They were not of the same blood, but they were linked somehow.

Maybe compassion was better than blood.

"Well?" the tracker pressed.

It's fine, she wanted to say. She wanted to *scream* it. If it meant having her voice back, she would speak to the tracker gladly.

"If you need *nerkoya*, you tell him." The tracker swallowed. "Grove knows I've paid for the entire experience."

"You pay for miracles," Galipa said, prodding at coals with a twisted black iron rod.

"A miracle would be a speaking girl."

"All in time, ah?" Galipa winked at Anna. "Do not fear. In time, you may regain everything, okay? You may speak."

"May," the tracker muttered.

"Yes, she may. Miracles take time."

The tracker brushed his hands over the coals. "A *miracle* would come before our ship."

Most benches were empty when Anna scraped her plate clean. Some guests were carrying their plates and leftover food to a trough on the far side of the room, while others huddled by the doorway, peering out at the sky and lacing up their boots. But the woman with the cinnamon wrap and a hawk's gaze sat rigid in her seat, her plate untouched.

"Go wait for the miracle worker, Anna," the tracker said. He jerked his head toward the curtains. "Farthest one back. The red one. He'll be in for you soon enough. Just don't go wandering."

"It's fenced," Galipa said. He unclenched his brow and looked at Anna. "No worry about this, yes? Go and sit. I'll take care of *this*," he said as he tapped his throat.

Anna slid from the bench and walked past the tracker like a beaten hound. She glanced over her shoulder to see if the hawk-eyed woman would ever move, only to find her being approached instead.

"You need to delay it by another day," the tracker said while wandering up to her bench.

Anna paused at the edge of the red curtain, half-slipping into a nearby alcove.

"Impossible," the hawk-eyed woman said. "They will not pay the fees in Nur Sabah."

The tracker leaned over the table. "Circumstances are *different*, if you couldn't tell. I've sunk good salt into the girl."

"So we sail tomorrow."

"She's worthless if she can't speak."

"Voice returns," Galipa said. He poked the coals absently.

The tracker ignored him and shook his head. "Get me another day, and you can have the last of my salt. I'll make a killing in the north."

But the hawk-eyed woman only blinked back at him. "Have you been there, *mohur*?"

"My sources have. My riders used to—"

"Used to." The hawk-eyed woman tipped her head back. "The north has changed. There is a reason that men such as Mohur Galipa are quick to flee the flatlands." She paused, surveying the tracker's veiled face. "Do you think that another day will change Hazan?"

The tracker cocked his head to the side. "One girl might."

Anna strained to hear more, but noticed the spark of tumbling coals as Galipa finished his raking and set the rod aside. She peeled away the curtain and slipped through its folds before the herbman stood.

All four walls of the room were hanging curtains, and it was cramped enough to be lit by a single candle on its iron chain. Directly beneath the candle was a square wooden table, and nearby sat a tray full of thread, rags, needles, razors. Black spots covered the floorboards like freckles.

But the most unsettling thing was out of sight.

Anna heard the coughing as a faint crackling noise until she stepped closer to the table. It came from the wall of maple-colored curtains ahead, and the fabric did little to dampen the sounds of fluid bubbling in the lungs. She'd heard the noise enough to know that it couldn't be helped, and their only escape was death. If she'd been allowed, she could've tried to mark them.

The curtains rustled behind Anna.

She whirled, breathless, to find Galipa drawing the curtains closed. *It's fine,* she told herself. *Not everything will hurt you.*

"Sit, sit," Galipa said as he ushered her to the tabletop. He grabbed a tin bucket from the corner and set it near the instrument table, sloshing some of its water onto the wooden floor in the process. "You are not hurting, ah? You do not need the pulp?"

Anna pushed herself up onto the table and listened to her body's aching. By now, pain was a constant thing, and she could hardly tell the difference between suffering and relief. Still, she shook her head.

"Good," Galipa said. He flashed a smile before sorting through a leather pouch on his hip. He produced a handful of flat green leaves, sprinkled them into a clay bowl, and mashed them with a black pestle. After a quick sniff, he gathered the paste on his fingertips. "This will help the skin to, how you say, form back? This will help."

Anna stared at Galipa for a long moment, then lifted her chin and peeled away the fabric around her neck. His fingers smoothed the ointment over her skin and prickly sutures, and the mixture cooled from warm to chill, throbbing over the wound.

Her lip broke at its edge, trying to smile. If not for her lack of words, she would've thanked him.

But Galipa seemed to see it anyway, patting her on the arm. His touch didn't make her shy away. "You are strong girl, ah? Shem says that he bring you food last evening. He says you are strong. This is very good. He does not meet many his age."

A flurry of whispers and coughing broke out behind Anna, just beyond the curtains. She turned her head and frowned, then looked back at Galipa. She could easily discern Shem's foreign words.

Once again, it seemed Galipa either read her thoughts, or the situation. His bright eyes dimmed, leaving his smile behind like an etching on his flesh. After a moment he looked away and patted her arm again. "It is good that you are strong. I need to head to market now, yes? Can you find your way to yard?"

Anna nodded, already working to rewrap her neck bandages. She returned his smile with as much strength as she could muster, sustaining the illusion until the northerner slipped through the curtain and his footsteps ceded to barking hounds and crying infants and cawing ravens, their wiry feet scratching over the roof tiles. Sitting in the gloom, taking in the piney odors of a nearby rag and the pulses of her torn flesh, Anna realized that she wouldn't wake up from a dream. She wouldn't learn why they'd sold Julek, or what the tracker desired of her, or why she was forced to live at all. Everything was wrong and much too real.

She pressed her palms to her face and sobbed.

She cried until she no longer heard the hounds, and until—

"Anna?"

Instantly placing Shem's voice at her back, she swiped at her cheeks with linen sleeves and cleared her nose with a hard sniff, swallowing the filaments of saline and hops-laden mucus. She gritted her teeth and tightened her hands in her lap, more angered than broken by her exposure. *If you cry*, she heard father saying, his voice muffled beneath river water, *do it in the far woods, Anna. Boys are too young to do anything but laugh.* Yet there was no laughter, only soft footsteps rounding the table.

Shem leaned into view with dimmed eyes. "Anna, why you cry?"

She glanced away. "Pain," she mouthed.

But the words drifted past him, his eyes scrunched as he parsed her face. "Thought pain?"

Anna lifted her head, studying the boy and his smile with blurred sight.

"I know stories." Shem kneaded his fingers shyly. "Many stories, and maybe you like them. Maybe they take away thought pain. They bring thought happiness, maybe."

Dark woods and dead brothers and wicked men. She knew too many stories already, cradled too many horrible thoughts to recover now.

But the boy's lopsided grin remained, and in spite of her shaking hands, she managed a nod. "Please," her lips spoke.

His smile widened. "Okay," he said, sinking down into a deep squat before the table. "I tell first story of beautiful girl. Very beautiful. Long, long time ago—"

A violent fit of coughing broke through the rows of curtains. Shem's eyes snapped to attention, flared, focused on something behind Anna with chilling intent. He dashed out of the stall with his young voice calling, echoing: "*Mat, mat.*"

And in the same way that Anna could mentally assemble true letters into basic words without being told, she translated basic words of his language without learning it.

He was calling for his mother.

Anna spun and listened to the wet hacking as it leaked into her stall. She heard fluids boiling in the lungs, spattering and drowning the sufferer, and Shem alternating between orders and soothing reassurances.

It was neither her responsibility nor destiny to help. It was in her best interest to let these things slip away. It was in consideration of her own safety and secrets to leave Julek unmarked.

You're wrong, father. She clenched her fists. *You were always wrong.*

She slid off the table, intent on Galipa's scalpels.

Chapter 6

She chose the cleanest blade on the tray, holding it an arm's distance from her face and staring into the silver, unsure of who was looking back at her. Three years ago, she'd seen herself in a rider's pocket mirror while he stopped in Bylka overnight. Even then, she'd stared into unfamiliar wide eyes, a lopsided smile, and a nose that seemed too crooked. Now her cheeks were less pronounced and her jaw was shapelier, but she still had that nose and too-bright blond hair. She had rough, world-worn skin, and a bandage where the world had left its mark.

She shook away the reflection as she lowered the scalpel, rounded the table, and pushed through the next set of curtains.

Shem stood over his mother with a wet rag in hand, dabbing at her forehead and the jagged lines of her collarbone while he sang lullabies. Several candles burned around the storeroom, illuminating his mother's crate-mounted mattress and half-finished tapestries upon the walls. The air was thick and hot and smelled of vinegar.

Shem's mother opened her eyes and smiled at Anna. "Come over, dear. Did Galipa send you?" She buried a cough deep in her throat. "Don't be afraid. You can stand closer."

"Sickness never spread," Shem said softly.

"Shem, she looks scared." His mother squinted. "What do you have in your hand, dear?"

Anna raised the scalpel and turned it in her hands, glinting light around the room. She noted the apprehension in Shem's eyes and his mother's bemusement, wondering if she could get away with putting a blade to a woman's throat and replicating the three points of her sigil, all under the auspices of healing.

She thought of father and mother and how they had hidden their blades in the rafters, just in case Anna decided to defy their wishes.

While mother and son stared at one another, Anna rounded the raised mattress. Glancing past the woman and into Shem's bewildered eyes, she gleaned that the tracker hadn't told them anything about her. She raised the blade to her own throat, pressing the point across her fabric, and mimicked the flow of her cuts. "Scribe," she mouthed, drawing out the motions of each sound. "I want to help."

Shem took hold of his mother's upper arm and frowned. "Not enough salt."

Shem's mother patted her son's arm in turn, trying to soften his mask of disappointment. "But perhaps where she comes from, dear . . ."

Shem's eyes were wide and bright, and the translucent lump in his throat bobbed with uncertainty. He shared quick, furtive looks with his mother, who seemed unaffected by the turn of events, if not relieved. "Maybe she is ill."

The woman put on a tired grin and smoothed over Shem's hand with her own, which had grown pallid and jaundiced. "Just get your *ba*, will you?"

Shem's eyes darted between his mother and Anna. Watching, waiting, blinking, he eventually stepped back. "No touch her until I return?"

Anna lowered the scalpel to her side and nodded.

Before the boy had even slipped between the curtains, the sigils on the woman's neck began to dance. They contracted and spun in tight revolutions, begging the blade to part the skin. They were gusts of cool air rising off a stream.

She lifted the scalpel, pressed it to the woman's throat, and cut.

Shem's mother remained still. She stared back at Anna curiously, perhaps wondering if she would die here and how long it would take. There was no pain in her eyes.

Anna followed the luminous trail as it warped and formed around her blade, teasing the edge deeper and further up the woman's neck. It was like chasing leaves in the wind, always one step behind but lost in the thrill.

She finished her stroke and turned the blade, joining the incision's edges. She watched the rivulets of blood halt halfway down the neck's milky skin, waver, then retreat into the wound. The severed skin pulled inward and reformed with a patina of smooth, pink scar tissue. Beneath Anna's fingers, the wound healed.

The rune burned with pale light.

"*Yishna'sul*," the woman whispered. Her eyes were wide and shimmering with tears, but they were not born from pain. Seconds before, her voice had been heavy with the fluids in her lungs. Now, with the rune's light, her words held only awe. Even her skin darkened, swelling with a rosy hue. "*Yisha'halam esul.*"

Something warm and trembling grasped Anna's hands while she stared into the woman's eyes. She looked down and saw the woman's hand—once pale, now lively and bronzed—clasped over her own. Anna felt the woman's heartbeat drumming across the back of her hand.

"You are blessed," the woman whispered.

Anna left her hand in place, comforted by the pulsing of her heartbeats and the way she looked at her. She stared at Anna like she was a gift, a miracle. She looked at Anna like her mother.

Footsteps creaked behind the curtains, and hushed words materialized from silence.

"*Mat?*" Shem asked. He wandered past Anna and leaned closer, trying to peer around Anna's hand and glimpse the hayat glowing behind the rune. His eyes snapped to Anna. "You did?"

There was no telling whether his shock came from anger or joy. Anna pulled her hand free, still clutching the scalpel, and edged away from the table.

Galipa hurried to the table, his bright blue eyes darkening. He gazed up and down his wife once, twice, three times, pinching his brow with each pass.

The more Anna watched their stares, the more she wondered if she'd committed a crime. She wondered if she'd somehow ruined things, or put hatred in the hearts of the only people who had shown her kindness.

Anna dropped the scalpel.

"The lungs?" Galipa asked. His eyes reddened as he laid a hand across her rune. "How are the lungs, Emine?"

Shem's mother, Emine, it seemed, reached up to Galipa and caressed his cheek. Candlelight reflected the glint of tears forming and breaking over her cheekbones. She inhaled a great gulp of air and released it smoothly. "*Dobra.*"

Despite the sobbing of his parents, however joyful it was, Shem wore a smile. His translucent lips peeled back and offered a clear view of his teeth, which were whiter and more rigid than any others Anna had seen. His gaze was one of boyish curiosity.

His stare fell to the rune, its lines appearing as scars in the reflection of his pearl eyes.

Galipa wiped at his eyes. "Have you tried the standing?"

Emine shook her head.

"Shem, stay." Galipa took hold of his wife's arm. "Hold her like this. Not too harsh."

"They don't feel *beskyah*." She glanced down at the arm on Shem's side, her eyes creeping over the limb as though she'd just discovered it. She flexed her fingers and wrist, marveling at the bones shifting beneath the skin. "You see, *canam*? Do you see?"

Galipa ran a hand over her other arm, tearful once more. "Yes, I see." As their flesh met, the sigils stirred and swirled near the point of contact.

She'd seen that on her mother and father before, each time their lips or arms met.

"Oh, child," Galipa whispered, studying Anna with misty eyes. "You left this mark?"

Their eyes weighed down upon her. She glanced at Emine, who seemed incapable of taking her eyes from her own limbs, and nodded.

Shem studied Anna with a furrowed brow. "He tell you this, *ba*?"

"He said nothing," said Galipa. For the first time, Anna felt the bite of Galipa's tone. It wasn't directed at her. "You are a blessed child, Anna. You are—"

He cried softly into his palms.

"*Ba?*" Shem pressed.

"Shem, *canam*, bring her whatever she likes," Emine said, rubbing Galipa's leathery arm and making the sigils dance. "Take care of her."

After a moment of silence, Galipa wiped his eyes and dabbed his cheeks with the collar of his tunic. "Yes, as your *mat* said," he managed. "I want you to take her up to the room. Stay with her, yes? Bring her anything." With a last glance at his wife, Galipa turned back to Anna. "You will not have to work another of the days, Anna. You will never want for any of the things in this world."

Once Anna followed Shem through the curtains, she heard the crying resume.

* * * *

Upstairs, on her new home of straw and linen, Anna tried to focus on the true letters. Shem sat on the floor in front of her and stared, touching his neck and trying to understand what Anna had done to his mother. After some time in silence, no longer keen on Shem's mumbled adoration, she'd requested a piece of paper and some writing utensils to resume practice. But the boy's curiosity hadn't dimmed.

Shem's head lulled to the side. "What did you do?"

Anna glanced up from her letters. She was halfway through writing, *We are going north.*

"My mother," Shem said, tapping his throat with two fingers. "I know what you are, but how, never how. I don't understand."

Neither did Anna. She'd seen sigils since she was a small girl, and she'd traced them in the dirt before her father had seized her arm and forbade her from doing so, but she'd never understood. She'd never spoken to any spirits, nor heard any words in her dreams.

She put her quill to the page, scrawled out the word hayat, and flipped it toward Shem.

"Hayat, *tek*," Shem nodded. "But how? How I have it?"

While the boy spoke, Anna watched his lips and tried to synchronize her new words and sounds to the twist of his tongue. She pieced together how to reply, slowly at first, then wrote, *You don't have it. You use it.*

Shem knotted his brow and gave a long exhale, as though the answer exhausted him somehow. He wanted to *know* something, and that was a sentiment that Anna could understand. It would take years, in all likelihood, before he realized that the world liked to keep people ignorant. "I want."

Anna set aside her paper and quill, then mouthed, "Impossible."

"Why?" There was no anger in his voice, merely the obsession that had seized him at his mother's bedside.

But some things were too complicated for lips alone. Anna tried for a few moments, then glanced away. For an instant she considered the pain of being normal, of being ungifted. She wondered if Shem was like her, beyond the flesh.

But he wasn't, and he could never understand.

"Can you do it to me?" Shem's clear eyelids flicked over his pupils but never quite hid them. "I want mark. I want rune."

Anna's fingers trembled. Not from fear, but anticipation. Her hands wanted to sculpt and carve, to draw the scalpel across his flesh. It was a mindless, gnawing impulse, but she had no reason to resist it. She scanned the floor for a blade.

"Yes?" Shem asked.

She wondered if the quill's tip would be sharp enough to break the flesh and follow his sigil's lines accurately.

Then shouting broke out downstairs. The eastern edge to the tracker's voice stood out among the others with horrific clarity. When he had spoken to Anna in previous days, his words had seemed icy yet restrained. Now they were sharp and cruel and burning with rage. With *murder*.

"And where is she?" the tracker roared. His boots thudded up the stairs, drawing Shem's attention to the curtain.

Anna hardly had time to drop her quill before the curtain flew open, revealing the tracker and his dark burlap covering. She hurried to gather her ink-marked pages and tuck them under the far side of the mattress, well out of the tracker's reach.

"Anna," the tracker said quietly, now looming over her. "Do you know what you did to the *sukra*?"

In the corner of her eye, Anna saw Shem bunching up his fists. She gave a subtle shake of her head, disarming him.

"Look at me," the tracker said. He squatted low enough to reach eye level with Anna. "Don't know if you understand this, but what you did was dangerous. And it was a fool's move. Do you know why?"

Because it was the right thing, she thought, but it was wasted. Some things, like mercy, were beyond his comprehension.

"You made a mistake," the tracker said. His drooping eyes spoke only of laziness, and the petals that he mashed and swallowed every night.

"She made saving of my mother," Shem said.

The tracker slowly wrenched his gaze toward Shem, having almost forgotten that the boy was in the room. "You mean that she *saved* your mother, cretin. Where did you learn your river-tongue?"

Shem, perhaps due to his translucent skin, gave no indication of embarrassment. "You show Anna respect."

There was a silencing impact to the words. Anna's breaths slowed, and she wondered if she'd imagined Shem's reply. Perhaps it had only been her desperate desire for somebody to defend her, to support her. But she could see the tracker's eyes narrowing in their burlap pits, and the fear set in.

"How surprising." The tracker rose to full height and turned on Shem. "And what would a Huuri boy know about respect?"

"Very much." His voice was factual and innocent, almost eager to provide the answer that to a question he understood.

"Come here, and we'll see what you remember." The tracker curled his hands into bony fists.

Shem slanted his head again. "I remember all."

The curtains parted once again. Galipa barreled through the doorway with both hands raised, breathless. And despite his best efforts, he couldn't conceal the trembling in his arms or the chattering in his jaw.

Beyond the curtains, Emine sobbed. A quick and foreign hush from Galipa forced her into silence.

The tracker cast a glance over his shoulder, eyed the herbman from head to toe, and laughed behind his burlap. "Now you come to bargain, I suppose. Is this how they handle their business in the north, Galipa?"

"She didn't mean to do this," Galipa managed. "It is a good thing, and I am glad, but—"

"But you're content to profit from her gifts."

"No!" He stared at Anna with wounded eyes. "She is a child, no? She is a blessed child. An act of kindness should be rewarded."

"To the proper owner, maybe."

"She has no owner," Galipa said.

"She is *mine*," the tracker said. "You can ask her, if you like. We made a fair bargain."

Memories of Julek's bargain turned over in Anna's head, but she pushed them away. If she could've spoken for herself, she would've said something, anything.

"You cannot have gifts," Shem said.

The tracker cracked his knuckles, still facing away from the boy. "Those gifts are labor, you know. If she provides labor, I need to be paid. That's honest business, Galipa. Now, you'll pay me properly, or I'll bloody this floor." He stepped forward and towered over the herbman.

Shem looked to his father, but the herbman shook his head defiantly.

It was maddening.

Anna scrambled to her feet and wedged herself in front of Galipa. She felt the tracker's warm, sour breath leaking through the burlap, the bloodshot tendrils worming in his eyes. But it wasn't enough to make her move.

"Step out of the way," the tracker said softly.

"Anna," Galipa said, laying a hand on her shoulder. "You should not be here."

Still, she did not move.

"Come, now," the tracker whispered. The tight weave of his burlap showed its age and fraying as he bent down toward Anna. "I'll go right through you, and I don't want to have to do that."

"Kill me," she mouthed. And it was true, she thought, now that the feeling was settled in her stomach. She would sooner die than move. She would rather be a meal for the hounds than the same girl who'd given up Julek.

If the tracker wanted to get to Galipa, of course, it was simple enough to shove her aside. But he wouldn't lay a hand on her, not out of violence, anyway. Instead he stared down at the girl and tore into her eyes with that lifeless gaze, trying to flood her with fear.

Fear was just a word.

Finally the tracker stepped back. "Oh, how I endure your antics." He looked past Anna, studying the herbman evenly. "Fine. No coercion, then.

I just want my fee, and I'll stand by it." Rage had evaporated from his words, but hatred remained.

Galipa patted Anna's shoulder and stole shallow breaths, trying to regain some sense of composure. He sighed. "And if I cannot pay?"

"I'll kill the boy," the tracker said.

"No coercion," Galipa hissed. "I earn hardly enough to put wood on the fire, *vesh*? And you come here—you want to take more than I have?"

The tracker laughed like distant thunder. "You were paid very well for our room and board. Now, I don't know what you saw in the north, but the mark on your wife's neck is worth something here. It's worth more than your life in any sense, Galipa."

"What does she want?" asked Galipa, a renewed fire in his voice. He stepped to Anna's side and furrowed his brow. "Look at this poor girl. What does she want, huh?"

"Do you really think it matters?"

"Of course."

"Well, she's free to speak up at any time."

Anna glared at the tracker, but his eyes offered nothing in return. She broke away from Galipa's hand on her shoulder, walked to the sheet, and gathered up her quill and paper. Their eyes were on her, but she wouldn't let the fear bleed through.

"What's this?" the tracker asked, glancing at Shem. "What did you do?"

Shem looked to Anna. "I teach her."

"Lessons, Galipa?" the tracker asked. "Is this what your mutt does in his free time, when he's supposed to be tending to her? What sort of arrangement am I paying you for?"

"This girl cannot speak," Galipa said.

"Right, and it was your charge to ensure that her voice returned. Have you been spinning lies with me?"

Galipa shook his head violently. "No, no, no. Shem was trying to be kind to her. She will have the speaking, this is true. But until then—"

"Until then she'll learn nothing, because she couldn't write her own years down if she wanted to. And if you think this *lesson* will pay for part of her services . . ."

Anna scowled and placed the paper up against the nearest wall, smoothing out its wrinkles with the back of her hand. She wrote with the quill's remnants of ink, and as the sound of the scratching nib filled the air, the conversation ceased. There was only silence as she scrawled out the four letters.

H-E-R-E.

"Huh," the tracker said after a moment. "So she learned a word."

"I want to stay with Shem," Anna mouthed.

The tracker wheeled on Shem. "What have you been teaching her?"

The boy blinked and looked at his father. "Words."

"What is it, then?" The tracker cast a hard glance at Galipa. "What have you said to her?"

But Galipa had no words to offer. He stood with his shoulders drawn up, his face red and streaked with sweat. "You see? You see what she say to you? She wants something. I can take care of her here, and she can stay with my son."

"That isn't an option. But she wants the boy, apparently," the tracker said, his dead eyes sweeping toward Shem. "I think she has a heart for your boy."

For the first time, Anna looked at Shem in this light. She only wanted his letters and his numbers, and the kindness he had given her—or so she thought. There was nothing inherently attractive about him, and he was far less handsome than most of the boys she had known, but the tracker's word resonated in her. She liked his *heart.*

"Shem?" It was a pained, wretched word, and it tore Anna's attention away from the boy. Galipa's eyes danced from one person to the next, swelling with new tears, and at last he focused on Anna. "What you mean? Please, please tell him. Tell him you want to stay with Shem."

"I want Shem," she mouthed, glancing from the herbman to the tracker when she could no longer bear Galipa's sobbing.

"That settles it," the tracker said. "Now, in addition to the boy, we'll be needing some salt."

Chapter 7

The debate had initially leaked through the walls in bitter snaps, broken up by bouts of sobbing or silence. The tracker's voice had been thick and steady throughout, but it never softened, even as he suggested putting the boy in chains.

When Anna focused, she heard fractured descriptions of the north and its violence, of how Shem shouldn't be returning, of how they'd barely fled the region. They argued about the weather, the food, the wars . . .

Every so often, Shem raised his head from sketches of cliffs and corpses. He never reacted to the argument, although Anna was sure he could hear the commotion even better than she could.

Inklings of an escape plan came over Anna just as she realized that the nearby room had fallen silent. Footsteps shuffled over the floor and the empty room's curtains fluttered. She glanced at her own doorway, where the curtains suddenly parted to reveal the tracker, followed by Galipa and Emine. The northerners' eyes were red and defeated, and in the candlelight, shadows etched out their swollen features and shimmers of sweat. Galipa held fast to his wife's arm.

"Anna," the tracker said, "come with me for a while. There are some closing matters to the agreement."

Anna stood and moved across the room, noticing something else on Emine's face. It was something she'd seen in Bylka, when men like the tracker had arrived and done their business in front of the children and parents alike. They'd taken the pouch of salt from the bogat's men, but their eyes remained on their children, steeped in memory and shame. She wondered if her mother or father had looked that way in their dealings. The night before, they'd tucked her and her little bear off to sleep with warm smiles.

"Make it quick, if you would," the tracker said to Galipa.

Emine met Anna's eyes again. The northern woman reached up, seemingly vulnerable, and covered the rune on her neck.

It crossed Anna's mind that it was her own fault, that her gift had done this. But maybe the tracker was right for once. Maybe she was valuable, and things had to cost something. Maybe a mother didn't deserve a child if she would give him up so willingly.

The tracker placed a hand on Anna's shoulder and led her toward the hanging curtain.

"Please, consider again," Galipa whispered as Anna reached the doorway. His eyes were shimmering and creased, just on the verge of breaking. "Do not take this boy."

But the tracker squeezed Anna's shoulder, guiding her through the open curtain and into the cool darkness of the corridor, and she wondered if she'd simply lost too much to understand him.

"Do you know what they're doing?" the tracker asked. They were halfway down the hall, just shy of the stairs, when he sighed. His rune glowed through the empty stitches in his burlap. "They're using tears for tears, girl. They think that if they cry, then you'll cry too. Just don't let them make you feel anything. Especially not for the boy."

Anna turned back toward her room, faintly aware of Emine's sobs from beyond the door hanging.

"Grove knows they don't have anything worth *gevna* in this place. He was a smart pick, when you get right down to it," the tracker said as he started down the stairs. "Droby are cheap in the north, but they don't know much beyond flatspeak. Maybe this one can learn his place."

Anna followed the tracker downstairs and into the common room, where the dying hearth was shedding the last of its warmth. The door to the streets was sealed and barred, and all that remained on the tables was a scattering of used plates and silver. Some of the inn's patrons rolled dice or picked apart herbs. To the far left, just in front of the curtain rows, was a circular table.

Smoke coiled out of the darkness and into the nearby candlelight. Something behind the haze shifted, and at once the hawk-eyed woman became clear across the table, inhaling from a standing pipe's long tube. Something about her deeply copper skin and delicate motions kept her concealed in the shadows.

"If you're hungry, you should eat," the tracker said. He gestured to the kettles and pans arranged around the hearth without pausing in his strides. When he reached the woman's table, he sank into one of the chairs and picked up a different tube, slipping it under his mask. "*Yak shen?*" he asked the hawk-eyed woman.

Anna eyed the pots for a moment, but her stomach was churning too much. She was unsettled by the hawk-eyed woman's stare, and despite her reservations, took the seat closest to the tracker.

"We're still leaving tomorrow," the hawk-eyed woman said, exhaling a ribbon of smoke.

The tracker cut his inhale short, and smoke dribbled through the burlap. "What happened to the salt I gave you?"

The woman fidgeted with her belt for a moment, then tossed a heavy leather pouch across the table. It landed in front of the tracker, hissing as its granules shifted.

"Oh," the tracker said. He picked up the bag and tucked it away in his tunic. "You shouldn't have come back unless you had good news."

"All news is good news." She ignored the tracker's snort. "Emine consulted me during the evening meal. I know your attention has rested upon this girl, but you should remember what she is."

Anna straightened in her chair, conscious of the fact that she'd been ignored, treated like scenery.

"She's a scribe." The words were buried under his breath.

"And a girl," the woman added. She tapped on the head of the tube. "You never told her how to behave, and it shows in her actions. Do you think it wise to take her counsel?"

Anna glanced down at the tube, wondering how the smoke felt to breathe. It'd neither felt nor tasted *good* when she stood too close to a fire, but perhaps this was different. She reached for the tube. The tracker slapped her hand, jarring her.

"Don't embarrass yourself." The tracker grunted. "What's the angle, Bora? Are you pulling for her because she feeds you?"

Bora offered no immediate reaction, but incubated the question with another bout of smoking. "I've known them for many cycles. They take good care of the boy."

"Their droba, you mean."

"Not anymore."

The tracker huffed. "He's Huuri."

"They claim him," Bora replied. "It would do them great harm to see him leave. Not only for their livelihood, but for their hearts. They would mourn him."

"Precious," the tracker said, "but this is business. I thought the north respected that."

"It does. Those who flee often value other courses."

The tracker smoked from the tube for a while, staring at Bora with still-glazed eyes. "Have you come here to tell me that you're backing out, then? Backing out over a boy?"

Bora raised a brow. "No. Severing ties is a luxury in these circles. But I'm sure you've learned as much by now." She turned her eyes on Anna, cutting into her thoughts and fears about the north. "I advise you to leave the boy."

The tracker set down the tube. "And what will he pay me for his wife's rune, then? A few loaves of bread?"

"Gratitude," Bora said. "It is a rare thing in Hazan, and timeless. You would do well to honor it."

"As you said, there are other courses."

"Then appeal to his business blood. Galipa has always been a trustworthy man. He would send you a portion of his salt for the rest of his days, if you accepted."

"The last thing I want is a trail to Hazan."

"Then his gratitude is the wisest choice."

Anna studied Bora, wondering where she'd been and what she'd seen. She had exhaustion in her eyes, but there was also an unfailing alertness, and she thought back to the coyotes in the fields around her home.

Bora looked at her, and she glanced away.

"You've got the night to say goodbye to him." The tracker folded his arms. "We sail tomorrow, you said." He stood, pulling at the sleeve of Anna's dress. "If you'll excuse us, I have to draw a bath for her. At the very least, she ought to look presentable tomorrow."

* * * *

When Anna finished bathing alone in a shallow metal tub behind the inn, finding little comfort in the red and yellow nebulae overhead, she hastily slipped on her new dress, a clean, oversized garment from Emine's wardrobe. Pulling the pleats past the cuts on her legs burned, but it was preferable to her old rags. The scent of the linen, eerily similar to the cloth Bylka used to wrap the bodies of stillborn babes, was distracting enough to keep her awake as she lay in her quarters.

Shem slept somewhere nearby, and the tracker rested in a chair just outside of the room, dedicated to some perversion of Anna's safety. In fact, he'd smirked at the idea of Shem sleeping in the same room as Anna, and it'd taken several minutes for the reality of her request to sink in.

In the common room in Bylka, she'd always slept with Julek nearby, but it was nothing like sleeping near a boy beyond her blood. Everybody knew what lovers did in the darkness, how they rolled over each other and sprouted babes in girls' bellies. Anna had never experienced it, or —beyond her mother and father—seen it happen firsthand. Her kin's insistence on secrecy, along with her own mistrust, hadn't allowed her to grow so close to anybody. Especially not to Shem, a foreigner who'd hardly passed beyond childhood, who stared with adoration beyond lust.

While drifting toward asleep, she had grotesque visions of the northern crypts, which had been illustrated in her mind by the tales of passing riders. She watched creatures picking at sun-bleached bones. She saw the sun screaming, water retreating from sand, boiling while it fled.

Anna sat up, her chest tight and robbing her of breath.

Escape became a burning urge. She could make it to the main city before dawn, and there, she could find the Halshaf. Some riders said that they took in young girls and boys, and they gave them food or shelter without any expectation of salt. It sounded plausible enough as she rose in darkness, supported by the wall. She could stay there indefinitely, *if* she made herself useful.

She crept toward a window and ran her hands up its slatted shutters. Cold air whispered against her fingertips as she felt higher and undid the brass latch. A breeze pushed the shutters open.

Scattered braziers and rooftop torch bearers dotted the dark sprawl. Hounds howled in unison, and foreign tongues snapped faster than ears could follow. In the main street below her, framed in the light that bled from open windows and doorways, she saw a young boy hurrying toward Malchym.

He was thin, probably starved, with the burnished skin of a northerner. His tunic ended just below his knees, and in the fabric's folds around his belly, he seemed to be carrying something. *Multiple things,* Anna realized as he wandered through another patch of light. His eyes were sharp and fearful, his shoulders huddled.

Before he could cross a bisecting alley, a shadow with a long cloak and brimmed hat emerged and blocked his path. It held a tapered club and swung its tip in lazy circles.

There was something familiar about his dress. *Agents of Malchym,* Anna recalled with a shudder.

Passing women pulled their children to the opposite side of the road, and conversations fell away without resolution.

Anna swung the shutters in a bit more, craning her head to glimpse the scene. She saw the man approaching the boy, the boy jerking his hands from his tunic and shielding his face.

Crusts of bread spilled onto the road, and then came the dull thump of the club breaking the boy's skull. The boy collapsed in a heap, motionless, and the agent walked onward, whistling. Hounds skulked out from the alleyways and fought for scraps.

It was impossible to breathe. Anna closed the shutters and slid down against the wall and listened to the wind wheezing past. Her breaths returned in jerks and prickled her lungs with frigid air. She brushed her sleeve over dry eyes. Malchym was no different than any other wicked place.

"Why are you awake?" Shem whispered.

Anna wrapped her arms around herself, suddenly vulnerable. She fought to quiet herself.

Fabric rustled in the darkness as Shem approached. He crept along the floor, his back painted with slats of moonlight, and paused at the edge of her sheets. For a long while they were both quiet.

During the last few days she'd grown used to silence. Perhaps she'd become afraid of her voice. But now, with the wordlessness hanging between them, she wished she could speak her fears.

Shem's hand rose out of the dark and brushed her cheek. His touch was gentle but probing, as though he couldn't fathom the strangeness of her flesh.

Anna reached up and wrapped her hand around his, holding fast to the skin's warmth and smoothness.

"Have you seen north, Anna?" Shem asked. He wrapped an arm around her shoulder. "My father say you take care of me." He paused. "I hope, because I do not like other man. Mother say he is not your father. So he may not take care. Not for you. So I take care of you, since you take care of me."

Anna squeezed Shem's hand, and the boy squeezed back faintly.

"When you make speaking again, perhaps you tell me about father." Despite the darkness, Anna swore that she could see the boy smile, see his heart shimmer through his skin. "I take care of you."

Anna willed herself to speak, tightening her throat until she felt pain, and the strands within her throat twisted and vibrated. Through the agony, she heard a low sound, barely enough to overcome the drumming of her heartbeat:

"I'll take care of you too," she whispered.

Chapter 8

They left the inn just before dawn. The streets were dusty and cool without sunlight, and the first caravans made their way toward Malchym in a sluggish trickle. Anna stood with Shem against the inn's front wall, their linen cloaks dancing together in the wind. The tracker, Bora, and Shem's parents settled matters of salt by the door.

Aside from a quiet *good night* to Shem, Anna hadn't ventured to speak again. Words sliced at her throat, and even the cardamom tea in her canteen failed to soothe the pain for long. Besides, she treasured the safety of silence.

Somehow Shem understood that.

To Anna's left, far up the caravan path leading to Malchym, the timber spires of watchtowers and keeps within the earthworks caught the sun's first light over the mountains. From here the city was pristine and welcoming. If Anna hadn't known its true heart, its corruption and malice, she might've tried to flee there.

Bora and the tracker stepped away from the door, allowing Emine and Galipa to exit. Emine approached and embraced Shem with hollow, dead eyes, while Galipa stared into the dirt with slack lips.

The tracker sighed and leaned against the corner of the building.

"Come this way," Bora said, wrapping a hand around Anna's shoulder and guiding her toward the street. Anna's gaze fell to the northerner's newly donned white cloak, which glittered with a hint of mica. Without warning Bora grasped Anna's chin and moved her head toward the city gates. "Where we're venturing, you'll learn not to stare. Some things are not meant to be seen."

Anna watched the gates and the endless procession of mules, horses, and giants. It was a fruitless attempt to block out the sobbing, the shouting, the shushing. Through it all, Shem was silent.

Maybe we are alike, Anna reasoned. It brought her no joy.

After traveling through crowds of herb-wreathed merchants and knife peddlers, Bora herded them out of the main procession and into a narrow side alley where chipped stairs led downward and out of sight. It was cool in the shade of the towering thatch-roofed and tiled buildings. Odors of burning dust faded beyond the main streets, yielding to saline and vinegar and over-darkened leather. Gulls squawked from the rafters and cut wide arcs over the road and nearby bazaars.

The tracker turned to Bora, shrugging. "She's earned it, I'd say."

Bora glanced down at her nails. Her shaven head was conspicuously free of sweat. "The judgment is yours. The *demicen* will have no quarrel with it."

"Right, then." The tracker unbuckled the cracked leather satchel at his waist. During his stay at the inn, he hadn't worn anything of the sort, certainly not with that kind of workmanship. A boy, it seemed, wasn't enough payment. After a moment of rummaging, he produced a handful of balled silver links and a knife with a wooden tang and iron blade. "Be good with these, girl."

Anna could hardly believe it. She'd nearly forgotten about the trinkets, but now she craved them again. They were worth more than salt, gold, or freedom. Her hands cupped with hesitation, ready to pull away if the tracker's decency was a ploy.

But there was no teasing, no tempting. The tracker placed the necklace and knife in Anna's hands with a sigh. "See, now? Honest partnership."

She wrapped the necklace's links around her wrist and formed a crude bracelet, pulled the cloak's sleeve over her skin to hide the metal, then slid the knife into the linen scarf around her waist. When she glanced up the tracker was already descending the stairs, and Bora stood waiting for Anna and Shem.

Honest partnership. She watched the tracker's silhouette disappearing around the bend in the wall, and for the first time she remembered the tomesroom, the light, who had saved her. She considered that he wasn't as evil as most men.

He did his deeds in daylight, while others worked in shadow.

His deeds . . .

Anna's stomach convulsed. She shook the thoughts away, watching seagulls swing over the marketplace in the rising sun's light. She couldn't forget the blood.

But Shem looked at her, and she looked back. The boy took her hand.

Bora led them down the stairs, through a narrower alley, and then into a courtyard lined with crooked pine trees and wooden fortifications, crowded by patrolling Agents of Malchym. There the ocean appeared. It was a vast and dark expanse through the gateway ahead, streaked with raw sunlight and stirring with the winds.

It's real, Anna thought, regardless of its childishness. It was easy to hear stories from travelers, but it was another to actually *see* something, to feel the wind rising from it.

"Come," Bora said. Her gaze followed the tracker as she navigated along the cliffs, along paths that were raised and carved from the rock itself, worn down by eons of footsteps and wagon traffic.

Below Anna, the waters churned and broke against the cliff's black rocks. The whitewash sprayed up as pale mist, tossing the wind through her hair and forcing her to step back. A day ago she might have released Shem's hand and taken the extra step, and nobody would have missed her, not even herself. Now the heights were dizzying, and she walked carefully along the cliffside with Shem, gazing out at the bloody, thrashing fish on hooks and dockside sentry posts.

The largest vessel in the cove was slim but tall, boasting sharp-angled sails and a dozen mooring ropes. Close to its boarding ramp, which Bora and the tracker had nearly reached, was a winding stairway carved into the cliffside, snaking down into the port and its shanty huts.

Something tingled through Anna's hands and stomach. It was *potential*, she realized. The potential for something better.

* * * *

Come midday she stood on the main deck and watched them cut the last ropes anchoring the vessel, smiling for reasons beyond comprehension. Somebody patted her shoulder as the ship lurched, riding a swell. She turned to see the tracker, whose eyes were still violet-tinged but placid. And in spite of everything, including the knot in her gut, she held his gaze.

"Honest partnership," he said.

That evening she ate dinner with Shem and a dozen strangers in the lower bunks. None of the strangers comforted her. Some wore strips over their eyes and huddled around the candlelight in silence, while others even looked like Shem, their hearts and stomachs pulsing beneath clear flesh.

Candles were sparse on the lower decks, the ceilings low, the hammock bunks stifling, all as the smell of rotting fish wafted up from the deep holds. But none of those things outweighed small blessings. The crew had segmented the lower decks with ragged curtains, allowing Anna to share a cell with Shem toward the boat's rear. If any of the crew members found it strange, the tracker made sure they withheld their thoughts.

Every so often Anna glanced at the hanging strands of beads and watched them lull to one side, wondering how much the boat tilted with each wave. When she set aside her canteen and dried pork, she found Shem staring at her.

"You cut?" he asked, his finger tracing his neck and exciting the sigils below.

"I don't know," Anna mouthed. Her fingers curled with nervous energy. They begged her to leave scars on the boy, to open him to the hayat and all its beauty, even if they'd already cost him a mother. *Light* flared through her skull. "I . . ."

The luster in his eyes dimmed. "If you do not want, I understand this."

Anna studied the sigils across Shem's skin, and hayat called to her in turn. "No," she managed as loudly as she could muster. "I'll do it." She tugged at the collar of her cloak and demonstrated a folding action, signaling Shem to conceal his rune upon completion.

Not that the tracker would dare to harm *her*. Little by little, Anna had observed his reactions: She was valuable to him.

"Does it hurt?" Shem asked, luring Anna from her thoughts. He glanced down at the blade's handle, which protruded from Anna's waist wrap.

Anna drew the knife and turned it over in her hands. Light glinted off the blade, and she realized somebody had polished the iron. She ran a thumb over the flat edge, marveling at how much of the grime and dried blood and rust had been scourged. It must have taken a grinding effort—and vinegar.

"Anna?"

She looked up and saw the fearful arch of Shem's brows. "Yes," she whispered. There was no sense in lying to him. "It will hurt while I cut you, but afterward it will heal."

"How you know?" Shem stared at the blade. "My father told me that *hayajara* not feel cuts, because they cannot have. Hayajara cannot make cut on hayajara."

She'd learned that much already. In the north, perhaps they knew more about it, or they could explain such things beyond telling stories. Perhaps there were more of the scribes, the hayajara, in the north.

Perhaps it made Anna less valuable.

Anna regarded the knife with another long gaze. "It's true," she said, her voice barely breaking above the waves' sloshing. Nothing moved in her throat when she spoke; she could no longer *feel* the words forming.

"When I've scarred people, the flesh has always healed quickly. They don't bleed much."

"So it not hurt?"

She sat the blade on the pitted wooden floor. "It might not be wise, Shem."

"You may make stopping if it hurts?"

Anna pursed her lips. "No, I can't. If I don't finish the cut, it'll be worse. You could die. And you can't make any noise." She saw the confusion in the twist of his brow. "They can't know. Nobody except us can know."

"But we are friends, both droby."

Rage flared through her. She saw the dark morning woods and the soglav, and felt hot breath on the back of her legs. She wrapped her hands around the knife. "I am *not* his droba," she hissed. When the boy shrank inward, frowning, she eased her glare. "Neither are you, Shem. You don't belong to him. But this has to remain between us."

Shem knotted his brow, candlelight shimmering across the flesh. "It is sworn."

His promise was the catalyst. Hayat surged through Anna, guiding her hand to the knife and restricting her vision to Shem's neck. The walls darkened and blurred around her, but every pore of the boy's translucent flesh came alive. When her knife touched his jugular, it was only a matter of tracing hayat's ever-fleeing glow, capturing fireflies.

Shem screamed.

Sigils fled from the blade. The boy jerked back, twisting the iron in his flesh, and a gush of clear fluid darkened to blood as it met the air. Hayat dissipated from the wound in a luminous cloud.

Come back. She scrambled forward, chasing the wound's open edge and stabbing toward the boy's neck. Every breath was thick with hayat's scorched scent, and she surrendered control of her fingers as the energy settled in her lungs.

Pain shot through Anna's skull, and the symbols vanished.

Wisps of hayat evaporated.

"I'm holding your suture," the voice said, cutting through the ringing in Anna's ears. It was a woman's voice, detached, certain. It was Bora, who now knelt on Anna's chest with hardened amber eyes. She held three rigid fingers against Anna's throat. "If you make another move, I'll tear your threading free, and you will bleed to death."

Even if Anna could've drawn a breath, there was hardly anything to say. Her head throbbed in slow pulses, robbed of hayat's euphoria, and she saw Bora only by the candlelight upon her shaved head and the murder in her eyes. Anna realized, distantly, that thousands had probably seen this image in their last breath.

"Nod if you can understand me," Bora said.

But Anna didn't dare to move; she could feel Bora's fingers pinching the knot at the tail-end of her suture. She forced a dab of air into her lungs. "I understand."

Bora's eyes hardened. "You can speak." Her posture was militant, her knee tucked into the crevice of Anna's ribcage and forcing the air out in a slow burn.

Pressure mounted behind Anna's eyes. Her throat tightened. Her vision blurred with tears. She clawed at Bora's linen, striking and slapping until her arms grew too heavy to move. In her last moments of breath, she flailed her legs and scraped her boots over the hardwood, unable to reach . . .

Bora withdrew her knee, stood, and stepped away. She loomed over Anna as a dark shadow, examining her every movement. But the attention wasn't curiosity; it was mercy.

Anna gasped as the crushing sensation fell away, and her first full breath arrived with sharp pain. Her fingers and toes tingled, all lifeless. The room slowly brightened around her.

"Shem," Bora said, glancing away, *"sharafen ha demecine."* When Shem opened his mouth to protest, she whirled on him. *"Shara."*

The boy staggered to his feet, little more than a blur in Anna's periphery, and retreated through the hanging curtain.

Anna squinted up at Bora, acutely aware of her throat's dryness. The salve had been her only barrier against pain. Stranded in Bora's shadow, it seemed that the woman had materialized from the shadows like a specter. There had been no footfall, nor any hint of cinnamon or sumac in the air.

"You didn't really believe that your handler would leave you to your own devices, did you?" Bora asked. "He may have reservations about harming you, but I'm not bound in the same manner."

"He's not my handler." Anna propped herself up on her elbows, tucked her knees in, and held onto her ankles, unwilling to look at Bora. "That man is a killer."

"What else?"

Anna squeezed her ankles. "What do you mean, what else?" She glared at the northerner. "He murdered my brother. And you work for him. You do everything for him."

"I work with him."

"Who is he?" Anna asked. Cold fear of the answer immediately set in.

"I don't know," Bora said. "He paid salt on the grounds that you are his dependent, and that you will be escorted with him. Anything else is concealed, child. I serve another."

Another. Surely they had to be far more wicked.

"All I know," Bora said, drawing Anna back to the moment, "is that he trusts you excessively."

Anna glanced to her right, where her blood-spattered blade rested in the candlelight. "You shouldn't work with him."

"Why? Because he's a criminal?"

"Because he should die. If he didn't have that rune, he would be dead." Anna's eyes watered, and she swiped her face with linen sleeves. "If you can hurt me like that, you can kill him. You should have killed him."

"You believe that I can destroy a rune, then?" Bora asked. "How did he receive such a mark?"

Anna wrapped her arms around her knees and closed her eyes. "It doesn't matter. You should help me, not him. He doesn't deserve help."

"If I murdered every wicked man alive," Bora said with a rigid brow, "then this world would be empty. We leave scars upon the worthy flesh in our circles. It would be a fool's task to choose justice in life."

The hypocrisy was too much. Anna gritted her teeth and stared up at the northerner, knowing that violence was hardly an answer. There were no surprises against her. "Just help me," Anna said. "Help me get away, and I'll give you whatever you want." She shook her head. "I'll give you a rune. I don't care. Jus—"

Bora sank in a low crouch, her hawkish eyes locked with Anna's. "You will not offer me such a thing again. You believe you're a good child with a bad man, but you wear the blood of the conquered. You are not a victim. You *create* victims. This is the truth of the world."

"What?" Anna whispered.

"You should be afraid of me, child. I do not fear pain, not as your handler does. I am not afraid to perish. The first thing you'll learn in Hazan is that you are not immortal. You never will be."

"I never claimed to be." Instantly she recalled the sutures across her neck.

"You still hold onto life within your breaths," the northerner replied. "You fear the end."

Despite the woman's hardness, there was something admirable about her. Something so essential to her survival that Anna wanted to say *teach me*, to beg for her knowledge. But there were scars that accompanied the lessons, surely.

"You have taken this boy from his family," Bora added, "and you now wish to take away his freedom with your cuts. I will not allow this."

"He asked me," Anna said. "He wanted this. You heard him."

. "He is a boy, and he knows little. Among the sands and plains, your cuts are everything." Bora's words emerged like tar, viscous and burning in Anna's mind. "For one cycle of immortality, men are willing to die. Men are willing to kill a thousand other men. Millions of innocents have died because of your cuts."

Anna scowled. "You're blaming me for these things, but I did nothing wrong."

"If you had marked this boy, you would have. In your new home, you will cause such deaths, and perhaps many more. It is the nature of your kind."

"I don't belong to any kind."

"The hayajara, child." Bora moved her head to block Anna's view of the wooden planks, staring back into her eyes with the same sharpness. "In the north, life is everything. And the lives you preserve will claim countless others. You cannot forget this."

Although Anna's fingers trembled, and her throat pulsed with the agony of speaking, she was struck with a sense of boldness. Bora's words had torn into her, but they only bled her fear. Somewhere beneath the surface, she felt power. *The lives I preserve.*

"Do you understand this?" Bora asked.

There was venom in her words, but Anna refused to show fear anymore, especially to Bora. She pursed her lips.

"You should not think of me as your enemy. You'll have plenty of those, you know." Bora leaned even closer. "I protect those who require protection."

"For salt."

"Do you believe that Shem gave me salt?" Bora asked. "If he were a hayajara, I would strike him as I struck you."

It was a pointless comparison, Anna realized. Scribes—hayajara, as Bora knew them—could never be boys. And they could never be like *him*, without man-skin or descended from the stag groves. Maybe that was why the tracker had always wanted daughters. Maybe he'd only wanted a chance at Anna's gifts.

"Heed my words." Bora waited until Anna met her eyes. "You should cooperate with me. In Hazan, this will be your saving."

"I don't need you."

Bora blinked. "I don't extend aid for your benefit. It would be irresponsible to let you roam freely, child. One does not release their hound into the streets without teaching it to return home."

"I'm not a hound," Anna said.

"You leave your teeth marks wherever you go."

"If I told my *handler* what you've said to me, he would have you killed."

"So tell him." Bora glanced toward the curtains, letting the candlelight wash over her hooked nose and firm jaw. "I don't care if I receive payment. I don't care what he may do to me. No man would be swift enough to stop me, if I resolved to do something." Her gaze passed over Anna like a knife's edge. "My oaths bear deep roots, child. You would be wise to take my hand when it is offered."

And so she slipped through the curtains.

Anna sat on the floor, motionless, unable to cleanse the feeling of being watched. Eventually she blew out her candle, curled up in the packed-straw bunk with her blade, and recalled how it had felt to hold Julek in his swaddling blankets. She'd been so surprised by the babe's warmth, and how her mother had trusted her so greatly.

In the darkness and the sea breeze that slipped through the vessel's cracks, her mind endlessly churning Bora's words, Anna wondered if she belonged in the land of the wicked.

Chapter 9

For four days the boat cut across the sea. Anna spent most of her time on the sun-bleached deck, playing dice with copper-skinned sailors and passengers, scanning the horizons, watching her forearms and ankles darken considerably in the sunlight. She caught only stray glimpses of Shem, whom Bora kept sheltered behind her white cloak.

Even so, she needed him. Julek had always given her the assurance that she would never be alone in life.

It wasn't long before Bora revealed her working voice to the tracker, but the man had only been gentle and encouraging in light of the discovery. "Easy," he'd whispered when Anna tried to explain, standing under the nebulae with her. "Let it rest, girl."

He was a shadow of the creature he'd been in prior days. When fish leapt out of the waves he gave a deep belly laugh, and he often brought Anna wine and honey cakes at dusk. In the evenings and hours before sunrise he wandered Anna's deck and put a blade to the throat of any man who crept too close to her bunk, giving her ample time to trace true letters into the floor's straw coverings.

On the fifth day, just before sundown, they reached Hazan.

Anna saw its shores as a black mass. Towers rose like a palisade, taller yet denser than in Malchym, bright with the glow of hanging lanterns. Northern air, warmer than usual, but hardly hot, flowed into her quarters and stirred her hair, bearing a scorched industrial odor.

Look how far you've come.

She envisioned her parents spending every morning scouring the woods for moss covered bones, hoping that their fruitless search haunted them while she created a new life. One of wealth, safety, prestige, all earned by her own hands and her gifts. Her father would've subjected her to a lifetime of labor in a riding post, anyway. *Your cuts are everything.* Bora's words made her cognizant of just how much her family would've squandered.

While the other passengers were busy packing their wicker trunks, Anna slipped on a poncho and gathered her meager possessions. On the upper deck, where Anna saw the lights and towers of Hazan, a thin wreath of smoke hung over the city and drifted westward toward emergent stars.

"Girl," the tracker called from the railing. He stood among a crowd of passengers, including Bora and Shem, appearing monstrous yet unremarkable beside scarred Morahrem worshippers and eyeless, blindfolded Gosuri. A nearby brazier, fanned by a sailor using a wooden paddle, lighted the threadwork of his mask. "Stay near me when we get off." He placed a hand on Anna's shoulder and nodded toward Bora. "She's our best guide here." The tracker stared intently at Anna's wrist. He took hold of her linen sleeve and unrolled it, concealing the silver bracelet. "Make sure it stays like that."

"I'm careful," Anna said. His touch, soft as it was, still startled her.

"Bad things have a habit of happening to pretty girls here," the tracker warned. He returned his gaze to the city. "Sometimes *careful* isn't enough." He drew up the hood of Anna's poncho, shrouding her in warm darkness and tucking her hair out of sight. "When we're on land smear some dirt on those cheeks. Bit too rosy."

Anna clutched at her belt and its hanging blade.

* * * *

The sun was a low hanging blister when they disembarked and left the mooring grooves carved into the coastline, their walkways manned by torchbearers and workmen with grating northern voices, surrounded by towering barges swathed in chains and strange black paste. Nearby were narrow city streets, where fading daylight reduced strangers to shadows and foreign tongues. They came to a shrill and sweltering junction of countless paths, hemmed in by buildings jutting out at one another.

Shem stood between the tracker and Bora, his eyes full of wonder at the commotion. He only noticed Anna after the girl had been watching him for a short time, but he flashed a smile verging on fanaticism. Even so, it was more welcome than the children gawking along surrounding rooftops and walls.

Thick, insignia-laden blocks of setstone formed waist-high walls at the opening of every street. Guards stood in packs behind each barricade. A man with teal face paint reclined in a hammock stretched between an alleyway's windows, while a nearby gathering of bare-chested, paunchy northerners inhaled powder and skinned pears and played the citole. Blindfolded falcons stirred within another group's cages.

Clumps of travelers, each distinct yet wearing similarly outlandish clothing, crossed the checkpoint stations.

Bora led them to a barricade adorned with a painted red paw. The men behind this checkpoint mulled in eerie silence. They wore iron plates with tan silk underneath, and only in the light of a brazier's pulsing coals did Anna notice their trick. Their armor carried a dull patina of sand baked into the metal, forming a speckled pastiche of sun-bleached ochre and soil. Bits of shrubs and withered grass hung from the armor in clumps.

"Fill our tins full," the tracker whispered in river tongue to the attending guard, "and tell *patvor* we're coming."

Monsters, she translated. Ghouls and demons lurking in the fen, as riders had once termed them. Every child knew the word from tales. She turned, staring at Bora expectantly, but received nothing.

As they passed, the guards shuffled back and regarded Anna with wide eyes. She couldn't ignore their hands resting upon dented pommels.

The market was a wide courtyard packed with net-covered stalls, and despite night's approach, buyers and sellers crowded the aisles, bickering. Candlelight illuminated vignettes of vendors' booths, the dim lights scraping up merchants' and craftsmen's faces to carve monstrous features.

A restless crowd clogged one side of the market. Bare-breasted women stood on daises, most of them young and frail and trembling, struggling to meet the eyes of the buyers in the audience. Some were still girls, though their long, black hair dampened the youth in their faces.

Anna wondered how much a pale-skinned, golden-haired girl would fetch in a market for Hazani men, but was quick to dismiss the thought.

"Best droby in Hazan," the tracker explained, shouldering his way past a beggar. He gestured for Anna to stay close. "Just one of them would cost a pouch, maybe two. But they're good at what they do. Worth the salt, the whispers say." He shrugged, then leveled a toying stare at Shem. "Look familiar?"

Shem examined the spectacle. "A little." He smiled as though he didn't understand the question. "In Tas Hassa, much quieter. They make the paying in coins. And in Qersul—"

"He's from Nahora?" The tracker narrowed his eyes at Bora. When the northerner declined to reply, he whistled. "Interesting. Who knew that a puddle of afterbirth could travel so far?" Shem continued to smile, oblivious. "Does he know Orsas?"

"Ashah meid'to baqa," Shem said in a rush of excitement.

Anna stared at the boy, but he didn't seem to notice. He was grinning proudly, willing to continue if prompted. Despite her best efforts, she couldn't mentally replicate the strange yet flowing sounds.

"*So korpa?*" the tracker hissed. "What did he say?"

Bora shrugged. "I don't know Orsas."

"But he does." The tracker stopped at the end of an aisle, scanning the boy up and down. He met Shem's grin with bloodshot eyes. "Around me, and around Anna, you'll speak only the river-tongue. And if you teach her a single word of eastspeak—"

"He understands." Bora seized the boy's wrist and pulled him closer.

"And he'd better take off that fucking grin."

The edges of Shem's lips lowered by a hair.

"Settle affairs at the kator," Bora advised the tracker, drawing Anna's attention. "I'll escort her."

The tracker moved his neck from side to side, producing a dull crackling sound like branches over flame. He sighed, slipped a hand into his tunic, and retrieved an apple-sized leather pouch bound with twine. "Should be enough for what we need. And then some."

Anna gaped at the salt, unsure of how the tracker had been able to accumulate so much. It was enough to buy a pair of oxen, if Anna went by Bylka's rates. Beyond the value of the pouch, however, she also found herself asking, *If he had so much salt, why was he tracking?*

The tracker tossed the pouch to Anna. It was impossibly hefty, rolling with the smoothness of a merchant's finely ground salt.

"Be sure she's at the rails on time," he said.

Bora eyed the pouch with distaste. "Naturally."

Hazani women grasped at Anna's sleeve as she passed their counters, vying for her to feel their fabrics: silk, cotton, wool. Some stalls sold spiders in bottles, while others offered horses so cheap that Anna could only attribute the price to their proximity to the plains, where such beasts were bred and tempered like sows. Shem translated at each stall, calling out prices for canteens, soaps, and dried provisions.

After two aisles they encountered a crowd thick with murmurs.

"Come along," Bora said, even as Anna crept closer to the outskirts of the gathering.

The peddler within the clearing was a tall, aging Hazani man with loose blue fabric draped over his shoulders. His cheeks were sunken and dark, and curling, wavelike sigils crawled over his skin. He offered a yellow-toothed smile before raising something long and metallic above his head.

Onlookers gasped and whispered, and a few of the more skittish crowd members shrank back, Shem among them.

Anna saw long-cultivated fear in the way Shem recoiled. He huddled beside her and clutched her wrist.

"What's wrong?"

"*Ruj*," Shem whispered. "Much harm."

Anna focused on the item in question. It initially appeared to be a rod or club, but it had the smooth edges of machined metal and a leather bulb at its rear. She listened in confusion as the peddler began his pitch in flatspeak. "What's he saying?"

Shem translated the peddler's raspy words, terming ruj as "wind," and relying on Bora's assistance to define the device's function. They claimed it harnessed magnetism, although Anna had only seen tin peddlers use that energy to attract two bits of metal together, and those were charlatan tricks.

She narrowed her eyes as the man uncorked a vial, poured its contents into the leather bulb, and reconnected the device.

The man pointed to a pig's carcass, which was strung up against a pockmarked and pitted stone wall with wooden reinforcement. He lowered the ruj to his hip, pulled a pin from the tube's spine, gripped the pouch with his free hand, and squeezed. There was a violent hush followed by the clap of wood fracturing, cracking, exploding into a thousand tiny shards, raining splinters across sand and rock.

Bits of the pig's carcass speckled the rock wall and backing wood layers. Tendons hung in loose strands, the fat and blood forming leprous spots across the dirt. The skull and ribcage were bleach-white shards of broken glass, dangling from the rope and peppered with glinting iron.

Wild clapping spread through the audience.

Once, it would've terrified Anna. Now it represented safety.

"There it is." Bora lifted her head and scanned the dispersing crowd. "Come."

Anna grasped the drawstrings of the salt pouch and tucked it in her palm, scowling. "I'm buying it."

Even in dusk, the crease in Bora's brow didn't go unnoticed. "Do you think this is a child's plaything?"

Anna's face flushed hotter with every retort. There was no longer a clearing where she could cry alone, or a mother she could run to. There was only spite. "I deserve something to defend myself with," she snapped. "In Rzolka, I wouldn't walk out to the fields without a knife at my hip. And here—"

"Here, you are not in Rzolka. You have many men who would die for you. Do not disrespect them with your childish games."

But Anna no longer cared for Bora's thoughts. Bora didn't understand what *burden* meant. Surely she had a family, confidants, a place she called home, people who loved her and wished for her safe return. A burden was an easy price for safety, for self-reliance.

Anna pushed her way past a weaver's booth, keeping the pouch tucked in her grip and out of sight. She approached the peddler head on.

He smelled of citrus, and his dark, yellow-ringed eyes brushed over her rather than acknowledging her. "*Desht?*" he growled, crinkling his brow.

Anna pointed at the ruj in his hands. Without attempting flatspeak, she turned her hand over, unfurled her fingers, and revealed the pouch.

The peddler's eyes widened in a slow daze, as though astounded that so much salt existed in the world. He studied her eyes, then the pouch again. Judging from how little he spoke, it seemed he understood their language barrier. His hands were soil-dark as he reached out to feel the leather.

Anna pulled hers away. She pointed once more at the ruj.

The peddler gripped the ruj in both hands and lowered it to Anna for inspection. He turned it over once, twice, allowing Anna to judge the metal's sheen.

Anna knew nothing of its quality, but pretended to examine it thoroughly. It was a simple tube, a leather pouch with brass threading, and a pouch of iron shavings. Satisfied, she untied her salt pouch's twine and held the open end over her palm, waiting to tap out the proper amount.

But the peddler tucked the ruj beneath his arm and snatched the entire pouch from Anna, leaving her fingers hovering limply. He peered into the container, smirked, then stuffed the pouch into a fold of his robes. Rotten satisfaction crossed his face.

Before Anna could protest the peddler shoved the ruj and iron pouch into her waiting hands. It was lighter than expected, but she was only dimly aware of the weapon. She was more interested in how the man had simply *known* the weight of the salt, rather than measuring it or tapping it out. There was little she could say, but she glared at the man.

He wheeled around and shuffled through the market, concealing himself among a sea of dark cloaks and vendor stalls.

"This is the price of being a poor shepherd for your salt," Bora said, suddenly at her side.

"*Ziemnish, korpa!*" Anna hissed. The regret sank in at once, and she could feel her cheeks burning, her tongue scrambling to take back the curse. She'd never even said it to the village boys, and—

Her face twisted before she felt the strike. It was a swift, stinging backhand, dissolving over her face in a wash of pins and needles. Her cheek throbbed, even as she pressed her hand numbly to the skin. *She struck me.* Surprise came over her as tangibly as the ringing in her ears.

There was nothing on the northerner's face. No anger, no cruelty, no exertion.

Nearby, Shem was staring, his shoulders bunched up and drawn back. His mouth was open in a vague display of unrest. For him, it was no easy thing, Anna reasoned in the daze. He could hardly take sides.

"Bora," a voice growled, so close it broke through Anna's shattered hearing. So familiar she placed it in an instant. "What'd you just do to her?"

The tracker's odor, burlap and sticky-sweet dusk petals, filled the air as he moved into view. His silhouette typically was enough to frighten her, but now he was calming.

An inkling of surprise filled Bora's eyes. "She has a foul tongue."

"Did I ask about her tongue?" the tracker asked quietly. He took another step forward, rising above Bora by at least two palms. "If I haven't lost my sight yet, I'd wager that you just laid hands on her."

Anna rubbed at her face, no longer stunned by the blow but by the ease of Bora's violence. If the northerner had desired it, death would've come swiftly.

"This child is not made from glass," Bora said, glaring at Anna. Spoken with more reverence, it might've been a compliment. "She is a cracked field. If you want manners to be instilled in her, they must be hammered down like stakes."

"Manners?" the tracker growled. "She has plenty of manners."

"In my tongue, perhaps the word has a different meaning. There is a shadow of decorum in Rzolka, but it is not enough to survive here. If it was, you would not have learned our ways."

"She seems to be doing fine so far."

Bora folded her arms. "This is Nur Sabah. In Malijad, she will be consumed while breathing."

The tracker lowered his head, letting the burlap folds slide down and crease. "What did you do, Anna?"

Gathering a deep breath, Anna retold her story with as much detail as she could muster: The man's yellow smile, his quick hands, her attempt to partition the salt in her palm.

But the tracker only rolled his eyes. "So it wasn't stolen," he said wearily, cracking Anna's defenses. "You offered it to him, girl."

"No, I didn't," Anna insisted with a frown. "He snatched it from me."

"It was her decision," Bora said, her voice level despite the latent scorn. "I told her to stay, and she disobeyed me to purchase this."

The tracker squeezed Anna's shoulder. "Poor girl has lost everything. And she doesn't deserve a spot of empathy? Apologize to her."

The wind brushed past with the bitterness of coal smoke, stinging Anna's eyes. Bora's silence was a slow, deliberate thing, seemingly eternal. Their eyes remained locked, and the northerner's amber stare burrowed into her. It held forthcoming violence, murderous words unspoken.

"My apologies," Bora said at last.

* * * *

The kator's railway sat upon the crest of the city's rise and stared out over the sprawling darkness of Hazan, revealing patches of forest among the hills, the black smears of lakes and rivers, the gnarled masonry of lamp-lit watchtowers. It wasn't as desolate as it had first seemed, but it was far from Rzolka. Much closer to Anna's vantage point on a setstone waiting platform, stretching from the railway station to the blackness beyond, was a set of parallel metal beams suspended above the valleys and gullies.

Sparks leapt from the shadows ahead, and a railed metal cylinder came speeding down the length of setstone, bellowing and deafening as it slowed to a halt. A length of railing swung open along the vessel's side, allowing the waiting passengers to board.

Shem gave an excited gasp, breaking the group's pall of silence. "Come, come!"

And because of the boy's smile, Anna was foolish enough to go.

Chapter 10

In her dreams, she wandered through the husks of her old life, passing soot-stained hearths and oak butcher's blocks stained pink from all the carcasses.

Julek's carcass, not pink but—

Anna woke in the darkness, trembling.

I'm here, she told herself, patting her arms and legs with tingling palms. *I'm fine.* She pulled the metal shutters up from the windows to ground herself, watching bone-white gorges and the innards of mountains screaming past, blurring together with heat shimmers on the horizon. Light revealed the pod's curving metallic ceiling, the pair of cramped bunks sharing a central aisle, the rear latrines.

Beads of sweat prickled her neck, reminding her of the dampness that would invariably ruin her leg's bandages.

Even when yesterday's heat had grown torturous, Shem had told his stories of Nahora and the terraced gardens and the birth of the world, how the man-skins were the apex of life, how his people's first tongue lacked the words for *man* and *woman* because there were only Huuri, even if Anna knew them as men. She loved his tales of such a faraway place, faintly smiling while he spoke, but his words never ceased, even when he wheezed and a film of dried blood covered his teeth.

"Shem," she'd whispered, sprawled out on her bunk, "you don't have to tell stories."

But the Huuri had only smiled with cracked lips, his eyes white and vibrant. "You like them," he said. "So I tell them."

There were a thousand stories to tell about Rzolka, but heat wasn't all that dissuaded her. Her memories were the rocks in Malchym's harbor, so sharp and far below her. All it took was a stray gust of wind. . . .

Metal whined in the darkness. The disc-shaped door at the front of the pod screeched and peeled back, flooding the compartment with light and wailing winds.

Anna recoiled, shielding her eyes with her hands to glimpse the sunlit figure ahead.

Bora's cloak dazzled and writhed in the breeze. Her stance was assured, relaxed. In a voice as sharp as the winds cutting across the hull, she spoke, "Come."

Shem rolled over, shrugging his shoulders out of cotton sheets, but Anna reached across the aisle and stilled him with a hand on his neck.

Anna squinted against the light. "I'll be back, Shem." She clambered out of bed, drawing her hunting blade and holding it at her side as she did so. There was no telling what the northerner wanted, nor what she was capable of doing, but refusal was never an option. And Anna would never repeat the mistake of equating compliance with helplessness.

"Come." Bora stepped outside the pod's door and waited, a pillar among the gusting. The edge of her lip crinkled. "And put your knife away, child. You will stumble and plunge it into yourself."

Child. How she hated the word.

Anger rose in her, but she was quick to suppress it. *Not now.* There was no sense in acting foolishly when Shem was nearby, when he could be harmed by any violence Anna brought upon them.

Anna lowered the blade and followed Bora outside.

Immediately she raised her free hand to her eyes, unable to see anything beyond the tears and light that blurred her vision. Bora's dark shape passed in front of her, wordless, before proceeding into a lane of shadows.

The sun was a high and blinding orb overhead, canted to one side of the kator. Bora's path along the pods' exteriors, bathed in cool darkness and guarded by metal railings, stretched along the entire length of the kator.

With her knife at her side Anna trailed the northerner in the shade.

The platforms linking the pods were forged from cheap metal, their swirled tempering marks covering the panels like etchings of sea waves. The railed walkways pivoted at key angles and joints, bound by rusting gears beneath the vessel. Mountains and cracked earth blurred past, wracking Anna with nausea. Scorched winds bellowed over the crest of the pods in bursts, laced with the odors of white coals.

Bora came to a halt halfway down the walkway, closer than ever before but warped by shimmering air into something grotesque and hopelessly distant. "Do you know what is done to children who bear their edges in the streets of Malijad?"

Anna gripped the blade harder.

"They are disarmed by cartelmen," Bora said, paying no mind to Anna's gesture, "and then they are beaten until they cannot walk, and their mouths are full of shattered teeth. If the child cries out, their blade is returned . . . in their spine, or the throat."

Anna took another step forward. "Did you bring me here to hurt me?" She angled her wrist to point the blade's tip upward. It was the way she'd learned to gut sows, driving up and through the belly.

Bora moved to the edge of the railing, staring off into the patchwork of bluffs and flats. Her breaths were even, ignorant to Anna's complete bemusement. "You're too quick to use your feeling mind."

Anna refused to lower the blade. "You're speaking nonsense."

"You would spill my blood without cause." She studied Anna's face, likely sensing the girl's fear that she'd been lured into the open. "Why do I scare you, child?"

"You don't," she lied. "But you're a killer, and none of your words matter."

"We are no longer in your lands," Bora said. Her words had been proven day by day: Violence was Hazan's only way, and cruelty its only law. "Words are sounds, child, and lying is a pastime in Malijad. You should fear the lightning that strikes you, not the thunder that deafens you."

"I don't fear either." Suddenly her blade felt woefully inadequate.

"This is your choice," Bora said. "But you should consider this: Words are free and cheap. Energy is a rare thing, and those who spend it properly are deserving of trust. Men with sweet tongues are the root of suffering, because they weave traps so cruel that they're beyond the thinking mind's comprehension."

Thinking mind. Whether it was a mistranslation into river-tongue or another oddity of Hazani, the phrase nested in Anna's mind. Anna exhaled, let her shoulders fall, and slid the blade into her belt.

The question wormed its way out of her.

"What's a thinking mind?" Anna turned her head and stared at Bora over her shoulder. "And don't tell me riddles. Tell me what it means."

Bora's gaze drifted across the sands. "Some have spent eons seeking an answer to that question, child. Yet you expect to know here and now?"

"Forget it, then."

"I did not say that learning was a wasted effort." Bora's eyes met Anna's, glinting in the sunlight with their amber sheen. "If you think that I live to torment you, you are wrong. You were brought here for a reason. So you could see your feeling mind."

"I can think too," she shot back, closing in on the northerner.

"And when you must, can you put aside feelings?"

Somewhere in Anna's memories, a young boy shivered in ankle-deep muck. His swollen red eyes called out to her, full of the same terror they'd once held during thunderstorms. Hands crawled up and over her, ready to take her maidenhood because it had been promised in honest dealings. "Always."

Bora turned her body toward Anna, letting the white cloak twirl over the railing's edge. She walked closer, her eyes lingering on Anna's wrist, inspecting the silver necklace.

"What now?" Anna asked.

Bora's hands shot out from the folds of her cloak, grabbed Anna's wrist, and tore the silver links free. Despite the violence of the seizure, Anna hardly felt her touch.

"Give it back!" Anna strained to scream but failed to break a harsh whisper. She lunged forward, her hands packed into fists. The northerner stepped back, but Anna was on her within seconds, throwing empty punches and swiping at folds of white fabric.

Bora took measured steps back in response to each of Anna's strikes. "Do you see?" She wove to the left, the right, into light and shade, her face and assured footing never affected. Her left hand remained high and bent, dangling the silver links. "Use your thinking mind, child. Think about what this is."

"It's mine," Anna said, half-crying the last word. Nothing could teach the northerner how it felt to have everything stripped away. "I'll kill you, Bora."

But Bora stayed one pace ahead of her. "Perhaps now you see why I worry about you. You're a hound, as I said you were. You bite at those who touch your scraps."

"Give it!" Yet the anger sapped her energy, sending shakes through her body, and the heat became unbearable, boiling the air in her lungs. Her arms slumped to her sides, resigned, and she fell into a walking pursuit.

"I will, once you prove that you have a thinking mind," Bora said. "Tell me what it is."

"It's mine," she huffed, "and you know it."

"Try again, child."

Everything ached and radiated heat within her, and it was only a matter of time until she broke. The words came from her without her consent, but she was far too tired to resist them: "It's a necklace." Anna's father, bearded in black patches, his eyes crinkled from the sun-scorched fields, flashed through her mind for an instant. She watched the sway of the silver links, imagining how many pinches of salt had gone into each curl, how much he'd been paid for Julek. "It's just a necklace," she whispered.

Bora stopped, seemingly satisfied. "Yes, it is." With a careless sweep of the arm she tossed the necklace over the railing.

It was a tumbling blur against a backdrop of beige. It was a metallic glint, revolving in midair, sinking lower and lower until it disappeared below the kator's walkway. Then it was lost to the expansive sands of Hazan, where a million things just like it had been lost and erased from memory. Where it would die without ceremony.

"Use your thinking mind," Bora said. Her face was smooth and bronze and untouched by sweat. "It was just a necklace."

Just a necklace, Anna thought distantly, staring over the railing at the nothingness. Her lips hung open, and she felt the hot winds toss her hair about her face, struggling in vain to pull her back to the moment.

Bora's soft words burrowed into Anna's left ear. "Child, your bindings endanger more than just yourself. My dreams are restless."

Anna grasped for words, still imagining the necklace in Bora's hand. "I don't care about your dreams."

"Look at me."

A rough hand took hold of Anna's chin and twisted it to the left, and Anna found herself staring up at the northerner. Somewhere deep inside, there was enough wrath to claw the woman's eyes from their sockets. On the surface, however, was only confusion. Nobody could be so cruel.

"You are free from your bonds," Bora said. "Let them go."

Anna's eyes crawled over the sands and mountains and ripples of heat, searching for the silver links. Malformed legs appeared in Anna's mind. "It isn't that simple," she whispered.

"It is," Bora said. A single rivulet of sweat ran her shaved head, coming to rest at her brow. "Once you learn the way, you can release it." Sigils stretched and shrank across her cheeks, almost as if they breathed with the northerner's slow rhythm. "In this moment, you are a wild animal."

"Let me go," Anna whispered, unsure if she meant it.

"Your soul carries a thousand packs, all of them filled with sand," Bora said. "You will be an animal until you learn to cast off your burdens."

There was no way for the northerner to understand burdens as Anna did, to see decaying boys in swamps and the recurring image of a father hoarding salt bags. In Anna's mind, there was no division between burden and memory. Releasing burdens meant releasing everything she accepted as real.

It meant releasing herself.

"Show me, then," Anna said faintly. *Only burdens,* she told herself, trying to focus on Bora's amber stare instead of her last image of home, with its misshapen door and wild grass springing up around the fences. *I'm not releasing Julek. I won't.*

"Speak with authority," Bora said. "This is a choice, not a command. You may have gifts, but your mind is spiteful, and it invites destruction. If you take my hand, we will tame your mind. If you run to the safety of your handler's wings, you will keep your burdens." The northerner gestured toward the endless stretch of sand and mountains. "If it's all too much for you, Hazan will not turn you away. Death is a simple choice for the living."

The survival instinct was a dulled but persistent force in her. Death was no longer the easiest course, nor the simplest. It was not merely a matter of ensuring her place in the Grove-Beyond-Worlds. After all the pain and terror and leagues of travel, she hated death. She hated its greed, its injustice.

Death wanted her yet didn't deserve her, or Julek, or the nameless millions who lost their battles each day.

"Show me," Anna repeated. "I want to learn."

"Very well," Bora said. No trickery, no chastising. "Come with me, child."

Bora led Anna to a bulbous red cylinder at the back end of the kator, this one twice as large as those around it. Light spilled through the doorway as Bora slid its door aside, revealing only the edges of a red and gold rug with a beaded fringe. Wisps of smoke curled up and into the light, unraveling in desert winds. Chanting issued forth from the chambers and matched the kator's thrumming.

Her hands trembling, Anna followed Bora into the darkness.

The air was thick and still. For the first time in days Anna felt sweat beading on her skin in cold dabs. Little by little her eyes adapted to the blackness.

At the far end of the chamber, lit by hanging candles and mounted on a table draped in red fabric, was a corpse. It was a dark, desiccated figure with its arms upright and fixed in crooked angles. Black pits represented a former mouth, nose, and eyes. But more unsettling than the body was the crowd of worshippers sitting cross-legged before the altar. They were so still that they appeared dead themselves. Men paced along the dark lanes of the chamber with ruji in hand, scanning.

Anna followed the northerner further into the chamber, listening to the gathering's chant as it echoed through the chamber. It was resonant and dull, far beyond comprehension. Their words were ancient and buried things, and by simply listening, she gleaned their secrets.

"*Medisyta sha olvef,*" Bora said, examining the worshippers with pools of candlelight and shadow across her face. "Meditation upon the end."

Anna lowered her voice in turn, then pointed to the altar's corpse. "Who is that?"

"Nobody knows."

Several worshippers turned their heads toward Anna in a lazy sweep. "They recognize your tongue," Bora said. "They fear it."

Anna was too fixated by the body to dwell upon their stares, however. She wondered where it was from, who'd birthed it, whether or not it had ever loved somebody. A hallowed corpse was nothing new to her. She'd seen pinemen in Bylka, which the priestesses covered in dark sap and dried on tables in the sunlight before stuffing them into hollows of oaks and thorn huts. But pinemen were special, their names known to those who sought their guidance on the trails. This was just a nameless husk, cracked and withering and forgotten. "If they don't know who it is, then why is it so important?"

Bora folded her arms. "What matters is that it has been swept from life."

"I already know that," Anna said. "People die."

"And so will you. You are arrogant. You live in fear for your own life. But life escapes us all. In time it will outrun the fastest among us."

"I'm not afraid to die," Anna countered.

"You are," Bora said. "The thinking mind will dull that fear, in time. But it is a rare thing to welcome death."

"So you do fear it." The notion came with a small sense of victory.

"A rare thing," Bora said, "but not impossible." The coldness in her voice said nothing to the contrary.

Those with bowed heads faced the altar once more, but Anna watched them closely, envying their stillness and the way their breathing never manifested in the folds of their robes. Their lungs were halls of stones.

"What about memories?" Anna asked.

Bora glanced down. "What of them?"

"The thinking mind," Anna said, choosing her words with as much precision as possible. "Does it dull them, too?"

"It dulls the pain," Bora said, "and it dulls the sweetness." Her eyes lingered on the corpse. "I suspect that for you, it would be a simple sacrifice."

As simple as letting go, Anna reasoned. She envisioned a fist unclenching, and from the open palm, handfuls of dried soil scattering in the wind. "How do I do it?"

"There was no trickery when I told you how long men have sought those answers." She gestured to the carpeted space behind a nearby worshipper, which also happened to be the furthest row from the body. "Each journey is personal and lonesome."

Everything had seemed so much easier when tasks were concrete, when memories were sweet and simple. Fetching wood and brushing horses and moving buckets were tiring things, but they could be undertaken and completed without much thinking. Carving a path in the mind carried no guarantee of completion. "Tell me how to start, then."

"Sit," Bora said. "Sit there, and set your eyes upon death. Think about how much you resemble the still body, and how life vanishes in your breaths. Focus upon this well. If you think of anything else, let it pass you. Turn your mind back to the end."

Anna stepped onto the carpet, unsure. Then, with a slow sweep, she glanced back at Bora. "How will I know when I'm done?"

The shadows formed dark crevices around Bora's jaw and eyes. "If you think that you're finished, then you haven't taken a single step."

After a moment to gather herself, lost in Bora's endless riddles, Anna wandered to the last row and sat beside a thin man with fluttering eyelids. The flesh beneath the lids was a dark yellow. *Hazani,* she recalled from the tracker's words. But the man paid her no mind, and Anna crossed her legs, suppressing the radiating pain from her bruised hips and scarred legs.

She fought to concentrate upon the illumined corpse. The body was a shriveled lump at this distance, partially obscured by the shoulders and bowed heads of the closest worshippers. Cardamom and distilled sweat tangled in the air, clouding the chamber like sacred smoke.

"*Malin sharame olven,*" the worshippers chanted. The man beside Anna let the words dribble from his lips, his eyelids moving feverishly. Their words were harmonized, but nothing indicated that there had been a prompt of any kind.

Anna held her breath and tensed her back, unsure of what to do. Standing up and exiting would've been simple, even expected. *I have free will,* Anna reminded herself, hardening her fists in her lap. *She can't hold me here.*

Yet she stayed.

Images of the desiccated corpse rolled through her mind, and gradually, the flesh reconstructed itself, its eyes reforming in bright bulbs. Skin sprouted over its withered shell in spores, then grew into a solid, rose-tinted mass. Limbs straightened out, yet the left leg remained malformed, and the right bent with a slight crook, still usable given the proper technique. Such details felt strangely fitting alongside its charcoal hair and freckles.

The corpse opened its mouth. "Anna," it whispered. "You left me?"

Anna's eyes shot open and revealed the altar and the shadows and the thin man. Her scream was a hoarse gasp, drowned out by sudden chanting. Tears ran down her cheeks in warm tracks.

A thousand packs, all of them filled with sand.

Then came silence again, and she stared down at the corpse with cool detachment. It was a collection of tendons and bones and cartilage. Memories of the end in the tomesroom washed over her, and she descended into dark liquid, basking in the crowd's hymns. She sank deeper, motionless, until the cold became numbing and she no longer desired to surface. Her body tingled and her legs wilted, her body swaying, tossed by the winds of Malchym's harbor. Like the western breeze that would pull her over the ship's railing, while the nameless men taught her to cast ropes and spit into the sea. . . .

With that lone gust, her body hurtled downward and into black waters. In the darkness the world gave way to a monolith.

She gazed upon its flat, harsh sides, trying to understand its true shape as she'd done with *light*. It was shrouded in fog and shadows, the darkness obscuring its angles. Every so often, segments of the symbol rearranged and fractured. Although the monolith did not speak, it emanated power, taunting her.

Anna wandered forward, desperate to unveil its form. Desperate to hold onto it and understand its mystery. She reached out, and as her fingers brushed the fog—

Bora knelt in front of Anna. Her lips were suspiciously tight, her eyes level with Anna's, a knot of concern twisting her brows into unfamiliar shapes. If not for the northerner's reputation, she might've appeared worried.

"Lower your head, and don't move," Bora said. She placed her hands, hard but smooth, like river pebbles, on either side of Anna's head. Around her, several worshippers stirred and glanced around nervously. Whispers spread through the gathering. "The first of many have arrived."

Anna focused on the amber eyes. They were dark and fearless and jagged, drowning out the world beyond Bora. The northerner's gaze was braced and ready, flickering back at something over Anna's shoulder.

"We seek only the girl," a voice croaked from the rear of the chamber. It was thick with the northern tongue, recognizable as river-tongue only by the hard curl of the *r* in the last word. Boots clanked over the metal panels and carpeted walkways.

"Head down," Bora whispered. She moved past Anna with an unceremonious brush, striding past rows of worshippers and converging on the source of the footsteps.

Against Bora's instructions, Anna craned her head around and saw the bright blur of the northerner's cloak billowing through slats of darkness. Six men stood by the pod's entrance, their faces shadowed and wrapped with beige cloth. Lean silhouettes of ruji rested in the crux of their arms. Some of the Dogwood men skirted around them to exit the pod, basked in moonlight to expose wide eyes, white lips.

"She's behind you," Bora said.

"Eh?"

It was all the leader of the new arrivals had time to utter, a transient bleat of confusion as Bora closed in on him and caressed the sides of his face, almost matronly. Then her hands were torquing and severing his spinal cord, drowning out the room's final hymns with a muted *snap*. The body convulsed exactly once before rolling in on itself and sinking in a heap. Worshippers shoved away from one another, scrambling to flee the rush of violence.

A man on the far side of the chamber gave a half-shout and fired his ruj, punching a dozen holes into the metallic hull and peppering the darkness with shafts of pale light. Wind screeched through the punctures in a ghastly moan as Bora lunged at the shooter, forcing him into an unlit corner and slamming his body against the perforated wall once, twice, three times, thrashing until he dropped his weapon and crumpled. Her arm was a crescent sweep as she snatched the fallen ruj and cast it across the chamber, the tube flashing through candlelight and shade and tumbling, end-over-end, before striking a man's open mouth. Fragments of teeth clattered across the floor. The man's comrade let off a reactionary shot, but Bora seized the casualty's arm and spun him closer, intercepting the brunt of the ruj's payload with a wet *whump*. Shards of bone and liquefied pulp drummed against the hull as Bora dropped the corpse's remnants and collided with the shooter, a mass of mica-laden fabric and dark flesh, grunts of terror blending with tangled footsteps and the clatter of ruji, the worshippers in full flight as they crawled from the madness and swiped at freckles of blood across their faces.

A metallic glimmer shot out from the blackness.

Anna ducked and shoved aside the yellow-eyed man, faintly sensing the whisper of broken air over her neck, the blade spinning past, the jagged edge scarring the carpeting between her ankles. The weapon tumbled off in a broken arc, dancing between patches of shade and flickering candlelight.

A pop thundered from the back of the chamber and washed out the darkness, leaving a white-hot filament of the blast framed in Anna's vision. Sound was a distant, muddled haze over the whipping winds. Visions of erratic movement materialized from a backdrop of smoke and raw, silvery desert. It wasn't until the kator turned on its track that Anna realized half of the chamber had been torn away, its edges a fringe of pulsing red and dribbling, molten alloy. Silhouettes flashed past the void with blades dancing and slashing, ruji firing in soundless puffs, bodies being kicked free of the panels underfoot and plunging into the night and its endless sands. Bora was a graceful whirlwind within the violence, a droplet of ink swirling into a stream.

A jumble of dark, sprinting shapes blurred past in the flats outside, drawing closer to the kator's railings in a cluster of hooves and snapping fabric. Five soglavs, this breed heartier and striped like the plains of their birth, raced over the rocks and kept pace with thrashing claws. Their riders were hunkered down in burlap saddles, ruji strapped across their backs and tattered hoods drawn up against the moonlight. Dust streamed in billowing clouds at their back.

Bora twirled and drove a blade into the final soldier's ear. Shoving the body free, she rolled to her left, retrieved a fallen soldier's ruj and leveled it at the approaching riders. Her shoulder shifted with the ignition.

Two riders, both flanking the kator's railing and preparing to dismount with feet unhooked from makeshift stirrups, absorbed the full blast of iron shavings. Blood darkened the curtain of dust. Tattered bits of cotton flaked into the breeze and coiled away, swallowed by the haze as quickly as the mangled bodies of the riders and dismembered beasts. The three men at the edge of their formation broke away and bore down into their beasts' necks with barbed gloves, hastening their approach. One rider reached back, grasped his ruj, and cradled it under a crooked arm.

The rose-shaped spark of a firing ruj blossomed in the darkness, and Anna's survival instincts assumed control.

She dove behind the shelter of the nearest worshippers, hands cupped to the back of her head and legs drawn to her stomach. Hollow *whumps* rang out as the bodies against her recoiled, slumping over and twisting and twitching. Her stomach convulsed as their cloaks bunched against her, slack.

Another explosion deadened Anna's hearing, this one surging a wave of smoke over the crowd and choking out the light that streamed from the chamber's rear. Tendrils of fracturing metal wormed along the upper crest of the pod. Everything smelled of blackened oak and forge bellows and rocks left in the guts of campfires.

Dazed, Anna lifted her head over the tangle of corpses and saw Bora, black against an argent sprawl, standing amid smoke and superheated panels. The northerner was swinging her knife in lazy circles, still eyeing the trio of riders.

One soldier, spurring his soglav to the far side of the pod and edging into the chamber's bleeding candlelight, jerked a cylinder out of his pack. After a hasty twist of the device's ends, the action nearly obscured by the smog and the swiftness of his beast's galloping, he cocked his arm back in preparation for a throw. Upon release, Bora's knife shot out in turn, revolving once with a glint before striking the device, sparking its edge, and detonating it an arm's length from the rider. The seed of flame was instantly swallowed by an ensuing black blossom over the flats, the aftershock and concussive wave tearing through the pod with deafening results. A film of dust erupted from the carpeting and bit at Anna's eyes.

She rubbed at her face, blinking away the debris in a wash of tears.

Her vision resolved with the final two riders drawing closer, undaunted by the explosion and the blackened fur along the sides of their beasts, oblivious to smoking armor panels beneath their scorched robes. They fished through their own pouches as the soglavs dashed over a rock outcropping, the pale snouts whipping and dark tongues lolling in the moonlight. Only one rider managed to produce a cylinder, but it escaped Bora's attention.

The northerner had turned back to Anna and was shouting, her warnings buried under the dulling press of the blasts.

"Bora," Anna cried, unable to hear her own voice. Unable to know if her muteness was derived from a broken throat or deafness. "Behind you."

The northerner failed to turn, standing still among the shroud of dust and shadow as the cylinder shot through the pod's sheared edge and tumbled over smoking carpeting. It spun in short cycles, drawing Anna's attention by virtue of its unassuming shape alone, coming to rest at the heap of bodies before her and nuzzling a corpse's bloodied palm.

Without a second thought, Anna shifted an oozing neck aside and grasped the cylinder. It was smooth, chilled by Hazan's plunging temperatures like trail canteens from so long ago. She fought her way onto her knees, drew back her arm, and cast the cylinder toward the pod's lighted gap.

After two tumbles, the cylinder exploded.

Anna felt the snap of heat, the cascading force, the—

Blackness.

"Waterskins in my quarters. Somebody fetch those." Heavy footsteps circled Anna and came to rest beside Bora. "Impressive work for just a few hours out of my sight, *sukra.*"

There was something familiar about the man's voice, and Anna hated herself for embracing it. *Remember what he is,* she told herself, the room's candlelight pulsing as she closed her eyes. Her throat was dry, stinging with acrid smoke. *Remember what he's done.*

Bora's callused hands took hold of Anna's temples, and in spite of the northerner's recent violence, the sensation was calming. "They descended upon us."

"Spare me," the tracker hissed. "Girl needs air you lot haven't breathed."

Disembodied arms dragged her feet over metal and carpeting and fine grains of sand, and soon warm air rushed past her. But now her eyelids were dark and free of the sun's orange press. The world was frigid. She opened her eyes to darkness and the boy, with his pearl eyes and moonlit arms reaching out to embrace her.

Through the shadow and closeness of death, Anna heard one thing:

"I take care of you."

Chapter 11

The first jinn emerged when the nebulae were at zenith, and the night sky was a field of cracked mica and smeared color. There were so many stars that Anna lost her peripheral sight of the deck and iron railing, drowned in the vastness of it all. Perhaps it was the wonder of the night that drew the jinn from their dunes.

Or, perhaps, it was to stare at Anna.

"They make tricks," Shem explained. He sat with his face pressed to the railing, legs in an awkward tangle, staring at the nebulous creature like a puzzle waiting to be solved. "Maybe you see them, the ones who make praising. They say jinn bring good luck." He wrapped his fingers around the iron bars. "I never know what is wanted by them."

Anna also rested against the railing, but she lacked the strength to hold onto anything. Her legs were splayed numbly out to her side, draped in a thin cotton sheet. She'd woken up in that position, but hadn't dared to move. Instead she listened to Shem's stories and ramblings, staring out at the dunes as they rushed past the kator and shrank away. She wanted to delve into her memories, but it was impossible. The blast swallowed her recollection of both the chamber and meditation alike, forcing her mind back to the immediacy of the starlit dunes and the wind sifting through her hair.

Anna strained her throat, begging the cords to twist and produce noise. "I can't see it."

Shem turned to her, his smile radiant in the starlight, and waddled closer. With a guiding hand he turned Anna's head to the left and rested her chin between the iron bars.

The jinn ran alongside the kator as a jumble of radiant, shifting streaks, purple, blue, amber. Its form was humanoid, to some degree, but not its flesh. It was a condensed storm of the cosmos; flecks like planetoids and suns and moons swirled beneath its outer shell. Tendrils of cerulean and emerald curled from its lips, and in one blur, it was a hound of the same composition.

Anna had heard about them in the songs, but the beauty of the moment was lost to thoughts of killers. She could hardly keep her eyes open, and heard only the hushed arguing ten paces behind her.

The tracker groaned. "Don't try my patience, *korpa*."

"Will you still my heart? We are not beholden to the same masters. My end would come quickly—"

"Mine wouldn't come at all," the tracker said. "Do you see what's on my neck, *sukra*?"

Bora's reply was unfazed by the curse, by the sudden anger. "Your end will be long, painful, and done in the nests of shadow."

While Anna watched the jinn and its shifting forms, which always came amid wisps of colored light, she tried to parse the dispute. Her vision blurred past clarity, but the abrupt silence at her back was her only concern. She realized that bloodshed would prompt a decision, and it would be one of absolutes.

Bora could throw the tracker from the kator, and Anna would be far, far away from his crimes and wickedness. It was a fantasy that played out in her head as she watched the endless sands and the jinn's wild galloping. And yet, if left only with Bora and Shem, death was certain. There was no place in Hazan for a girl who couldn't understand flatspeak, and certainly nobody who could protect her. Her value in these lands came from the tracker, who'd promised her so much for all of her suffering.

From the tracker, who put himself in front of blades and Malchym itself to protect her.

But Bora's slaughter would do nothing for Anna either. Whether for her own survival or Anna's, she'd stood against killers and emerged. She'd braved blasts that would've sent Lojka's best men running for cover.

For a fleeting moment Anna wished she could utilize the force she'd seen in Bora when the men arrived. One day, when she knew the names and faces and crimes of every wicked man, she could make them answer for their evil. She could burn their fields, scourge their flesh with whips, and make them beg for breath before—

Anna's eyes jolted open. She heard the tracker's heavy boots clomping toward her, rattling the thin metal of the deck.

"Anna," the tracker said gently. He moved to her side, just within her range of vision, and sank down onto his haunches. His burlap mask rustled as he turned his head to the side, presumably eyeing the jinn. "Your kin ever tell you about those cults in the peaks, girl? They say that there are gods. Not just the Grove and the Claw's spirits, but real, walking gods. Some say that they took these gods to bed, had babes with them. Some bring their babes into the forests and slit their little throats." He shook his head, suppressing a laugh. "The *kretiny* in the flatlands are just as superstitious. They think fortune and miracles come from jinn." The tracker huffed. "Those from Rzolka have more sense."

"Sense?" Shem asked from behind the tracker.

"Sense," echoed the tracker. "The sense to walk away when you aren't needed."

"Anna needs me."

"Shara, Shem," Bora called. "We should leave the Rzolkans to their sensible dealings."

"I'll be fine," Anna said, closing her eyes against the breeze. "Don't worry about me, Shem."

After a moment of hesitation, Shem's little footsteps pattered across the deck. "I clean your bed," he chimed, his voice fading. "Very clean."

And when the footsteps of the two northerners disappeared, it was only Anna and a wicked man.

"She nearly killed you," the tracker said. His voice swirled around in the shadow of Anna's closed eyes, each sound forming into true letters. "The northerners have a thousand ways to tunnel into your skull, girl. Like sedating you when hired blades are on their way."

Anna opened her eyes and found that the jinn had vanished. "Who were those men?"

"They wouldn't have been a problem if you weren't there," the tracker said. "Flatspeak is a language of lies. She lured you out there."

Lured. It was a pebble in her mind, baiting her thoughts. Distantly, she formed a reply. "She saved me."

"Tried to crack your thoughts." The tracker settled himself down beside Anna. Sweat and rotted dusk-petal mingled with the breeze. "Isn't that the first thing we do to a headstrong mare, Anna? Burn away its wild blood?"

"You just want to hold the reins," Anna whispered.

"*Ne prava,*" the tracker shot back, stunned or perhaps, if Anna stretched her imagination, hurt. He cleared his throat. "You know better."

Anna opened her eyes and gazed at his burlap mask. For the first time she saw him as ridiculous, a cowardly man who would sooner pursue a thousand kindnesses than admit his own wickedness. She glared at him. "If you cared you would've been there."

"Not even the wisest man can out-think a Hazani's schemes."

Anna hardened her stare. "Those killers had man-skin."

"Perhaps," the tracker said, "but not like our kind. Not even like the easterners. Their people breed with Hazani, with Gosuri . . . probably with the ten-legs. Throat-cutters and whores are the only honest workers in the flatlands. Here, in this place," he waved his hand over the railing, encompassing the entire swath of sand and stars above, "truth is a cracked word in Hazan, girl. That's the first thing to learn about Bora's kind."

I've learned about lies from my own kind. She watched the tracker's beady, violet-ringed eyes through the burlap holes. "You didn't notice that she left?"

"Under false pretenses." The tracker paused. "False reasons."

"I know what a pretense is." If only from caravan drivers. "Don't treat me like a child."

"Right, then," the tracker said. "Bora said she'd bring you there to calm you down."

"She did."

"Not as expected." He tilted his head to the side, the wind tugging at one corner of the burlap. "Look at you. Two paces from the Grove."

The Grove-Beyond-Worlds. Its mention stirred old longing in her, beckoning her to a calming refuge past this life, with its soft moss and ever-present shade. With her *mishu*—her little bear—and parents who hid their children among the brambles and under-roots. Without salt or wicked men or the recurring sense that Anna had forgotten something at home, but could not recall its name. "It would ruin you, wouldn't it?"

The skin around his eyes creased. "Say it plain."

"You need me." Anna stared at the burlap around the tracker's neck. Pale light seeped through the threadbare patches, forcing impossible calculations of hours into Anna's mind. Nothing could last so long. "I don't have an *investment* to look after."

"Don't nitpick over words. We've been partners from the start."

"What happens if you arrive without me?" Anna asked. "Bora was right, you know. A rune won't always protect you."

The tracker's brows tightened, turning his eyes to bloodshot slits. He took in a long breath. "Such little faith in your own marks. If you knew the quality of these lines, you'd sing different songs. You carved something endless, Anna."

"And without me," Anna said darkly, "they'll make your torture endless." Riders who had fought alongside the Moskos had never been shy about their exploits, especially after a few drinks in the presence of old comrades. A dark cell, a bullwhip, and a captive were all they needed.

Now, gazing at the tracker, Anna wondered how many men he'd tortured. She wondered if he could imagine the merriment that wicked men would find in an unfailing body.

He did, it seemed. His silence sang.

"You wouldn't touch me." She weighed his eyes, twisting her blade into the new wound. It was the humanity she'd once seen, but never dared to chase. The reins she'd been holding, unknown even to her, since their first meeting. She straightened herself against the railing. "If I want to rest in the Grove, I will."

"You wouldn't."

"I'll make that choice," Anna said. "You can bring me there in bindings, but it still won't matter. My father told me what happened when the bogat of Korkowice found a scribe. She was a small girl, and she didn't want to leave home. She didn't even want to work for salt. They tried to break her bones and hurt her mother, but she wouldn't help them. She couldn't be forced to do it. Once they broke her, then what?" She stared through the railing's bars, watching the sand shimmer in the starlight. Her throat hummed with the flurry of activity, awakening from days of slumber. "Then they only had a girl. All they could do was kill her."

"Partnership, girl," the tracker hissed. "Nobody said you were a droba, even if I've saved your bones enough to own them." He struggled to breathe without grunting. Behind the violet blossoms in his eyes, there was rage. "In Malijad, you'll have as many barrels of sa—"

"I want more than salt," Anna said.

"What, then?"

"Truth," she said. "I need to know why they took him." In the silence that fell over the deck, Anna felt something bizarre and nostalgic. It was a tingling swell in the back of her throat. *Sadness.* Julek's weight, light, almost unnoticeable after so many seasons of carrying, fell upon her back, and the question of *why* became vital. When memories of a crooked-legged boy eating unripe blackberries and marveling at fireflies faded, there had to be something for her to understand. There had to be truth behind the pain, reason in an senseless world. She blinked to hide whatever tears might emerge in the moonlight. "And I want to know why they need me. I want to know why they need the runes." More blinking. "I need to know how wicked you are."

The tracker let out a whistling sigh. "You think I'm wicked?"

"It's subjective," Anna whispered, fighting the cracks in her voice.

"After all I've done for you, I'm a wicked man." The tracker lowered his head. The anger was gone, leaving only a husk of bitterness. "Do you want to know what's wicked, Anna? Malchym is wicked. Kowak is wicked. The bogaty are wicked. *Rzolka* is wicked. It's rotten to its core, but you're too young to notice. Still covered in womb blood, aren't you?" He raised his head. His eyes were devoid of their dusk-petal haze. "But maybe now you're old enough to see it. Just take a good look. You've found the last honest man in Rzolka."

"You're not honest," Anna said. "You're a liar."

"Only one of us broke our deal."

By now truth had become so warped in Anna's mind that she couldn't recall what she had, or had not, done in the marshes; his lies were as valid as her memory. But she could never call him an honest man.

"Do you really miss home, girl?" the tracker asked. "Do you miss Bylka and its pretty flowers? Do you miss the all-wise bogat who paid two handfuls per child? And how about your father, who put the ink to the bogat's writ?"

"Don't talk about my father," Anna snapped. "You chose to come to our village. You could have tilled fields, or made knives, or caught fish at the ford. But you chose to hunt us, and that makes you wicked. Just like those *killers*."

The tracker sighed. "Imagine that. Me, the wickedest man you've ever met. Did you ever consider who put us on the hunt?"

"I want to know everything," Anna said, unsure if she could stomach the truth.

"Huh." The tracker folded his arms, creasing his mail undershirt. "Here's a compromise, then. I'll tell you who wanted the crack-leg, and who wants you."

"Not just who," she said. "Why."

"Right. That too. But keep both ears open, because I'm not fond of repeating myself. Once you've heard it all, you'll decide who's wicked."

Anna nodded.

"What do you know about Radzym's keep, girl?"

"The bogat?"

"Yes, your bogat," the tracker said. "Don't tell me you've never been to his keep."

"Never," Anna replied. "The riders used to say he was taking boys, but not why. They said Malchym didn't know. I just know that he has too much salt."

"Moskos don't understand *too much*. Truth is it's not in your blood."

"You wanted some of their salt. That's the truth."

"Truth is muddy," the tracker reminded her. "Listen close, and you'll see my point." He turned his gaze to the dunes. "Before the war, Radzym was a shadow. Any man old enough to use his prick would tell you that he never had two fingers to the throat of your land. Never put sweat into the fields, and neither did his kin. Probably never saw the eastern fields until they gave him the writ, in fact. And bury my name if he could pick out Bylka on a map." The tracker gave a hollow laugh, as though he had attempted, and failed, to mimic true amusement. "The *korpa* has barely thirty years, and he's held the writ since before your first breath. How he got his hands on the parchment . . . well, it depends on the imagination. Each tale is different, but I've seen the way his eyes crawl around in his skull. My guess is that he turned on Adym once the war broke out, but not with a blade. Too bold for him. He probably told the Moskos how to surround the keep, stack their straw, and burn out the family." The tracker shrugged. "That was how the Moskos divided up the land, girl. They didn't care who could thresh wheat or crack an enemy's line. Crooked-tongues were rewarded. Crooked-tongues like Radzym."

Radzym's name had drifted through her father's post once or twice, but nobody spoke much of him. What little Anna had heard of the bogat, however, vindicated the tracker's story. The riders, and sometimes Anna's own father, had called him the *novy sinka*—the new runt.

"What did he do to you, then?" she asked.

"Not a thing," the tracker replied. "Not personally, anyway. He's a crooked-tongue, and he worked with Moskos, but I've no blood-wish with him. I only met the *korpa* when he needed trackers."

"You're not a tracker," Anna said. "I'm not sure what you are, but you're not one of them."

"According to what?"

Wind whistled over the kator, filling the silence. But Anna's first night in the ruined keep was enough to make her point. Somewhere in his heart, the tracker knew it too. "Why was he taking them?" She couldn't summon the nerve to ask about Julek specifically.

"Enlightenment." The tracker cocked his head to the side. "Do you know that word?"

Someday, I will, she assured herself. "Go on."

"Most would wager he wanted something warm in his bed," the tracker said. "All of those young boys . . . a few girls, just for thrills. A quick-lipped messenger near Veszula thought he was forcing *duzen* broth down the boys' throats, adding more giants to his pens, but it didn't explain why he'd take the maimed ones. A few cycles in, words slipped through cracks in his walls. Words that called for skilled *help*." He took in a measured breath. "The bogat is young, but he's no hare. Doesn't need to fuck every pretty creature that walks through his gates. That's what his *sukry* are for."

"You didn't—"

The tracker held up a callused hand. "There's a certain slowness to the truth of things, girl. Tales within tales." He looked back at Anna. "The whisperers said that Radzym had gone mad for runes. Not just these," he said, gesturing to the luminescence beneath his burlap, "but of another breed. Radzym's scribe carved up his neck five, six times each day with what I'm carrying, but they wanted what they couldn't have. New marks."

As Anna listened, the symbol that screamed *light* danced in her periphery, begging for attention. "What do they look like?"

"Don't know. Radzym doesn't know either, far as word went. At the heart of things, the problem was simple: Nobody had ever *seen* them. It was chatter slipping through old walls. Words from Nahora, from some sunbaked wanderer in Desh Safar. Doesn't matter a grain though, because there was never any proof of them."

"It doesn't make sense," Anna said, seizing the natural break in the tracker's words. "Did they think Julek was a scribe?"

"Of course not. He was scrap parchment."

"I don't understand," Anna said, a thread of anger worming through her chest. His riddles were tiring.

"You said you didn't want to be treated like a child," the tracker said, more comfortable than ever. "Listen here, then. Radzym thought his scribe could figure it out, if he just kept at it. Rumors about their shapes were everywhere. Moon-curves, mountain-teeth, waves, they tried everything, but none of them worked. Nobody even knew what they might do, if they ever found the fucking things. And each time they failed, it left another ruined neck. Nothing but scar tissue, if they even lived."

As far as Anna knew, there was no reason why marks were confined to the throat. It was just the way things had always been, how they'd been justified by a dozen different legends. She slowly raised her hand to her neck, feeling over the stitches and rough flesh. No matter what she'd once felt about her voice, she felt fortunate in that moment.

"So they cycled new blood in, new blood out," the tracker continued, oblivious to Anna's gesture. "They always needed fresh bodies. It wasn't just Radzym doing it, you understand. The krolgaty turned a blind eye."

Seated ones of Malchym, Anna recalled from her father's sparse explanation of the term. *Bogaty among bogaty.* So much power was beyond comprehension.

"You'd be hard pressed to find a bogat that wasn't looking for those runes, or churning through whole villages to work at them," he went on. "Even Malchym, you know. Maybe their low swords don't know, but their council, all of the krolgaty, must know." He gave a dark laugh. "Defenders of justice. Why do you think their men were searching that tomesroom? The korpy thought that a looted keep might hold their answers. I don't know what those runes do, girl, or if they even exist, but everybody wants them."

"They're just symbols," Anna said, watching *light* squirm in the darkness. "Maybe they should be afraid of them. If they exist."

"Now *there*'s a shred of thought," the tracker said. "But they're just hounds. They're so hungry for a kill, even if it's leaking pus. Loose words say the runes will set Rzolka aflame, and each bogat's hunting for the torch."

Anna pulled herself back from the man's words, suddenly realizing how they'd spoken of Julek. How they'd called him *parchment* and whitewashed his death. He meant nothing to men who answered to no one.

"Those among my circle tasked me with watching Radzym," the tracker said, disinterested. "We have one attached to nearly every bogat, and four in Malchym. Three in Kowak. But I was correct, girl: There was nothing to Radzym besides a crying, tit-hungry boy. My work near Bylka was a waste." He stared at Anna, his violet irises churning. "Until I found you."

"You were looking for me?"

"No," the tracker said, waving his hand in dismissal. "But what a merry little accident it was. Moment I found you, I knew it was time to head north. Time to bring home the one respectable thing in your backwater pit."

An accident, she thought numbly, mulling over the words. It calmed her to think that she hadn't been the reason for the trackers following her. In some ways, she figured it would've resonated in her gut to hear *you're not worth killing for.* Yet there was no solace in the explanation. There was no reason for anybody's death. The more he spoke, the more Anna recalled her meditation, and the fleeting nature of life.

Perhaps in a just world, one without scribes, wicked men would not outlive their victims.

"Goes without saying that you're special," the tracker said. "And partnership means fair treatment. So the honest way of it is, you're a good sort of special. Anything you want, anything you need, anything you whisper in your sleep, my circle will have it for you. How's that for an earning?"

Earning. The word was cracked coal and mashed dandelion in her mouth, so bitter that her throat clenched. "Don't try to buy me," she whispered. "Not anymore."

"You have your *truth*," the tracker said.

"No," Anna said, "I have your words. One man's words."

"Cooperation from an honest man puts you off, eh?"

Anna's stare was unwavering. "Tell me about your circle."

His eyes were creased with the enjoyment of a man in the thick of dice-gambling. But upon hearing *circle*, the veil evaporated. He tilted his chin up with slow resolve. "They'll save Rzolka." His voice was deep and determined, his words rehearsed.

"How?"

The tracker's pupils, darkened to black droplets in the night, drifted upward to watch the sky. "Take the simplest truth, girl. Politics are a tired game."

Her father had said as much. Not even the bogaty seemed interested in dealing with the missives from Malchym. But Anna had always heard of Malchym's councils, which supposedly seated as many women as men. Like all half-truths about Malchym, it had a certain element of foreign allure to it. Malchym was a place where all things could've been true, because she had never been inside of its walls or able to dispel the illusions.

"Besides," the tracker said, closing his eyes, "we wouldn't want to overfill your mind."

"Tell me," Anna said. She did her best not to sound like a petulant child, but it was fruitless.

"There's no need, girl."

"Yes, there is," Anna shot back, her voice a hoarse whisper. "I don't know what you want to save Rzolka *from*. I don't know how they plan to save it, or why they want my help. I don't know what politics has to do with anything. I don't know—I don't know a lot of things, and you owe me the answers. And I want you to stop calling me girl."

The tracker arched one eyebrow. "Oh?"

"*Panna*," she replied, recalling the term she'd once heard among bloodletting women in her village, often directed at her mother. A term of respect, if not deference.

"By the Grove," he moaned. "It's what Malchym calls its women, its girls, its cockless animals. Leave it in the shit, where it belongs." He sighed. "And since when did you bleed, girl? Your sheets are as white as bone."

"You'll call me *panna*," she whispered. "And you'll tell me about your circle. About your politics." Even if she didn't understand, she would pretend that she did. She couldn't surrender her advantage.

She couldn't surrender the truth.

"It'll breeze past you, *panna*," he began, practically spitting the word, "but you want the whole truth of it, so I'll indulge you. It's not like anything

I tell you will reach inside and twist your little heart, though. It's all history and songs to you. You don't know a breath of this world." The tracker laughed like a hound that'd lapped up its water too quickly and sputtered. "Before you crawled from your mother's slit, Rzolka was strong. Not perfect, you understand. I've never been one to drown things in honey.

"But strength was what we needed when Nahora reached the eastern shores and started undermining the markets in Kowak. It was what we needed when the Hazani slugs crept down the Flats and put their seed in every girl from here to Chemna. When the Gosuri burned a trail toward Malchym, and their krolgaty did nothing to stop them. When the north haggled every log and strip of kindling out of the Splinters, and Malchym gobbled up their metals in return." He sneered. "Can you see the way of it, Anna? Out in the fields and pinelands, there are plenty of decent bogaty who knew how soil felt on their hands. Blood, too. But the runts under the Mosko banners were city-born, and they only knew salt. Only wanted to spread their legs for the north. Those runts hardly had a dozen holdings outside of Malchym, but that was all it took. Writs from that marble cesspool had a way of stirring things. And in Kowak, you could already see the end. Huuri crowding the slums and salt changing hands a thousand times over, paying off foundlings to put a blade through any honest bogat's spine.

"Malchym threw coins at the bogaty near Kowak, and the men danced for them. And do you know what happened when the old wolves tried to cull their litter, to pick up the Moskos and their fleas by the scruff of the neck? The fucking runts bit at them, bled their own fathers dry. Kowak's proper lot held out for a while. Until Nahora stuck their cocks into the affair, sent galleys across the straits to show the runts how to fight. Those pups bit and bit and bit, and they lapped up the blood at Malchym's side. Imagine that, Anna. Two cities, Kowak and Malchym, both hobbling under the Mosko standard, putting villages to the torch to bring *peace*. Roasting the old wolves in their armor, and stuffing blackened flesh into their wives' mouths. Hanging boys from the lantern posts and standing around with their sacks in hand, laughing. All of that, done for order, and unity, and peace.

"Now they say their den is safe, but it's cracking again, just as it always did. Both cities want their scribes. They want payment and foreign masters and fat bellies. The cities are a cancer on Rzolka, *panna*. They're runts who bitch and moan to their mothers when fists turn to blades. They're the reason for the trackers in the mist. They're everything you grew to hate. They're why you grew up among thorns, not honeysuckle. They're why your father needed the salt." The tracker grew still for a moment, his eyes glazed over and shadowed. "They'll crawl out of their dens soon enough, and they'll tear each other to bits. But there won't be any old wolves to tug at the scruff of their necks."

Anna held her question in the back of her throat, piecing together the words carefully to avoid whatever rage still festered in the tracker. She'd never seen him in such a state. It was a trance of sorts, thick with loathing and memory and hatred. "What did you mean about my father?"

The tracker didn't look up. "Was that all you heard? Like I said, politics are beyond you."

"Why'd he need salt?" Anna asked. "We had plenty."

"Enough to haul you to Malchym in safety? Not a chance."

Anna froze. She could feel the truth like the season's first snowflakes on her tongue, chilling her and fading in the same instant. "Malchym?"

"So I suspected," the tracker said. "Your father told some sod about heading for Malchym a full cycle before we laced up our boots. Radzym bled the *korpa* for everything he knew. Do you have any idea how much salt the Malchymaz would pay for a scribe like you? Your kin wanted to pawn you off, *panna*. Wanted to fill their pouches and move along."

Not even the kator's whistling registered. Anna leaned back against the iron railings, tilting her head up and toward the nebulae. She saw her father by the hearth, his face warm and soft and lit by the orange glow of quarter-split logs aflame. His phantom hands combed through her hair, asking, *Where have you been, kohana? Did you gather the sap for your brother?*

"Look here." The tracker rested a hand on Anna's ankle. "No reason it had to be that way. This is the litter's fault."

Where is the sap, Anna?

Anna's eyes throbbed. "Your circle."

"What of it?"

"You call it Patvor, don't you?" Anna whispered. "I heard it. You call yourselves monsters."

"Fear is the only thing the runts can understand," he said. "Imagine when we swell up from the soil with your army, girl. When we make them pay before any runt has time to burrow, before they dredge up our names at all, and they hear that death's riding on the back of *monsters*. When they cry out for mercy from *monsters*." Another stifled laugh. "Just like the old songs, eh? We'll cull them and raise a better litter, a better pack."

Anna thought of the old wolves and the pack and the runts, trying to anchor her hatred onto a mass without a face or name. There were countless runts, she imagined, but their numbers didn't lessen their crimes or her losses.

Burrowed or not, she would bring their judgment.

Chapter 12

Her first glimpse of Malijad was a raging fire. Unlike the autumn bonfires she'd fed in Bylka, where she joined the other girls to collect kindling and fallen branches and withered roots in the clearing, this fire would see no huntsmen bring their kills. This fire was violent, clogging the skies with black smoke and burning the air into a melting haze. The peaks of Malijad's setstone structures were obscured by the smog, even at twenty leagues away.

She'd woken early that morning to find the tracker sitting cross-legged in the pod's central aisle, staring at her with those cavernous burlap eyes. It'd been expected, considering he'd carried her back to the pod, covered her, and waited for her to fall asleep. For the first time in cycles she woke with purpose, with the vague hope of saving Rzolka and hanging wicked men.

She'd wandered outside with a telling glance from Bora, full of unspoken caution about the flats and the men who might roam them while she was so exposed. After the attack, however, the Dogwood guards had become far stricter about keeping passengers in their pods. Freedom was a luxury.

The world beyond the pod reminded her of home, where winds moved in sleepy gusts and the sky was a starry pink veil. But blotted along the horizon was smoke billowing from deep channels in the flats, gathering like tufts of black cotton. The scope of the destruction was mesmerizing.

"*Jesh*," the tracker said from behind. The closest translation was *eat*, and Anna had only ever heard it from her mother.

Anna glanced back to find him standing in the doorway and slipping a chunk of hardtack under his mask. He didn't need to eat, if the stories about men with runes lasting over a day were true. Then again, he also didn't need to sleep, or even breathe. Living habits were difficult to abandon. "Don't you see that?" she asked.

"Skies don't take the sting out of your belly." The tracker sighed. "Come on."

Seeing the monoliths bathed in smoke was surreal, but perhaps it was a common thing in Hazan. In her new life. "Do you think it was an accident?"

The tracker eyed Anna wearily, then stepped aside and nodded toward the doorway, his stare lingering on the smoke. "Head inside. Shouldn't have to say it three times."

They ate in silence, leaving the pod's door open to fill the room with cool air and light. Anna sat on her bed and picked absently at the hardtack. Moving the food to her mouth, chewing, and taking occasional sips from her canteen were all perfunctory actions. Her mind was cluttered with fears about Malijad and its immensity, about meditation and symbols, about Shem and how he watched her from across the aisle.

"Shem," Anna said, hoping to distract him by pointing out the lowered window shutter, "is that fire from heat?"

"No," Bora said. She was leaning against the doorway with a tract of sweat running down her temple, the tawny landscape reflected in her eyes. "This is an old sign, unique to Malijad alone. To place spark-salts in the canals is a warning to interlopers."

Anna frowned. "Interlopers?"

With a quickening heart, Anna parsed the tracker's indifference, why he'd been so cavalier about the smog. *He's trying to spare me panic.*

"Welcome to the flatlands," the tracker growled. "Everything's mystical."

Anna was still gazing out at the inferno when Shem reached across the aisle, his arm flowing with gentle sigils, to place a piece of hardtack by her feet. She was reminded of a hound bringing a kill back to its master.

"No," Anna said. She picked up the hardtack and offered it back. "You should eat it."

"You're bones and hair," the tracker said, pacing near the latrines at the back end of the pod. "Eat it, girl. Or maybe that's a warning too."

"The orza will fill her plates beyond need," Bora replied. "You are not from the flatlands, where a child often lives with only bones." Her hawkish glare turned on Anna. "The mothers of Hazan know a simpler test. She has breasts, so she will live."

"Barely," the tracker said.

Anna pulled the edges of her cloak further around herself, then looked up at Shem. His brows formed a mournful curve, and he swiveled his head from side to side, unsure of what he'd done to upset them.

"That is the root of your concern, then." Bora nodded. "Her body doesn't please you."

The tracker squared his shoulders, pausing mid-step. There was familiarity to the stance, especially in the shadows pooling along the folds of his mask and obscuring his eyes.

"Both of you, stop it," Anna croaked. She watched the tracker's hands wander dangerously close to his blade. "I'm not hungry."

"Perhaps I should feel something for you, child," Bora said. "I'll be leaving you in the clutches of an animal."

Anna stared at Bora, tracking a bead of sweat as it formed on her brow and ran down her cheeks, her graceful neck. There had to be a reason for her barbs, some mechanism behind the provocation. It was as though she could pull levers within the man.

"Pretty face you have," the tracker said. "No small wonder it hasn't been carved off yet."

"Where is yours?" Bora asked.

The tracker grunted, burying the noise deep within his burlap.

"Let it go," Anna whispered. "Please."

Shadows crawled over the tracker's mask and unarmored tunic, occasionally slashed by the light that came through Anna's shutters. For a long, creeping moment, his hands lingered near his belt.

They fell away.

"Get your pack ready," he whispered.

All of Anna's breath left her in a rush, her chest aching. She thought of the blade in her belt, wondering if she could've retrieved it in time.

More than anything, she wondered who she would've helped.

* * * *

As Anna stood against the railing and looked down the line of waiting passengers, some Hazani with unstrung bows and others Huuri with flowing hoods, it occurred to her that she wasn't so different from them. Not anymore. Her fair skin and light hair were concealed, and she spoke a faraway tongue. She'd even taken on some of their mannerisms, standing still to avoid overheating and breathing solely through her nose. She wanted to learn their ways, to thrive like the thorny plants that some passengers carried in jars.

And beneath it all, the heat, the blood, the fear, she *wanted* a life here. She wanted a life anywhere.

The tracker stood motionless. There was something disturbing about a violent man at peace, about his mail shirt slung over one shoulder and head tilted skyward.

All eyes now rested on the coal-dark cloud above Malijad. It cast shade over the kator, over mud-baked huts and granaries dotting the landscape, over smoldering iron skeletons where canvases had once covered the channels. Ahead the city loomed like a cliffside worked in pastel paint, a blur of ochre and turquoise. Bridges draped in tapestries and trinkets spanned between towers, and as the kator lanced through another veil of smoke, now riding high above the flats on an elevated track, Malijad's outlying villages, no doubt expansive enough to rival Malchym, slipped under the vessel in a blur.

The world bled together in a mass of beige and black. Entire streets and marketplaces streamed beneath the tracks as vivid smears. Setstone gouges grew into shadowed pits and thin fractures became chasms, snaking over sun-bleached colors and exhaling crystalline dust in the breeze.

She closed her eyes, lost to the winds, the shouting below, the kator's reverberant humming, eternally ascending setstone, a black sky, smiling Gosuri children.

Everything ceased.

Anna opened her eyes to the crowd, and the platform just beyond the railing, a dull ring overtaking the city's noises. She rubbed the tips of her fingers together beside her ear canals, listening for the crackling of skin-on-skin to ensure she hadn't gone deaf as her mother had always done after bouts of thunder.

Broken sunlight bathed the left side of the platform, where a group of Dogwood soldiers waited with ruji, dark glass bottles, and a makeshift desk of wooden crates draped in red sheets. Vertigo struck her as she stared over the railing and watched crowds moving in formless, hazy streams far below them.

"*Yelsh*," a Dogwood captain called from the platform. He was older than most, with a lean, sun-darkened face and blue fabric covering his neck and forehead. A red sash covered sand-freckled armor.

A group of men shrouded in flowing white fabric, exposing only their eyes, disembarked alone. They moved like a palisade around a group of brown-robed passengers, most of whom were half their size. *Children.*

"Bora," Shem said. He tugged at the hem of the northerner's cloak and leaned over the railing, grinning. "They remember me? They remember songs?"

"No," Bora said. "There are many faces within the Alakeph. These men are not guardians of Qersul."

Anna studied the white-clad men with scrutiny, spotting the outlines of long blades beneath their robes. *Alakeph.* Rzolka's Halshaf branches had never needed the protectors, as far as she knew. Their leader spoke to the Dogwood guard seated behind the crates, his gloved hands emoting gracefully, and their exchange was so casual that it could've been between blood-kin. The foundlings milled about freely.

But when Anna looked at Shem, she saw his sale as a droba in Tas Hassa and in Qersul, which she'd never seen but feared nonetheless. "You said you were a droba."

Shem nodded. "I was. They make the buying."

Anna looked confused. "Galipa fought with them?"

"No," Shem said, equally bemused.

"He discovered Shem at the foundling hall in Qersul," Bora explained, her words tainted with frustration. "Galipa donated his salt to prove that he could care for such a child. He is a good man." Bora cast a hard glance at Shem, and Anna realized that the annoyance hadn't arisen from Anna's questions; it was from Shem's lack of reverence for his father. "These men are perceptive. Through eyes alone, they understand the way of a man's hands."

Anna squinted at the warriors, who'd finished conferring with the Dogwood guard and were filing into the building through a covered stairway. There had to be a Halshaf monastery somewhere within the sprawl, she reasoned. "What if they misunderstand someone?"

"They never will," Bora said. "They're far too good for Hazan."

The children followed the Alakeph up the steps, through a hanging curtain, and into darkness. When the last white-clad warrior carried a lame boy inside, the Dogwood guard near the kator raised his hand, called out something in flatspeak, and waved for one of his comrades. A youthful Dogwood guard approached the metal gangway with a cutting gaze, scanning until his attention came to rest on the tracker. After a hushed exchange with the tracker, the guard waved Anna and the others onward. "Right this way, my friends." In river-tongue, which Anna assumed to be his native language, the guard's voice was smooth and saccharine. It bore youthful maturity that Anna hadn't found elsewhere in Hazan, especially since flatspeak sounded as raw and spiteful as its birthplace.

Even so, a flitter of grymjek had leaked out from the tracker's whispered dealings, and it didn't fade so easily in Anna's mind:

Patvor.

The guard led them to the covered staircase, and as Anna glanced back over her shoulder, she noticed the kator's disembarking passenger queue had ground to a halt, stalled by Dogwood attendants. While Anna ascended the steps hand-in-hand with Shem, she tried to imagine a clean bed and cold water, which now seemed as luxurious as her promised riches.

The young guard paused halfway up the steps. "She wants to see the new faces with haste." He grinned at Bora. "She had your quarters prepared, *morza.*"

It was lost on Bora, it seemed. "I'll remain for now."

The guard offered a parting grin, revealing some of the whitest teeth Anna had ever seen, then proceeded. He stepped aside at the doorway and draped the fabric curtain over one arm, allowing the tracker clear entry. "Watch your head, *pan.*" He offered a reverent bow to Bora as she passed. For Shem, he smiled so fully that it put creases under his eyes. "Right ahead, *novy pan.*"

But when Anna moved to follow Shem into the darkness, the guard's elbow dipped to bar her way. She peered up at him, reading his brown eyes and the playfulness in his brow, unsure if he'd moved his arm unintentionally. Triangles with soft edges swam beneath his skin. His lips formed a lopsided crescent of a smile.

"My, my." His smile expanded. "The stars blessed you well, *panna.*"

He offered a wink so coy that Anna nearly missed it, and she wondered if she'd imagined the moment. "Thank you," she whispered.

He squinted at the steps behind Anna. "You seem to have dropped something."

She twisted around to scan the steps, and saw nothing. She patted at her hip for her knife and at her shoulder for the straps of her pack. There was nothing else to drop.

"Here it is," the guard said, digging down into a leather pouch on his thigh with his free hand. He grunted with mock exertion, and after a moment of rummaging, produced a violet-shaded rose. "This must be it."

Anna stared at the flower. It was a lovely color, and she'd never seen something like it in Bylka, even at the harvest festivals. The petals were fresh and new, swirling inward to form a black crease at the center. Its stem was a vibrant green, bordering on miraculous in a dying place.

He twirled the flower between his fingers. "Do you like it?"

A smile played on her lips. "It's beautiful."

The guard tucked the flower into the neckline of her tunic, making sure to point its thorn away from her skin. "Well, that looks quite nice." He gave Anna another wink, far more pronounced this time.

"Anna?" Shem called from inside.

She leaned around the guard, holding up a finger to signify *wait*, then looked back to the guard. "It couldn't have grown here."

"Oh, no." He gestured to the surrounding city and its endless, dust-clouded streets. "But in there, in the *kales*, the orza grows them like weeds. I found a single bulb many years ago, *panna*, and it sprouted well in its new home."

"Oh." Suddenly it didn't seem so remarkable.

"Don't mistake me," he said with a smile. "Not just anybody can have them. Each day captains pick five of them at the orza's request. We hand them out as we please to her visitors."

Anna glanced down at the purple folds, lost in their beauty and deep coloring. "For what reason?"

"Whatever we like, of course." The guard lifted the curtain higher, offering Anna passage. "Sometimes for a lovely *panna*."

She held the guard's gaze for a moment, envisioning him without armor or sun-darkened skin, wondering if those things were intrinsically part of him or merely acquired traits, and if he was Rzolkan beneath it all. He was alien to her. His kindness was as misplaced as sunlight under a full moon, and—

"Something's the matter?" the tracker grunted, breaking Anna's focus. He stood behind Shem, his vacant eyes cycling between her and the guard.

The guard flashed Anna a knowing smile. "Apologies, my friend. She was asking about the *kales*."

"Doesn't need words right now." The tracker Shem pulled free of the doorway. "We have places to be, things to do."

"Precisely," the guard said, lifting the fabric higher and offering Anna a concealed wink.

She glanced down at her boots and stepped into shade, her cheeks unexpectedly warm. She was quick to lock fingers with Shem's waiting hand, which waited patiently at her hip. After the tracker finished a few muted words with the guard and led them down the corridor, Anna stole a glance over her shoulder.

Only the guard's dark eyes and smooth lips were visible through a gap in the fabric, but that small sliver of a gaze and a grin was enough to fix Anna's stare.

Shem guided her around a bend in the corridor, and she saw only dark stone and Bora and the tracker ahead of her. It was a cold, dying place once more. *Hazan*, she reminded herself. Exhaustion and hunger returned in fierce waves. Thoughts of charming men suddenly seemed childish and hopeless.

Especially when she heard the monsters ahead.

Chapter 13

Muddled shouts echoed down the corridor, joining a wash of footfalls and foreign tongues and cavernous echoes. But the shouting voices stood apart from the din with their familiarity. Although Anna couldn't tell one speaker from another, nor see the end of the passage, she swore she understood them.

A full sentence in river-tongue, unmistakably male, sliced through the clamor. "See, now? Hush up with it. I told you they'd be here."

"Teasing runts," another voice, this one lower yet timid, was quick to reply. "Say something."

"Fuck's that flatspeak gibberish?" a third man wondered, almost as though speaking to himself. "No news, bad news? Something like that."

The tracker hissed a curse. "You can quit your yipping. She's behind me." He glanced back, though his inspection seemed to miss the uncertainty clouding Anna's eyes. "Don't make any sudden movements, and don't go prodding at her. Give her some room to stretch her ribs."

"She's a hound, then?" the third man asked. He released a slow-burning cackle that was met by the first man's belly-laugh.

Something about their laughter raked down the back of Anna's neck, so she gripped Shem's hand tighter, eased by the sensation of pumping blood in his fingers.

Bora looked back at Anna warily. Her amber eyes were as sharp as ever, crystalline with the light that poured from the tunnel's exit and threaded over stonework.

"Ah, ah, ah," said the third man. "I see pretty fingers."

Rustling fabric and the clapping of tacked boots against tile echoed from the back of the corridor, heralding the approach of the next group of passengers. The tracker, seemingly jarred back to the urgency of the moment, led the group onward.

Before they emerged from the passage, however, the ceiling slanted up and away with a gilded sheen, glittering with sunlight from an unseen window. Lacquered ivory and jade swirled along the walls.

Anna broke free of Shem's grip and shouldered her way to the tracker's side to glimpse the majesty of the chamber. *Chamber* wasn't the right word for it. Tiles extended in all directions, flanked by staircases that wove through one another like a spider's web. Men in bright sashes streamed past carrying parcels and banners, while women carried the folds of glimmering skirts. Children chased one another up stairwells, through lanes of fountains, into gardens nestled within the walls amid pillars and murals of warfare. It smelled of the sweet dust kicked up by horse hooves in summer.

She was distantly aware of the three men before her, but her sight was lured by the sunlight dancing down through the dome's iris. *A palace.* She prayed to the celestials and the Grove, begging for a life here.

"Sweet little Bylka girl," the third man cooed, breaking her focus. His head was bald and sunburned, his nose distinctly porcine. Freckles on his cheeks hemmed in two beady eyes, which were jaundiced and tired, while his smile was a curiously white yet lopsided jumble of teeth. Something resembling a beard covered his face in patches, left to run amok about his chin and neck. A crescent of his gut hung beneath his blue shirt, reaching down to his pants of loose beige twill and red striping. His exposed flesh bore sigils of tangled leaves.

Hearing of home put a chill in Anna's chest. Looking away from the man was harder than she expected, however. She'd always learned that hounds bit when you turned away. "Who are you?"

"The manners of bogland girls," a thin man murmured. He stood on the left side of the trio, draped in a purple overcoat with a gold-beaded sash around his waist. His hair was dark and pulled back with a knotted cord, revealing the harsh angles of his face and hooked cheekbones. Around his eyes he had pinched, leathery skin and thick brows. He was clean-shaven, but it only lent a porcelain illusion to his face. His sigils were jagged waves.

The last man, presumably the first one Anna had heard speaking, simply watched her from the center of the formation. He wore a cylindrical wicker hat and lacked any visible earlobes, which only made his dark, drooping eyes and black-painted cheeks more conspicuous. His orange robe was similar to the thin man's, but his hands were shrouded in leather wrappings, much like Anna had seen on the beakmen who handled crows. "Manners," he said. "How soon will we see it?" His bulbous sigils moved at a crawl.

The tracker looked at Anna. "When she's ready."

"And what is this?" the thin man said as he looked over Shem, the edge of his lip curling.

"A droba," the tracker replied. "An herbman in Malchym sold him to us."

The thin man. "You wasted our good salt on *that*?"

"Dealings of a different sort," the tracker said. "Don't lose sleep over it, Nacek."

"The orza should not wait," Bora cut in.

The freckled man's eyes bulged, and again he flashed his crooked smile. "The goddess speaks! We thought you'd never come back to us."

"To the orza," Bora said.

"So you say, *ladna morza*." He gave a lecherous grin, but it was lost on the northerner.

"Waited long enough on you and your lot, *kretin*," the wicker-hatted man grumbled. He turned and made his way to the nearby staircases, muttering curses as he went.

The thin man, Nacek, sighed and followed at a brisk pace.

"Much better," the freckled man said. His eyebrows danced as he looked over Anna once more. "Come, we can walk there together. Maybe talk about those tender little marks on your neck, hmm?"

"Must be a dozen dancing girls to meet along the way," the tracker said. "This one has blades."

"A touch of pain never dulls the pleasure!"

"Walk, Josip."

Eyes swinging between the tracker and Anna, the man offered a mocking bow and strode away.

The tracker eventually followed, his fists balled. As Anna kept to his side, absently observing the opulence around her, she considered the three men. They were cruel, stupid men, but perhaps deep in their hearts, they held the same dream as the tracker. Perhaps they could organize the messages, transportation, and the blades needed to retake Rzolka. Perhaps they were powerful enough to grant Anna anything she wished.

Almost anything, she thought while climbing the tiled staircase.

They moved through antechambers and along balconies, passing ballrooms and bathing halls and indoor markets with the smell of anise. Passing visitors wore vivid colors and intricate patterns Anna had never fathomed.

The sight around the corner stunned her.

Hundreds of bodies, men and women alike, formed a living wall that reached the ceiling and spanned the width of the gateway. They were silent and rigid and smeared in red paint, and with closed eyes and sealed lips, they resembled strands of crimson webbing. They grasped at one another's ankles and wrists and necks, discernible as living beings only by ripples of breathing. Upon hearing a series of *mola* shouts from Dogwood guards, the wall's occupants condensed downward and crept out on painted hands, forming an outlandish diagonal ramp to the upper level of setstone.

Nacek started up the path immediately, and the living wall held the weight, light though it was, without any indication of strain. His comrades followed.

"I don't understand," Shem whispered at Anna's side. "The man-skins shall be cherished—"

"Shut him up," the wicker-hatted man growled. He cast a hard look over his shoulder before continuing up the living ramp. His steps were sure and forceful, kicking the flesh beneath him.

As Anna teased her first step onto the ramp—the wrist of a muscular man, its painted surface free of boot prints or scarring—she heard footsteps receding. She spun around to find Bora heading back down the corridor, her slender form reflected on the tiles as if it were a still pond. Several of the soldiers cupped their hands to the backs of their heads as the northerner passed, but none ventured to speak.

"*Chodge, panna,*" the tracker said, significantly higher on the ramp. In the palace's light he appeared more monstrous than ever, covered in his ancient clothing and threadbare mask.

And yet he was her path to safety.

Grasping Shem's hand, Anna ascended the living ramp. She kept her eyes fixed ahead, ignoring the odors of stale mineral paint and sweat. When she stepped off the flesh and onto setstone, which had been coated with a patina of ivory, she couldn't help but smile.

Truly smile.

Birdsongs filled the air, incense coiled up in ribbons, and light streamed into the chamber through segments of amber glass. Light framed a ring of columns and awnings, and smaller gardens flanked the perimeter of the chamber, filled with pebble bedding and violet rosebuds. Curved windows of emerald and sapphire stained the desert light into something celestial. Trees molded into pregnant mothers, complete with sap-stained and bulging knots, cast shade overhead.

"Come closer," a voice cooed from the shadows. It was a woman, assured but comforting, bordering on maternal. Despite masterful river-tongue, her northern roots bled through. "Don't be shy."

Nacek was the first to step onto the pebbled path, still carrying the pleats of his robes at shoulder height.

"Not you," the woman said. It was neither comforting nor biting. Even so, it halted the thin man and forced a demure retreat. "Just the girl. This is an important day for her, and she deserves some attention." She drew in a longing breath. "Proper attention, so to say."

All eyes turned on Anna.

She tucked her gaze low, unwilling to indulge their wicked leering, and stepped onto the pebbles. Rather than scrutiny, she sensed appreciation in the woman's voice. A breeze threaded through the gardens, chilling the sweat across her skin. Shade fell in long, sweeping blades over the walkway.

An orza, she thought, stealing cursory glances at the woman and her throne. Perhaps she was more powerful than a bogat, or even a krolgat. The idea was jarring, and as she drew closer, her mouth drying and fingers picking anxiously at slick palms, she wondered what to say. How to stand, how to stare, how to smile. *If* she should smile.

Memories of what she'd endured, so recent and yet so far away, arrived between thoughts of decorum. She prayed that her life was like the old stories, where wickedness was the heat that tempered iron, or the darkness before an inevitable sunrise. Where, after so many hardships and trials, those without wickedness in their hearts would be rewarded, and the wicked would be punished.

A stone slab, creeping vines, and the orza's sandaled feet came into view. Anna's breath coiled in her throat.

"Let me have a look at your eyes," the orza said softly. It was an invitation rather than a command.

Anna looked up, debating whether to meet the orza's eyes or stare over her shoulder, but such a choice was futile: The orza's gaze was inescapable.

Her green eyes had the dark, placid nature of a pond, but they were inviting, questioning. The dark skin beneath her brows was smeared with crimson and violet powder, creating the illusion of a burning stare, and the whites of her eyes were vibrant like Shem's, neither jaundiced nor bloodshot, while her nose was slender and straight, her lips darkened with unknown dyes. Most pronounced was the black hair forming a crown around her head with the aid of pins, gold thread, and folded lace. Strips of purple cloth formed a loose gown. It was jarring to realize how *normal* she appeared, beneath her elegant theatrics and powders.

Her sigils were graceful, tumbling blades of grass.

Anna imagined her own reflection staring back, dirtied, light haired, laced with scar tissue, and wondered what the orza saw.

"You have pretty eyes," the orza said. She gave a measured smile before leaning back in her throne, which rose from its stone base like a flower in bloom. "How do they call you?"

Pretty eyes. Simple words, but resonant. She couldn't recall the last time she'd been complimented by anybody of worth, let alone an orza. It took all of her self-control to remain composed in her smile. "My name is Anna, orza," she said in her strongest whisper.

"Please, dear, don't concern yourself with titles," the orza said. "Only Anna?"

"Yes." Her answer was instinctive. Her cheeks burned as she replayed the response in her head once, twice, three times, realizing how insulting it was to answer an orza with one word. "I mean, no," she stammered. "Anna, First of Tomas."

The orza let the moment play out uninterrupted, offering only the slightest smile as encouragement. "My words step in error," she said, sighing. "I have not asked the name of a river-blood in some time. Your people don't carry a single word through their lineage." She thought for a moment. "A Gosuri name is just as fitting, I suppose." She paused, thinking. "*Kuzashur.*"

Anna blinked. "What does it mean?"

"Southern star."

Anna grinned. This name was far better. There was no mention of Tomas, no mention of sibling order, no mention of bloodlines at all.

Only her light over Hazan.

"Kuzashur," Anna said, if only to feel the name pass her lips. "It's a pleasure to meet you."

The orza inclined her head. "What lovely words you have." She gestured to herself with painted nails. "Dalma Emirahni. Among those without lineage, Dalma of Thirty-Three."

"It's a pretty name."

The orza studied her neck and arms, frowning. "Tell me, do you hurt?"

"No," she said. "Not anymore."

"Our herbmen can inspect you. It's no trouble."

Anna tipped her head. "It's appreciated, but I think I'll be fine. I've learned how to take care of them." She glanced at her legs. "The scars, I mean."

"Yes, it seems that way." The orza inhaled deeply. "How very enduring, you must be. But what about your body? I heard that there was a rather unfortunate incident on the kator."

"I had a good night of rest."

"Only one? The Gosuri rest their warriors for six days after battle." The orza frowned at Anna's dusty cloak. "You must be starving. And parched, of course. River-bloods are accustomed to liquid at every *hesh*." She gave a pitying smile. "Have no fear, Anna. In this place, liquid is as common as the sands. Wine, water, arak, boza, kefir. You will be nourished, no matter how your body may yearn. Outside of these walls, such things are impossible. But not here."

Anna didn't realize her thirst until that moment. It was true, after all: Beneath the fabric wrappings and dust, she was still a river-blood. She was suited for Rzolka. But this place was better, and she'd earned the right to stay.

"What do you think?" the orza asked. She must have noted the confusion on Anna's face, as she offered a sweet smile and added, "In regard to these walls, dear. What do you think of this place?"

"It's wonderful," Anna said, her reply too earnest to be embellished. Too laden with hope for a liar. "Until we came inside, I couldn't believe that it was real."

The orza laughed. "Trust your heart, Anna. It's quite real. As real as death, they say among the plains. These walls have been my bastion for years. I trust that they will provide for you too. We've even arranged a handful of theatrical performances, just for our special guest. Have you exchanged words with anybody within these walls?"

"Those men." She tilted her head back at the gathering near the ramps.

"Ah." The orza's lips tightened. "There are many things to say about them, but none are so pressing. I'm sure they've left their mark upon you. If it comforts you, their quarters are distant from your own."

"It doesn't trouble me," Anna said.

The orza laughed under her breath, concealing her lips with a practiced hand. "And others? What about the Dogwood officers? I instructed them to greet you with radiant hearts."

"One of them did," Anna said, feeling the young man's grin and aura flood back to her. Remembering the beautiful flower tucked into her tunic. Imagining his eyes before her, strong and spirited and playful. "He was very kind to me."

"Konrad." The orza smiled, then pointed to the flower in Anna's tunic. "Isn't it beautiful?"

Anna couldn't hide her excitement. "I've never seen anything like it."

"Konrad gives them to the girls who catch his eye," the orza said, hers bright with implications.

"It's really lovely," Anna said, steering the conversation back to the flower. She could feel the warmth of her blush spreading back through her cheeks. "He said that you have a garden here."

"We have many gardens. Consider them yours, too."

Anna glanced down at the violet flower, unable to envision an entire bucket, let alone a garden, filled with so many of them. "It's very generous."

The orza leaned forward as though sharing secrets among friends. "You know, it's a rare joy to find such bright spirits in the world. If it pleases you, I would love to converse in the company of tea and sweets. There are so many things to discuss, and so much to learn about you. This I can feel in your essence."

Anna could only nod in return. Her mind swelled with all of the good fortune, with the possibility of sleeping in a bed tonight, alone and secure and well-fed.

"But first," the orza said, her voice flattening, "I wish to see one thing."

The break in the orza's tone chilled her. "What is it?"

"It's nothing, really," the orza said. "It's a banal task, dear."

Anna squinted. "For me?"

"Yes." The orza rested her elbows on the throne's golden arms. "Don't worry. For one so special, this is hardly a task at all. But the men who delivered you here are eager to see it, and we shouldn't disappoint them. It will be done in a wind's breath."

The certainty of the orza's face was enough for Anna, but she examined the woman a moment longer to wait for her thinking mind—the clarity she considered thinking, anyway—to speak. Underneath the kind gazes of wicked men, there was callousness, a scheming edge. But there were no veils between them. "What is it?"

The orza nodded toward a passageway set into the far wall. Six Dogwood guards, who Anna hadn't even detected until her eyes fell directly upon them, stood beside the vine-shrouded columns. "Come for a walk with me, Anna," the orza said. "It's just inside."

Anna fought off pangs of discomfort. "Will those men follow us?"

"Simply to observe, dear."

"Observe what?"

The orza rose from her throne, collecting the trailing strips of her gown and draping them over her wrist. She motioned for Anna to follow as she moved toward the doorway. "We require your aid."

"How so?"

"One who is familiar to us has been harmed."

Anna looked backward as they walked, watching the three men, the tracker, and Shem drawing closer. A set of guards trailed the men. "Badly?"

"Oh, yes," the orza said. "Grievously."

She led Anna past the Dogwood guards and into the passageway, which was darker and colder than expected. On the other side was a small, candlelit chamber with metal doors on the accompanying three walls. Cushions were arranged in a crescent, and in the center of the floor was a metal grate. Half-moon brackets forged from dark iron were bolted onto the walls at eye level.

The chamber's silence was haunting.

"Where are we?" Anna asked. Aside from the limestone walls, which were bathed in a furnace's red glow by the candles, it seemed entirely detached from the *kales*.

"There are many spare rooms within these walls," the orza explained. She paced around the chamber before selecting a beaded white cushion, settling down, and folding her hands in her lap. "My builders alter designs as they see fit."

Anna's eyes lingered on the metal brackets, certain that spare rooms were never so deliberately engineered. "They must have altered it for something."

"An introduction area," the orza said. "Just stand in the center, dear." She extended a thin arm to pat the metal grate, her fingers skeletal in candlelight.

Anna did as instructed, but her steps were guarded. Days of being misled, misdirected, and misused bred enduring suspicion, and even more permanent was hatred. She searched the orza's smile for the barest flicker of betrayal.

But a jumble of footsteps broke her concentration, and the stream of men entered behind Anna, along with Shem. They fanned out and claimed their cushions, Nacek and his two comrades doing so with routine efficiency. Shem settled at Anna's right, straining forward with star-bright eyes and hands woven beneath his chin. Seated beside the other men and the orza, he faded into the gathering as another phantom silhouette.

Following a period of unnerving silence, the sound of jangling metal rose from beyond the chamber. The clanking grew louder, becoming so clamorous that the seated men glanced nervously around from their cushions, desperate to locate its source. But something more unsettling lurked beneath the metallic sounds. Something inhuman and urgent, blurting out fractions of words before devolving into groans.

Anna's fingers bunched up at her sides. She cast an uneasy look at the orza, who was quick to respond with a placating nod. *He needs aid,* she told herself, ready for whatever came through the doors.

It was the price of safety.

The door to Anna's right swept open, nearly striking Shem. Two men in Dogwood uniforms stumbled into the candlelight with chains in hand, their feet scraping against the stone floors in violent steps. Grunts of exertion and muttered curses filled the chamber as they fought their way between a gap in the cushions and into the chamber's center, the rusted chains pulled taut and shivering.

A man wrapped entirely in black fabric, secured to the opposite end of the links, shot out of the passageway. His arms were bound to his sides beneath the wrapping, but his legs kicked and strained against the floor, adding to the cuts along dust-caked, red-splotched feet. His screeches were stifled beneath the covering, clipped and swallowed and suffocated, like those of a drowning man. As he writhed in the candlelight, his belt-hitched chains slowly reeled in by the guards, something flashed near his head.

A metal ring had been set into the black fabric covering his neck, exposing a lone oval of flesh.

Anna's stomach clenched as she watched the guards move to opposing sides of the room, hauling their chains in spite of his muted screams and curling toes and thrashing, which only made the task of clamping his chains to the brackets easier.

The guards stepped back to wipe their brows and shake out their tired arms, and the man hung before Anna like a spider's cocooned prey. No matter how far he kicked or threw his weight around, he was trapped. His cracked and bruised toes barely scraped the grate.

"Anna." The orza was leaning around the captive in a bid to lock eyes. Her words were soothing, breaking through the man's cries and the thumping of Anna's heart. "Please, don't be alarmed by his madness. He's one of our foremost captains."

"Behold the Dogwood," Nacek said while picking at his nails. "Rzolka's bottom-shelf export."

Anna stared at the captive's bundled body, wondering what Hazan had done to him and how he'd ever been a captain. She nearly forgot that she was expected to help him. "What happened to him?"

"*Har-gunesh,*" the orza said. "The sun, dear. His unit was lost to the sands for nearly a cycle. There are many stories to be told about—"

The man's tortured grunts overtook the orza's voice. Without delay, the guard to Anna's left moved closer and drew a cudgel from his belt.

The guard swung the weapon high and to the side, then delivered three strikes to the captive's face. After a muffled cry of agony, the captive fell silent and hung his head, shaking.

"Domik," the orza snapped. "Mercy be upon him. Which mind do you seek?"

The guard bowed his head, the metal rod hanging by his side. "*Uzgun.*"

"*Afymet,*" she said in return. Momentary anger drained from her eyes. "Now, then. There are many tales to be told about the sun. I knew a Gosuri herbman who claimed that it infused him with celestial wisdom. Others, upon whom I tend the field of assent, believe that it scorches the mind." She drew a defeated breath and pointed to the suspended man. "My hayajara is serving alongside one of my regiments until the end of the *ru*. I would wait for her return, for I hate to frighten you, but this man's breaths may vanish in that time."

Anna met the shadowed faces of the men around the circle, even pausing to gaze into the tracker's eyeholes. "Is this a test?"

"This man requires your help, certainly, but we're all mystified by your gifts." She surveyed the hungry stares of those around her. "They wish to see your work, dear."

"On with it," the wicker-hatted man growled. "Show us the marks, girl."

In the ensuing silence, Anna drew the blade from her belt. A dry mouth made swallowing impossible. Everything about the man terrified her, even as he hung still, barely breathing. Even as . . .

Light surged from the back of Anna's mind in a flash, incinerating every other instinct. It flowed into the recesses of her memories and whispered, sweet and omnipresent: *Be still.* It calmed her hands and warped her vision to a sliver of the chamber, intent on the man's neck and its patch of flesh.

His sigils were twelve-sided and asymmetrical, flickering past and jumping with every heartbeat.

Her blade plunged through the skin, through muscle and surface vessels and sprouting hairs. Hayat's tendrils spun around her fingers and flooded her airways, dense and pooling with its secrets. Cryptic symbols and true letters and cracking landscapes claimed her mind. Her hands moved with ruthless resolve, no longer worried about blood or life but desperate to unearth *light*.

The blade drew closer to the starting incision, but the hayat bloomed, screeching to stall the rune's end, to hold her hand, to follow *light*. And so she flicked her fingers, chasing.

Light was just ahead of the blade, taunting her, begging to be tamed. Her hand moved in ways she'd only traced over hay or dirt or paper, obscured from her feeling mind.

Faster, faster, the lines came together, converging.

Blood droplets sizzled against the hayat.

Anna finished the cut.

She pulled her hand away, examining the marks clearly for the first time. The man's sigil was perfectly carved within the oval, and it pulsed with luminous white energy, pulling the blood and ragged skin back together. Dark blotches of bruising shrank and disappeared. But below the rune was something cryptic. Branching points moved down and away from Anna's cuts, extending to the metal ring's lower curve. It was a series of octagons crowded haphazardly into an oval.

In Anna's mind, it was *light*.

She dropped the blade, a wave of euphoria coming over her.

The man threw back his head and screamed. His arms contorted in spasms beneath the fabric, and his legs kicked wildly at the grate, the tendons beneath his skin tensing and snapping.

No, no, no. . . . The word crashed through Anna's thoughts.

A pair of white orbs burned behind the fabric on the man's face, exactly where his eyes should've been. Brighter than Shem's, surging with uncontrollable energy. Flaring so intensely that it blinded Anna and seared the walls with crystal-shimmering refractions.

Raising both hands to shield her eyes, Anna had to squint to discern anything in the chamber. It was brighter than daylight, washing out the flames that danced above candlewicks and bleaching the limestone walls. Screeching drowned out her frantic breaths, and as she gazed around the chamber for reassurance, she discovered that everybody was transfixed by the captive's radiant eyes, marveling or recoiling or laughing.

Except for Shem.

His eyes rested squarely on Anna, awestruck before his new god.

Chapter 14

Every nerve in Anna's body was primed, detecting subtle things that most would ignore, latching onto movements that showed the truth of a person's mind. Movements like the trembling in the orza's hands as she closed the doors to her study.

The Dogwood men had been quick to hurry the screaming man out of the chamber, but their unease was obvious. And while Anna thought distantly of the man she'd marked, wondering who he truly was, if he'd ever recover from sun madness, if the glow in his eyes could be extinguished, she was unafraid. It was liberating to mark somebody without consequences.

Nacek, Josip, and the wicker-hatted man had gazed upon Anna as though she walked the Grove itself. They were simple men to read: They wanted her gifts. In the proper applications, it was a harmless wish.

Shem had watched as a supplicant, desperate to receive the blessing of her cuts. For better or worse, he would do anything to hold her favor. Even as he was escorted to his quarters, he longed to tell Anna sweet things.

The tracker, by way of his mask, had been the most difficult to read, and it concerned Anna. The room had fallen silent in the aftermath, and while she'd mostly seen a mass of rotted smiles and eager eyes, she glimpsed nothing in him. There was something darker than disinterest in his silence. Bylka had never been a hub for news within Rzolka, but life altering developments—the burning of the northern fens, the assassination of bogaty—had always reached the town within a cycle. Rumors of other runes, which extended beyond the power to safeguard life, had never arrived in Bylka. For somebody as fanatical as the tracker, who knew so much about the bogaty's hunger for such runes, there had to be *some* fascination with her deeds. Even if news of similar runes was lost to the sands of Hazan, there was little question that the orza would hear of it eventually.

But the tremors in the woman's hands told Anna that her markings were the first of their kind.

Something deep within Anna revealed this truth. She couldn't explain it any more than how she'd formed the rune, but she felt power, relief from some cryptic pressure. She'd been led to the study in a state of ecstasy, walking with the confidence that she was valuable and limitless, even if she couldn't control the hayat. She welcomed its wild whispers.

It helped me come this far, she thought, remembering the way that the man's eyes burned with *light's* glow. *I won't ignore it.*

The orza sighed. "I apologize for the lack of servicing." She her way back toward the table, having locked the door with a sliding latch. "Most duties are attended to by Them, but I'm sure that the need for absent ears is apparent."

Anna nodded, unsure if the orza knew that even Rzolka's droby received names. It was jarring to hear the orza order her droby around with the collective word *Them*, or, in the singular form, *It*. She wondered if flatspeak's intricacies were lost in translation. "It's fine, thank you." She'd already poured herself two cups of mint tea, and had nearly finished a third by the time the orza settled into a rattan chair across the table.

Droby seemed necessary for servicing the study: It had countless silver kettles, spoons, plates, and pipes to contend with. The walls were high and stacked with wax-sealed scrolls, all neatly tucked into cubbies and labeled, and the floors were covered in ox fur. Overhead a lantern glowed within the shell of a stretched skin, diffusing light with a yellow pallor. The room smelled of citrus and smoke.

"Please, indulge yourself," the orza said to the tracker, who sat uneasily on his own side of the table. Her smile withered as he remained silent. "What a remarkable day."

Bora stared down at her silver plate. Her skin glistened, suggesting she'd arrived from the baths.

In spite of Anna's awareness, Bora remained unreadable. But there was a probing curiosity about the northerner, and every so often their eyes scraped in quick brushes.

"Bora, have you seen him?" the orza asked.

Bora looked up with militant obedience. "Yes, orza."

"Release your thoughts."

She bowed her head reverently. "I've witnessed nothing comparable, orza. It is most unique." A sliver of contempt, likely beyond the notice of both the tracker and the orza, crept into her voice.

"My thoughts align." The orza turned to the tracker, smiling. "She must be a gift from your gods. From your Grove, *pan*. Do you know what you've brought us?"

Anna gripped the edges of her chair and fixated on the word *brought*, wondering if the orza thought of her as another crate of cargo, or one of her *Its*. "I just want to help the cause," she said, drawing the attention of the entire table. It was strange how her soft voice was commanding. And *marvelous*.

"So driven too," the orza said. "And what did he tell you about this cause?"

"There are wicked men in Rzolka," Anna said, taking a moment to sip her tea and savor the fact that nobody challenged her or spoke out of turn. "I want to stop them."

"Ah, yes, of course. There are very wicked men, dear. Have you witnessed their actions?"

Witnessed. Anna drew in a long breath. "I have."

The orza put a hand to the fabric above her heart. "How horrible. The stars weep for you, Anna." She took a moment to compose herself, but her eyes crawled as though formulating questions, thinking. "Where did you learn to make such markings?"

"I'm not sure," she replied. "It was just what I felt. That's the only one."

"Bora, have you seen these before?" the orza asked. "The markings, that is."

Bora flicked her head to the side. "As I said, *Nur Morza*, they are most unique." Her pointed look wasn't lost on Anna.

"Yes, that's a fine word for it. Did Anna show you these markings while you traveled?"

"No."

"Humility is the compulsion to heap sand upon miracles," the orza said. "Or perhaps you were too shy."

The woman's easy manner, which had seemed like a blessing at first, served the same function as the animal skins above the table. They clouded her demeanor into something imprecise, making it difficult to read her intentions. Most people carried their past in limps or knotted brows, and with one glance, Anna knew if they'd been maimed or coddled by life. Joyful faces were suspicious in Rzolka.

Not everybody is damaged, she told herself, noting the delicate arch of the orza's brows and her soft smile. *Not everyone's past is shameful.* "Perhaps."

"Do you know what your attendant explained in his message?"

"Which message?"

"While you were so terribly harmed," the orza said, pouring herself a cup of tea, "your attendant instructed mirror-glints to be sent to our riders. They sent the flashes with urgency, and now I see that it was done with good reason. He told us that your hayat carvings would last through the *heshi*, enduring without any sign of weakness." She nodded at the tracker, satisfied. "And how true his words were, dear. Look. Even now, his markings remain."

Although the rage from that foggy morning had faded, the orza's words were still bitter. The woman knew nothing of the rune's origins, of a young boy named Julek, of kin who would sell anybody for a bag of salt.

"Now, upon seeing you, what have we found?" The orza tucked an errant strand of black hair into place. "The Celestials knew your gifts, dear. You've spun hayat out of its primordial state, and now, now it may grow."

Anna glanced into her empty cup. "I'm not sure I understand."

"These markings have never entered the world," the orza whispered. "Under your steady hands, your shadow, new worlds will blossom."

It was overwhelming. In some ways she'd only been a vessel for the rune, surrendering control to its energy, its demands, allowing her fingers to move as an instrument for something grand. But even as she resisted her importance, she recalled the symbol from her meditation, remembering its shape within the fog, the way she'd once seen *light* as unreachable.

"She stays with me," the tracker said, drawing a sharp look from both northerners.

"Yes, of course," the orza said. "That was always the arrangement. Your chambers are in the northern rise, and as with the others, your sleeping quarters have been stocked with some provisions from home. River-blood delicacies, I should say."

"What about her?" the tracker asked.

Anna glanced at the man, but he stared too intently at the orza to notice. A telltale glossiness in his eyes spoke of dusk-petal withdrawal, which would leave his mind more addled than usual. Until he found a new vendor, anyway.

"She'll be quartered in our finest chambers." The orza nodded up to indicate a higher floor. "It's just beside the spire keep."

"Beside me," the tracker said. "I want an eye on her."

She gave a reproachful hum. "She'll love her quarters, and you'll grow fond of yours. I can assure you, if safety's the thorn in your mind, that the Dogwood Collective will keep uninvited specks of *sand* from getting into her chambers. There are guards from the first dawn to the final moon, and—"

The tracker shook his head. "No."

"Then what?"

"Won't do to have her sleeping in those parts."

"And why not?" the orza asked, sipping her tea and adding a pinch of black sugar. "Certainly you'll be able to visit her as you wish, and you'll be paid in full for your contract, *pan*, but you have no reason to escort her so closely."

"Fuck the contract." The tracker pushed back his chair and cracked his neck to one side. "Our breed drafted it, so she ought to stay with us too. Their blades came close to her."

The orza's smile hardened. "We're in a bastion of friendship. *Breed* should not separate us."

"She's right," Anna cut in. She leveled a scrutinizing gaze at the tracker, remembering his promises of warmth and luxury and safety. Of unified effort. "We have one cause. And Bora kept me safe."

The tracker's slippery eyes danced around the gathering "She won't sleep near the *sukra*. Not a chance."

"Such things aren't your decision," the orza said.

Bora stared at the tracker, likely full of a thousand barbed thoughts. But the orza's presence stilled her.

"Word was she'd slip back into the sand," the tracker spat. "What's the right of it?"

"Bora has always maintained quarters in this place," the orza said. "She moves around as she wishes, of course, but she's a close-hearted friend. If she wishes to stay, then I'll hear no more about the matter."

Bora glared at the tracker. "For now, I would remain, orza."

The orza smiled. "And so it is."

"So it is," sneered the tracker. He stood and turned his weary eyes on Anna. "Come our way when you want your own blood." He glared at Bora, then the orza, his stare thick with cruelty. "Not one whisper to her. And you'd better believe I have their ears, *sukry*. You push us, and it'll be the most expensive dungeon in the flatlands."

The orza sampled her tea. "I suggest you honor our cause's arrangements, *pan*."

Whatever it meant, it only sharpened his glare. Without another word he stalked over to the doors, threw open the sliding locks, and disappeared around a corridor's bend, leaving an uneasy void in the study.

The orza spooned black sugar into her cup. "I'm sorry, dear. As I told you, *Har-gunesh* is a cruel god. He harms the mind as much as the flesh. In time his mind may heal, likely by your markings' guidance. As it stands now, there's little to be done for him."

Amid the clinking silver plates and fire-hardened glass, Anna realized that it wasn't *Har-gunesh* destroying his mind. It wasn't his exhausted supply of dusk-petal, or his feeling mind run amok. She was hesitant to call it *care*, or *affection*, but there was a sense of protectiveness, one bordering on the paternal, perhaps, bolstering his anger. And now, no longer sailing or riding kators or walking on trampled moss paths, there wasn't a business incentive for him to protect her.

Anna looked at the riveted double-doors through which the tracker departed, studying the dark wood as though it might offer some unconsidered answer. Much like Bora's words in Nur Sabah's marketplace, there was violence undone in his exit.

The orza cleared her throat, breaking Anna's focus, then smiled at Bora. "Come, Bora. We'll show Anna to her quarters. We should let her rest before this evening."

"This evening?" Anna asked, wary.

"For your cause," the orza said. "Before you enjoy the night and its wonders, there will always be the small matter of providing service to your cause. Tonight we'll just witness your gifts once more."

"What will my gifts do?"

"Our warriors require simple aid," the orza said. "Tonight, we simply wish to see what you did to your attendant. A protective marking. Some of the men from the cause will be in the path of harm, and they require your care."

"You want me to mark the Dogwood," Anna said. It was the second most common use of scribes in Rzolka, outranked only by the protection of bogaty. On its own, there was nothing distinctly harmful about the request.

The orza gave her a polite look. "Is this acceptable?"

With some delay, Anna returned the gesture. "Of course."

"Lovely. And how do you feel about lessons, dear?"

It was hard to say, as Anna had never received formal lessons in all of her years. It was something for the wealthy children in Malchym and Kowak. That wasn't to say they didn't fascinate her. There was always buried desire associated with Shem's true letters, learning the functions and interlocking way of words between tongues. "I like them."

"Good." The orza added another pinch of black sugar to her tea. "Bora can teach you many things, of course, but we have other radiant minds in these walls. Some of them may surprise you."

For Anna, the word *surprise* was rarely associated with good things. "It sounds lovely."

"And," the orza said with an exaggerated wink, "I'll show you all of the joys within our districts. These halls are built for more than vaults, of course. Without celebration, what point is there in living?" She laughed as her eyes traced the tabletop. When she glanced up, the severity in her eyes turned her powders to war-paint. It made Anna's hand constrict around her teacup, white-knuckled. "You have a wonderful heart, Kuzashur. This is easily known. But not all are so kind, and not all hold such radiant hearts. With every star's blessing, you'll live a joyful and prosperous life here. I simply ask that you consider each action carefully. Some men demand permission to be received rather than forgiveness sought." The weight of her words haunted the study and formed a fragile silence, broken only when the orza herself stirred and sipped her tea. A glimmer of playful youth returned to her eyes as she lowered the porcelain, but the shift was forced. "Your days of southern darkness are over, dear. You should know that *Malijad* is the Gosuri word for womb, and you've arrived so near to the Days of Seed. What an auspicious path to rebirth."

It was spoken as though the mood hadn't soured moments earlier, and Anna did her best to overlook the lingering unease. Although the bile hadn't settled in her stomach, she pushed her cup away and offered a thin smile, her fingers reaching up for the comfort of the purple flower in her tunic's weaving.

A thorn cut into Anna's thumb.

Chapter 15

Anna's legs ached as she crossed the waist-high grasses of a balcony terrace, boots in hand and eyes pinched against the sunset's fire, exhaustion blurring the orza's palatial tour into a half-forgotten dream. Through the towering buildings she saw the dimness of approaching nightfall, kators moving in chrome flashes along hovering tracks, mirror signals glinting between posts, nocturnal markets sprouting in the aftermath of the sun's terror. It was almost enough to distract her from the shouts, bestial and thick with drunken rage, that had been echoing from the lower levels since morning.

The orza wandered to the black iron railing that encircled the terrace, gazing out and holding Malijad's sunset in her irises. "Is there such majesty in the south, dear?"

Far off in the haze, smoke and glass erupted soundlessly from a setstone high-rise. Seven seconds later, its dull clap reached across the sprawl. Nothing crossed the orza's face. "No, I don't think so," she said finally. Dark bunches of Dogwood armor crowded her periphery, their mass no more than twenty paces away. "Do they have to come everywhere with us?"

It was an innocent question, but its implications sent knots through the orza's brow. She was quiet for a time, presumably working to construct an agreeable answer for the cadre. "In time, you'll grow accustomed to the scope of their presence." She glanced back at them with a saccharine smile. Then, as though bleeding her own ambiguity, she hummed and stared back over the railing. "Most soothingly, their aid is always within reach. Even if you don't imagine that you'll require it."

Anna was unwilling to press the woman's veiled words, given how easily doubt could corrupt hope. Rare hope, no less.

In a descending capsule, its motion as fluid as the kator yet strangely weightless, Anna mentally recited her mantra with dogmatic insistence. *Save Rzolka, save Rzolka, save Rzolka.* Only her cause provided enough energy to stay awake, to blink away exhaustion, and ignore her blistered heels in the orza's presence. For better or worse those words were her only link to the south, her only goal. She could become comfortable in the *kales*, of course, but her mind would be restless until she rooted out every trace of wickedness in the south.

That was how it had to be, she told herself.

On the designated floor, Anna wandered down corridors wrought from setstone and dark mortar. *Save Rzolka.* The masonry was chipped and blackened in spots, its support pillars bent into crooked spines. Reckless shouts echoed from the chamber ahead. Most of it was in the river-tongue, but inklings of flatspeak and grymjek bled into the din. No matter what they'd promised her, she knew she'd be terrified by her task. She fought to embrace Bora's teachings, to stifle her fear and act with necessity.

Save Rzolka.

The orza's steps echoed in pursuit, and Anna glanced back to meet her painted eyes. "I'd like to do this alone, if it's all right."

The orza's brows arched in surprise; she was faintly impressed. "As the winds carry you." She took a step back, her smile as vibrant as ever, and Anna continued onward. "And dear," the orza added, forcing her to turn, "do as they ask." Concern, thick and pooling in the twist of her lips, dampened the smile.

Anna's throat tightened.

Their faces were haggard and streaked with black paint. Sigils pulsed beneath coal-dark smears, more luminous than candlelight on their sweat-stained skin, or their bloodshot, *nerkoya*-infused eyes. They hardly noticed the new arrival as they continued their rituals, shaking one another by the shoulders, sharing bulb-shaped flasks, flicking oils into their pupils, driving pins into fingers or palms. Some chanted praise for the bear's fury and the ox's tenacity in the grymjek, while others knelt in half-circle formations and burnt withered grass as an invitation to the Grove. A scattered few—mostly Hazani and dark-skinned northerners—were tossing mica into lantern light to form glittering stars as they cinched tunics and wicker breastplates, inspected ruji or short blades, laced up boots, pulled on leather gloves and rose dark hoods.

Toward the back of the hall, standing beside his three comrades with a painted mug in hand, was the tracker. If not for their garb of pressed shirts and laced pants, the four men might have also been taken for warriors.

They drank and joined in animal calls, fueling the room's energy. Their faces were shadowed and sharp in candlelight.

Anna slid through the crowd, dodging men who sloshed liquor and exhaled smoke. She was shorter than them, but her course was calculated, directing her feet through the scuffle.

When she emerged into the chamber's clearing, ostensibly the ritual's nexus, the eyes fell upon her. The clearing's inner ring paused with bottles at their lips and half-spoken sentences unfinished. Then those in the outer circles peered through the mass, catching sight of Anna and angling their bodies in turn. The tracker and his comrades, swept up in fond recollection, were among the last to notice the growing silence.

The tracker stepped forward. "*Chodge tu, panna.*"

Those who stood beside Anna shrank away, granting her some freedom in her movement. Even those who'd pounded the tiles and screeched fell silent, giving the room a distinctly eerie feeling.

She met the tracker further in the clearing. Once again, she noticed telltale rings of violet in his eyes. She saw the feeling mind in his shaking hands and the way he tried to compose himself. His stare flitted away, little more than a momentary spasm of the eyes, but Anna read its buried message: shame.

The wicker-hatted man stumbled toward the tracker. "Do you see it, *shest korpy?*" He spun around, nearly collapsing with his drink in hand, and swept a finger over the crowd. His eyes were glassy. "Look at it, boys. This is *death*! The death of Nahora, the death of the Hazani cartels, the death of the two cities! This is Rzolka's lifeblood. Look at it, and remember the face. Remember that your life is a gnat's in her shadow! If a hundred men strike at her, a hundred of you *korpy* swallow the blades. This is your fucking goddess now, *rosumesh?*"

The chamber echoed with a unified, deafening bark: "*Tek yest!*"

The wicker-hatted man took a long swallow from his mug, then twisted his face into an angry snarl and thrust a fist skyward. "Are you bleating goats, *che subraty*? Let them hear it in Kowak!"

"*Tek yest!*" rattled the air.

Satisfied, the wicker-hatted man drank, spat his mouthful onto the tiles, and skulked back to the other men. In his absence was only the tracker and his subdued stance. Fresh energy set the bunkroom to murmuring and cackling.

"Right, then," the tracker said in a low rumble, managing to captivate the audience all the same. "They tell me you've had to burn bodies on nights like this."

Scattered nods and agreement filled the bunkroom.

"All over now," the tracker continued, tossing a nod at Anna. "She's a good one, and you'll treat her like it. This isn't the orza's scribe. These marks don't fade as soon as they hit your throat." He lifted the hem of his mask, revealing a still-glowing rune. "Most of you are here because the old days are in your hearts. A few might be here for the salt, or the tits, or whatever they pack into those pipes." He paused as chuckles broke out. "Your wants and needs aren't any of my concern. Do your tasks, and do them well. Earn your fucking desires."

A wave of approval spread through the men, softer than before but more directed in its purpose. They weren't maddened; they were *motivated*.

The tracker approached Anna, struggling to regulate his walk. His withered eyes looked down at her. "The miracle stands before me."

Anna surveyed the crowd. "I'm here for the cause."

"You might as well *be* the cause, *panna*. They're all talking about what you did today, you know. About how you put fire in the *korpa*'s eyes." His voice sobered for a moment, graver and deeper than before. "Never seen one like you, and I guarantee the flatlands haven't either. We ought to parade you around as a god. These sods would throw salt at hares, if they learned to jump high enough. Imagine what they'd do for your marks."

Rather than salt, Anna saw bloodshed. She saw burnt bodies and orphans and entire cities laid to waste. Bora was right to say that life was precious here. So precious that it warranted murder. "I just want to do my part."

"Did you get tired of the *sukra*?" the tracker asked. Anna said nothing, still clinging to the woman's kindness as the tracker substituted his own answer and huffed. "And Bora said you'd never understand this place. Stick with your own breed, and you'll stay sane. That's a solid truth from sand to swamp."

They aren't my breed, she thought as she stared at the masses. Her blood was the same, but that was where their kinship ended.

"Remember what I told you about superstitions?" the tracker asked. "The orza wanted to bleed the mission because there are clouds over the stars. Not to say that we expected anything else, of course. Give any *sukra* a painted face and silk, and watch what happens."

"She hasn't done anything to you," Anna said coolly.

"Things move slower in the flatlands." He took another sip from his mug. "Grove knows she'd love to boil the river-blood right out of you." He pushed past the confusion on Anna's face. "You're a smart girl, must know Bora was trying to crack your mind. We placed bets on what the orza told you during your private time today." A cold laugh. "Fuck the flatlands."

Anna steeled her gaze. "She hasn't tried to persuade me of anything."

"Yet. Come off it, girl." He grunted. "*Panna.* I'm looking out for you in this place."

"I'll look out for myself."

Laughter like winter winds issued from his lips. "My, my, we're headstrong today. Where is the *sukra*, anyway?" Anna glanced back toward the corridor and the orza, but the crowd blocked her vision. The tracker waved a hand to call off her search, struggling to control his lids' spasms, then gestured to the clumps of soldiers around her. "Let's get to it. Just like you did to me, you understand. Some of them need their sight."

Anna looked past the tracker, watching his comrades intently. "Tell me why I'm marking them."

"For the cau—"

"No," Anna said, halting the words as they dribbled free. "I want to know specific things. Don't be vague."

"Hard to explain."

"You explained things already." She recalled the kator and its moon-bathed deck as something distant, far from the palace's beasts. "Tell me why I'm marking them. Tell me how it helps the cause."

The tracker's head lulled to the side. He twisted his shoulders to turn away, and just as it seemed he'd resigned himself to silence, he raised an unsteady arm and indicated a mass of black-clad warriors. "Look, *panna.* Do you see how they're dressed?"

"For fighting." But upon closer inspection, she noticed rows of pockets along the front of their shirts, all stuffed with squares of blackened ceramic. "They're armored."

"*Tek,*" the tracker said. "This must be coming up on their hundredth mission. Do you know enough numbers to count the men in here?"

She couldn't tell if it was an insult, but she shook her head all the same. "Why does it matter?"

"They used to have twice as many in their ranks."

"The orza has her own scribe," Anna said.

"Wetwork is never as quick as it should be. Runes fade." He cleared his throat. "I've been talking with their captains, and they had a lot to say. About the raids, about the tactics, about the orza. Overall, they're a savage lot. Thirsty for death trophies, and salt too. But they're going up against tens of thousands."

Again the numbers slipped past like water in her hands. But she recognized the amount was daunting. "Are they attacking Rzolka?"

He gave a bitter laugh. "Not tonight, *panna*. Not for a while. But if you put the blade to them properly, then it'll happen. They can take it all back. The peaks, the two cities, the rivers."

"Where have they been fighting, then?"

Before the tracker could answer Josip stepped into the clearing and danced with awkward hops. The warriors cheered and clapped for him, calling him "painted doll" in the grymjek. Errant arms and legs nudged Anna's back.

"Step off, step off." The tracker reached past Anna to shove away some of the men. He then folded his arms and turned back, raising his voice over the foot-stomping and clapping and cursing. "It's all in Malijad, *panna*. Six districts are pressed against the Dogwood's. We're not here to yoke them; we just want them turned to dust." The tracker spoke like a man addressing his equal. His explanations were sparse, but they were born of drinks and dusk-petals rather than deception. "Each one of those districts is a hive, Anna. Some send metal to Malchym, some give beds to the *korpy* from the plains. To men like Radzym."

Spindles of hatred broke through her thinking mind. She held an imagined version of Radzym's face in her thoughts, picturing him surrounded by mountains of salt and dancing girls, lining up young boys and girls to bleed them like lambs. "Radzym is here?"

"Might've been," the tracker said. "They come by the dozens, *panna*. They like to talk about deals, sell their timber for whatever trinkets the Hazani are peddling."

She held onto the distant hope that Radzym was in Malijad, and that he would die tonight. Not before he answered for his crimes, though. Even as his image stung her, she held it close to her heart. "Where are they going tonight?"

"Bilge."

Anna was unsure if she ought to recognize the name.

"Down south, we knew him as Grymor Bilge." The tracker tilted his head. "Now he calls himself Orzi Bilge. The flatlands are his dusty fucking fields, and he has it comfortable here. Yellow-eyed new woman, salt from Malchym every cycle to keep their metal flowing, giblets and crumbs to stuff his bloated—"

"So they're targeting his supplies," Anna said.

"Too many streets and levels in that district, *panna*. Not even these captains know where they are. And Bilge has enough blades to put a fire under them once they break down his doors." He huffed. "No, they're going for his skull. Signed his death writ the moment he tucked tail."

A renewed round of cheers and jeers went up as Josip's legs tangled and bowed, sending him sprawling to the tiles. His mug shattered nearby.

Anna wanted to protest the tracker's logic, her thinking mind adamant that vengeance was misguided passion, but she couldn't muster the wisdom to fight back. *This is Radzym's fate.* This was the fate of every wicked man in Rzolka, and if the tracker told the truth, then Bilge was the first of her wishes. "Is it just him? He's the only one they'll kill?"

"Bilge, and anybody who stands in front of him," the tracker said.

Anna nodded, even as her thinking mind flared with the approaching violence of that reply. "I'm ready." In the same breath she watched the Dogwood warriors shoving one another with primal noises, brandishing ruji and long knives and hammers. She saw her rune still pulsing beneath the tracker's burlap. There was no way she could mark them all in good faith. And between Nacek and Teodor, drinking from his flask as though he'd never see another drop in his life, was Konrad. His manner mirrored those around him, as did his black paint, but he remained as handsome and youthful as he'd been on the platform, and Anna swore that he glanced in her direction. "I'll only mark the captains," she added as the tracker tried to turn away.

The tracker scratched his burlap. "Sun have you cracked yet?"

"Only the captains."

After a moment of hard gazing, the tracker hummed and rocked back on the heels of new boots. "That's the southern way." Before Anna could ask what he meant, he added, "Lead from the head of the spear. Right. That'll keep them in place. Lowest rungs might be too prideful to like it, though."

"We don't know if we can trust them yet."

"Nobody worth a pinch has heard of Dogwood betrayal. You can trust them."

"Until they desert you," Anna said. She sensed the cracking shell of the tracker's certainty, and she chipped away with concerned glances at the crowd. "If I mark them, they might just slip away. And they'd be safe too."

The tracker considered the scenario for a moment, surveying the warriors and their antics. Finally he gave a nod. "There's some sense in letting the captains hold the whips." He lifted the edge of the burlap and drained his mug. "Mark the captains, *panna.*" His voice became more ardent with every word. "This is where it begins." He looked past Anna and toward the men at her back, raising his mug with a heavy swing. "This is where it begins, *dibelka!*"

The warriors rattled metal against metal, let out wild screams, and pounded their heels against tile. Anna couldn't center, let alone hear, her thoughts.

But the tracker left her abruptly, wandering into the center of the clearing and letting candlelight form black tracts across his mask. He motioned for Anna to follow, using his mug-bearing hand to lead salutes, and sparked a chain reaction of belly-born cries.

Anna stepped into the eye of the storm, swimming in the fervency and ocean of gazes. Tremors in her fingers niggled at her thinking mind and its illusion of detachment. Her heart, which now served only as a distraction, pumped faster and faster, reaching a crescendo as she noticed Konrad at the forefront of the circle.

It's only because he was kind to you. It's only because he showed you attention and gave you a flower. It doesn't mean anything.

Somehow, to another part of her, it meant everything.

The tracker addressed the crowd—with success, if waves of applause were any measure—but Anna's attention was elsewhere.

She thought of Radzym and Bilge and even Konrad, who had to survive because he didn't deserve death. *It will obey,* she thought of hayat, unafraid of its abilities in spite of the day's prior testing. Having made the marks, her compulsions were muted. There was only the familiar humming in her fingers, waiting to form another vessel through blood. Deeper still was the bitterness behind her gifts, the knowledge that she could always spare others, yet her own flesh was deprived of its power.

That she might always be a victim.

The tracker's speech ended, masked behind a haze of shouting, and six captains emerged from the crowd. They formed a line, streaked in black and wordless, their only hint of emotion found in Konrad's curled-lip grin.

Something metallic glinted at Anna's side, and upon hearing a distorted command from the tracker, she absently reached out and seized the object: a thin, clean blade. All other thoughts faded as Konrad stopped only a hand's width from her. Youthful eyes shined, and the luminous triangles across his flesh, their edges rolling, formless, smooth, grew brighter by the second.

He was staring at her, flashing those impossibly white teeth, encouraging her.

He'll come back untouched, Anna told herself as the blade touched his skin. She lost herself to the hayat and its staccato impulses. The wisps pulled her hand and lulled her out of thinking, out of feeling, out of concern for anything except perfection.

Upon finishing Konrad's rune the crowd erupted in cheers. A parting, boyish smile was all Konrad gave her before he fell back in line. The next captain approached, and Anna realized that he too would come back untouched.

She lifted her blade.

Chapter 16

Her door was a reflective slab of tempered iron, or steel, or some alloy never seen in Bylka. The orza produced a small brass cylinder and traced a design across the door's surface, concealing the exact pattern from the accompanying Dogwood guards using her body. In turn, mechanisms clanked and whirred, followed by slamming noises from the top to the bottom of the slab, sending tremors through the tiles.

The slab swung inward.

Anna stared at the now-empty space, her vision hazy with the lingering burn that accompanied hayat indulgence. The door was nothing like ruj, or the kator's humming, and she hoped that her instructors would explain its workings in the coming days.

The orza stepped inside, then glanced back over her shoulder. "Please, dear, do enter. It's your home, after all." A subtle sweep of her hand discouraged the Dogwood from accompanying them inside.

Home. It was bizarre to hear the word after cycling through cities and quarters. After assuring herself that she had no home, and didn't want or need one.

All of that seemed irrelevant when she entered.

It had high ceilings, opaque white curtains, cushioned couches and exotic skins across the floor. Tables with fruit-filled golden dishes filled the atrium. Through a curtained archway was a bed and desk. *Her* bed. Beyond that, a balcony stared out at the city, shrouded by a leather awning. Cardamom and honey filled the air. The walls were lined with alcoves, scroll cases and bookshelves, jars, vases, tapestries, mosaics.

She was lost in the opulence of it all, but when Anna remembered Shem, reality returned like descent in the capsules, cold and sinking in the pit of her stomach.

"The Huuri," Anna reminded her. "He's a friend of mine, and I'd like to know where he is."

The orza's eyes lit up. "Ah, yes, of course. It's a sweet boy. Bora was instructed to bring It back to these chambers once It had finished Its tasks. It should be in the private chambers, just over there." The orza pointed to a small, gold-inlaid door across the room, nearly indistinguishable from the wall's patterning.

"He," Anna snapped. "He's my friend, not an It. His name is Shem."

The orza nodded slowly. "Such confusion is regrettable. The Huuri, in these lands, do not often progress beyond their natural role."

Anna thought to apologize, to blame exhaustion, but she thought better of it. Her head throbbed with remnants of cheering and the fatigue of hayat, but it wasn't enough to pacify her. It broke her to think of Shem working all day, tireless though he was. In Shem's stories of Nahora, the Huuri were architects and equals. Here, they called him It. Anna looked away and slumped into a nearby chair.

"Things will be fine, dear," the orza said. She moved to the doorway, her smile flickering. "You'll find comfort in these walls."

Anna studied the woman's maternal eyes, her sheepish hands joined at her midsection. "I know."

"Anna," the orza said with a guarded edge. "Could I extend a question to you?"

"Of course."

The orza's gaze roamed the wall tapestries. "Your attendant—"

"He isn't my attendant," Anna said. She saw the orza's unease burgeoning behind makeup and dim lighting. There was something coy about her question, and Anna was too tired to feign restraint. "Do you know his name?"

"Dear," the orza said curtly, "I'm sure you know that such men have preferences buried in their spirits. This man prefers to live without his given name. Does the understanding reach you?"

"You know it?"

"It has been heard," the orza admitted. She cast a glance over her shoulder, scanning the empty doorway for visitors. "Yet I would prefer not to say it aloud. I can't imagine that you would either, Anna. If we can cooperate without the minutiae of given names, then I see no reason to dig for the heart of his truth."

"You're right," Anna lied. She'd shelve the issue for another day. There was power in names, after all, especially for living creatures. Even children couldn't love a hound without naming it. "I'm sorry. You wanted to ask about him."

"Just one thing, dear. I don't mean to inquire too deeply, either. . . ."

Studded boots clacked over tile, coming to rest in the doorway without revealing their wearer. A fragile silence crept over the orza's words, her voice tapering off in a hum.

"Merely gift suggestions," she finally said, though there was no luster in her ensuing smile. She offered a shallow bow before moving to the doorway. "Dreams guard you, Kuzashur." She exited without waiting for a reply, the door's mechanisms giving a final shudder as the slab locked in place. Then all was quiet, and only the hum of Malijad's nightlife remained.

Anna stared at the space where the orza had been, anxieties churning, before turning toward Shem's chamber. She moved quietly to the gold door, opened its latch, and stepped into darkness.

A single candle threw light upon the low ceiling and windowless walls. It was suffocating, but its design mirrored that of the larger chambers, with gold furnishings and a desk by the bed. In some ways it felt like a mockery. Shem was curled up peacefully beneath a single cotton sheet, the smooth curve of his skull and ever-visible eyes illuminated. Red-splotched bandages covered his hands.

"Do you see your teeth marks?"

Anna's body tensed. She recognized the impassive voice hiding among the shadows to her left, only detecting the northerner's sigils and shaved head once her eyes adjusted to the gloom. "Did you bandage him?" Anna asked. She moved to Shem's bedside and met his glowing eyes through the skin, wondering if he could still see in sleep. "Bora, did he—"

"Six *heshi* of cracking coal, operating levers, and moving the iron rods that emerged from flame." Bora stared at the boy's hands. "They are instructed not to wait for the air to sap their heat, child. Their flesh eventually builds upon itself in time, so that they no longer feel the pain. Shem's flesh does not have such training."

"I can take care of him, Bora." Chills emanated from the darkness around Bora. "He won't work anymore."

"I want you to look upon him," Bora said. "See what he sustained for you."

"It wasn't for me," Anna said, even as she turned and examined the bright red stains leaking through the bandages. She frowned. "You don't think I made him do this, do you?"

"It was for you," Bora replied. "Every *hesh* of his labor, he asked for you. He didn't want my bandages, because he said that you would mend his broken flesh. He trusts only you."

"I didn't ask for it to happen," Anna said. "I stopped it."

"You cannot stop zeal," Bora said, rising from her chair and taking a step toward Shem's bed. "Even if you spare his hands, he will give his back for you. He will give his sight and his speech for you, child. Just as the men on the kator did."

"That wasn't my fault."

"Not in any conscious sense," Bora said. "But your shell bears responsibility. You were at fault from the moment you crawled out of the womb." Her eyes sparkled in the candlelight, sweeping back and forth over Shem's body. "Fate may not be the truth of this world, but a swinging axe must eventually come to rest, whether in sand, or timber, or viscera. Violent things have predictable courses."

"You said you could teach me how to think. It was working too, I swear it. I'm doing my best."

"Perhaps," Bora said, "but your best does not absolve your marks, child. I don't seek to condemn you."

"So why accuse me?"

"Part of my teaching is consciousness. How do you expect to see the truth of this world if you're unaware of the harm that you cause?" Anna opened her mouth, but the thinking mind pulsed in her, latching onto Bora's words and calming the anger they stirred. "He will not be the last. My lips moved with certainty when I told you about the flatlands. Many will kill for your markings, many more will die."

Anna frowned. "And you respect the orza enough to let me live?"

"No," she said. "It is not a matter of respect. If I saw a threat in you, I would seize your breaths. And if I saw evil, I would destroy you." She looked at Anna from head to toe. "I see a mind in flux."

"So teach me," Anna said. "Show me to the tome-men."

"It isn't so simple." Bora's eyes drifted back to Shem. "Until today, I thought that you could be leashed, given proper time. You were reckless, but malleable. Your meditation was beyond anything I had ever seen, child. The way you centered . . ." She appeared steeped in reflection. "It is a rare thing to descend into the thinking world, but even rarer to remain for hours." Bora tilted her chin up, the candlelight corrupting her features into grim shapes. "I saw what you did to the captain, child. There is no cage in the world that can stop this."

"He was wounded," Anna said. "Without me—"

"Truth is a murderous thing."

"I saved him."

"For what purpose?" Bora asked. "He wore the garb of a man who exists for pain, answers, and nothing more. Few shadows of this place are beyond my reach, and yet they stayed my hand upon his hood. What lies beneath his covering, child? Why has their brother been confined to darkness?"

"Because he's *sick*," Anna said.

"Not from the sun, I assure you." Bora's words were inescapable. "He is not of Nahora, surely. The orza is not foolish enough to take one of theirs."

"I only did as I was told," Anna said. "Why does the man matter so much?"

"Even I cannot be certain anymore." Bora looked away. "Perhaps your next marking will blacken the fields beneath their feet. Perhaps it will make trees grow from their flesh."

"I can control it."

"Words are cheap, child," Bora said. "A focused mind will only expand its grip on you. Enduring protection of the flesh is a rare but understood matter. Bringing new markings into this world will be seen as the work of gods, of prophecy. Blades from every stretch of land will march upon this place, once they uncover what your markings might do."

Anna glanced at Shem, then back at Bora. She spoke the truth: Her gifts would bring war, if discovered. But she couldn't bear to lose Bora's teachings, to risk returning to a terrified, primal state. She couldn't immerse herself in darkness after days of light. "Do you know where they're keeping the man?"

"You will cause harm on your path, whether you spare or slaughter."

"Just tell me how to find him, and I'll do the rest."

Bora's brow twisted into a rare angle. "It would be safer to continue to teach you," she explained. "If I released you now, I would be freeing a rabid hound. Into the hands of assassins, no less."

Assassins. Anna shuddered at the word. "The orza isn't wicked."

Bora folded her fingers. "No, but we are all beholden to masters. Your life is not solely within the orza's control." She drew a long breath to steady herself. "I have seen potential in your mind, child, but it would be a wasting of energy to force you onto a path. I can only show you the truths I detect."

Anna considered the northerner's words carefully, realizing why she'd baited the tracker into his rage. Her thoughts settled around her like dying leaves, but there was no judgment in her perception, only understanding. "I marked their captains tonight," Anna said softly. "Was it the right thing to do?"

Bora's eyes shone like glass. "Right and wrong are shadows of truth, child."

"Tell me," Anna pressed. "Was it *right* if I want to help Rzolka?"

"Such dreams are burdens."

"It's all I have," Anna hissed. She could feel her cheeks warming, the tears coalescing behind her eyes. "Just tell me what to do."

Without meeting Anna's eyes, Bora moved for the small door out of the chamber. She stood as a silhouette for a long, wordless moment, as though forgetful of her intentions. Finally she replied in her enduring flat tone: "It will take some time to locate where they've moved this man. For now, meet me on the terraces at sunrise." Her back straightened even further. "Alone."

Chapter 17

She drank cold tea on the still-dark balcony, unable to sleep through the thumping of explosions and roars of collapsing setstone, the dreams of lolling tongues and pale bodies with bright blood. The wind pulled at her cotton nightshirt and bore the odor of smoldering metal. In the distance she noted the black monoliths of spires and buildings, but the barest sliver of orange wormed out from the horizon, creeping so slowly that it seemed frightened of what it might reveal. Sporadic popping eventually ceded to the whining desert breeze.

Just before *Har-gunesh* lanced through the cloud cover and spilled orange light across her rug, she tied her hair back with twine, tucked it into her hood, and headed for the corridor. Shem's creaking door stilled her before she could leave.

The Huuri boy stumbled out of his chambers in a pair of twill pants, letting sunlight flow over and through the sinew of his torso. "Hello, hello," he said in a sing-song voice.

Anna worked to put on a smile, unable to look past the fresh blood seeping through his linen. "Good morning, Shem." Her smile faded. "Those bandages need to be changed."

He beamed. "You fix me."

"The orza's herbmen will do it for you."

"Cut." Shem drew a line across his throat with a bandaged finger. "You make me better? I can earn cuts."

"You don't work for me," she said. "You never had to." She gestured to the table, desperate to pull the boy's haunting eyes away. "Eat, Shem. Rest today, and have your hands bandaged. I'll be back in a few hours."

Confusion swam in his empty gaze. "I want work."

"Shem." It was a harsh, unanticipated crack. She immediately regretted it, but forced herself onward, angry at her loss of control. Angry at her anger, she supposed. "Stay here until I get back, and don't work." Her voice softened as Shem drew in his shoulders, crestfallen. "I want you to feel better. I know you care."

His face brightened as he sat directly where he stood, crossing his legs over the outstretched paws of a bear's pelt. He hunched over, propped his chin up with both hands, and grinned at Anna. "I don't work, then. I *help* in gardens."

Anna glanced at his maimed hands, wary. "If it hurts, you have to stop."

"Yes, of course!"

Her smile flickered just enough to imitate happiness, and she slipped out of her quarters without looking back.

Dogwood guards crowded the corridor, milling about in silence. They were speaking just before Anna's door opened, judging by the half-mumbled words and collective disengagement that capped off their dialogue. Anna counted fifteen of them in total, eyeing her and offering smiles if their gazes met.

She pulled her hood higher and quickened her steps.

* * * *

The skies were a sill of bluish chrome when she reached the terrace, underlined by familiar orange. She wandered through the grasses and stake-supported vines, searching for Bora amid clumps of men and women walking backward with white robes and mica pendants, muttering chants in flatspeak and bowing with each step. The worshippers' clenched eyes and crescent-shaped trinkets shed a buried truth: They were retreating from something.

From *Har-gunesh.*

Anna turned away, undeterred by the warmth across her hands. It wasn't long before she noticed the lone figure seated beside the terrace's railing, just past a stretch of black grapes and curved red fruits, and approached.

Bora's sweat-riveted head turned as Anna drew closer.

A smirk tugged at Anna's lips. "You could hear the grass."

"Do you think I employ tricks?"

The joy faded instantly. "I was just trying to figure out how you did it," Anna explained. "The way you're so alert, I mean. I thought it was impressive."

"Impressing you is not a primary concern."

Anna frowned. The northerner's voice was neutral as always. Even so, Anna imagined that even killers had a tongue for small talk. "Am I interrupting something?" No reply. "Was I late?"

Bora's chin dipped. "Sit."

Anna did as she was instructed. She folded her hands over her lap as she'd done on the kator, and with some effort straightened her back. From her rear came the low thrum of the winds and the rustling grass. "Bora, what are we doing?"

Bora's eyes were fixed ahead. "Sitting."

"Wasting time."

"Experiencing the truth of the world is far from *wasted*," Bora reproached her. "Life is always slipping away, child, but you'll die an animal if you don't learn to observe." Her voice lowered. "To detach yourself from the needs of the feeling mind."

It was beyond what Anna understood in any meaningful way, but she trusted Bora with her lessons. She watched the sunrise through the setstone. "Those people," she said, jerking her head toward the now-absent worshippers, "why were they praying to *Har-gunesh*?"

"Not to *Har-gunesh*," Bora said. "To *Aya-soluk*, the Pale Crescents. Shy creatures in need of coaxing to return in the evening." She too stared at the sunrise. "Eons have passed since they spoke to *Har-gunesh*, but their priests and priestesses say that bargaining is a wasted effort. Worshipping is madness. It's a cruel, hateful god."

"You don't believe it, then," Anna said.

"I believe it kills," Bora said as she tilted her face toward the cruel god's light. "I know it, in fact. But this life is too meager to be spent cowering, child. Bargaining cannot delay death."

Anna closed her eyes and let the sunlight filter through in a pale orange wash. She thought back to the forest and the tracker and Julek, seeing the truth of Bora's words through a pang of discomfort. There was something soothing about inevitable death, knowing that Julek would've had to die somewhere, even if he'd survived the trip to Lojka.

But the living endured the consequences of death. The living dreamt of remains left to rot in marshes. The living felt rage.

"Do you believe in gods, child?"

She considered it carefully. Nearly everyone in Bylka believed in the Grove, of course, but that was a place beyond gods entirely. A scattered few—those who endured the mocking and the spitting, that is—believed in the Claw and its thousands of gods, sacrificing to rivers and fallow fields for good fortune. But most of those worshippers were selective, latching onto the gods they could trick or easily satisfy. Her father told her that most of the Claw was gone, and she'd heard from passing travelers that worshippers who lived during the wars were fed to hounds alive, mocking their animal sacrifices. But most who spoke of the Claw had a nostalgic glint in their eyes.

All Anna knew was that she'd never join their fold. If there were gods, they'd been given enough innocent blood to bless the entire world.

"No," she whispered. "Not many of us do."

Bora stared ahead, the silhouette of her forehead and nose avian.

"Have you ever seen one?" Anna asked.

"I don't seek them out."

Anna picked at the grass around her legs. "So you do believe."

"There's no sense in believing in them." Bora's wary eyes turned on Anna's hands and their tufts of plucked grass. Anna tucked them away. "Either they exist, or they do not. Our perceptions cannot change this world."

"But if they exist, you would worship them."

"You extract your own words, child." Bora's chest rose and fell and rose again. "Some say that gods are beyond our understanding, but there is a simpler truth to worship: It is a contract. And being indebted is a damning thing."

It was an odd sentiment, even for Bora. But Anna thought about her words, remembering how she'd seen the Claw's worshippers bathe themselves in boiling water and drive daggers through their feet. Whether or not they existed, Anna wasn't sure she'd ever pay such a price. "What about me?"

Bora raised her brow.

"Scribes," Anna said, a chill in her voice. "Some say that we're descended from gods. You even said it."

"I said you would be *seen* in this light."

"Then how did we come into this world, Bora?" It was an age-old question, circulating around Rzolka and the north and the east for hundreds of years, but no answer had ever emerged. "What made me?"

"Womb and seed."

"It doesn't explain our marks."

"A veil of self-importance," Bora replied. "You exist. Anything beyond that is an illusion."

An inkling of bitterness rose up in Anna. Her own gifts were difficult to grasp, but there was some prestige to be found in her role, in the things she could do. "You've seen what my marks have done."

"I've seen many marks of the hayajara."

"But mine are enduring," Anna said, borrowing the orza's description.

"Yes," Bora said, "they exist. What of it, child? Do you want to be worshipped? Not all who hold power are gods."

"Power?" Anna whispered, taken aback somewhat. "We can stop death, Bora." The northerner said nothing. "Not even the gods can do that."

Bora remained quiet for a long while, betrayed as mortal only by the rivulets of sweat running down her cheekbones and temples. "As I told you," she said, "being indebted is a damning thing. The wise have already signed a contract with this life, and they don't venture to break it."

We're all indebted to death, Anna thought. No matter how many others she saved—or indebted, as Bora would have it—she could never save herself. She'd never be saved by another. After all she'd done and seen, knowing the consequences of thwarting death with her marks, perhaps it was childish to wish for similar immunity. Still, she couldn't repress her feelings of jealousy, or the sense that Bora wasted her ordinary nature by refusing runes. "Bora," Anna said, snuffing out her thoughts, "what do I *do*?"

"Breathe."

She bristled, but obeyed. Concentrating on her toes, her calves, her stomach, her arms, rolling relaxation through every muscle, Anna slipped into a calm and shut her eyes against the sunrise.

Shards of tarnished memories glinted beneath consciousness, but she didn't reach for them. Her hands were already raw and streaked with oozing gashes. Instead she saw the dark pond of her mind, where fog peeled away in long sweeps and reeds sprouted from the muck. Her thoughts were gnats, circling and thrumming against her skin with their telltale whispers of cool air, flitting past in endless circles.

Abandon your burdens.

She raised her hands to bat away the pests, but it was futile. The swarm grew denser, louder, congealing into a hum that swallowed all but the most wayward words.

Abandon Rzolka.

Her arms moved in wild streaks, cutting through the black cloud only to find it reform with greater thickness. She screamed into its collective mass and heard her voice reflected back at her, feeble and childish, unable to overcome the mangled cords in her throat.

Abandon Julek.

Anna drew in a breath, but the gnats poured into her windpipe and her lungs, filling her with visions of drowning and Malijad's ruins and dead gods.

And as the black cloud settled in her, she closed her eyes and ceded control.

Anna opened her eyes to the monolith hovering over the pond, burning away the low carpet of fog and consuming any glimpse of the horizon or nearby oak trees. Although familiar, it was too perfect to have been engineered by men, too ethereal to exist in woodlands. She'd seen it on the kator, but it was more tangible now, having cemented its form and leaving only a wreath of fog before her. Its name was a great and terrible thing, she sensed, too horrifying for a mind so fragile. All the same, she envied it. She craved it.

With shivering hands, she reached closer, edging.

She stopped herself. It was foolish to chase things without knowing them. Her thoughts crackled at the edge of awareness, threatening to drown her once more.

Anna turned her attention to the water and its unbroken, reflective surface. She thought of rain falling somewhere in Hazan, wasted on the sand and its gluttonous thirst. She thought of the rivers in Rzolka, the thunderstorms that swayed the oak trees, the tears that Galipa cried as he released Shem.

The symbol that screamed *water* formed from the blackness of the pond's surface, pulling itself into swirling loops and crescent bands, and she glimpsed it fully, knowing it in a single glance.

There was a howling, a whistling, a—

"Child," Bora said. It pulled her back to the world.

She was acutely aware of the sweat pooling beneath her cloak and cotton tunic, the hot breeze of Malijad at midday, the pure blue sheen of the skies. More than anything else, she observed an arrowhead's point staring at her just a hand away, its toxin-infused tip glinting with freckles of dull purple.

Bora's hand held the arrow in place, shaking, and her gaze trailed a group of shadows scurrying away on a surrounding rooftop. "Practice will be done indoors."

Chapter 18

Ten eyes, flawless, slick, raw beads of ink, reflected the tremors in Anna's hands. Mandibles twitched and crackled with each rub, their dark hairs as thick as the bristles of a horseman's brush. The creature loomed over her with the same measured patience as its kin in Rzolka, who were known to spin webs in windowsills and leave behind desiccated fly corpses. The azibahl was a sleek, sand-shaded tangle of legs and chitin, impossibly large, smelling only of weak vinegar and copper, its ribbed throat clicking in dead tongues.

She looked back down at her parchment, frowned, and scribbled an angular break between two Kojadi characters. Her first mistake in weeks.

"The correction is marked," the lecturer croaked in flatspeak, its voice so alien that it could hardly be termed an accent. The sounds were guttural, stitched together in the least organic way possible, but coherent. "Which verb form is utilized?"

Anna gave her way to deep thought, rummaging through the four cycles of lessons she'd accumulated since arriving in the *kales*, through the thirty tenses of Kojadi and its winding, sharp strokes. "Preterite past, with the inflection of awakening," she replied in flatspeak's ninth-tier dialect, which seemed to require twice as many words as the most formal river-tongue she knew. She wondered how her own syntax had mutated since that distant arrival.

"The correction is spoken."

Relieved, Anna set down her quill and flexed her fingers. It brought her some measure of pride, but not enough for her to smile. Especially not with a dozen other students watching so intently from the amphitheater's front rows.

They were mostly the children of merchants and artisans, tall and olive-skinned and clad in multicolored robes with sashes. Their faces seemed too elegant for Hazan, as though engineered with the north's most handsome traits: bold, black brows, sharp cheekbones, rich hazel or gold irises. Unlike the children in the south, their skin was free of blemishes and pockmarks, giving them an unsettling porcelain sheen. Separation from their circle had seemed cold in earlier lessons, but after four cycles of leering stares, she was grateful for some distance.

Lecturer Gir crept back along the wall in silence, his spindly hind legs slinking over limestone while his forelimbs adjusted a five-pointed cap. The northern students, muddied by fading sunlight and an amber-tinted dome of glass, gave a few parting mutters before turning toward the stone dais.

It was no secret that they hated her. She'd gleaned several phrases from study hours in the tomesrooms and eavesdropping on Dogwood conversations, allowing her to pick up whispers such as *parchment-skin* or *field-whore*. But more damning than her oddness was her standing, reflected in the constant throng of armed escorts and tea invitations from the orza.

Still, it was a rare thing to feel accomplished in the *kales*. She had every sweet and trinket and fabric she wanted, all without payment, and learning—either in lectures or through Bora's guided meditation, where she'd gleaned new yet untested symbols like *howling* and *decay*—was her only chance to be productive. Her flowing Kojadi script was tangible proof that she was teachable, even if it was in a dead language. Flawless missives written in six of flatspeak's twelve dialects sat in the brass tube beside Anna, and the lessons were only growing easier as she approached the servant and laborer dialect of ruinspeak: single words that relied upon inflection rather than written meaning. It had to do with the cost of a word, the orza had once explained in her study. "There is a price associated with being articulate," she'd said between sips of mint tea. "How much water can a man afford to bleed from his mouth?"

Her second missive tube, which she'd never shown to Gir or any of the other lecturers, contained the results of a hundred hours spent in the tomesroom's depths. The names and reputed family trees of Rzolka's bogaty, the maps of holdings she'd never known to exist, the condensed Nahoran histories of five wars and coups in the south.

"Kuzashur." Lecturer Gir's voice dribbled through the amphitheater like a door on failing hinges. Anna's attention rose to the dais, where the azibahl stood upon immaculately stacked mountains of ink vials, tomes, and spare parchment as a jumble of burnished legs. Lamplight formed glimmering motes in his eyes. "You are requested by an adherent of the orza."

Anna, taking her cue from her classmates below, glanced at the auxiliary entrance to the left of the amphitheater.

A figure stood in the threshold once sealed by a sliding wicker screen, burning a long shadow across the desks and haunted faces of the students. Bora lingered, her posture impeccable, before backing out of sight.

Silence hung over the chamber as Anna gathered her belongings under her arm, hurried down the steps, and moved into the marble corridor, making sure to seal the wicker screen and its surge of murmuring before she heard too much from the others.

"It couldn't wait?" Anna asked in river-tongue. She joined Bora at the railing that overlooked a shaded statue garden and its pack of roaming bear cubs. The cloisters were deserted that afternoon, their hanging pots either extinguished or bleeding their final wisps of burnt marjoram.

The northerner looked up from the cubs and studied Anna sidelong. "It was a *qaufen*."

Anna cycled through her Kojadi, wondering if her vocabulary was being tested, but recalled nothing with a similar sound. "What?"

"The arrow that nearly stole your breaths," Bora said. "The craftsmen in nearby districts know them as *qaufen*." She weighed Anna's confusion. "Mongoose, child. This is your tongue's knowledge of such words."

She thought of the clawed, brown-furred animals a beast-peddler had once brought to Bylka as part of a wandering menagerie, trying to reconcile the creature with a murderous arrow. "Who launched it?"

"Such things are not known." Bora eyed a Hazani guard on the far side of the cloisters, moving away from the railing and motioning for Anna to follow. Her voice, while casual, had the measured volume of hired blades, giving Anna a strange sense of eavesdropping as they walked. "The alloy of this arrow does not exist within the district, nor Malijad's entirety. Whispers say that it hails from Leejadal. There are few forces capable of acquiring such a thing, child."

Anna recalled Leejadal from her rudimentary studies of Hazani provinces, knowing it only as a mapmaker's dot above the plains. "Then you must know who did it, right?" She glanced over her shoulder, spying the Hazani rounding a pillar and entering their lane of shaded tiles. In a lower tone she added, "You must have ideas about them."

"These thoughts are wasted. Their flesh is beyond your reach."

Even if true, the sentiment was infuriating. She glared at Bora, regarding her sharpened awareness and latent power—a spring, waited to snap free—as wasted, despite her countless hours of meditation. The wisest course was one of unspilled blood, Bora had emphasized, but Anna could only guess at the wisdom of allowing would-be assassins to roam the city. "You found out who did this, and I'm still just waiting for them to kill me."

"Vigilance has never been a passive thing," Bora said as she steered them through a linking corridor and past a row of partitioned powder dens. Her gaze tracked from side to side, vigilant of the shifting silhouettes and smoke and cackling that leaked from behind silk screens.

"Bora," she sighed, "I can't watch out for every shadow."

"You should." Bora stared ahead as they stepped out of hardwood shadows and into the vibrant, sunlit grasses of the third tier's artificial garden. She scanned the gentle knolls, the bright tufts of hazel trees, the snaking streams born from grommets in the walls and threading below bridges. "You wouldn't see these blades, child, even if I told the truth of their forms. Your only defenses are a hare's vigilance and lightness of foot. If you recognize the hatred in their eyes, your breaths are already stolen."

Anna couldn't fathom seeing the world in the same manner. Her eyes fell on weary tutors leading young students around the greenery, or on red butterflies flitting from one flower to the next, too lost in her own love of the gardens to consider killers. Perhaps it would be her undoing, she considered. "Then call it curiosity."

Bora led Anna through rows of poplar trees. The northerner had an odd habit of slipping into silence without explanation, and Anna had accepted it over time. But there was a soft slope to her lips, words teasing with escape. "Nahora is an unfailing suspicion. There's nothing to be done about their malice, child."

"But why?" Passing a poplar tree, Anna met the piercing green eyes of a hooded grower. She lowered her voice and glanced over her shoulder as the woman returned to trimming the tree's branches, humming gently with a Hazani lilt.

"Nahora's aims have always rested in the taming of Hazan," Bora told her. "If they sensed new blades moving against them, they would release the burden of casualties and make war with this land. One child's life is not worth thousands." The northerner was icy in her resolve. "If war is sparked with Nahora, I will not build its kindling."

"So we sit and wait for them to come back," Anna whispered. "We know who it is, and we just wait. You expect me not to do anything."

"Wariness is its own blade," Bora replied. "As is mistrust."

"But you expect me to trust the orza and the people around her." Anna recalled four cycles of private tea sessions, of receiving trinkets in satin-embossed boxes, of never being asked about her life in Rzolka or discussing things with gravity. She recalled the hateful stares of the orza's own scribe, a skeletal woman with a lower jaw woven from scar tissue, always watching from the doorway. "What about her scribe?"

"What of her?" Bora asked. "I've seen the shape of her shadows. Your fears are unfounded."

"But Dalma *must* have some enemies."

"The Emirahni always have," Bora said. "Such men already left their mark on her lineage, child."

"Who did they kill?"

"The wounds were born of salt, not blood." Bora's eyes swept the approaching sprawl of sitting circles, where children meditated in silent clumps. "Your tomes will never know the true way of things. They're words best left buried."

"If they could break them once, why not twice?" Anna asked. "They could've slipped people inside. Enemies."

"The practiced eye sees them everywhere." Bora's gaze rested on a Dogwood guard at the far side of a nearby bridge, his ruj tucked against his shoulder as he stuffed a wooden pipe.

"We're talking about killers, Bora." Anna watched the rosy-cheeked guard huffing, his fingers trembling as he struggled to hold the pipe still. "Whatever you think of them, they wouldn't try to hurt either of us." *I hope.* "They don't have enough men anyway," she added, as though bolstering her confidence.

Bora noticed her doubt, and gave a faint hum. "Perhaps the orza's men outnumbered them at one time. But without salt, they had no reason to remain. Does it seed you with fear, child, to consider that these men guard your breaths?"

Anna watched the Dogwood guard drop his pipe and spill charcoal ash into the brook. "The orza has more than enough salt."

"Now, yes," Bora said. "But it was not earned in Malijad."

"So how does she pay the Dogwood?"

"Rot cannot grow without dark, festering shelter." Bora regarded the Dogwood guard with a passive face, her disapproval well-hidden. "The *kales* casts enough shade to nurture such a thing, child. Even the most virtuous minds, in times of wicked drought, can be reached."

They can be reached. It made Anna shudder. "Are they the only blades left here?"

"The largest, surely," Bora said. "Before their arrival, there were only the Alakeph." She pulled in a slow breath. "There were few of them, but the way of their hands was known."

"So they're hired," Anna said, strangely disappointed in the realization. "They're no different from the others."

"Such words are misguided." A rare note of scorn slipped into Bora's words. "Their blades preserved the orza's flesh, just as the walls of the *kales* preserved the Halshaf hall. That exchange was one of known hearts."

"You said that the Katil Anfel could be anybody," Anna said. "You can't be sure."

"I am. Their lives are sworn to ideals that you cannot fathom."

"They're sworn to children, aren't they?"

"To those without kin," Bora corrected her. "Without their blades, it is not known whether Shem would have lived. He knows the truth of their hearts. If you ever fear them, ask Shem where his joy resides. Ask if their ways are pure."

They walked through bathing halls and tiled lounges until thoughts of killers faded in Anna's mind. When they drew close to the market square above the bestiary, surrounded by hundreds of moving bodies that could've easily tucked daggers into folded palms, Bora disappeared into the masses.

It was the northerner's latest trick, forcing Anna to recall the layouts of endless halls and chambers to return to her quarters. She drew a long breath and headed for the eastern gateway, free of fear as she scanned the fists and bulging cloaks and sweat-beaded faces of those around her.

She abandoned terror for hope.

Pure hearts existed within the *kales*, and she would seek them out. She would leave behind memories of guilt, of foggy mornings and wicked promises. She would redeem herself through the way of their hands.

Chapter 19

At the edge of a sweet-smelling *nerkoya* hothouse, its gloom arrayed in rows of buds and slick bundles with tepid water underfoot, Shem pointed out the foundling hall.

They were gazing down from Shem's favorite balcony, a secluded stone half-moon that had taken several cycles of garden exploration to uncover. He'd claimed she could see all the way back to Rzolka on a clear day, but Anna didn't believe it, and wasn't sure that she wanted to try. All the same, she was glad for confined space after her conversation in the indoor gardens just a day earlier. Here she could dangle her legs between the balusters and, ordinarily, count caravans with the Huuri, which was a constant but demanding game in light of how much trade pumped through the courtyard at any given time. But on that day, she merely watched the blinding, bone-white trickle making its way from the main keep to the outer wall.

Around the Alakeph were their flocks of foundlings, dense wagon lanes, a limestone barrier that encircled the space, dozens of nondescript buildings huddled against the inner wall. Beyond them and their courtyard dwelling were the true streets of the district, threading through setstone heights in dizzying patterns. Travelers, she noted, rarely wandered into sunlit streets. It was a city where travel routes changed by the hour—the *hesh*, according to northerners.

The foundling hall was little more than a speck of color against the haze, its red tile roofing smothered by a cluster of nearby crafting huts. It was a blotch on the sand-swept burg, seemingly in danger of being swallowed by the surrounding cityscape. Yet if she'd slipped out of Galipa's inn on a night so long ago, she might have ended up in a hall just like it. A child in robes, or a Halshaf sister, living under the protection of the Alakeph and their white veils.

It was the perfect place to remake herself, she'd considered as she lay awake the night before. To be defined by pride rather than regret, by works rather than birthright.

"Could you take me?" she asked. She thought to tell him of her own fascination, perhaps even about a bid for penitence, but decided that it could only cloud his joy. Not that he would understand an ascended being's need for atonement.

If only he knew how low we could descend, she thought as they made their way to the capsules. *It would break him.*

* * * *

After reaching the base level and worming through the premier markets, which consisted of countless stalls selling distant spices, beasts, blades, jewels, woods, and ores, Anna spotted a Dogwood patrol station. The dark-lipped attendant flashed a dutiful smile and led them to the concourse away from the trade gates, making sure, as the others did, to waggle his pocket mirror and apprise his comrades of Anna's movements.

Cracked mud buildings filled the inner perimeter of the courtyard, raked by the hot winds and airborne grit. Kitchens with circular roasting pits operated alongside drying huts, and every so often was a counting house, where men behind shielded grates dispensed painstakingly measured lumps of salt to merchants. A diamond-shaped lattice of dark metal formed the courtyard's towering main gate, permitting entry to lanes of giants, some hauling caged soglavs or bear cubs. Drop-peddlers wandered with their arms out, adorned with dozens of swaying canteens that resembled spores along their wrapped flesh. Traders from the less-settled routes were marked by their packs, which used jutting metal rods and stretched skins to form movable awnings, cumbersome yet granting salvation from *har-gunesh.*

Don't fight it, she thought as she saw an imported hound panting in its cage. It was slumped against the wire mesh with shallow breathing, unlikely to survive a day. *Let the heat drown you.*

"There!" Shem called. He took off running, sandals kicking up whirls of dust as he slipped past a soot-faced glazier. Before Anna could make sense of his wild dash and catch up, the Huuri crashed against the foundling hall's iron door and drummed with a balled fist.

In Rzolka, nobody dared to question a closed door. Here, it was a mere suggestion of privacy. Anna drew closer and wandered behind Shem, breathing heavily with her hood drawn high and sweat seeping into her undershirt. "Give some warning next time," she said, her rare smile making the boy giggle and flash his pristine teeth.

A metallic whine stilled Shem's laughter. The door swung in, revealing an aging woman in a white robe. A white hood similar to those of the Alakeph, yet concealing far less, was draped over her sun-creased skin and small yellow eyes. Her nose was slimmer too, her lips nonexistent. Blooming heptagons moved under the skin.

She spoke with Shem in a strange, clipped dialect of flatspeak. Between each sentence, the woman nodded thoughtfully and hummed in understanding. When Shem finished, she stepped aside and motioned for them to enter.

Anna wavered in place, wondering if the sister, as Halshaf legends suggested, could read the truth of her heart. She held her breath high in her chest, praying she couldn't.

Once Anna stepped past the Halshaf sister, the air became cool and breathable, tinged with honey and herbs far too delicate for Hazan. The atrium's lighting was soft red, tinted by rows of candles in ornate metal jars, and the walls were covered with quilts and wood panels. Images of blood-covered newborns, breasts, and women's loins adorned nearly every surface, carved into tabletops and sewn into ceiling tapestries.

Chanting echoed from the adjoining chamber, but unlike the kator, it was joined by laughter.

She heard dozens of children's voices, as carefree as any she'd heard in the south. She listened to their footsteps clopping over tiles as they ran and played games, and she heard them shrieking with delight, speaking with a jumble of accents and dialects and ages, from first-years to those in Shem's range. Behind their words was scattered singing and bouts of string music.

Anna turned to Shem, who seemed lost in his own world as he paced around the atrium, staring at the artwork and muted colors. "Do they remember you?"

His face glowed crimson with the candlelight. "She welcomes me."

Maybe they could read her, after all. "Am I not allowed?" she whispered. After all, what place could a wretch have in—

"All may pass through this place," he said. His eyes were wide, awestruck by the chamber's beauty. "All are loved."

Such warmth broke Anna's heart, in a way only the guilty could comprehend.

A heavyset man appeared in the doorway ahead, his dark hair thinning and beard hanging in patchy tangles. He wore a dark smock with his sleeves rolled up to the elbow and, most remarkably, possessed sigils that resembled interlocked fingers. *"Onur'ane Shar—"* His voice fell away, and Anna realized he was staring directly at her, eerily reverent. "High-Mother Sharel," he said, this time in accented river-tongue. "The third mass shall be of the convening soon. Our young guest may like to accompany you."

The Halshaf woman moved to Shem's side, and took his hand in her own. Shem looked back at Anna with a smile, and accompanied the woman as she led him into the chamber.

"Hello," Anna said uncertainly.

The man inclined his head. "Low suns upon you, Kuzashur."

"You know my name." Even more perplexing.

"Ben'karim," he smirked. "My wife has told me of you." He entered the atrium with a limping gait, wiping his hands on a rag. "In fact, most here know about you by now. She's very fond of you."

"Oh." Anna paused. "Your wife?"

The man stopped cleaning his hands and glanced up. He was completely befuddled. Then came a thunderous laugh. "Forgive me, Anna. Such humor is a very southern thing. I've been reading scrolls of these laugh-words, as of late. I nearly missed this."

The man hobbled off, waving for her to follow.

Anna obeyed with latent caution. She passed into the main chamber, where children ran in circles and danced with colored ribbons and gathered for stories. The presence of Alakeph around the chamber, even with long blades and unfeeling eyes, put her at ease. *Pure hearts.* She followed the man along the rear wall of the chamber until they reached a curtained doorway, where he stepped aside and allowed her entry. His scent reminded Anna of licorice and crushed mint.

The office was cramped but well-stocked, with columns of leather tomes and ribbon-wrapped scrolls piled to the ceiling in places. He had a stool and a metal podium as his work station, surrounded by spare candlesticks, jars of lantern fuel, and ink bottles.

Sidling past Anna, he kicked aside some crates to form a crude path. He dug through a collection of papers and measuring sticks in the corner, grumbling curses in flatspeak, before producing a second stool. He set it down, brushed it clean using his rag, and settled onto his own seat.

"Please, please," he said, reaching for a flask by his feet, "sit and bring comfort." He uncorked the flask, filling the room with nostril-tingling fumes, and poured some of its clear contents into an empty ink bottle. "Arak, Anna?" He held the bottle up for her approval.

Anna politely shook her head and sat down.

The man shrugged, swilled the bottle's contents, and grimaced. "I would not even give this to hounds." He pinched his left eye into an awkward wink. "Is this a southern thing to say?"

"Yes," she said, "something like that." While the man set down his bottle, Anna cleared her throat. "I don't mean any disrespect, but I really don't know who your wife is."

"Ah, okay, okay." The man rested his hands on his thighs, wide-eyed and smiling. "It was not humor?"

Anna shook her head.

"She is Dalma Emirahn. Now I am *sure* that you know of her."

Emirahn. Anna combed her memory to no avail. Perhaps it had been one of the various noblewomen walking through the palace, or—

Dalma. Orza Dalma.

Anna's cheeks flushed. "Your wife is the orza?"

"Yes, that's right." The man's humble smile remained. "My name is Jalwar. Should I be offended that my name is beyond her lips?"

"Maybe she told me before," Anna explained. If Hazan's bonding system was anything like Rzolka's, she'd made an even greater mistake. "Is that your palace?"

He laughed again, his voice almost melodic. "A joint holding. But Dalma has far more interest in politics and trade than myself, ah?" He grinned to himself this time. "It is a world of shifting sands, and my mind has no way about it." He cleared his throat. "Sands, always shifting . . ."

"My apologies," Anna said, clinging to her still-raw embarrassment.

"For what?"

"I haven't addressed you properly."

"I am called Jalwar." He laughed. "Names are not such a binding thing within these confines, I assure you. And as I said, political events hold little of the shaping for my world. The title *Orzi* has not been used in some years."

Anna stared at the man, taking in his rounded stomach and hairy jowls. Surely he did something more than sit here in his office. "Do you command the armies?"

"Oh, never. Bloodshed is too bitter." He gestured to the office around him. "My place is within these walls."

"Doing what?" Anna asked. It sounded harsh, but the man took no offense. There was a kindly understanding to him, and a lack of decorum she found refreshing.

"I sweep tiles," Jalwar said, scratching at his beard. His thinking expression dissolved a moment later. "Ah, it is more humor, Anna. I lead this place. Surely not the brightest, or the wisest, but such a duty is a

rewarding task, I assure you. And, as you can see, it's a rather quiet affair."
He shrugged. "I was surprised to see that you visited us."

"I came with Shem." Yet as she spoke her mind latched onto the phrase:
A rewarding task. She pored over the concept in her mind like a long
lost trinket. Then she saw the growing confusion on Jalwar's face. "The
Huuri—Shem is one of the Huuri."

"Ah, of course." His rolling eyes suggested the name was obvious
yet carelessly forgotten at some time. As if Shem was a treasured child
from long ago, despite the two surely never meeting. "He'll find the mass
uplifting, I'm sure. But what about you? I've heard many things about you,
but I never developed the strong heart to seek you out. I could not find
your trail at the First Moon Gala, either."

Anna paled, realizing she'd spent most of the night in her chambers
reading a tome on numbers. "I didn't think Dalma was so fond of me."

"Yes, oh, yes." He shifted his jaw thoughtfully. "You are good friends
with Konrad, yes? He tells me of you."

"I didn't think he knew much about me, either," Anna said, hoping,
somewhat foolishly, that he did. Despite four cycles of relative nearness,
he'd never sought her out, nor had he spoken to her while she was in the
lecture areas. However imagined, she blamed an upsurge in duties. "There
isn't much to tell about me."

"Is that so?" Jalwar asked. "I heard you're from a family of venturers
in Rzolka. You must have seen quite a bit of the land."

Anna held back a frown, unsure who'd told Jalwar such a story. Venturers
were a hard, determined breed, more suited to colonizing mountains and
hunting monsters than tending to riding posts. But such lies weren't started
without reason. "I saw some."

"I know very few who have traveled to these lands willingly. It takes
a brave girl to do this."

A braver girl than Anna, it seemed. "It isn't as harsh as I was told."

"To its credit, my friend, you are in the softest corner of Malijad. There
are some areas of Hazan that exist only for sand and sun, ah? You could
ride your horse for a thousand leagues and find only disappointment."

"I suppose."

"So why did you come here, my friend?"

It was almost impossible to hide the unease. "A change. Something new."

"Ah, forgive me." Jalwar waved his hand. "I meant to here, to this hall."

All at once, the lingering urges born from cycles of monotony and
nightmares and guilt surged up in her. She didn't know whether to sob or
to tell a tale that opened on a foggy morning, with a trail of blood leading

from Bylka to the northern cities, to thoughts of escaping and finding
refuge in Malchym's red-tiled halls before she took a wicked man's hand in
partnership. She wanted to tell him about Bora's certainty and the blackness
of her own heart, about how she could find forgiveness and change within
their embrace, about how many lives she'd stolen and could never repair
without devoting herself to their hall.

One breath away from release, she faltered.

"I just wanted to accompany Shem," Anna said softly, glancing away.
"He came from one of the halls in Qersul."

"Qersul?" Jalwar asked. "What a journey for such a young one. I've
met the head of their hall; he's a charming man. Perhaps, in the coming
cycles, your friend may visit Qersul again."

Anna imagined Shem's eager face upon hearing the news and couldn't
help but smile in turn. Even as her own eyes dimmed, surely imperceptible
to anybody but Bora. "He would love it."

"I'll see what can be done." Jalwar leaned forward. "Did Dalma tell
you of these halls?"

"Very little." Her thoughts sank back into gardens and talks of Katil
Anfel. "Can I ask why you wanted to see me?" She realized the apparent
rudeness of the question. "Why you were eager to meet me, I mean."

"The hayajara—forgive me, *scribes*—hold a special place for the
Halshaf," Jalwar said. He glanced down at his missives with a nostalgic
smile. "A most sacred one, you see. Did Dalma tell you of this, I wonder?"

Anna leaned forward. "She didn't."

"Curious." Jalwar's face grew stone-like. "Perhaps if you have time to
speak with her alone, she can say more, ah?"

Alone. The sentiment behind that word chilled Anna. Away from Patvor,
away from men who were frightened by the most placid thoughts . . .

"It's easily understood, I assume?" Jalwar continued. "The Halshaf
make worship of life. And what more life-love could the avatar of such
a cause possess, I ask, than purest saving of life?" He glanced at Anna's
hands. "Your kind is honored with good sense."

Anna thought of the men in white robes, of the blades secured beneath their
fabric. "Does every hall have a scribe? To keep the warriors safe, I mean."

The northerner's eyes crinkled. "Warriors?" He considered the word.
"Ah, ah, the alakeph, no?" Anna nodded. "They do not accept these marks,
child. They make deference to those in need of the scarring."

Those in need. Emine's boiling lungs, soldiers stalking in the night.
. . . "Shem said that they guard the halls. But this hall is near the gates."
She squinted with coy innocence, trying to approach Bora's information

about the orza's sworn guardians as obliquely as possible. "They protect the *kales* without any markings?"

"Fear is not so strong to them," Jalwar said with a shrug. "Death is accepted. Their pockets receive no gemstones, no salt. They receive only love from those who are guarded. And, of course, adoration from the life-givers. From the World-Womb itself." He inclined his head in reverence. "Strong men may take many paths, Anna. Theirs is most noble, I think. Many come from fortunate wombs and warm families. They know little of hardships to which they're bound."

Fighting with no promise of recompense seemed outlandish, but Anna couldn't deny the beauty of their mission, and deeper still, the hope of redemption through selflessness. She felt a sudden twinge of shame. Compared to the Alakeph, what had she really done? "You said something about my kind," she said, steering her thoughts to that of aid. "Do they mark the foundlings?"

Jalwar gave a weary smile. "They would, if such things were not tales."

"I'm sorry," Anna said, straightening in her seat. "I don't follow."

"Your arrival—ah, of one such as yourself—is a thing told by many halls. One may almost term it prophecy." His eyes narrowed. "If one believes in these things."

Anna leaned closer. She'd heard numerous tales of scribes' origins, but none were true, and certainly not the work of fate. "Prophecy?"

"An old tale, my friend. Likely nothing."

"I'd like to know anyway."

"Well." His eyes dimmed. "In some stories, a hayajara has stumbled upon the Halshaf's halls and given marks to the sick."

"There's only one *tale* about it happening? It hasn't really happened?"

"A tale may hold some wisp of truth, no?"

One tale. The singular nature of the story put Anna on edge, suggesting that no other scribe would be foolish enough to offer their marks in charity. But upon realizing how many blades had been aimed against her, it didn't seem so unlikely. She belonged to a rare type, demonized and revered and hunted, and few had the chance to give away runes without attracting the eyes of the powerful. As with others, she'd learned that fact the hard way. "In this tale, did the scribe have a name?"

"It depends on the teller, yes? In some variations, they did." Jalwar looked down in thought. "It's an easy thing to say, ah, yes, destiny led them. The stars led them, the jinn. It is a question beyond me, certainly."

"Maybe they wanted to help." Anna struggled to meet Jalwar's eyes. "Maybe they wanted a different life than what they had."

"Perhaps," Jalwar said. He lowered his voice, eyeing her considerately as he spoke. "In this tale, they healed the foundlings. This is a sacred task of the Halshaf, ah? To heal those who are not strong enough to mend themselves. Some simply do not have enough food." Something jarred his expression—sudden remembrance, maybe, or the hopeful bloom in Anna's eyes—and forced a dismissive wave of the hand. "But in this hall, such a tale does not sustain our hope. Your gifts are suited to the *kales*, my friend, and Dalma has always been generous with her donations."

"I see." She hadn't expected to be so swiftly cast aside, especially after hearing the legends about her kind. It was a place where she was *prophesied*, and that was sure to erase a heart's crimes. "If you're an orzi, why do you need donations from Dalma?"

"I live in the way of the Halshaf," he explained. "A donation is worth more than taking, yes?" Anna shrugged. "Your point is strong though. In many places, only the High-Mothers lead the halls. They do not have the proper, ah," he said, searching for a word, "*connections* to secure their supplies. Such halls, in time, will expand in the shadow of towns and cities. I'm sure of this. Many will rival Qersul: A lovely city, and not in want of anything, ah?"

"Shem said it was beautiful," Anna said. She envisioned the Huuri boy on dustier streets, without aid or warmth or the promise of a next meal. "What would've happened if he went to a hall in the south?"

Jalwar's eyes wrinkled. "I cannot say, Anna. Not all in the south are so fond of our philosophy. We have some allies—of this, you must know—but many halls struggle. Medicine is a rare thing in Rzolka, ah? They lack herbs from the plains."

"Do the children survive there?"

His stare crept away, uncertain. "In some places, yes."

As Anna sat on the stool, listening to the laughter and harps and knowing the power that rested in her fingertips, she felt a pang of sickness. She imagined what the south and north would be like if rulers never existed, and those with gifts were used for benevolence. If they were rewarded for service, not submission.

"Are you all right, Anna?"

"Yes, just a bit tired." Visions of such a world were wasted thoughts. Even so, they nested in her heart, unwilling to dismantle themselves so easily. *When the time is right, they'll surface,* she assured herself. "Are there sick children here?"

"Always. There are seven halls in Malijad, and we are the most capable, yet."

Anna studied his wariness, wondering what could plunge a man into silence so quickly.

"Not all illnesses can be cured through herbs," Jalwar finished.

Something conspiratorial sat in the air, as though his mere suggestion, and Anna's implicit understanding, had swept them both into something dark. Anna glanced over her shoulder, her movements demure so as to avoid raising the northerner's guard. "I could take a look."

But the moment vanished with Jalwar's warning hum. "Quite sweet of you, but Dalma has very clear instructions."

"What are they?"

"Far too burdensome for one such as yourself, I assure you. Not all of these instructions are created by her alone, you see?"

Anna frowned, already knowing the culprits of that statement. "But I could help." *I need to help.*

"I know, my friend. You have a warm heart about you." The northerner gave a sad smile. "Alas, your markings are not made for *this* world. They belong in Kales Emirahn," he said, gesturing to the palace outside. "Dalma has told me of your cause, Anna. It's a wonderful thing. A very rewarding thing." Regret dampened his words.

"I could speak to her," Anna said. "I could ask if—"

"No, no," Jalwar said, gently but firmly. "Some rules cannot be smeared, unfortunately."

"Not all rules are right."

"Ah, this is true. And yet . . . and yet . . ." Jalwar shrugged with heavy shoulders. "The Halshaf smile upon anybody who wishes to lend aid, Anna. Your gesture is enough."

"What about my hands?" Anna smiled as she raised her arms. "Did she say I can't wrap bandages?"

"Fair words." Jalwar rubbed his chin. "Such things are not beneath your rank?"

But rank had nothing to do with it. She remembered all too well how to sing eastern lullabies and tuck blankets around crooked bones. "It would be an honor."

When the Halshaf sisters introduced her to the gathered mass using ruinspeak, she became keenly aware of her strangeness. Some had seen her kind here before, she gathered, but others crept up to prod her and scamper away with wild eyes.

From their stares alone, Anna envisioned worlds of ash and famine. Some had eyes like those of Bylka's abandoned cavern effigies, hollow and weathered into pits, carrying secrets that she didn't dare to probe. Few carried their birth-given names.

"Hello," was all she could muster in their dialect.

At first there was only a rustle of movement among their ranks, children picking at rug tassels or sharing uncertain blinks in the candlelight.

Perhaps they read her and the brutal way of her own hands. In the end, she'd only break them, only—

A Hazani boy with burn-mottled flesh crawled free of the gathering, filling the silence with hardwood creaking under fragile palms. He wrapped a hand around Anna's ankle, looked up to meet her stare, and offered a budding smile.

Hours passed in the cloisters, and her fingers grew shriveled and red from pressing sponges to the foreheads of dying children. String-wrapped bundles of herbs, burning atop the braziers and candles around the cloisters, gradually nauseated her. She was surrounded by blistered and scarred northerners who knew nothing of her yet approached her with scrolls to read in the river-tongue, or bearing carved toys they offered as gifts. Some of them ventured to climb into her lap, nestle in its crux, and drift off to sleep with gentle smiles. They clung to her shirt as if she were their mother.

The thinking mind lectured her while she worked, assuring her that many of the foundlings would die before the next cycle, and that her efforts bandaging, feeding, and washing were a mockery of her gifts. It whispered that their affection was premature and unearned, and worse yet, the product of kinless children who knew little of love, who could only offer the same imitation that Anna supplied in return.

She cherished every moment.

Her perception of time returned when withering daylight crept through the cloister windows. When she heard a craftsman screaming for mercy, for his breaking bones, for the missing young girl he knew nothing about. Three Dogwood men soon burst into the atrium with primed ruji, their ceramic armor and dark veils making them indistinguishable from the soldiers who brought ruin to Rzolka's enemies in the night. "Kuzashur," they bellowed in unison, hoarse river-tongue drowning the protests of the Halshaf sisters and Alakeph, "you have been summoned."

Chapter 20

Drunken shouting and the clattering of metal on stone echoed through the *kales* as Anna and Shem ascended the living stairway, flanked by Konrad and his detachment of soldiers. Konrad's unfailing boyish smile should've calmed her, but the rune shining faintly through his neck wrap made his role all too clear. He'd been waiting at the market's capsule with his regiment, the only one among them to keep his blade sheathed and hood pinned back.

"Don't worry," Konrad whispered as they drew close to the upper lip of the ramp, stepping over painted spines and thighs. "Who could be angry with a face like yours, *panna*?"

Anna saw exactly what she'd anticipated. Exactly what she'd feared.

The tracker, Nacek, Teodor, and Josip stood among the orza's garden, surrounded by throngs of unarmored Dogwood captains and dancing girls. All of them held flasks or goblets or bunches of dark grapes, stumbling through the archways and over exposed roots, their features flushed red and glazed by liquor. Some collided with columns, shattering porcelain mugs in their hands, while others played pipes or grabbed at breasts.

At the center of the spectacle, the orza sat slumped in her throne, her eyes haggard and her face unpainted. And just behind the throne stood the orza's scribe, whose hood concealed everything except her scarred jaw.

"She returns to us!" Teodor yelled, his lazy stare the first to fall upon Anna. He drank from his goblet with one hand braced on a tree, a wicker hat lolling atop his head and boots brushing the soil. "Our goddess, our goddess . . ."

Even in the gloom the tracker's violet irises flashed from across the chamber. His arms had moved with a careless sway, yet upon noticing Anna and stumbling past a painted girl, he grew still.

Nacek gulped down his wine. "Bring her here."

The pipes and broken singing and cracks of trampled foliage gave way to Konrad's boots on tile. "Come along, *panna*."

Konrad approached the orza and Dogwood men followed in turn, spurring Anna on with a guiding hand upon her shoulder.

Shem watched the gesture with bold eyes and hardened fists.

Anna squeezed his hand. *Don't do it, Shem. Not now.*

"Took you some time," Teodor said to Konrad. "Now we know you're clear of hound's blood. Can't track a single girl."

"Where was she?" Nacek asked.

"With the foundlings," Konrad replied, stepping before the orza and bowing to both women. "How goes the evening?"

The orza met Anna's eyes, but spoke to the others. "Tiring, I'm afraid."

Teodor gave a deep, grating laugh, then set his goblet on the stonework surrounding the orza's throne. "We've had enough mirth here to last us ten fucking lifetimes, and yet our prized guest was nowhere to be found. It bruises the heart." Teodor stumbled to the orza's side, bent over, pressed his lips to the orza's hand, and kissed so forcefully that her fingers clenched the armrest. "Did you know where she was?"

"No," the orza said. "She was in safe hands, surely."

"You can ask Jalwar," Anna said, pulling up short of Konrad's side. She stared at Teodor, then at the tracker, who had neither spoken nor wandered closer. "It was just a visit."

"Just a visit?" Teodor asked. "Disappeared on your guards."

"We told them," Anna shot back. "We didn't do anything wrong."

"Then how will you have fun, dear?" Josip said, giggling beside a column and seizing a dancing girl by the wrist. His hungry eyes were upon Anna, and failed to recognize the terror beside him.

The orza cast her gaze to the floor. "Do you hear it, then? All is well. Perhaps we should call on Them to prepare your quarters."

Almost in unison Josip let out a cry of protest and Teodor grunted, pointing to the dim shafts of light spilling through gaps in the ceiling. "Where's the night, then?" the latter growled. "We're hardly out of our beds, and I still have the sleep in my eyes. We're staying here till we're done."

Anna watched Teodor take another swig and felt the same repulsion as in her old home, where riders spat their chewed pulp on her father's floor. Their lapses in common decency were maddening. Especially from the tracker, who refused to even acknowledge Anna beyond timid glances from the shadows. While she hadn't expected him to cast his words behind her, she was enraged by his shyness, by his shuffling between the trees like a spooked deer. His burlap mask made him pitiful and strange, as though playing the part of the orza's commissioned fool. "There are other places for you to gather," Anna said, still glaring at the tracker.

"Oh, aye," Teodor growled. "Other places for you to *gather*, too. Instead you slipped away. Weird way of it."

Anna edged past Konrad and onto the orza's stone circle, unwilling to bury her scowl. She leveled a finger, peeling and bloodied and pink, at Teodor. "We told them where we were going. I wasn't hiding from anybody."

"It was miscommunication, perhaps," Konrad said softly.

"Curious," Nacek said at Teodor's back. "You oversee the missives between your units, Konrad?"

Konrad cleared his throat. "Yes, but I can't ensure that every man reports properly."

Anna shot the captain a pointed look, certain that his attendant in the market's post had used a pocket mirror to flash movement reports up the central column.

"Aye, aye," Teodor said, kicking over his goblet and shattering Anna's recollection. "Fuck your reports, Konrad. Our goddess doesn't want to be found."

Josip wandered closer to the spectacle, still dragging the young dancing girl with a white-knuckled grip. "There must have been something delightful in the foundling halls."

"I was just helping Jalwar," Anna said, stunned that she'd even have to defend her kindness to men without a conscience. Patvor's four-cycle crusade had swallowed entire districts and brought ruin to countless men, regardless of whether or not it was justified, yet they feared an afternoon in the service of broken children. They condemned the joy she'd brought to foundlings, who had likely lost their kin in similarly *justified* circumstances. "They don't have enough aid, you know."

"More than they deserve," Teodor said. "One of the first things our saltmasters struck off the ledgers. How much could those slugs possibly feed back to the *kales*?"

Nacek groaned. "Twelve fields of salt per cycle."

"I don't mean salt," Anna shot back. "Hands and medicine. You can't buy everything."

"So what can you give them, girl?" Nacek said, his eyes sharp and dark, his teeth wine-stained. "They haven't even seen stirrings of Rzolka in their dreams. Leave them in their swaddling."

"She gave the helping," Shem said, skirting past the Dogwood men to stand at Anna's side. "What is wrong?"

"This was one of them, no?" Nacek asked, his face was composed as he looked over Shem. "Strange little beasts."

"Nothing about the cause says we can't help people," Anna said.

"Common sense," Teodor cut in. "Us or them. Doesn't look one hair good when you run off after their spawn, try to go where we can't see." His hat's brim threw long, distorted shadows across his face. "Tell us how it looks, girl. Tell us that you care."

"I do care," insisted Anna. "I've done my part."

"And then some," the orza said, paying no mind to the wicker-hatted man looming nearby. "Perhaps this should be discussed tomorrow."

"Speak your mind on it, Dalma," Teodor said. "Do you think she ought to be marking their babes? Jalwar's runts?"

"I didn't mark any of them," Anna hissed. She glanced toward the tracker for support, however ridiculous the plea seemed, but found only violet wisps in his eyes. "I wouldn't."

"It's so difficult to be sure these days," Josip said in a singsong tone. "I am most curious as to why our portrait of beauty has left us without informing us of her path, or her intentions. Most curious."

"We see it," Shem said, cocking his head to the side. "We see foundling hall, and we visit. Good thing."

"That's what we want to fucking hear," Teodor said. "You make flash-crack choices, girl. We're trying to win a war, and you're lured by whatever shiny-and-brights you see. Do you want to see Rzolka come back?"

Anna unclenched her jaw, tasting stirrings of blood. "Of course."

"Settled, then." Teodor's face dissolved into its drunken mask once more, the rage and earnestness and mistrust evaporated. "We just need more *order.*"

"You can trust me," Anna said, sensing the end of worthwhile hours and redemption in the drunkard's words. She considered that their cause was the proper path, no matter what sacrifices it demanded, and that she'd feel purified when her fingertips brushed Rzolka's field-stalks once more. But there was no way to soften the chaos. There was no purity in drowning healing for hatred. "I won't mark them, you know, any of them."

"Words are so fickle," Nacek whispered.

"I could look after her," Konrad said, filling the gap left by Nacek's words as they trailed into a hiss. He glanced at Anna, and for a moment his warmth and soft words reminded her that she wasn't alone. His newfound innocence held the glowering of wicked men at bay. "I could personally ensure her safety, and report back whenever you need it. Doesn't that sound reasonable?"

Teodor, for all his boldness, seemed unsure of what to say. He glanced drunkenly to Nacek, then to Josip, and finally to the tracker, though his gaze was too fogged to convey any meaning. "Huh. A keeper."

The orza straightened in her throne and stiffened her lips. "He's a good man, and a good soldier."

"Needs more rules," Teodor said, chewing at his. "For her safety, of course. No more trips to that hall. Too many foul spirits in the air, and we'll carve up that place if she steals their illness. No more trips to the markets, or the barracks. Might cut yourself down there. And no more trips to the chambers with the Hazani *sukra*." Teodor examined Anna's twitching eyes. "That's right, girl. We know about your meetings. We always knew. Needs to stop now though, as there are blades in every corner of every avenue in this fucking city. Can't risk what they might do with free access to you."

Anna searched for friendly faces that didn't exist, shelving any notion of telling them about the *qaufen* arrow strike cycles earlier. There was only Shem, whose stare was devoid of comprehension and hidden designs alike. "I can still speak to her. With Bora."

"Keep her at an arm's reach," the tracker said, wandering through the foliage without preamble. His boots mashed the grasses and crushed the roots and reminded Anna of the land he'd trampled underfoot so long ago, hunting. "There's a bad way about her."

Anna met his violet eyes. "She's my friend."

Teodor gave a sputtering laugh. "Her breed of *sukra* doesn't make friends. Break away from her, girl. She can die in the foundling pits if she wants to lecture something."

"She provided the safety that your circle could not." The orza met the southerners' eyes evenly, undaunted. "She has never given me reason to doubt her loyalties."

"With all due respect," Teodor growled, slurring *respect* so horridly that it sparked Dogwood laughter, "I'd sooner piss on a northerner's loyalty than trust it."

Josip and Nacek shared toothy smiles.

Anna thought of her lessons, of the mornings she'd shared with Bora when the sun crept in bright brands over the setstone, begging her to close her eyes and retreat to the quiet place she'd constructed amid anarchy. Where time was unimportant, and where loss and memory were foreign concepts she delayed indefinitely. Those moments vanished in the cracks of Teodor's rotted teeth. "How do you expect me to spend my days? As your servant?"

Teodor's laughter slowed and fell away. "You think you're a servant?"

"The days don't change," answered Anna. "Either I'm being escorted down the same passages, or I'm waiting to be called in the same quarters. There's nothing else for me, and you know it. You all know it."

"Nothing?" Teodor bent over, picked up another goblet, and drained its contents. He surveyed the grasses before tossing the goblet out of sight. His mouth hung ajar in a ragged line. "Your bathwater is cleaner than anything the spoiled sows in Malchym have ever seen. You have more ink than a tomesroom. More lessons than the budding pricks in Nahora. More music than a bogat's troupe, and more fabrics than a trade galley on the Byryd, and more salt than you know what to fucking *do* with. And you say you have nothing, then? To anybody in Rzolka, you'd have the life of a goddess."

Anna took a step forward. "That isn't what I—"

"But you still think you have nothing. Maybe it's been too good, girl. Maybe you've *had* it too good here."

"Teodor," the tracker growled. "That's the solid end of it. We've staked out our lines."

Teodor whirled, wicker hat flopping. "The stubborn sow will always uproot its posts, *brat*. Remember that."

"She is stubborn," the tracker said, pausing to walk toward the throne and stand beside the orza's scribe, "but stubborn is better than drained. We need that fire, if we want to torch the wretched cities. Nothing else to be said."

Josip peeled his fingers from the dancing girl's wrist. "Oh, truly." He winked at Anna. "Everybody adores a good challenge."

It wasn't the first time she sensed the threat in their circle. In Nacek's crooked, bitter words, in Teodor's brazen taunting, in Josip's lust, in the tracker's apathy. But now the danger had grown, manifesting in the unreadable glimmer of Konrad's eyes. She'd promised herself to never be used again, but the promise faltered at every opportunity. Even the orza, who'd once seemed so strong and steadfast against such men, fought to resist shrinking away like a beaten hound in her scribe's shadow.

"It's done," Anna said at last, glaring at the entire gathering. "I'm sorry that you couldn't find me, and I'll find new pastimes in my quarters and lessons."

Teodor's eyes widened. "That so?"

"You have free steps wherever the Dogwood roam," the orza added, not without a pointed note of distaste. Words regarding the Dogwood, as they had in preceding weeks, set her jaw to churning.

"For now," Teodor said, sniffling. He nodded at Konrad and took another drink. "And you'll watch her."

"Within reason," the tracker cut in. "You'll stay out of her quarters."

Konrad pressed a hand to his armor, although the gesture seemed insincere, given his smirk. "Absolutely."

Anna suddenly craved Bora's analysis, her dissection of the sly smiles they passed between one another, just barely within Anna's range of detection. "And I'll bathe alone," Anna said. She stared at Konrad, making his smile dim. "Understood?"

His voice was low, earnest. "Very much so, *panna*."

Teodor's eyes were too muddled to betray any of his thoughts. "Good." He wiped his mouth with the back of his hand, then beckoned a dancing girl to his side. "Enjoy sleeping with your silks, girl."

Anna looked to the orza, holding her tongue. "Good night, Dalma." She turned away, glimpsing only the slightest crease in the woman's brow, and made her way back down the stairwell with Shem at her side. The scattered footsteps of Konrad and his Dogwood attendants followed.

"Hold onto that fire, goddess," Teodor yelled from behind. "But don't let it burn you."

Terror and rage and uncertainty flooded her, but Anna surrendered the sensations. She saw only the darkened gold of the hallways, felt only the human stairs bruising beneath her, and heard only Shem's whispers of assurance as they walked.

She existed for the moment, unwilling to hold onto gathering fears.

Holding on meant death.

Chapter 21

The most troubling aspect of a restless mind was its intangible wandering. Thoughts of collecting firewood and rubbing sap from cold fingers rose in Anna's mind, yet she indulged the vignettes, imagining the frozen edges of riverbanks and horsemen trotting down a dirt path. A thinking mind would've dwelled on Konrad and his muted regret as he wished her goodnight, his face disappearing in the ever-diminishing crevice of the door, or on the wicked men no longer bound by the orza's leash, or on Shem, whom she'd ignored as he retired to his chambers with sullen eyes.

She didn't notice that her mind had strayed. Not until the sound of a small bird's flapping jarred her back.

Anna rolled over, eyes combing over the balcony, breaths trapped beneath rigid lips. Standing near the wind-tussled door hangings was not a bird at all, but a shadowed figure in a wash of moonlight. Anna clenched a fistful of silk and tried to draw the sheets in front of herself—her trembling subtle enough to be disguised in the darkness—and wormed her legs over the edge of the bed behind her.

If she could get to the ruj, which she'd wrapped in cotton and stored under the frame . . .

"You keep them unlocked."

Bora's crisp voice halted Anna. The latter exhaled into her silk covers. "What?"

Bora's dark shape loomed, stepping through the double-doors and approaching the bed like one of the specters from Anna's nightmares. "The doors. You've left them unlocked."

Anna pushed the covers aside and glanced at Shem's door, wondering if the Huuri was alert enough to guard her from assassins. It was an awful burden to place on a boy. "Doors don't seem to stop you."

Bora moved to the table near Anna's bed, lit a brass lamp, and sat stiffly beside her. "I saw what happened today."

"It's getting worse," Anna whispered.

Bora gazed across the room, leaving a dark orange trail along the profile of her face. "We shall speak of that later. I meant your visit to the foundlings. You spent most of your hours in their hall."

"And what?" Anna asked. She waited for a glare of censure, but there was only the quiet rustling of the wind. "It felt good to help them."

"Such things are noble."

It was surprising to hear from Bora, although Anna wondered why. In last month's tomesroom scouring, she'd learned about Saloram. It was the philosophy Anna had learned on sun-laced rooftops and sweltering kators, the path that had molded Bora. It shunned runes and gods, and although it embraced the present, there was a driving force behind consciousness: the reminder to use one's lifespan in a constructive manner. For all of Bora's wisdom, she seemed hesitant to aid anybody but herself.

"You should be cautious, child," Bora added. She studied Anna with hard eyes. "The animals in the orza's company are always watching."

Anna stared down into the flame-lit folds of her blankets. "They told me that we aren't allowed to meditate together."

"Nor to speak," Bora said.

She could hardly believe it. "What do you mean? They never said that."

"Not in your presence," Bora said, "but they made it clear to both the orza and myself. It is a divisive thing, but in coming days, it's essential for you to maintain your practice. Focus your mind often."

It was difficult to imagine pressing onward without Bora, but judging by the northerner's appearance in the dead of night, she wouldn't be without guidance forever. She nodded with respect. "I will," she said. "Where were you today?"

"Watching things you cannot notice," Bora replied. "If truths should be exposed, then know that my dreams are decaying once more. There are dark whispers in their eyes, child. Horrible things."

An enlightened mind echoing Anna's thoughts was damning. "I can't just leave again, Bora. I won't go so easily this time."

"It's a simple thing to be resolute, but simpler to be blinded by it. Don't lose sight of this world."

Anna stared through the open double-doors and watched the smoke curling up from between the setsone spires, a greasy black stain against the lighter darkness of midnight skies. She took in the soft roars and clapping of combat, so distant yet so close to her and her gifts. "Do you think I should stay?"

"No."

It was the answer she'd expected, but the truth she hated to hear. "You brought me here," Anna whispered, leaning closer. "You helped him to deliver me. How can you say that now, after everything?"

"All things are impermanent, child. Even loyalty."

"Would Dalma want me to stay?"

As much as Anna craved a false answer, a sense that the woman loved her and wanted her to remain in her protection until the stars burned away, there was no sense in believing such things.

"Whether or not she desires it, she would use you." Bora blinked. "Never rely on another for your existence, child. Not even when you fail yourself."

Anna thought to ask what it meant, to prod at the growing weakness in Bora's eyes, but she could only nod. "I need to see the foundlings again."

"To what end?"

"My own," Anna answered truthfully.

"Speak your truth, child. Would you abandon your precious homeland for one hall?"

"No. It's not about choosing. This will be worth it in the end. I know it will. But when I was with them, I felt peaceful. Something like that, anyway. Things felt peaceful for the first time in a long while." She picked at her quilts, slipping into silence and letting the sounds of another distant strike filter through the balcony glass. "I can still hear their laughter, you know. When it's all quiet, I hear it. And it's been so long since I felt anything like that, Bora. Even longer since I did something."

"You've done plenty."

Anna bit back a retort. "This is different. You were right about them, you know. The Alakeph."

"Your visit was no coincidence, then."

"No," she admitted. "I had to see it for myself. You said that they were pure, that they'd give their lives for children they didn't even know. They made me feel like they'd do the same for me. And there's so much I want to learn from them." As soon as the words passed her lips she imagined Bora's chiding. There were a thousand fallacies in those words alone, but she lacked the energy to stop herself. "There's so much to learn in that hall."

Bora's voice was gentle. "I understand."

Anna looked up in surprise, searching for compassion in Bora's face without success. "Maybe we could speak to them. We could ask them to accompany me." The northerner's silence bore through her. "Anything. I just need to return."

"They will not listen."

"Then I'll find a way," Anna said. She pointed at the balcony and the heights of Malijad beyond it. "How did you get here? In this room, I mean."

Bora's visage was like a statue in the light of the small flame. "I came with intentions of showing you. Though perhaps for a different end."

Anna narrowed her eyes. "What?"

"There are some revelations worthy of being witnessed rather than explained, child. I would show you them. This path may take you to your desired end, but there are truths to be observed along the way."

"What sort of truths?"

"Miserable truths. Truths that you weave."

Anna studied the light as it flickered over Bora's eyes, and a cold pit deepened in her stomach. "I've never tried to weave anything."

Bora stood, walked toward the balcony, and waited. Her silhouette was a stark, silvery burn upon the horizon. "You may forget reality," she said, "but it does not forget you. My sources know where they're holding the marked man."

Memories of ever-burning eyes trickled through Anna's mind. She unclenched her fists, wondering about the man's current state. Whether he'd been tortured or healed, as the orza had promised. Her own predictions sickened her. "Bring me to him."

* * * *

Eastern flurries broke the monotony of lukewarm desert air as they crossed setstone ledges and quilts of baked clay roofing. She followed Bora's shadow with her cloak wrapped tightly around her, staring out at Malijad and the puffs of smoke within skyscrapers. She couldn't bear to look down, fraught by dune-borne gusts and darkness and memories of the gut-twisting drop at Malchym's cliffs.

They moved quickly yet carefully over cracked shingles and rotted panels and crumbling walkways that had been abandoned mid-brick, all living remnants of the *kales'* twelve rotating architects. The tomes had all described the Emirahni rooftops as being ornate, gleaming like molten alloy above the city, but that had been long before vaults ran dry and materials grew scarce.

"Here," Bora said at the end of a long, windswept corridor flanked by crumbling arcade pillars. The skies were black, the streets below a dusting of lamplight and fires. In the gloom, Bora stepped onto an adjoining walkway over the void. "Mind your steps, child. The world falls away if you wander too far."

A crooked staircase wormed down and away from the corridor, snaking into neighboring districts with the support of a ruptured arch. Bearing Bora's weight seemed a miracle, given its lack of integrity, but the northerner's ease suggested that she'd made use of the steps on countless nights.

"This reaches the foundling hall?" Anna whispered, teasing a step onto a shattered outcropping. Flakes of setstone skittered into the breeze.

"It reaches many places," Bora said, wandering past, "but on this night, trail my heels. Hold your words till they're needed."

Eventually they reached a distant tower estate beyond the Dogwood's district boundaries, its red marble chambers melted and fused by unimaginable heat. Glossy stalactites stabbed down from the ceiling, sometimes encasing statues or porcelain tubs with a crimson varnish. Wind moaned through the surreal gallery as Bora led Anna into an entombed dining room, through a doorway, and down a lightless stairwell.

They emerged into a courtyard in eerie silence. Collapsed buildings rose up in barbed tangles around the square, looming and black. Mounds of gray ash collected along the foundations and licked over walkways on the breeze. Bodies rested beneath the powder, shriveled and blackened and curled in on themselves in a final act of preservation. In the silvery press of moonlight it was a dream from Anna's youth, the buildings a mass of snow-capped firs on the far edge of a field. But the odor was sulfurous and stifling, and Anna pulled her tunic over her nostrils to block out wisps of charred twill.

"They're keeping him here?" Anna wheezed.

Bora wandered forward, leaving a set of dark, delicate footprints in her wake. "Not only him."

Far in the distance a pair of lanterns bobbed down an alleyway and cast a pale sheen across the setstone and ash. The lantern bearers approached a low doorway set into the masonry and rapped on its surface twice. When the metal slab creaked open, a wash of candlelight spilled out over the alley to expose a mass of ash-laden corpses along the packed earth. The two men entered, shut the door, and bolted the latches.

Bora approached the alleyway, granting Anna a moment of chilling indecision before she followed. The grisly shapes at her feet offered no thoughts of refuge in the contents of the building, and Anna's marks revolved in her mind, screeching: eyes gushing light, men chained to walls, blades carving flesh with torturous streaks.

This is my consequence.

Soft voices bubbled out of the silence as they drew closer to the alleyway. Distinct words were muffled by cracked mud walls and metal fixtures, but grunts and winces emerged through a wash of conversation. The bodies around the doorway were innumerable; in their piles they coalesced as shapeless, dusty hills and valleys, staring up at Anna with hollow eye sockets and withered flesh. Stiffened fingers rose up from the ash like talons.

While Anna was still picking her way over the corpses, shuddering each time her cloak snagged on bones or cracked skulls, Bora knocked on the metal door twice. The tinny sound rang down both corridors.

"So?" a voice growled from within.

"The orza has requested an inspection," Bora replied.

Keys jangled beyond the riveted door. The latch mechanism clicked and thudded aside, followed by the grating sound of a crossbar being lifted from its brackets. Before the latch unhooked, a smattering of annoyed river-tongue leaking into the night air, Bora threw her weight against the door and forced it in. Something solid collided with the metal, rattling the hinges. A man screamed from within, but Bora wrenched the door open and drove it back into place with a bracing shoulder, stifling the noise with a *snap*.

Anna shrank back, glimpsing the motionless boot of a guardsman through the doorway as Bora stepped inside. Violence was nothing new, but Anna stared at the southerner's body in confusion, edging closer to glimpse a bearded, split-flesh face in the candlelight. *One of the Dogwood,* Anna surmised from his black uniform. She watched as Bora moved over the corpse and through a fabric hanging, hearing the faintest mutters of alarm in the wake of the northerner's entry.

Yet as Anna stepped inside, skirting around the expanding blood pool beneath the doorman's hair, the dull ripping of a butcher's cuts filtered through the curtains. A man's gurgling fell to nothing after a fall of soft footsteps and the sputters of a carved airway, far too familiar to Anna's ears.

"Come, child," Bora called from beyond the fabric.

Anna turned and gently closed the door, making sure to avoid the dead man's leg. Standing in the midst of violence always made her feel exposed, especially when the light of the guttering candles made the body so luminous. She picked her way over the body, smearing her boots with blood, and entered the adjoining chamber.

The stench of bile and decaying flesh was so overwhelming that Anna hardly noticed the bodies sprawled at her feet. Blood coated the floor in black smears and still-wet puddles, and spattered across the pitted setstone walls were dark blotches whispering horrible tales. Chains hung in tarnished loops and broken-link stalactites.

Along the wall just beyond Bora was a row of bodies, their arms suspended above their heads by rope bindings and faces shrouded with black fabric. Nothing covered their torsos aside from a latticework of infected scars. The skin was dark, swollen with rot and stretched over jutting ribs, and their heads darted from side to side upon hearing new voices. They were blind, maggot-like creatures, responding only to stimuli and hallucinations. One body, tucked away from the others in the chamber's corner, was free of injury. A pair of bright orbs glowed through his blindfold.

Anna's breath caught in her throat. "Who are the others?"

Bora stepped aside. "Ask them." She gestured for Anna to approach the nearest captive. Despite trembling jaws and whimpers, the men retained their muteness. "Speak slowly. Your tongue is not familiar."

Glancing away from the still-bubbling slit of an open Dogwood throat, Anna approached the nearest suspended man. She noted the pus ringing his cuts, the mottled blossoms of pipe-burns across his chest, the clustered freckles of a sadist's needlework. She managed a guarded whisper. "Who are you?"

"Tasir." The reply was swift and panicked.

"Why did they bring you here?"

"To ask." The edges of his lips shriveled, threatening to break. "Please help."

Anna looked to Bora, but the northerner's attention rested on the Dogwood corpses, examining the puddles and broken bones she'd created. "What do they ask you?"

"Names. They wish to know where my brethren are."

"What did they do? Your brethren."

"They handled salt for men of the south." The captive rattled his rope bindings, his forearms tensing with bands of striated muscle. "You must release us. Please."

The other captives murmured in flatspeak and ventured to try the river-tongue, mostly managing broken phrases about freedom. The marked man, plain in the darkness due to his burning stare, remained still.

"Do you know where you are?" Anna asked.

Tasir's head fell lower, tucked into the curve of his collarbones like a hound anticipating the next kick. "Our home," he whispered, his voice fraught with high cracks. "They are all *deshaf*."

"Ash," Bora translated, kneeling beside the Dogwood bodies as she rifled through their packs. "The Dogwood Collective raided this district on the former lune."

Anna trailed his scars and slick incisions. "They couldn't all have been guilty, Bora."

Bora halted. "They weren't."

"So why did they come?" Anna whispered among tortured groans. She stared at the shadows pooling in the folds of Bora's neck scarf.

"There are hunters among the Gosuri who pour boiling water into holes in the rock. They seek to drive elusive prey above ground." She met Anna's eyes with a pointed glare. "Yet there are always unseen beasts that suffer in turn. The heat is not selective."

For once the story's meaning was apparent to Anna: Whatever names resided on the tracker's list were sure to create a hundred more casualties. And as Anna gazed around the room, lost in the blood and rot and blighted skin, she realized the absurdity of it all. These men were pawns in a game far larger than themselves, guilty only of handling salt for their masters.

Their sigils trickled beneath the flesh, calling to her, begging for reconstruction.

"Don't, child," Bora warned.

Anna glanced down at her own hands, mere hairs away from the tang of her hunting knife. Witnessing their agony was unbearable, but to acknowledge her own role was crippling. She lowered her hands. "What about him?" she asked, nodding toward the man she'd marked so long ago.

His burning eyes seemed to rise and swivel in Anna's direction, but the motion was lost to the candlelight and tricks played by dancing shadows.

"He knows your tongue," Bora said, rising from her search of the corpses and moving to Anna's side. Something smooth and curved glinted in her hands, but she kept it angled out of full view. "Speak to him, child."

Anna edged forward slowly, certain that the man glimpsed her from behind his veil. When she drew close enough to feel the warmth rising from his skin, a slow, simmering wave behind the heat of lit wicks, her lips fell open. "Who are you?"

"Kill me."

No, she told herself, even as her heartbeats drummed up her throat, *I won't do it.* She couldn't do it. The hayat preserved itself. "We can help you."

"Kill me." It was more urgent now, passed through gritted teeth. With every repetition the surrounding captives grew louder, their murmurs bleeding through the chamber and out into the night.

"Bora," Anna said, whirling on her heels. She spotted the northerner near the doorway with a familiar cylinder in hand, hefting the device up and down. "We need to get them out."

"They are beyond aid," Bora said. She was a blur among the darkness, but the surrounding drones of pain gave her a wraithlike aura. "Use your blade, child. Slit their throats."

Anna's jaw trembled as she looked over the row of captives, screaming and groaning behind strained rope. Everything about the chamber told her it wasn't another test from the northerner; she was expected to bloody her hands and end them, as mercilessly as the men who'd brought them here.

"Kill me," hissed the man with glowing eyes, remaining still in his bindings despite the thrashing of those around him. "Kill me."

The noises grew too inhuman for Anna's ears. She staggered back, watching their bodies writhe in candlelight like a cluster of maggots, slick with perspiration and red smears and discharge. "Do it," Bora ordered.

Chants of *Kill me* swelled with rage. Burning eyes flared through the black veil, flooding the chamber's corner in ethereal light, while rivulets of sweat ran down skeletal calves and drained onto the floor.

"The price of completion, child." Bora's footsteps hardly registered. Her hand clamped around Anna's arm, and jerked backward. "They'll be here soon enough."

Anna plunged backward through the fabric and into the cool antechamber. Their screeches were overwhelming, but she turned and followed in a mindless fog as the northerner dragged her over the bodies, toward the doorway, into the darkness of the night. Echoes of desperate men mingled with her shallow breaths.

Bora moved to the lighted doorway and tossed a heap of violet fabric across the corpses, covering their wounds with a graceful shroud. It seemed mocking, given the horrors rolling forth from the chamber, but there was no time to parse the fabric's significance. She tossed the cylinder through the threshold and moved aside, guiding Anna with an open palm upon her shoulder.

Anna wandered forth, her body numb, her vision lost in the dark. She stumbled over ash-capped remains and the crumbling husks of peddlers' carts, following Bora's silhouette, each step taken blindly. An explosion thumped through the earth, pulsing up Anna's legs.

She spun to find dust spewing from the open doorway, its particles frothing in candlelight and the flames of burst lanterns. No longer did she hear the screams of doomed men. She envisioned their bodies, mangled and dismembered, hanging from ropes like carved portions in a butcher's stall.

Surely one would remain through the carnage, silent and hateful.

Anna lumbered toward the doorway in a daze. "Bora, we need to—"

"He will be claimed." Bora took hold of Anna's shoulders and stared down, the moonlight turning her eyes to shards of jet. "Don't dwell on it, child. You've seen the face of your path. That is enough."

"It's not enough," Anna snarled. "We could have helped them!"

"By placing them in new ropes. There are no safe havens for them in these lands, child. Not anymore." Bora inclined her head toward the tower behind Anna. "It's time to return."

Just then Anna noticed the lights of approaching lanterns. Foreign voices, indistinct yet shouting commands in neither Orsas nor flatspeak, rose from the shadows beyond the cluster of ruins. "Are they yours?" she asked, shaking.

"They are known," the northerner said, "but I would not seek their compassion."

"But one had my runes." Anna thrust a finger at the den. "What are they going to do with him?"

"Nothing new."

Anna gaped at the smoldering doorway, aware of the world only through tingles of wind across her neck and the biting odor of burnt hair. She watched the dust curling and dissipating, shreds of Bora's planted violet cloth drifting off into the breeze.

"Let's go," Anna said. There was sickening comfort in the idea that the captives were mutilated beyond saving. She followed Bora over broken bodies and dusty cloth and pockmarked earth, pausing only to vomit at the foot of the looming watchtower.

From the walkways spanning Malijad's ruined district, a sprawl resembling starlit ocean and blurs of lamplight, she saw Bora's associates filing in and out of the den in dark robes. The only deviation among their uniforms was a bare-chested man with shackled limbs, two pale eyes burning through the blackness as soldiers whisked him into a setstone labyrinth.

Chapter 22

Nightmares of burning eyes and decaying flesh jarred her from sleep each night, and it wasn't long before she ventured back out to the comfort of the blackness and the lamp-lit void below. Back to a place of freedom, in spite of its proximity to death in every loose brick and clawing gust of desert wind. Bora hadn't reappeared since that night, leaving Anna a phantom atop the battlements and winding paths.

After a week of exploring Malijad's vantage points, toying with thoughts of escape or stepping over the edge, Anna headed to the refuge she'd seen in calmer dreams.

She clung to the shadows along the outer wall, where small, prickly leaves sprouted through the crafting huts' foundations and crunched beneath her boots. Hundreds of carts flooded the trade paths, and the main square was so congested that the Dogwood guards could barely make their rounds.

Anna followed a pair of Alakeph into a tanner's lane and its odors of sun-bleached flesh, shouldering past tattooed men and pelt-covered racks, soon noting the wails overtaking the dry scrape of knives on pelts. The rear of the foundling hall and its open window slats bled candlelight into the darkness. She couldn't shed a sense of wrongdoing, the notion that she sought out the hall as penance.

Anna purged her thoughts as she peered down both avenues of an intersection. She secured her hood, dashed to the door, and knocked with the flat of her fist.

The door swung in with some delay, revealing Jalwar's face in ribbons of lamplight. He stared past Anna with a furrowed brow and parted lips, a familiar sluggishness lingering in his eyes.

"Jalwar," Anna whispered, staring up at the irregular black hair under the man's chin.

"Oh!" Jalwar flopped forward. He braced himself on the door frame, stared down at Anna with one eye determined to wander away, and smacked his lips. "Anna, what you are doing here? What this is?"

Anna glanced around. The only observers were a group of Hazani men chuckling at Jalwar. "We should go inside."

Jalwar stumbled back and cleared the way for Anna. Beyond him was a darkened atrium, its beautiful wicks and lamps extinguished. A lone candle burned on a tin plate near Jalwar's feet. He picked it up, grunting, and chuckled. "Come, then."

Guided by the dim light of Jalwar's candle, they crossed into the main chamber. It was not as lifeless or decayed as the tomesroom near Bylka, but it was eerie nonetheless, given the sleeping schedule of the majority in Malijad. Those within their district tended to rise in the afternoon and work when the sun was past zenith. Yet the children were all asleep behind veils and locked doors, guarded by the ghostly shapes of the Alakeph.

Inside the office, Jalwar stumbled over to a lamp near his podium and tipped the candle toward its wick. Rivulets of candle wax spattered as the lamp glowed to life, but soon the popping faded, giving way to an even burn.

Anna sat on the familiar stool, surprised at her own presumption. She'd visited only once before, but felt that she'd earned her position through risk alone.

"Yes, right, okay," said Jalwar. He settled heavily onto his own stool, holding out both arms to ensure he wouldn't fall. "This is unexpected, I must make known."

"Have you been drinking?" Anna asked.

Jalwar muttered something in flatspeak, then scratched at his lips and shook his head. "It grows on the plains. Something from the boar-clans." He surveyed Anna closely. "This time of darkness is a rare one for you, Anna. You should not be here."

She folded her arms, examining the patchwork mess of documents arranged on Jalwar's podium. "It seems like the wrong time to do work."

Jalwar sighed. "During the scorching times, I am with the young. During the blessed time, I wait for shipments and scrolls. It is a very boring thing, you see?"

"I suppose," Anna said. The sheer reality of reaching the hall dwarfed any disappointment she felt for the man. "I've come to discuss helping here. I don't have much time."

"Falling stars," Jalwar huffed, rubbing his eye with the back of his hand. "Anna, they have sent men from the *kales*. You must not come to this place." Midway through his rubbing his left eye widened. "Oh, no.

You are *here*, Anna. You are in this place. In this place you cannot see."
His chest and stomach swelled with gulps of air. "Oh, oh, oh . . ."

"Calm down," Anna said. She stole a glance over her shoulder at the
fabric hanging, noting the ragged hem at its bottom and searching for
exposed boots. Nothing. "Jalwar, I want to continue working here."

His face flushed beneath bronze skin, darkening slowly like a kettle left
over the fire. Thick hands covered his eyes. "How did you even reach me?"

"It's unimportant," she said. "Will you allow me to work?"

One of his hands fell, revealing an eye with fractals of broken blood
vessels. "In what manner, Anna? It is not permitted. They sent men—"

"Forget their men," Anna said. "I want to keep helping these children.
What can I do during the night?"

"They would see me killed for such a thing," whispered Jalwar. His
eyes combed the floor, aimless and broken yet somehow curious, ignorant
of Anna's passion. "You too, perhaps."

"I don't care," Anna said. The bitterness of her words struck at once.
"What is there to do at night?" she pressed.

"Nothing that would respond to the warmth of your touch," Jalwar said.
The words were unexpectedly lucid. "Look, Anna." He swept his arm over
the podium, indicating a mess of crumpled parchment and documents.
"This is my blessed time."

She gazed upon the documents, unable to stave off a sense of defeat. This
was what she'd traveled so bravely to see, the new face of aid. Even so, her
mind explored a dozen branching paths, imagining what the letters said and
how she might formulate her replies in written flatspeak. "I could help."

Jalwar's eyebrow crept up. "It is only ink-work, Anna."

"When do you sleep?"

"Ah?"

Anna gave a hushed sigh. "When do you have time to sleep?"

"Not so often."

"So let me help," she said. "I could attend to them for you. I could
check the ledgers, and write new missives for you. You could tell me what
to say." The more she spoke, the more feasible it seemed. She could aid
them, with our without scabs on her hands. "Nobody will have to know,
Jalwar. Who else visits this place?"

He shrugged. "It is only the Alakeph, I must suppose." A generous
pause. "Such a thing is so sudden, Anna. Perhaps in a moment I will
awake from this dream, and the leaves will be sweated free of my skin."

"It's not a dream." Anna frowned. "Just say yes, Jalwar. Say yes and sleep, and I'll do the same. I don't have long, Jalwar. If you believe in prophecy, you'll do this."

Speech and heavy breathing and the subtle pacing of the Alakeph's boots fell away.

"You may have stubborn blood of Gosur, after all," he responded. "Arrive when your eyes may see the queen upon her web."

Anna recalled the fifteen stars over eastern Hazan. They were so bright that they burned through the smog, regardless of the devastation in the districts, and so immutable in placement that Bora had forced Anna to meditate upon the constellation. "Okay." A nagging smile pulled at her lips. She wasn't pleased with coercing him, but there was always a satisfaction in successful negotiations. "Is that it?"

"I hope," Jalwar huffed into his hands. "Now go, Anna. Be quick of this."

Anna stood. She stared down at the podium, contemplating how to arrange its contents, how to address missives, how to write with a steady hand. How to tuck words beyond the awareness of wicked men.

Chapter 23

That night she recalled the packed floor of her old home and the soft pattering of rain on the thatch above. Mother and father were away, their destination unclear. She didn't care. She just stood by the fire, rubbing her hands clean of the blood of chickens she'd beheaded on the stump. The droplets sizzled on the embers below. Every patch of the home's interior was painted in sigils and runes, overlapping till they formed hideous webs.

A forest spirit with pitted eyes arrived with an offer: If she never left the house, Julek could wander out of the woods and stand by their window's shutters, free to speak and live beside her.

He stood with a lopsided smile, his freckles and dark hair and pale skin so vibrant in his new life. Strength kept him straight and upright, and he rested a sleeved arm on the windowsill.

"What do they say?" he asked about the sigils upon the cracked and burnt slats of the house's walls. "You realize that they're going to flay you, don't you?"

Anna opened her mouth, but spider legs bristled across her tongue. The black creatures raced down her chin and into her neckline, then burrowed between the notches of her ribs. *I don't care about that,* she wanted to say, but the spiders poured and poured, filling her mouth. *I love you, little bear.*

Sunlight bit through her eyelids, jarring her from sleep. As she sat up in the bed, the covers arranged neatly around her, she realized she hadn't been resting at all. No, it was far too gentle of an awakening. Her heart barely stirred, and the air in her lungs was warm and used, as though she'd been breathing steadily for some time.

Dreaming had been her meditation.

She'd worked so hard to visualize the boy like a trinket in her mind, coming closer in her dreams to holding and speaking to him. *To atonement born from untruths.* And with that, she knew the thinking mind would never allow her to dream of the boy again. Much like a boy honing his first knife, she'd sharpened the edge and tested it upon her own thumb, drawing blood before she felt any pain.

And though the thinking mind couldn't comprehend it, Anna cried into the safety of her blankets.

When the vengeful god rose so high that its shafts no longer spilled into her chambers, Anna rose from bed, gathered her hair in a thick knot, and secured the clump with a length of gold ribbon. As she ate flatbread and honey she found her attention drifting back to Shem's door, where she had visions of the hanging boy, disfigured by smirking Dogwood men. They could've gotten to him while she was sleeping, while she was at the hall.

She pushed aside her plate, walked briskly to the door, and knocked. Her breaths slowed. She pictured his body lifeless, broken. "Shem?" she whispered.

The door flew open, revealing the boy's animated smile. He was shirtless and shoeless, dressed only in his cotton pants and a brown sash. Lean muscle bands across his chest and arms had evidently been formed in the lower gardens, where he volunteered his time with older women in the *kales*, but Anna hadn't noticed. Whether she'd ignored his growth or hadn't seen it under folds of fabric, it was startling to behold.

How much else have I missed?

"Anna!" Shem spread his arms wide and hugged her with more force than he'd needed, though he meant nothing by it. He was strong and eager, and he cared. "They answer my calls."

Anna waited until the Huuri released her, and stepped back. "They?"

"The Venerated," Shem grinned. "In the darkness, I could not find rest. I looked for you, but you were gone. I worried that you leave me. So I pray whole night for the Ascended to be returned to me, you see?"

Since the kator, she'd hadn't heard Shem discuss his faith. The Venerated were like Anna —man-skins, Ascended, however they were known—and existed somewhere among the other planes. Anna paled when she considered Shem's words, and not from the idea of being deified. Not even from his devotion. "Shem," she said, "I was doing something important last night. Did you tell Konrad or the orza?"

His eyes darkened to silvery ash. "No, never. I only pray."

"Why?"

"To make sureness of your safety." His jaw shifted. "Do I upset you, Anna?"

Anna sensed the hurt she'd beaten into him. "Listen to me carefully, Shem," she said, speaking to him in a way that most of the Dogwood men would have found patronizing, if not outright spiteful. "I'm thankful that you care about me. You're a good friend, and I appreciate that. But you can't check on me every night."

His eyes twitched. "I don't understand it."

"You'll need to stay in your quarters, Shem. Somebody could be hurt if you try to follow me."

Shem lowered his head. "What if I cannot wander to dream-place, Anna?"

"Stay in your quarters," she said in a milder tone. "It's a sort of trial, Shem. A trial of faith and patience. It will bring you closer to ascension." She could hardly say the words without cringing. Even if she dismissed his faith as a lie, it was cruel to manipulate his innocence. To shut him away, despite his allegiance until death or beyond. She fumbled for new words, grasping at anything she could muster. "It's like training for you, Shem. We'll both become stronger if you do it."

For once there was suspicion in his eyes. At times Anna wondered how far she could prod the boy before he lost his blind obedience. With a sinking knot in her gut, she realized that the moment had come.

"Yes, Anna," he said, turning away and retrieving a fresh shirt from his cabinets. He dressed himself, then stared at her from across the room, his smile buried under sills of relaxed muscle fibers. "I wonder something."

Anna waited.

"Konrad." Shem wrung his hands. "You like him?"

"You're asking if I love him," Anna said, unable to keep the rebuke out of her voice. She took a step into Shem's room. "No, I don't." He didn't look up. "Shem," Anna pressed. "Why would you think that?"

The orbs of his eyes receded behind tissue and bones. It pulsed in cycles as he laid his thoughts bare. "I hear such things. In gardens, in hallways. I hear, Anna."

"Whatever you hear, it isn't true. I don't want any of them. Remember this."

Shem nodded, and it was done. For then.

As the two of them wandered the corridors, escorted by a set of thin Weave Wars veterans who worked for their powder of choice, she couldn't stop glancing at Konrad. It wasn't his appearance that drew Anna's attention.

It was the idea of him and his type. She realized, on some level that Bora had blunted, that a girl her age would be expected to marry soon. In Rzolka, anyway. Her tomes told her that in Hazan, bonds came later in age, and often had little to do with love. They had to do with alliances and cartels and territory, and often joined numerous partners. But both options were frightening. She wondered if her mother and father had been more loving before the war claimed her father's tenderness, and if love would propel her to her fated twin like in the old stories, or if she'd have to deceive herself into loving a violent man.

Shem departed from the group with two Dogwood men, cheerful as he climbed into the open capsule. The new escorts held each other's stare as the door slid shut, and Shem plunged deeper into the *kales* for a day of mindless gardening.

"Where are you heading today, *panna*?" Konrad said. He slowed to reach Anna's side as they continued on. "Lectures, perhaps?"

"Just to the tomes," she whispered, although she'd read most of the scrolls within her literacy range. Speaking with the Dogwood, even Konrad, filled her with an urge to flee.

"And to your bath," Konrad added.

"Yes," Anna said, suddenly cognizant of how well Konrad knew her schedule. Of how well he might burrow into the minds of captured men.

"*Panna*, forgive me if I'm derailing your plans somewhat, but how would you feel about something more exciting? The council has been a bit strict on you lately, and it's a pity."

Anna narrowed her eyes, trying not to envision the ash-covered streets. "What is it?"

"Well, I turned it over in my head last night," Konrad said. "If Malijad's a desert, you've only seen a grain of sand. A quiet, boring, and rather serious grain of it. You should get the most out of such a place." He shrugged. "Don't forget that I was once a boy from Rzolka myself. So I know what you think. These streets might seem daunting, but we both know how special it is. Someday it might feel like home to you."

Anna slowed. "You're allowed to take me there?"

"I know the city as well as any northerner," Konrad grinned. "The orza's district, anyway. They have everything and anything." He gestured through the nearby columns at the cityscape. "They have menageries with all sorts of creatures, and shade-squares with music you couldn't imagine. Every block has tailors or bakers, or craftsmen with an eye for toy-making."

Anna gazed at the endless streets, then Konrad. She'd seen the districts well enough, and hearing about lighthearted things only made his suggestion feel perverse. "I've outgrown toys."

"And the rest, *panna*?"

She watched sunlight paint long slashes along the setstone, wondering if every Dogwood man was as wicked as the guards who'd staffed the torture den. Perhaps Konrad was ignorant to their crimes, just as her father had spoken of being innocent amid his comrades' misdeeds. Being tempted by baubles and flutes would draw Bora's scorn, but Anna didn't care. She needed him to be innocent.

"Show me," Anna said.

* * * *

They passed through the main gates within the hour. Konrad assured Anna that there was nothing scandalous about their trip, but insisted that their presence remained understated. Anna wore her hood and dark yellow scarf, which most Hazani donned regardless of the weather. Konrad traveled without armor but still had a guarded sway to his arms and neck, much like her father's. It was the gait of a man who'd killed, and escaped death. Beyond the gates was sprawling chaos. Squat bunkers and sturdy watchtowers, manned by teams of mercenaries, fractured the flow of traffic and towered above the passersby. Down the eastern street, an endless valley between setstone heights, the crowds gave way to a mixture of bazaar stalls and residential quarters. In the sunken dens of some buildings, men smoked from pipes and scar-matted hounds thrashed and bit at one another, surrounded by presses of Gosuri and Hazani and Huuri.

They walked in quiet rhythm, surrounded by the dull thumps of cloth being felted and sacks of grains being loaded. Eventually they reached a quiet plaza with vendors and stone benches. Bushels of palm plants and thorny roots sprouted in the shade.

He led Anna to a wide cart with two sheet-covered tables of merchandise on display. Most items were darkly-stained wood carvings, but some were carved gems, others trinkets with dried claws or drilled bone fragments. The peddler was pale-eyed and thin, his hands tucked behind his back and chest puffed out.

"Do you like anything here?" Konrad asked Anna. He had little interest in the square's other carts. Nevertheless, he shared a smile with the peddler beneath the cart's awning.

Anna prodded at a painted shell. "What are they?"

"Just nice things." Konrad glanced at the vendor, then said something both elegant and unexpected. It was not the harsh tongue of flatspeak, nor a Gosuri dialect. It was as fluid as the words Shem spoke so many cycles ago.

"Where did you learn that?" Anna asked.

Gentle laughter passed between the two men, but Konrad's eyes darkened at the question. His smile remained with a nervous curl. "Learn what, *panna*?"

"You just said something to him." Anna studied the vendor's face: It was more angular than the Hazani, even with their mixed breeds and differences, and framed with elevated cheekbones. "It wasn't flatspeak."

"Ah," Konrad hummed. "Orsas. Isn't it beautiful?"

"It's rare," Anna replied. She still recalled the tracker's rebuke in the markets.

"The Dogwood learn things from all over," Konrad said, picking up a necklace with a sliver of jade and turning it over in his gloves. "Things from Nahora tend to be the most exceptional." He studied Anna's face. "Have you heard stories?"

"Some."

"It's better than any story," Konrad said. He held the necklace closer to Anna. "What do you think?"

Afternoon light tumbled through the gem, painting Konrad's glove with bands of refracted color.

Anna gave a delicate smile. "It's nice."

"Do you want it?"

"Maybe someday." Anna watched the colors twisting, splitting into beautiful ribbons of light. "Besides, I didn't bring anything with me."

"Forget your salt," Konrad winked. "I'd like it to be a gift."

"For what?"

"For a pleasant walk," he said with an arched brow. "Is it too egregious?"

She shook her head. "No, but—"

Konrad drew some coins from his coat's lower pocket, spoke in Orsas to the vendor, and completed the transaction with a nod of appreciation. He held the necklace out for Anna by its dark string, grinning.

"Thank you," she said, taking the necklace with some reluctance.

Before reaching the *kales*, undaunted by the crack of explosions and plumes of black smoke from neighboring districts, Konrad helped her secure the necklace. He swept her hair gently aside and knotted the string with a dexterous twist, then lifted the gemstone in his palm so it caught a glint of fading daylight. Anna had never cared for gifts, having always rejected offerings with disguised intentions, but she wondered if Konrad's intentions were disguised at all. She smiled at the jade fragment.

When Anna braced her door to close it that evening, they stood in silence till Konrad took the initiative, an impish curl in his lips. "Sleep well," he told her.

"The same to you," Anna said. Then, before fully sealing the door, she spoke out once more. "Konrad, some of the men talked about a place in the city. They said that traitors are questioned there."

His expression darkened. "There are several, *panna*. I've never visited, but they exist."

"They said something happened to one of them."

Konrad appeared off-guard, but was quick to compose himself. "Sour matters. I wouldn't dare to force them upon you."

"Do you trust me?"

"Of course, *panna*."

"I heard they found evidence of who did it," Anna said. "Purple cloth."

He offered a smile to placate her, but it was wasted. "Rumors about Nahora have always been rampant. Don't be afraid of their blades. Nahora isn't what they say."

"I see." She cradled her necklace in her hands and thought of Bora's violet fabric, of the *qaufen* launched over setstone valleys, of men who struck kators by night. *Nahora.* "Thank you for the day, Konrad."

It wasn't until Anna engaged the lock, turned away, and lifted the jade to the candlelight that she noticed Shem across the room, staring.

But Anna was far too busy thinking of killers to focus on a bruised heart.

Chapter 24

Each night, Anna's hands crept closer to the unreadable monolith, plunging deeper into its wreath of dark mist and probing for substance. She murmured her secrets as sacrifices to the fog, which sheltered long-dead memories like the flames of wind-stricken candles. Recollections of shrieks on a cold morning, flesh torn open, promises made freely and brokenly unfairly.

End was all it whispered back.

Then she always woke to blackness, her chest aching and forehead clammy, to make the long trek to the foundling hall. The regular nature of her visits made crossing the rooftops habitual, leaving her unwanted opportunities to think. On some trips she thought of Konrad and their daily talks, where he shared inklings of Orsas and stories of his childhood near Kowak. He'd been an apprentice to a fletcher, but when Anna had described the rigid feathers of the *qaufen* arrow, his face stiffened and he fell silent. Even so, he granted her enough comfort to wear his necklace, even as she slept, and to think of a life beyond vengeance and guilt. Sometimes she thought of Shem, who hardly spoke to her but glared at her necklace. She thought of the orza and Bora, whom she hadn't seen in several weeks, and how she hadn't been summoned to mark new captains. It was as though she'd melded into the masonry of the *kales*, becoming yet another wastrel.

The work for Jalwar consisted mainly of sorting mailing compartments and correcting his grammatical errors in the river-tongue, but it was exciting to read messages from unknown cities and regions. Some were from Alakeph captains relaying their recruitment numbers, while others were from Halshaf monasteries requesting supplies. Anna wasn't averse to redirecting sacks of grain or herbs to outlying chapters, falsifying the logistical changes on the hardcopy sheets handled by the *kales* and its saltmen. She had a deft hand capable of forging nearly anybody's signature.

For a while, even without Bora, it was good.

But the truth of her existence, the knowledge she couldn't hide in the shadows forever, visited her in a burlap mask one night. It came as ragged footsteps and murmured arguing between Alakeph men, ending with a shadow falling across Anna's podium.

She glanced up, entranced by the lamp-lit gaps in the burlap and the swirl of purple irises. But she wasn't frightened as she surveyed the tracker. "What?"

"Should've known," he said. A pair of Alakeph men stepped behind him in their opal robes, but Anna was quick to motion them away. "How long has this been on?"

"A few weeks," Anna said, dipping her quill into the ink for a new line. "You came without them?"

The tracker haunted the doorway for a moment, then moved closer with a grumble. He settled into a wicker chair, the folds of his black cloak pooling around the armrests. "They'd see you flayed."

"Beaten." Anna glanced up. "They wouldn't kill me."

"Beating could break those pretty hands," he whispered. "But you're right. Chances are, they wouldn't have a pence of a solution. Fine little mess you've managed to make."

Anna resumed writing to the monastery in Yelasim. "How'd you find me?" She thought immediately of Shem, however unfair it was. Bora's insistence on realism meant expecting betrayal.

"That's the curious thing about this." His rune was still burning cool white, untarnished by age. "Even if your mind fogs, your body never quite runs down. Sleep isn't an easy thing, some nights. So imagine my surprise when I spotted that tucked bright hair near the courtyard a few nights ago."

"And you never followed me?"

"Tried. You're fast, girl." He huffed. "Much too fast for these legs."

Anna studied his eyes, noting the way they caught her stare and then drifted, before returning to her work. "You found me."

"It took some time, I'll admit," the tracker said. "I should have checked here sooner."

"What's my punishment?" Setting down her quill, Anna hardened her gaze. "Or will you let the others settle it again?"

Not even his breaths fluttered the burlap. He sat perfectly still, hands meshed upon his thigh. Deep thinking never cooperated with the press of dusk-petals. "I'm not planning on telling the others."

Anna's eyes flicked up.

"Words are steady things to me, girl," the tracker said. "See, now, that's what you won't get with the northerners. They'll weave lies into prophecy."

"What do you want, then?"

"It's a concrete thing," he replied. Despite his tone there was nothing threatening in the slump of his arms or the sprawled tangle of his legs. "You'll be called upon by my brethren for another marking ceremony, just before the Days of Seed, some sort of northern song-and-dance nonsense. Do what you do, and we'll all be right for it."

Her guts lurched. There was no way for the tracker to know what she'd seen in the chambers, and her cooperation was already expected. Its phrasing as a request put her on edge. "What makes it different?"

"Different, eh?"

"I've never turned a mark down," Anna said. "You make this sound like a new deal. You don't gain a thing from keeping my secret."

"Maybe I just like you. How's that?"

"You like what I can do," she whispered.

The tracker gave a wobbling nod. "Right. And if you stop marking, we have a problem. *We.* You and I. We're good together, but if this all falls apart, it's done."

"You would lose more than me," Anna said darkly, picking up her quill again.

"Can't fight that," the tracker agreed. "But we have so much to gain, you see? It's growing close, Anna."

Before the quill's nib touched the parchment, Anna froze. "Close to what?"

"We could have it all," the tracker said, his fingers tensing and loosening upon the armrests. "Fifteen traitorous pups cut down in the night, and another ten on our draw of the battle line. Not a single cartel in Malijad can say they don't know us any longer. We're either bound to them, bleeding them, or buying them." He nodded into the folds of his cloak. "There's just this festival and the last strikes. Then it's southward, Anna. Then it's back home."

Anna's nib hovered, a rivulet of black ink drooling onto the parchment as she squeezed the quill. She could hardly envision it. Moving back to the lakes and forests and mountains, speaking her old tongue with strangers, being welcomed by friends and distant kin by virtue of her flesh's shade alone.

And yet she recalled mother and father. She imagined what she'd do to them, or what she'd order her subordinates to do. She saw troops marching under her banner and killing at the movement of her wrist, dens of agony and infected scars, men screaming into the blackness for help that would never arrive.

The ink pooled, and she glanced away. "You just need me to mark them?"

"Simple cuts, Anna. We're close enough to lick it."

She lifted her quill. "What do you know about Nahora?"

Stillness came over the tracker in a cold wave. "Runts," he said at last. "Something you need to say?"

Despite the memories of the *qaufen* wavering in Bora's hand, and explosives rupturing the kator's shell, Anna held her tongue. There was numbing safety in the tracker's vision of the future. "They're just mentioned in the tomes."

"Wasted words." The tracker looked around the office, scrutinizing ledgers and stacks of missives. "But what I told you, about liking you . . . you believe that, don't you?"

Anna glanced down at her papers. "I think so."

"*Pravda*," the tracker muttered. "Trust me. When I say mark, I mean it." His voice slipped from drug-slurred advice to grave warning. "Keep the breath in your throat, girl. We're so close to it. And whatever you think, I can't control what happens to you forever. Consider this an ounce of my heart-blood."

Anna nodded.

The tracker slid his chair back, grating the wooden legs against the floor. He gathered up the pleats of his cloak and stood, one hand bracing his knee, the other combing the air for balance, before wandering to the doorway. "Tell me, girl," he said. "What do you think of that captain?"

Anna hadn't stopped watching the tracker as he departed, but now she felt exposed, his eyes whirling back on her without reason. "Which one?"

"Your faithful *hound*," he spat. "Konrad."

Anna reddened when she heard the name, but managed to bury the truth in the rapid tapping of her quill. "He's a good man," she said. "He's respectful, and he does his job well."

Shadows thickened in the creases of the tracker's mask and cloak, leaving only his rune amid the blackness. "I see," he whispered at last. He backed away and ducked through the threshold.

As Anna attempted to return to her writing, she noticed a trickle of pale white amassing in her periphery. She glanced up at a cluster of Alakeph men in the doorway, their hands resting on the grips of sheathed blades.

Only then did Anna turn her thoughts to writing. She wrote letters with words she'd never fathomed and addressed them to monasteries she'd never visit, her every missive informed by her thinking mind's certainty of the bloodshed to come.

Chapter 25

Their world was one of murder. Numberless warriors filled the chamber that evening, gathered around the main circle and crowding tiers of scaffolding that stretched into darkness. Brazier light gave way to savage glares and slashes of paint upon dark flesh. A soft pall of *nerkoya* smoke clouded the air. The silhouettes and quick movements flashed through the haze, never shrouded enough to be ignored. They scarred their flesh with needles and screeched and slashed their palms, smearing blood across the floors and walls.

They wished to be animals.

No longer did they check their equipment or tighten their straps for battle. They didn't pore over ruji barrels, nor the cutting edge of short blades. Flasks made dizzying circles around the gathering, and puffs of mica flared in the lamplight, but the rituals were vestiges of a dying world, surface gestures of a time when faith and fear had been real things, when appealing to gods or stars had been essential to survival. After so much hunting and killing and returning without losses, they were no longer afraid. They fed from the sadism of splintering doors and dragging their enemies into darkness.

Over time they'd adopted a singular goddess.

Anna, who brought ruin and broken bones and blackened setstone to every stretch of Malijad. Anna, who'd granted them violence and immunity superior to the conquerors of the old songs. Anna, who couldn't fathom how many had perished at her hands.

She stood in their circle, rigid as a great oak. Beyond the ring of dim lanterns the wolves shifted and crowded her, threatening to break the thinking mind's concentration on her blade and the droplets of sweat snaking between her fingers. In Anna's mind, she was a branch bent, but never broken beneath the press of snowfall.

"It's a surprise for us both," Konrad had said on the way to the chamber, his smirk playing beneath eager eyes. "You'll do spectacularly. It's for the Days of Seed, they say."

Anna glanced up from the dusty and bloodstained tiles, her vision crawling between lamp-lit rings until she spotted Konrad. Beside him was the tracker and his companions, who were all distracted with twine-wrapped bottles and herb-stuffed pipes, their faces swollen and red from arak.

Closer to the circle's inner ring was the orza, who appeared skeletal in the lamplight. Grooves of stress and sleeplessness scarred her young skin, while her eyes sank into their sockets, untouched by the beauty of ceremonial paint. Even her gown, a trailing mixture of silver thread and crimson, was merely draped over weary limbs and knife-jagged collarbones. As always, the woman's attending scribe revealed nothing beyond a pink network of scars beneath her hood.

Anna's gaze circled the crowd.

Bora's stone face was a beacon among chaos. She stood among men, camouflaged by a harsh stare and shaven head. Her brilliant white cloak was all that marked her, glowing through the grit and smoke that encircled her.

Anna focused herself to the task at hand. *They're here to see me,* she reminded herself. *I'm their gift to the world.* Her hands grew slicker as those truths set in.

"Rein it in!" screamed Teodor.

A sudden wave of murderous voices crashed upon Anna. Her breaths congealed in her throat, and her vision shifted, blackening at the edges and racing across the crowd for refuge. Yet Konrad was fixed on Teodor's hollering, while the orza glanced down with bruised empathy, and Bora had disappeared from her standing place.

Focus, the thinking mind whispered, worming through her consciousness and soothing primal thoughts. *You'll not die here. It will come to you, but not here.*

Anna's heart slowed. She locked her eyes on Teodor, watching the ridiculous man stumble back and forth before his cadre, his too-large boots twisting beneath fat ankles and crooked knees. He was as much a mockery of grace as the warrior spirit he'd once embodied. He was a broken, bitter old man.

"Down, down," Teodor spat, met by pockets of laughter. He had a way with the men, settling them like raucous dogs with a mere drink from his flask. "We're drawing up on the northern festival. Days of Seed, they are. Have you boys earned some rest, then?"

A thunderous *no* descended from the farthest heights of the scaffolding, reverberating through the chamber as the decree of a dead god. *No, no, no, no. . . .*

"Fucking right," Teodor called. He paced within the circle of lamps, retaining a comfortable distance from Anna. "Thinking about your cut of farmland in the south yet? Putting the heft back in your stones, dreams of your future wives? The ones in the beds of traitors, this very moment, while you bleed in the sand?"

Laughter and wretched screams and jeering filled the chamber. Nacek and Josip shared a golden flask as the tracker stared at Anna through ragged slits.

Anna stared back.

"You *korpy* are a strong lot, no two ways of it," Teodor continued. "You've served your goddess well." He swung his mug toward Anna, sloshing dark liquid across the floor. The crowd stamped and chanted Anna's name, pulsating the floor and the cartilage within Anna's chest. Teodor gave a wild shout to cease the clamor. "You've put an end to it, boys. You've cut the fucking head off their serpents, ripped the hearts from their babes while they slept!" Teodor waited for the cycle of applause, shrieking, hushing. "This city was the start. Rzolka knows our fucking names, and they think they're ready for us. They think they can spot our numbers a thousand leagues away, like we paint ourselves as Hazani whores." He took a deep breath. "Even if we did, we'd still run up on them and fucking *gut* them!" The cheering rose, punctuated only by stamping boots. "Hang them from oaks, burn them in groves. Fuck them! Fuck the cities!"

The room's energy seeped through Anna, far more pervasive than a winter morning chill. Something dangerous was in the air.

"Blades are pledged," Teodor shouted. "Patvor is the fire at *sukry's* doors. Some tuck their young ones away, laughing at the idea of old wolves rising in the sand. Fifteen, twenty, thirty thousand *blades* are pledged across Hazan. How many of the half-spines in the south will pick up new crests when they see our banner, eh?" Teodor crossed his arms, the mug dangling limply in his grip. "Tonight, you'll burn because *you can*. You'll bleed them because you fucking *can*. Whatever your sick stones desire, you'll take. Earned this city, *korpy*. This night, you keep what you seize. This is your prize. Sink into your fruit before the new harvest, you mutts."

Pommels and clubs and tacked boots drummed over the tiles. Their voices were a hum of rage and ecstasy, a collective energy, mounting and primal and spiteful, with no outlet except the mad calls of a beast.

Anna fought the shaking in her legs, as well as bristling of small hairs along her arms, but it was futile. Her body was as much a slave to the room's fury as those around her, and though her thinking mind worked in a shell beneath the chaos, none of her thoughts or mental tricks stayed the terror. She stood before men intent on a prize. There were no limits.

She realized how right Bora had been, how strong the desire to live truly was.

She looked to Konrad, and the southerner stared back at her. His eyes were an oasis in the lamplight. The world moved in torrents around him, but Anna ignored it all.

"What are mutts without handlers, though?" Teodor cackled. Several boos sprang up, but the man brushed his wicker hat in dismissal. "Our dear goddess has brought us so far. The dream of Rzolka's still bright in her pretty fucking eyes." He pointed to Anna. "Road ahead will have its lumps, but she'll be there. You'll never stop being her blades, her shields, her sows for slaughter, if she craves it. But she serves Rzolka well, and it serves her back. If the gods didn't want us to burn the *sukry,* they wouldn't have sent their punishment our way, ah?" He ended his question with a scream, his face blood-red and lips darkening to purple. His hat cast ragged shadows over his brow. "So she serves Rzolka tonight, before the true war begins. Before the cities burn and the traitors bring offerings to her fucking feet, kissing flesh and praying for mercy from the wolves. Before she warms her proper throne."

Even Konrad's eyes shriveled. He glowered and shot sidelong glances at Teodor. Whether or not Teodor had shared his plans with the others on their council, it was clear that the Dogwood were ignorant. The surprises of a madman were never welcome.

Bile oozed through Anna's gut.

The lamp-lit movement of burlap drew Anna's attention. The tracker was nodding with a frantic pace, but Anna was certain that his vigor didn't stem from bloodlust; what may have seemed like agreement to outsiders was really a furtive plea.

Do as he says, the shakes of his head screamed. *Do as we planned.*

"Patvor," called Teodor with a cupped hand against his lips. "Hobble over here, you cunning *korpy.*" He aimed a crooked finger at the tracker, laughing. "And you. You stay. You've had your time."

They want me to mark them. The realization bit into Anna, and all of a sudden the blade in her hand felt formless. Her body resisted. For once the two minds stood in unified opposition. The feeling mind conjured visions of these men torturing innocents in dark, hidden dens, forcing themselves upon their wives and young girls, spending nights vomiting up barrels of liquor that would kill lesser men, all funded by the salt of their people. Deeper still, the thinking mind foresaw their corruption. It saw excess and rage and anarchy in their eyes, waiting to be unleashed with the promise of immortality.

Victorious conquest turned all men to monsters, Anna knew, but there was no telling what became of conquerors who'd already transformed.

Beyond her veil of thoughts was the ever-present nodding of the tracker, pleading with her.

Mark them.

As the three men gathered in the inner circle, fed by the screeching of the Dogwood men and dancing shadows among the scaffolds, Anna looked to the orza and her scribe. She could hardly read the orza's face, which was angled so far down that not even a sliver of her eyes emerged.

The wicked men stood in formation. They smirked at her, drunk and brash and hideous in lamplight, their features slurring together and mutating into black scars with the every shift of their lips.

These men will save Rzolka, she told herself. It was not a reassurance. It was a mockery of the truth they told, and the absurdity of their claims. *I could do better.*

And from that the cogs of her mind locked in place.

I could do it.

The wicked trio before her were intermediaries, stepping stones to a cause, holding lanterns as Anna did the hard work of splitting timber. They were attendants to a goddess.

Anna slid the blade into her belt. "I will not."

Amid the murmurs and hollering, her whispered voice was lost on most of the outer circle. Only the three before her, close enough to hear her words over the din, had any discernible reaction.

"You fucking *what?*" growled Teodor. His lips curled back to reveal crooked, wine-stained teeth. "You take out that blade, girl."

Those in the first rows noticed the commotion, their voices growing softer, their cheers less animated. The drug-dulled eyes of the Dogwood fell on Anna in slow waves, and silence followed in turn.

"She must be toying," Josip laughed. He glanced at Nacek and Teodor for assurance, but received only the unbridled fury of their stares.

Anna held her ground, even as Teodor stole a step toward her. Even as she felt his shadow slinking over her, *drowning* her.

"Right now," Teodor hissed between his teeth, spraying a mist of wine and drool in the lamplight. Still her hands rested idly at her sides. "You fucking pup. Take it out."

Nacek folded his arms and surveyed Anna, then flashed a pointed look at Teodor. "Are you glad you never smothered her flame, *brat*?" His eyes were serpentine, dark, unblinking slits.

Through it all Josip kept up his nervous laughter.

Teodor's face grew redder and sweat-streaked as Anna kept her peace, but the crowd was quick to respond. Some of the Dogwood men cackled, drinking swills of beer and spraying out mouthfuls like surfacing whales. Others gave mock jeers in the old tongue or flatspeak. Those among the scaffolding released the most grating laughter, their joint hysteria circling the chamber and bearing down on the humiliated men below.

A wry smile crossed Anna's face. She spotted the tracker between a pair of lamps, but the man was no longer nodding. In the time she'd spent at his side, she'd become adept at reading him through ragged eyeholes and the slump of his shoulders.

His eyes were extinguished, his shoulders hanging in ruined slopes. An unsettling air of helplessness hung over him.

Once again Anna's throat went dry.

Teodor shouted something restrained and half-muffled, but Anna ignored him. She was busy looking to Konrad, whose usual charm had ceded to fear.

Even the orza's gaze had risen from shame, examining Anna with dreadful prescience. It was the stare given to those marching to the hanging hill, to those with cuts too deep to be stitched. Her lips parted, as though whispering, then trembled. The orza sealed her mouth and watched with an ashen face.

"From every pillar in this fucking keep," Teodor was hissing, having drawn even closer to Anna in her distraction. "Do you fucking hear me?"

She glared back at him. "You won't have it."

"The ceremonies are finished," the orza called. She faced the entire crowd, arms outstretched and eyes hardened to cuts of opal. "Gather with your captains and disperse." Bouts of mumbling and disorder spread through the ranks, but the orza was quick to clap her hands above her head and drown out the noise. "*Gefahl sha'hur!*" she ordered. At once, the Dogwood mobilized in a cascade of footsteps and clinking metal.

Teodor remained. He scanned Anna up and down, the hatred smoldering in his eyes. One hand, wrapped tightly around his mug's handle, was a patchwork of red and white, the other a shaking fist. His every word was acrid, dragged up from his throat and choked free. "She got to you, didn't she? The fucking northerner."

Anna watched the orza directing the masses away from the scaffolding and outer circles, but was quick to return her gaze to Teodor. She thought intensely about where Bora had gone, and while she intended no disrespect, there was little to be lost. "Which one?"

"Traitors have their day," spat Teodor. "We'll give the runts something to scream about, girl. Mark those words." He turned away from Anna and stalked toward his comrades, spiking his mug into the side of a lantern as he went. Curses in the grymjek filled the air long after he convened with the others.

"Come, *panna*," Konrad's soft voice said. He stood by her side, his armor's sand coating dazzling and starry in the lamplight, and cast a hard look at Teodor. "We need to get you back to your quarters."

Anna's eyes fell in the same direction, but she thought nothing of Teodor. Instead she met the tracker's gaze and felt its frigid touch across the circle. In spite of the things he'd done to her, he was an honest man, and there was danger in disobeying the advice of an honest man.

"Let's go," Anna said. She headed toward the lift with Konrad in tow, half-expecting the plunge of a Dogwood knife through her spine with every step. But her concerns were far from her own wellbeing.

She thought only of the runts and their screams.

Chapter 26

Before Anna could close the door to her quarters, Konrad caught the edge of the slab and held it in place. "It might be best if I stay for the night, *panna*."

Anna searched the captain's eyes for the rash energy so many soldiers were unable to resist, and found only concern. There was none of his charm or flourish as he glanced down both lanes of the corridor. The courtesy of seeking her approval was enough, she supposed.

"Come in," she said, taking a step back. She waited until Konrad had sealed the door, then folded her arms. "What are you so afraid of?"

Konrad reached down to his belt and undid the fastenings of his sheath, placing a leather-bound short blade on a nearby table. "Bruised pride," he said darkly, next removing a knife strapped to his lower back, a pair of blades along his shins, and a sling in one of his pouch pockets. By the time he was finished the table resembled a weapon merchant's shop display. "I promise you I'm here for the proper reasons."

Anna looked over the blades, all of them polished and fitted to worn handles, before peering up at Konrad. "I believe you. But do you really think they'd come here?"

Konrad shrugged. "Not by themselves."

Over the past few cycles Anna had grown close to some of the Dogwood men. Speaking with them was rare, but they often recognized one another, and occasionally gave her sweets or flowers. It was hard to believe they'd be swayed to violence so easily. Against innocents, even. "If they wouldn't go after me, what about the foundling hall?"

"My men are good men," Konrad said. "The men under most of the captains are respectable too. But let's keep the source of the salt in mind. Even if their only allegiance to Patvor is a pouch per cycle, it's a strong bond." A mournful smile cut his lips. "Could be nothing, of course. Teodor's prone to his fits, and when he wants a few of us to do something against our grain, he'd have better luck kicking an old hound into a hunt." A touch of Konrad's boyishness returned as he grinned down at the table, surveying his motley of weapons. "Just in case. The Alakeph can handle the little ones."

Anna could hardly understand the threat. Despite their scorn for Rzolka's filth, it took surprisingly little for the trio to turn on their own, or on innocents who had nothing to do with their war. There was no telling whether they'd employ a beating or murder. Whether the Dogwood would pick her lock, or blow the very hinges from her door. Whether Teodor was lashing out like a spoiled child or planning her demise carefully.

The unknown made Anna shudder. "If they come, will it be tonight?"

"The iron is certainly hot," Konrad said, making his way back to Anna's door and inspecting its magnetic strips. "If we don't hear anything tonight, then, with stars' guidance, the old prick might've forgotten about it."

"Was it right to do?"

Konrad faced Anna. "What?"

"Denying them. Was it right?"

He gave a mischievous grin that somehow eased the tension. "It doesn't matter to me, *panna*. I'm not your judge." His grin deepened to a full smile as he stared into the larger portion of Anna's quarters. "Is there an escape here?"

"There's one way," Anna said. "If we need it, we'll be fine." She thought of using the balcony path to alert Jalwar immediately, but she couldn't risk betraying her holdout to anybody else. Not to mention the eyes that surely combed the foundling hall now, waiting to strike.

Konrad's eyes flitted around the room, searching for the possible route, then turned back to Anna. "So we will."

"Do you really think it'll come to that?"

"No," Konrad sighed, "but my old field warden would see me hanged if I didn't ask in advance. *Always have a way out,* dead men wish to tell the living." He rolled his eyes, verging on laughter. "More words of advice from the honey-blossom himself."

Certain things were only humorous to men who'd known death and befriended it, Anna supposed. Despite all of her training she was terrified of meeting her end amid the rage of a wicked man.

"Anna?" The gentle voice preceded the hush of a door on magnetic hinges Shem stood in the half-darkness between his quarters and the main chamber, lamplight penetrating the outer layers of his flesh and diffusing rainbow shades across the tiles. His burning eyes tracked Konrad. "Why is he here?"

"Protection," Konrad said, paying more mind to the shape of the room. He paced around the bed, the tables, the cabinets, hands looped firmly through his belt.

"I make protecting," Shem said. "He should go."

Her heart sank when the boy looked at her. "You can both protect," she said softly. "There might be bad men coming here, Shem. He's only here to help us."

The Huuri's shoulders, bare and strong and rippled with bands of light, sank in a heap. "You trust him."

Anna hardened her eyes. "I trust you both. Be reasonable, Shem."

"*Ol'achim mosham Orsas?*" Konrad asked, peering at Shem curiously.

It gave Shem some pause, but he regarded Konrad with the same cold manner. "*Kep,*" he said quietly.

Konrad rattled off more Orsas, the regimented edge to his voice slipping away as he went on. There was some familiarity to his tongue, if not camaraderie. Anna couldn't imagine that he'd learned his dialect from anything less than a professional tutor.

After several exchanges in Orsas, Shem glanced at Anna. Nothing in his eyes suggested the bitterness had gone into remission. "Trust me. Not trust him."

"I trust both of you." Harshness bit into the end of her words. It all seemed so ridiculous, warring for a girl's trust, arguing, when trained killers were intent on her door and throat. She wondered how Shem would feel if he had to stand over her body, ruminating over every pathetic whine he'd made that night. Anna gritted her teeth. "Isn't that enough for you?"

"Me, not him," Shem said.

"I don't belong to you," Anna hissed. She pointed a shaking finger at the Huuri, her arm drained with the effort of staying upright and taut. It was her last ounce of nervous energy, her last fuel in the war against exhaustion. Her arm collapsed at her side, and she stared at Shem, eyes watering. "I'm not yours to claim."

Shem's brows shifted, beneath which his eyes grew and shrank in slow cycles as though he couldn't understand her words. Finally his gaze grew still. "I go."

"Where?" Her voice faltered.

"The hall," Shem said. "Always wanted in the hall."

Anna watched the boy slip past and disappear behind the closing slab, leaving behind only the whirs of the bolt mechanisms.

"*Panna,*" Konrad said at last. "I advise letting it settle overnight. He's capable."

She nodded dimly. The boy's absence was palpable. "You'll sleep by the door."

"And so I will," Konrad said, unbuckling his final knife from a strap beneath his cuirass and twirling it in the lamplight. He slumped down against the door, hardly casting a glance at Anna.

She extinguished the lamps early that night. Rather than sitting on her bed and meditating for an hour before sleep, she simply crawled under the covers and pulled them close to herself, then rolled over to face Konrad and the main door. Moonlight filtered through the fabric on her balcony doors, staining the captain in pallid gray and sharpening the glow of his neck rune. From her vantage point and angle, she was shrouded in enough darkness to stare at Konrad without being detected. Even so, his eyes were so vigilant that they chilled Anna. Rarely did he stand or stretch, and when he took such liberties, his patrols were swift.

Yet over several hours, through the distant pop of explosive shells and the flashes of light from disintegrating stars, he didn't notice that Anna remained awake beneath her blankets, scheming. She calculated logistics she'd already put in motion, trying to form the proper words to twist a man's heart to her own ends. And when—

A pair of soft, wispy lights blinked into existence behind the balcony's glass, cooling from white to pastel blue in a matter of seconds. A flicker of blackness hinted at blinking eyes, in some form or another. They hovered on the railing, gazing inward, giving little form to the metallic framework housing them.

There was nothing immediately threatening about them, nor as overt as the breed of cruelty the Dogwood employed. Anna sat up in bed, staring back, gauging whether it would be prudent to fetch her ruj.

"Anna," a tinny voice droned. Its words were wracked by quick, constant ticking. "The Council brings goodwill and the desire for salvation. Open this barrier and hear our words."

The Council. It wasn't about Malchym's council, surely. The river-tongue was too fractured, too sweet and flowing to be southern in origin. No, it had to be the Council she'd probed in tomes, with origins buried alongside terms like *statehood* and *obligation.*

Nahora.

Anna slipped out of bed, retrieved her ruj, and approached the balcony's door. As she drew closer she discerned the speaker's true form: a narrow, chattering raven composed of brass plates and cogs and silver tubes. After reading about Kojadi machine schematics, it was too tempting to ignore. Despite her dread of a Dogwood ploy, Anna threw open the doors and aimed at the bird. "What are you?"

Its brass head twitched to the left, followed by a spooling noise. "Her voice is known." The cast beak clicked open and locked in place. An eastern woman's voice, marked by its grace and sense of whispering, emerged. "Make no sounds, dear, for we bring salvation. The Council of Nahora hopes that this message will find you well. My name is unimportant, but my offer is not. The Council extends full amnesty for your service to the interlopers, as well as citizenship upon the terraces of Golyna. You would be loved and attended to." The spooling noise slowed, and with it, the words gradually deepened and slurred. "Our voice is limited here, but consider our words carefully. Say the word *peace*, dear, and you will be preserved. Remain silent, and we will be forced to destroy you. Our home is a living body of breath and bone."

Anna could only gape at the stagnant creature. Beyond her confusion about its mechanisms was a sense of urgency, an impulse to scream *peace* and make it carry her, on gleaming wings, away from this world and its wickedness.

A dream. It must be.

But its fading words resonated in her. *We will be forced to destroy you.* It was the same as all the others. Nahora, the great and powerful, would put a blade to a child's throat. How many others had they snuffed out? Anna inhaled sharply, now glaring at the bird and its hypocrisy. Visions of its engineers and hateful Council passed through her awareness, clouding the machine's true form.

You're all the same.

"Are you—"

Before she could finish speaking, the small bird sprung up and fluttered back, catching a gust of wind as it banked away from the tiles below. It twisted and soared off into the blackness, then vanished.

She stood still, staring, wondering if she'd burned the world's final kindness. "Come back," she whispered, unsure if she meant it.

And when she finally slipped back into bed, waiting for the bird's return, it was with a ruj cradled in her arms.

When the sun rose and shards of orange light fell across Konrad's face, Anna hurried into the antechamber. She found the southerner sitting with a lopsided smile and hands folded across his lap. Disoriented memories of Nahora's bird came to her, but they were too outlandish to be true, too mired in wishful thinking to exist beyond dreamscapes.

"I have to visit somebody," Anna said. "Can we go?"

Konrad bent a brow. "The Huuri?"

A wave of panic rolled over her. Shem hadn't returned home during the night. She swallowed the lump in her throat and fought to stay composed, even as nightmares long gone resurfaced in her. "He'll be there." Foolish as it was, she clung to the hope.

"Oh. The recluse. By now, I'd wager they want his head."

Anna walked to the table, littered with Konrad's assortment of weaponry, and caressed a dagger's flat edge. "If you don't take me there, I'll find a way."

Konrad stood, groaning, and moved to Anna's side. His shoulders loomed over her. "The old hounds didn't take kindly to your last trip. The last that they knew about, I should say. Do you have any idea what they'd do to you?"

"No." She envisioned cracking bones, the stretching and splitting of flesh.

"They believe it's his fault," Konrad explained. "Your fire, so to speak. They think the orza and her husband have dark plans for such an important girl." He grew quiet, and cleared his throat. "You shouldn't feel condemned for what you chose, *panna*. Whatever happens to him—"

"Is my consequence." Anna traced the dagger's handle. "I'll reach him, one way or another. Make your choice."

Konrad circled the table, inspecting the array of iron and steel. "And you'll tell him?"

"To be vigilant."

To take the foundlings. To leave and never look back. She kept her true intentions folded beneath her tongue, confident that the Dogwood captain was ignorant of the lies.

"Pertinent to many of us," Konrad said. He met Anna's eyes across the table, dark hair spilling across his forehead. "You know, they say that in Hazan, only the wind and the jackals can outrun their fate."

"I don't care for fate." Anna moved to the door. "If we leave now, they'll have time to make themselves ready." She held her plan behind sealed lips, since cracks in a wall tended to widen. Cracks about the Days of Seed, about upcoming festivals with more than enough distractions to conceal the movement of a few foundlings and their guardians. Then again, the north was a cruel place. The sudden absence of anything pure would arouse suspicion.

It was their best hope, Anna reasoned.

And hope had a habit of souring in Hazan.

They crossed through a branching courtyard flanking the *kales*, its low walls crowded by hooded growers with beige gloves and trowels.

Konrad led her along a stone path, watching the growers sort seeds and bulbs, tuck roots into patches of fresh, black soil, dig small channels with wooden coverings to ferry water from the nearby canals. For once the air reminded her of Rzolka, where soil was always churning and sprouting and darkening, and water remained after hours of sunlight. It was a rich, raw smell that came every spring and summer, but only existed for a few moments in Hazan.

The Days of Seed.

What should have been rebirth.

"With all intended respect," Konrad began, over the crunching of soil beneath iron spades, "I think the storm may have passed."

Anna frowned. "Meaning?"

"Teodor's likely found his wits in an empty flask," Konrad sighed. "This could be risk without any reward, *panna.*"

"It's riskier to assume that," Anna said. It was a forgone thing, whether she would live or die. Now she focused her mind to things beyond survival and personal importance, working through scenarios of misdirection. She wondered, distantly, if the Nahorans could've helped the foundlings. "When do the Days begin?"

"If I had to guess, the orza's judgment is the only timetable for Malijad. For Hazan, might even be. Cartels everywhere have hands on the scruff of their neck."

That was all it took to remind Anna that, at his core, he was still a soldier. No matter how many smiles he offered or flowers he brought from the orza's garden, he was still sworn to Rzolka above all else. Above *her.*

"Just don't do anything rash." Konrad's words jarred her back to the wash of pungent earth and clay. "You know how a southerner's temper is. White-hot one day, quenched the next."

"Of course," Anna said. Her thoughts flickered back to the Marchblade's words about chaos, about their *sort.* Teodor and the others, southerners warped by a lifetime of war, had devolved beyond tempers. They held spite and cruelty and sadism.

She'd seen their hearts in ash-laden districts.

* * * *

When they slipped through the garden's low doorway and reached the dusty expanse of the main courtyard, the foundling hall's door an iron square in the distance, Anna froze. Her toes curled and rooted her in place; her hands shook within damp sleeves.

White-hot one day, quenched the next.

Their ranks were arrayed in endless columns, a sea of shrouded glares and black wrapping and dangling blades. Ruji jutted up from the gathering, a forest of barren pines, with their spines and pouches supported against ceramic-plated shoulders. Behind the mass of head scarves and crow-like sentries on the distant walls, the trade gates were sealed. Every stretch of the courtyard was swallowed by dark leather boots and silent, anxious killers. The only gap in their formation was a narrow, twisting path leading to the foundling hall.

"Kuzashur," the voices droned in unified river-tongue, rattling the earth below Anna's feet and piercing the air. "You have been summoned at full dark by Orza Dalma and the eminent liberators of Patvor. You will be escorted to the theater for a night of wonder. Garments will be provided. If you decline, slaughter will follow."

Until that moment, Konrad had seemed anything but feeble. Yet his hands, slack to grasp his blade, revealed how many heels he lived beneath. How many complex layers of wickedness and betrayal were woven into the *kales*, and how one man could never sway every heart. His sullen eyes stared at their front row.

"Wait for me," Anna said. She forced herself to walk forward, certain that if she waited for the captain's reaction—indeed, if she heard her own thoughts at all—she would flee. Wicked men had a passion for ritual fear, and Anna felt it under the press of a thousand soldiers, under words that echoed through the distant streets with a phantom's wailing. But fear was preferable to subjugation. Blinking against *har-gunesh* and a thousand dark gazes, hearing only her clipped breaths and the scrape of soft leather on earth, Anna approached the shaded walkway.

With another breath to steady her hands, Anna entered their ranks. It was a familiar world of stark shapes and gloom, of trees rising up through a haze, of oncoming death. The air was caustic, muddled by polishing oils and the urine they used to soak their garments.

They haven't killed you, Anna thought, trying to swallow past a dry mouth as she neared the end of the path. *Therefore it isn't real. Don't fear the unreal.*

Anna was still deep in Bora's proverbs when she reached the doorway. She drummed out three quick knocks, unwilling to turn or focus on the killers staring in her periphery. There was a nauseating stretch of silence before the door's hinges squealed, leaving High-Mother Sharel with luminous heptagons in the doorway.

The northerner smiled at her, and the terror evaporated.

In the main chamber, Anna strode past children learning to sit still and use their quills with practicing ink. She eyed packs of Alakeph and offered them a bowed head, recalling the threat in the courtyard when she noted how vigilantly the Alakeph watched the atrium's doors. They'd spill blood if the Dogwood entered, but there were dozens of invincible fighters for every one among their ranks.

Jalwar's office was stagnant, animated only by the heavy sweep of the Hazani's hands over his podium. Documents sat in neat stacks along the shelves with ribbon binding, just as Anna had left them days before, and a shaft of daylight fell through a wall slat and across Jalwar's arms.

"Jalwar." Anna stood in the doorway, one hand holding the hanging open. Jalwar peered up and caught sight of Anna, but before he could set his quill aside or finish the thought hanging on his open lips, Anna stepped inside. "We need to talk."

"Please, do sit," he said, his relief souring as he gestured toward the stool. "Who brought you here?"

"Nobody." She seated herself, trying to make sense of the missive before Jalwar, which was covered in half-finished sentences and erratic characters. "I came by myself."

"To negotiate?"

"To talk. You and I."

With a shaking hand Jalwar picked up the sheet and tossed it to the floor. "When he came, we should know better."

"There was no way to know." Anna thought of the tracker and his wounded eyes. "And he didn't tell them. He wouldn't."

"You trust him so much?"

"No." Anna glanced away. "I understand him."

"Yet things are known." Hardly any white remained around his eyes, now darkened by bloodshot clouds and veins. "You see the many men they have gathered outside of our walls. What interest do men take in foundlings, Anna? What war do they fight?"

"They wouldn't do it," Anna said, more hopeful than assured. "Did Shem come here?"

"It is said you defy these men," Jalwar whispered, ignoring her question. "I cannot speak to Dalma, nor my cousins within the *kales*. These men are hateful." His gaze refocused. "Surely it was not Dalma who organized this."

"Does it matter who did?"

"It may," Jalwar said. "Not all can be reasoned with."

It was true enough, she supposed. Chilling, but true. "How did this happen, Jalwar?"

The northerner's eyes flickered with curiosity.

"With Dalma," Anna continued, "with the Emirahni. The scrolls said they've controlled a district of Malijad for generations. And now what?"

"I was a fool," Jalwar whispered. "A fool's fool. Such things are over, my friend. Their line was damned before the first bricks of this hall were placed."

"Just explain it," Anna said. "I'm not a child. I need to know what they wanted out of this place. Why they chose Dalma, I mean." Deeper still, she needed to know the approaching designs of wicked men. Of men who were beyond reason, but perhaps seeking conquest untarnished by bloodshed. Perhaps it was all they wanted. After all Anna had seen, her greatest terror wasn't the promise of violence, but that she'd be spared from it. "Is there anything to gain from breaking the same line twice?"

Jalwar seemed wary to speak. Something twisted sat in the approaching words, burning his tongue and forcing him to silence. "They had nothing to do with her line's fall. Long before those men drew breath, the Emirahni were strong."

"I read that."

His stare was sluggish, crawling over the desk as though ignorant of who'd written the crumpled missives and ledgers. "Strong made enemies. Things have a slow way in the north." He reached down, produced a twine-wrapped bottle of arak, and poured out a jigger's worth of the liquid. His hands quivered and spilled clear droplets over faded papers. Dark blots spread beneath his palms. "My family's seven fathers owned great sheds, where they made the drying of spark-salts. In time their vault pits fell empty, and they sold their sheds. But our ledgers still breathed. They had a good hand for words of untruth." Jalwar drank the jigger slowly, his face unaffected, before setting down the glass. "I saw this art in the way of your fingers, too."

To Anna, memories of falsified ledgers seemed so distant now, so absorbed by more severe crimes that they barely existed.

"It's a wasted tale, my friend," Jalwar said at last.

"Tell it." Cycles past, she wouldn't have believed her own demands. But now, after all she'd seen, she feared her wrath, her potential to do harm.

"What is there to tell? The Emirahni had storehouses and salt, and we needed such things. In ink, it was miracle of salt for the Emirahni. Twelve bloodlines had been woven into their name, eight beautiful women and four handsome men, and I was the last of the joining, my bloodline and all of the spark-salts we never held."

Anna weighed the northerner's guilt, already welling up in the flare of his nostrils and the second jigger he poured for himself. Her stomach tightened.

"Every bloodline stole revenge on that day. My blood was not the only ledger of mistruth. Each joining had been another lie. All of the Emirahni salt and lumber and ores, taken, used, carted away. Yes, Anna, yes, we stole it all away. They had only the husk of their *kales*, and Dalma's father, so dishonored and wrathful."

Anna failed to stem her scowl. Before those words, Jalwar had seemed more honest than anybody she'd encountered in Hazan. His purity drained away with the second jigger's swish, tipped back and thudding on the podium in a single sweep. "You ruined her."

"I didn't have the knowing," he shot back. "I was the only innocent of thirteen hearts, Anna. Dalma's father failed to breathe before the ending of the season, and she was left with nothing. Not even enough of salt to make the hiring of Katil Anfel and avenge their plight." He gripped the neck of the arak bottle and rolled its base across the desk in lazy circles, watching the liquid tumble and bead against amber glass. "Malijad law let the others leave. Ruin of bloodline's wealth is reason for dissolving, you see?" He sighed. "I stayed, Anna. I stayed because I knew the pain of being utilized."

"So you brought these men here," Anna said. "You used her even more."

"It was not *me*." His knuckles burned white on the glass. He locked eyes with Anna, beads of sweat tracking down his stubbled cheeks. "I speak only to Halshaf. I placed my heart in this hall, Anna. Not once have I cursed such a path."

Anna's couldn't soften her eyes, nor unclench her jaw. How much of the northerner's truth had been warped by time, reworked and mellowed as the mind did to all guilty memories? "They didn't just *find* this place."

"Loose winds carried the orza's tragedy to the plains," Jalwar said faintly. "One day, they appear at the gate with wagons and cold eyes. Foundlings hide from them and cry. They make the offering of salt and blades to broken bloodline. To woman with nothing but shame. Salt for shelter. Shelter for riches when they make Malijad pay for words of untruth."

Make Malijad pay. It seemed too ironic. Anna wondered if the orza had received what she desired so long ago, gleaning completion from the violence and chaos and rage, or if she'd only become aware of a new trap around her ankles. Perhaps, worst of all, she hadn't noticed a trap at all.

"Then their dealings are over," Anna said.

"Yes," Jalwar agreed, his mouth ajar, eyes roaming. "Over."

Silence dusted the chamber, leaving the word circling in Anna's head until she could no longer bear it. *Over.* "They're not going to let her live, are they?"

"Would *you?*" She wondered if anybody, anybody who'd truly cared for another, could ever lose that stare.

"If I could," Anna whispered, their shared knowledge of a rune's impossibility sinking in with a dull ache. She fixed her gaze on the gloom around Jalwar's desk, only returning to his eyes when the quiet carried on for too long. "We can't save everybody."

But Jalwar's eyes were too distant to accept hard truths, lost in the arak's clear depths. "Do such things matter now?"

Anna breathed in, but her chest refused to grow. She let the dampened sounds of sisters lecturing fill the stillness, trying to make sense of the plan that had fallen apart just minutes ago. "You need to leave," she said. "With the foundlings, I mean. I thought there was another way, but it's all coming down now. Maybe you can still get them out."

Jalwar's eyes drifted to his papers as his thick hands nestled on his lap, leaving the quill abandoned in a blot of ink.

"I've written missives to most of the halls in Hazan and the plains," Anna said, hoping to earn even an ember of Jalwar's warmth. "They've started to stockpile their supplies for new arrivals, and they'll take you in. No matter where you take them, they'll be cared for."

Jalwar pressed a finger into the still-slick ink of a nearby page. "This is our life, Anna."

"Life changes," Anna said. "You know that most of all."

"For how long did you plan these things?" Jalwar asked, his voice strained. "You have known for days?"

"How long did *you* know about their crooked deal?"

"I never deceived her, Anna," Jalwar said. "Your ink bears mistruths."

"You have to go, Jalwar. Take them and leave, however much it costs. This place isn't safe."

"Without blood, without my heart—"

"Just like the foundlings," Anna cut in. Something surged in her chest as the man spoke, and she remembered how much she'd burned when she walked away, when she accepted that her blood and roots were perception. It was rage, and she had no pity to spare.

"Perhaps I could send them away," Jalwar said with a defeated hum, scratching absently at his beard, "but I cannot leave this place. The spirit nests itself."

Nests, in Anna's mind, were built to be burnt. She glared at the northerner, but his attention was elsewhere. "You'd send them off alone?"

"With the Alakeph, Anna. These are strong, brave men, of course. They give all breaths for one young heart."

"They're warriors. Not like you."

"Look outside," Jalwar said. He filled a third jigger with increasingly steady hands. "They need warriors."

"Go with them," Anna pressed. "They need you to guide them."

"And how you say this?" Jalwar asked. "Before your approach, Anna, the hall was of peace. And now—"

"It's not my fault," Anna snapped. She rose from the stool and towered over Jalwar, her teeth grinding. She didn't know if she believed herself. "I don't have time to argue with you, and the foundlings don't have much time at all. Especially not for somebody being stubborn. Bad things will happen if you remain here."

He raised the jigger to his lips. "Certainty. So much certainty."

"Because they'll want to punish me," Anna said. "They'll take away anything I care about."

Jalwar drained his arak, tossed the jigger into a heap of cloth in the office's corner, and began to sift through layers of stained paper. "Ah. Then they have victory."

"They don't. They win if you remain, and they can get to you."

"We live in fear for all of our breaths," Jalwar said softly, "so that you may be defiant. And yet you speak of bringing such men to Dalma, of ruining her—"

"Don't do this to me." Beneath the venom, there was a note of pleading. "I'm only trying to help you out of this mess."

"You have brought more than aid upon our hall." He sighed. "Prophecy is for wary fools and hopeful fools alike, but always fools."

Anna turned away. "Make plans now. When Dalma holds her performance, you can leave with less attention." She made her way to the door hanging, drowning her thoughts in the latticework of amber threading.

"Anna," Jalwar managed as Anna reached the hanging, his lips scrunched against bitter words, "these men brought a dreadful thing when they came to us." Their eyes met, cracking whatever veneer the northerner had managed to construct. He angled his face away from the glow of lamplight, away from Anna's terrible realization, away from everything but humid blackness and liquor fumes. Sweat trailed down his temple, glimmering. He laced bloodless fingers together and forced out a breath. "Go to the infirmary, Anna. The boy's life may depart with *har-gunesh*."

Chapter 27

In the hall's western chamber, sealed behind a wicker door and soothed by Halshaf sisters with rosewater-swollen sponges, those afflicted with pulp-lung came to die.

Anna wandered down its rows of frail bodies and fever sweat and woven herb shawls, a slave to the rotting sunlight filtering through its shutters. To Bora's slender form standing watch over tattered quilts, her stare as pensive as ever.

Sills of soft light fell across the coverings and dark wood of Shem's cot, but the boy's flesh held none of its prior glimmer. Blossoms of fluid, cobalt and crimson, swelled beneath his face. His youth was now a tapestry of angry fists, of swollen club strikes, of crushing boot heels, of chipped bones and milk-white cartilage clusters.

Not even his eyes shone beneath bruised lids.

Tears muddied her vision and ran in thin, hot lines down her cheeks, and she realized that she couldn't help him, couldn't put him back together, couldn't take back the words she'd spoken in anger.

I did this to you.

"Take what you can store in a pack," Bora said. Amber eyes flicked up at her. "There's only the end for you here."

"And out there?" Anna thrust a finger at the shutters.

The words passed over Bora like a gentle wind. "Such things are not certain. But here, the end is certain, as is suffering. Look past your heart and be intelligent. Use the mind I've granted you."

"I did," she whispered. "But you left me."

Bora cocked her head to one side. "I watched over you and heard their whispers. You must leave."

Anna glared at the northerner. It was impossible to restrain the thoughts that clamored for attention, that had swelled ever since Bora began her war on emotions. "Leave?" she whispered. "Your faith puts others above the self, Bora. You never cared for anybody but yourself."

Somehow, Anna expected to break Bora's mask. It was a draining thing, and she waited for the words to shatter the woman's illusion of calmness and reveal a semblance of humanity beneath, complete with its fear and pettiness.

Bora only blinked. "I could flee without you, child. I could slip into shadows so deep that the light never reaches them." She surveyed Anna. "I choose to save you, and those who you may save. Ready yourself, child."

Anna saw herself assembling tunics and flasks and linen-wrapped loafs of dark breads, traversing the rooftops with her destination unwritten, the entirety of the world open and unbound by prophecy. She saw Shem lying in his bed until a merciful Dogwood soldier brought an ax down upon his skull, snuffing out his inner light. She saw Jalwar's orphans being flayed, scalped, bled, and the gentle old man's corpse abandoned amid Malijad's burning ruins. She saw the orza's mutilated body hanging from rafters.

Anna tightened her lips. "I can't go."

"Think of your marks," Bora replied. "Think of how they may be used. Pain alters belief, child."

Anna imagined the scourges and needles and rusted blades flow upon her flesh, certain that she *would* feel pain. She would endure it. "My beliefs won't." Anna stared down at Shem. "Can you take him with you?"

"No."

"You have to!"

"His injuries are severe. Too severe to cross the heights, or to run. If you wish, I'll make his end quick. Huuri are constructed well, but I have no trouble locating the life vessels."

"No," Anna snapped. "Not yet. I'll do it myself, when the time comes." Tears bit at her eyes, but she found focus in Bora's amber stare. "When the performance begins tonight, Jalwar's going to leave with the foundlings. Make him."

"He's a stubborn man," Bora said. "And there are forces that work beyond your sight, child. Some secrets are beyond the reach of your master, and beyond the orza herself. They're wolves that haunt my dreams."

Anna drew a shaky breath. "The Nahorans."

"You've seen them," Bora said with narrowed eyes.

"It was real." Anna stared at the quilts covering Shem. "They offered me safety. Could they have given it to me, Bora? All of those things they promised?"

"Yes."

Anna let out a shaking breath, unable to meet the northerner's eyes. She envisioned everything that could've been, all of the blood unspilled. "Those without gifts will always pay your price," Bora continued. "Here, you may be destroyed by their rage. There, you would be cherished." Her eyes fell to Shem. "Those born to normalcy would see no difference."

"But you chose sides," Anna reminded her. "You left their fabric on the bodies."

"Plans must be fluid," Bora replied.

Anna thought back to how the Nahorans had oscillated between killing and capturing her, to how they'd exhausted every possible method of reaching her. To the bird's last words in her chambers, haunted by the inevitable. *Destroy.*

A hideous plan emerged from Anna's memories, obliterating every other thought. "Bora, were you working with them?"

The northerner drew a slow breath. "Not me," she said. "Konrad."

By now, there were hardly any lines drawn between enemies and allies, traitors or friends, foreigners or natives. Even so, it was Nahora, the nation for which Rzolka could never muster sympathy. It was a land of conquest, and meddling, and—

And beautiful Orsas, which had lulled Anna out of her terror.

"You didn't tell me?" Anna whispered.

"He cares for you," Bora said. "He gave you a necklace, didn't he?"

Anna raised her hand to the small lump above her chest, where the jewelry rested under layers of fabric. "Why?"

"It's a tracking stone, child. His own key will change hues as you move further from him. Such devices are among their simplest tricks."

The pieces converged with an inevitable crash, and Anna remembered the way Konrad had looked upon her, making her feel wanted like nobody else and making her dream of his stare, of sharing a life that she'd never have with him. She realized he'd manipulated his reports, ignoring her trips to the foundling hall until it created rage. She thought of the flowers he'd given her and long walks taken through the streets, where he'd smiled at her and taken away her fears of wicked men in the world. He was a lovely, charming man, and there was nothing in his heart for Anna.

Just as she slept with visions of Rzolka, he slept with dreams of Nahora. *Liar.*

"I need to get ready for the performance," she said finally. She thought to tear the necklace away, but its weight was too welcome. "I'd like to be alone for some time."

With that, the northerner turned and made her way toward the balcony, her white robes trailing her in a flurry.

"Child."

Anna glanced sidelong to see Bora standing in the full light of the glass panes, radiant and statuesque. "The end may come for one of us before our steps cross again," Bora said. "If you meet your end, my memories of these days will pass with fondness. They were most illuminating." She looked toward the hall, strangely unsure. "And if I meet my end, then forget my name. Never look back to the jaws that claimed me." Something delicate came over her, a smile, on anybody else's lips. "Carry only the mind you cultivated."

Anna watched as the northerner strode away, her shadow shrinking and disappearing among the endless cots. And when Anna was alone, her mind a wash of celestial patterns and forsaken gods, she knelt beside Shem's bed and prayed and cried.

Near dusk, an Alakeph captain tapped his heels in the doorway. "A bath has been arranged."

Purging herself of the broken boy's image, if only to stay sane, Anna dried her swollen eyes and followed the Alakeph captain to the bathing chamber: a space wrought from black, reflective rock that reminded Anna of quenched steel.

Her actions were perfunctory, limbs moving as though contorted by a puppet tinkerer, coarse hands dragging soap and tepid water and rose petals over herself.

He's dying.

She focused on the Dogwood-issued garments folded on the nearby table, the tainted Nahoran necklace bundled between her cloak and shirt. It was too much. She gazed into churning bathwater, where ripples met the marble basin's edges and—

A pink-red strand swirled under the surface.

She'd always known it would happen, but some things seemed too monumental—too intrusive, perhaps—to occur in the foreseeable future. Childish as it was, she longed for her mother. She longed for the festival that should've accompanied the blood.

They'll call you panna, her mother whispered.

Knots crawled up and down Anna's throat. She rested both hands on the marble basin, wondering if she could fade from existence if she was quiet enough. If Bora would materialize from the shadows, sensing that her refusal wasn't absolute, and show her the lone thread that unraveled a tapestry of fear.

Anna dried herself with bleached cloth, blotting between her legs with a linen towel, and pulled on her new clothes: a flowing beige tunic with opal beads along the sleeves, a dark satin skirt, and long white stockings. When full darkness fell and she returned to the chamber, lighting Shem's lamp to see his frailty in orange hues, Anna drew her blade and held it over the boy's tender neck.

There was no feeling in the act.

When it was done, Anna stared at the bloody mess on Shem's pillows. She tried to make sense of the splotches and small scraps of flesh, no longer aware of what lay in the bed beside her.

"Anna?" The Huuri opened his eyes, their light shining like lanterns in the deep forest. He smiled and slapped his hands against his chest, where the bones were crooked but forged with fresh angles, their cracks and fragments and splinters pressed into unbreakable threads. His rune pulsed above and below the bruising, its own star in a nebula of murky, blooming scar tissue. "You save me. You have given the gift to me."

Anna dropped the blade.

Whatever he was, he could never be a boy again.

Chapter 28

She wandered among the living with a corpse at her side. Every so often she gazed at the Huuri and lost herself to the radiance of his eyes or his toothy, crooked smile. Her hands still bore the weight of the short blade, and her fingers brushed and dragged against one another, tacky with blood that she'd already scourged with soap. Alakeph and foundlings had crowded the doorway, murmuring with awe, but Anna hardly discerned their voices; she'd only heard echoes of Shem's laughter and worship:

Blessed Anna, my life is yours.

She recalled Shem dressing himself with strong, healed arms, flexing his fingers, grinning as he stared into every mirror and prodded at his face and rune. She recalled him wrapping a neck scarf once, twice, three times around the mark, trying to block out any remnants of its light despite his obsession. She tried to imagine what Bora would say to her selfishness, to the ecstasy and beauty of dying beside somebody who cared for her. Somebody who didn't deserve her fate.

They left the hall and approached the spires of the *kales* in silence, the courtyard lit by braziers and deserted aside from innumerable sentries along the walls. Only Konrad had been left waiting at the door, an escort that offered no safety and even less comfort.

The escorting captain's surprise at Shem's appearance was enough to absolve him of guilt for the attack, but little else. Even his compliments on Anna's white dress and silk hair wrap felt empty.

Even from the higher towers, Anna heard the low rumble of the masses, the staccato drumming and low tones of the instrument sections. The night carried the ceremonial trappings of an execution. When they drew closer to the theater, Shem's hands, scarred and warm, wrapped around her own. Anna met the boy's bright eyes sidelong, but couldn't smile.

Attendees hurried past in silk-adorned clumps, crowding ribbon-strewn corridors to form a crowd before the double doors and their Dogwood guards. One by one, each patron was identified, patted down for blades, and ushered into the theater chamber, all to the shrieking of the orchestra's opening movement.

Each time the doors opened to allow entry, harp strings resonated in Anna's chest, and drumming pounded into her bones.

"*Oz'asin*," a captain called.

Konrad skirted to one side of the gathering, sweeping his arm to clear a narrow path for Anna and Shem. When his eyes met Anna's, they were so genuine that it hurt.

Anna moved through the gap slowly, aware of the gazes falling upon her. Her grip tightened on Shem's hand, and the sensation dragged her back to dead forests, dead dawns, places she feared even more than here. At the end of the crowd, Anna emerged into lamplight.

The Dogwood stared at her like a sow that had survived its bleeding.

A shriveled-skin captain in their unit stepped forward and smiled at Anna. His rune took the shame out of his yellowed teeth and the broken-bone twist of his nose. "Enjoy the performance, dearest *panna*." His voice was too gruff to be softened by a Lojka accent. "They've worked so hard to keep the tale authentic."

The tale? Then the Dogwood attendants pulled the twin doors open and drowned the corridor in noise.

Konrad stepped past Anna and rested a hand on her back, guiding her forward despite the tension in her legs. Every step was unsure, fighting to break away from the orchestra and its horn blasts, its low strings that resembled mourning in a dead tongue. She wandered into shadow and haunting melodies, the faces of the endless crowd barely visible in candlelight against the glow of countless sigils. All along the walkways, braziers burned in deep pits and basins. She craned her neck to see the farthest rows of balconies and seating circles, but it was impossible, for the rows of patrons and their sigils receded into darkness on all sides. Below her, growing closer and more ominous as they descended a walkway, was the curved stage.

Lamplight painted the dais in warm yellow light. Performers with flowing, hooded robes plucked their instruments on the shadowed terraces behind the main stage. Frail voices rose occasionally above the music, always peaking with a broken crescendo.

This place was worse than death.

Konrad led them nearer to the stage, and as Shem squeezed Anna's hand she sensed her pulse running rampant along her wrists. She became cognizant of the dryness in her mouth, the shifting vision that made everything more threatening. Focusing on the present would be Bora's only advice, but she wanted to be anywhere else.

There is nowhere else, she thought. *Nowhere is safe.*

And so she walked, tucking her gaze to the walkway until they reached a deserted front row, waiting before her like the teeth of a bear-trap.

"Are these reserved for us?" Anna whispered.

"As a matter of fact, the orza chose them," said Konrad, his voice mellow.

Anna wondered if somebody so kind and wise could hold cruelty in his heart. *Anybody could,* she suspected. As Anna slipped past Konrad and sank down into one of the oak seats, she became certain of it: Anybody could be reached. Everybody was wicked in their own way.

Shem sat beside Anna and poked at her shoulder. Light flickered through his face and fed the spark in his eyes, granting warmth to his smile. "All is fine."

Anna smiled back. Just as Bora had always pressed, she lived in the moment, in the flash of comfort from his presence. "I know." She looked at the Nahoran agent to her right, who offered the same grin he'd worn for days with pretense.

In their own way.

Anna stared at the glowing stage.

The music faded, and curtains blocked out the lamplight.

Darkness consumed the theater.

Trickles of footsteps and blurred shadows moved across the stage, followed by the hissing of something being pushed across stone. Feet tapped in ever-diminishing rhythms, the shadows slinking away and blending back into nothingness. Silence. Then dark orange lamplight flooded down from the upper tiers and sides of the stage, revealing a scene lifted from storytellers' archives.

Desiccated trees cluttered the stage, their branches long and gnarled and cracked. Smoke curled from urns placed behind prop trees and formed a carpet of swirling fog. The orange light sifted through the fog and carved notches of shadow into the forest, bathing the scene in an eerie glow. Behind the main stage was a painted mural of gray woods at sunrise. In typical Hazani style, the sky was cloudless and streaked with stars.

Yet something was familiar.

Whether at a bonfire, within a festival hall, or in one of Malchym's alleyways, Anna had seen it all before.

She could always sense the characters, the tragedy, the end of theatrical tales.

String music and gentle drumming rose from the quietness. As the lanterns panned back and forth, guided by the hands of black-robed performers along the stage, shadows appeared in Anna's periphery.

She gazed at a raised booth to her left, nearly level to her and more secluded than any other section in the theater. Even at her distance, through the slight haze of pipe smoke that dribbled over their railing, she knew the occupants. She recognized them in the baggy, lopsided corners of the tracker's mask; the wide brim of Teodor's hat; the chewing jowls of Josip; the ornate, pin-fastened peaks of the orza's hair; the scars of the bitter scribe, which emerged as Teodor's pipe flared with harsh light.

Anna averted her eyes to the stage, trying desperately to fight the urge to vomit. Her throat constricted as the harps grew louder and sharper.

They're watching. To them, the performance was her terror. It was the trembling in her fingers and her mockery of elegance. They fed on it with hidden smiles and shadowed eyes.

Anna straightened her back and focused on the stage, losing herself in the curls of the smoke and echoes of the drums. She set her heart to a slow rhythm as her thoughts fell away, sinking to the riverbed.

A pair of running figures burst onto the stage, their hands linked and bodies wreathed in fog. The lead actor was pulling their partner, who nearly fell as they crossed the stage and approached the audience. Mere steps from the stage's edge, their worn tunics and outlandish faces became clearer. Overstated eyes and mouths were painted onto wooden masks, the features distorted and horribly warped to convey a singular reaction: fear.

One of the actors, the smaller of the two, had a feminine face with sapphire paint to form tears around her eyes. Knots of straw-colored burlap formed an impression of light hair. The other, a wide man with bent legs, had a rosy-colored and boyish face lined with dark freckles.

Disbelief set in so quickly that Anna, however foolishly, waited to awake from her dream.

Her mind lost its focus in the masks and their eternal shock.

In their lantern-washed panic.

In her reflection.

Singers joined in with the strings, their wailing an imitation of dark birds that haunted Rzolka's forests. Then came the flutes, piping and thunderous, to match the exaggerated breaths of the actors.

"He approaches!" cried Anna's actor, the Hazani-accented river-tongue only deepening the madness.

Anna's mind rushed to purge any trace of—

A third actor crept out from behind the trees. A fresh burlap mask covered his features, and in his hands he held a rope that snaked down into the fog, twisting.

The soglav lumbered past him, brushing the stone floor with knuckles and chipped claws. This beast was trained, its movements assured, the collar studded with rounded iron nubs and its muzzle absent. Dark, groomed fur hid its body, and it gazed upon the actors as little more than the scraps of meat it had been fed during its training cycles. And as it moved toward them, lithe and strong and far too tame to frighten anyone besides Anna, the strings shrieked.

The tracker raised his arms and called out, his Hazani tongue thickening the words: "At last, the traitor is found." He took a step forward. "The traitor, and the innocent wretch who shares her blood. How might she be made pure?"

"I'll not stand beside you," Anna's actor said. "I wish ruin upon your people."

"Then you must be destroyed," the hooded actor said, leveling a finger toward them.

"No!" the woman cried. "I cling to my life, and I fear my wicked end. Take this pitiful life in my place, and I will serve your cause!" She shoved Julek's actor to the ground, her hands bent into claws and back bent with a primal arch.

Anna's heart pounded faster, faster, her throat swelling.

"A bloody deal," the hooded actor said, "but one born of your vile nature."

He released the soglav's rope, and the beast sprang to action. It thundered past a pair of prop trees, all four limbs and snout raking the stage, before hovering over the fallen actor's body. Over the man who was not Julek, who struggled to stand and back away from the creature, who made no sounds but scrambled so fiercely that his panic couldn't have been born from stagecraft.

Before the man staggered two paces away, the soglav dove forward and slashed wildly at him. Cloth tore open and flapped in the lamplight. Bloody streaks opened beneath the soglav's blurs of motion, ripping and shredding and flailing, its claws and forearms staining darker as it pressed on. And still the audience was silent, the music growing louder, the horns and strings blaring, the smoke boiling up in waves and bleeding over the stage's edge, the actor dying in silence as his arms fell away and flaps of skin dangled.

The soglav's head jerked forward, its jaws snapping open and sealing around the mask before the man could defend himself. A crack, then a crunch, and the mask fell to the stage in splinters. The actor's remaining eye, surrounded by puncture marks, swept over the front row. Through his daze Jalwar managed to glance at Anna. Intricate black stitches sealed his mouth, the lips and surrounding flesh bulging through the sutures in purple lumps. Yet the sutures didn't stir as blood drained from his wounds and he fell backward, his eye losing focus and arms going slack and sigils vanishing, the music roaring on behind him.

My consequence.

Konrad's voice was a muffled drone in her ear; his hands were numb upon her shoulders. Shem looked to her, lost in confusion that neither Anna nor the world could remedy.

He should have left.

Everything rushed over Anna like gale winds. She heard only her heartbeat and the strings, high and grating and bloodcurdling in the madness. Then she heard them. She heard Teodor's rumbling laughter, Josip's vicious giggling, Nacek's fits of chuckles. Turning in her seat and brushing away Konrad's arm, she saw them puffing on pipes and thrusting fingers out at her, laughing and laughing.

Reality's levee broke.

Anna stood and wandered toward their booth, lamplight blinding her with its orange glare. At first her feet dragged along the floor, unwilling to function, but soon they were pushing her forth, sprinting away from Konrad's muted pleas and into darkness, letting her thoughts congeal into a single impulse, forcing her body toward rage, toward a drumming heartbeat and tense shoulders and aching fists, toward violence she'd only glimpsed in dreams and forgotten forests.

And then she was upon them, scrambling up and over the low barrier that separated their silhouettes from hatred.

One last puff of Teodor's pipe lit his bulging eyes and brows twisted in confusion. It etched out Nacek's hanging jaw. It revealed Josip's cheek-cutting smile, his head cocked to one side like a listening hound.

Shadows hung over the others, irrelevant to Anna.

She vaulted toward the fading glow at the tip of Nacek's pipe, where flakes of black and gray *nerkoya* leaves broke away and fluttered into darkness. Where the man's hat brim was flopping backward, a word of the grymjek escaping his lips in a bitter roar, his—

Anna's knees crashed into the man's chest. She curled the fingers of an open hand down toward the palm, angling the ridge at the base of her hand outward as she'd learned in the archive tomes. In the darkness and rage, she remembered the Gosuri fighting technique and imagined it within her hand, how she'd seen the diagrams drawn in dark brown ink. The palm's ridge had to be driven into the narrow band between the nostrils and the upper lip.

Her hand made contact. It crashed into the target region and sent vibrations up her arm, rattling her to the elbow. The flesh split beneath her strike, and she felt the front teeth twisting and cracking at their roots, the lower cartilage of his nose shattering. She savored the present and the dragging sensation of skin and bone and spittle against her palm.

Teodor's pipe spun end over end toward the floor, the still-lit wad of *nerkoya* flaring.

Anna swung again with her left fist. Bone gave way beneath her punch, the impact rolling her hand upward and into the soft orb of Teodor's eye. Without regard for the pain she bent her fingers at the midpoint and dug her knucklebones into the socket.

He screamed, and the eyeball pressed back until it surrendered and broke beneath Anna's touch. Warm fluid gushed over Anna's hand.

"*Korpa!*" Teodor screeched. His voice devolved as he screamed and kicked, those precious seconds woven into an eternity by the torment.

For Anna, the eternity was one of vengeance.

A hand seized her hair and jerked her to the side. Her scalp burned and she cried out, tumbling off Teodor and colliding with a set of knees, her arms wildly thrashing and striking at the flesh above her, no longer thinking but desperate to inflict—

"Skin her!" a man screamed in flatspeak, the expression cutting through the pain and the darkness.

Through the aching pulses in her head and feet kicking at her, catching her in the wrists and shins and ribs with deadened sensations of impact, she heard the crowd calling out and clamoring. She sensed panic in the vibrations of the floor, in the way the herds shifted and stampeded down the aisles, in—

A piercing whistle rang out among the madness.

For an instant the feet ceased to kick, and Anna pulled herself along the floor on elbows and knees, the hand upon her hair still tethering her to the booth's crawlspace. She rolled onto her back, pried her eyes open to a cluster of silhouettes, and drove her heel into the closest shape.

Nacek roared, tearing his hands away from her hair to clutch at his face. He stumbled back and nearly collapsed into Teodor's seat, but was stopped by another shadow behind him; the swift, looming shape descended upon him, one hand wrapping across his face and hooking beneath his jaw, the other clutching the base of his neck, jerking upward with enough force to slacken the body. Nacek slumped to the floor in a heap.

There was no time to identify her savior.

Anna whipped her head back, granting her an upside-down glimpse of the orza and the scribe bolting out of their seats and fleeing the aisle. She pushed herself up in turn, the pain and breathlessness striking her before she regained her footing, and pulled herself over the railing.

The fall was short but damning. Remnants of air were crushed by the impact, flooding out of her in a stream of muted breath and wheezing. Agony tore through her ribs, her throbbing knees, her scalp.

Screams filled the theater, and through blurry eyes she saw the crowds dispersing and trampling one another, knocking over lanterns or braziers holding white coals. Dogwood soldiers sprinted down the pathways with ruji in hand, but none turned toward Anna.

Wincing, Anna forced herself to one knee and stared out at the chaos. Onstage was Jalwar's body, the actors fleeing for the curtains, and the soglav, which now stalked timidly between the prop trees as the room overwhelmed its senses. Ahead was Shem, running with an awkward gait and eyes wide with panic. To her right was the booth, where something—no, somebody—drove a wedged blade through Josip's cheek.

Bora.

Anna saw it in the sheen of her head, the elegant butchery of her stabbing and thrusting with the dagger. In a flash of wayward lamplight she recognized the cold stare, the tight incision of her lips, the effortless motion that buried the blade's hilt in the man's face and left his tongue lolling.

Darkened shapes moved along the opposite side of the theater, and Anna realized why the Dogwood paid her no mind: Dozens of incoming soldiers, their markings and armor decidedly Nahoran, had taken up cover behind the seats and booth rails. A woman with auburn hair called out orders in a flowing tongue, thrusting her finger in Anna's general direction. Above their firing line, spindly legs raced over the walls and ceiling and rafters, dashing through the shadows and passing through candlelight along the curtains.

Tan scales of chitin and forged iron protected the azibahli flesh, and the creatures put all six of their limbs to use as they swept over the pillars and vaulted arches, burrowing back into darkness so rapidly that the Dogwood soldiers claimed their own cover and pointed their ruji helplessly at the ceiling.

"Anna!" Shem cried. He slid down at her side, patting at her arms as though curing her with touch alone. Youth bled through in his panic. "Anna, you are hurt?"

Just over Shem's shoulder Anna spotted Konrad escorting the orza and her scribe away from the madness. He was holding Dalma close, as though preparing to yell a desperate order, when he plunged his blade into the woman's neck. Before the orza could wrap her hands around the gushing wound, Konrad brushed past her and set upon another group of Dogwood men in cover.

The orza's scribe gave a knowing nod to Konrad before fleeing.

"They killed him," Anna mouthed. She couldn't draw air into her lungs. Couldn't care for the deaths she glimpsed across the theater. She met Shem's eyes and thought only of the glistening punctures in Jalwar's head, of Teodor's laughter and the rattle of breaking bones. "They did it."

Shem clutched Anna's arms. "You need safety. We leave this place."

Ruji broke the air with bitter hisses. Fabric tore apart and fluttered in the air; stonework sparked and disappeared into whirls of dust; flesh turned to pink mist and gristle. Fleeing patrons collapsed or vanished in mid-step, their dismembered lower halves illuminated by the spreading flames from toppled braziers and broken lamps. Plumes of smoke and grit erupted from the walls as the two lines exchanged fire, leaving dimples and pits and gouges across timber and stone alike. Azibahli wove through the storm of iron fragments and picked their way toward the Dogwood lines, unfazed.

"Anna?" Shem whispered.

Just before the first azibahli dropped, a Dogwood soldier produced a canister from his vest and spun toward Konrad. He lobbed the device and shrank behind cover. Within a second, the canister tumbled end over end, arcing toward Konrad's face, glinting in the fire.

It exploded.

The air broke with a clap, and the world pulsed beneath Anna, and a black cloud shifted where Konrad once stood. Hearing trickled back to Anna through the ringing, but she heard only Shem's voice, muffled and lost beneath water, and the dribbling of debris as it rained down around her.

Konrad surged out of the smog with half his face intact. Blood vessels and nerve clusters and muscle fibers wormed over his skull, repairing him in tandem with the remnants of his exposed chest and heart. Bits of his armor had been sheared away or pockmarked beyond repair. He stumbled midway through his run, but as he neared the cluster of Dogwood men, he increased his pace and drew a blade from the sheath on his lower back. Three ruji payloads to his chest and hands couldn't halt him.

Another explosion ripped through the far side of the theater, where the doors had been torn from their hinges and failed to stem a tide of fresh troops. This time a crowd of patrons was framed in the flash.

Azibahli dove from the rafters and thrashed through the crowds, letting out hideous screeches as they impaled Dogwood troops with forelimbs and cast them aside. Growing flames were reflected across their chitin, in the beady clusters of their eyes.

"*Shara,*" a voice commanded.

Anna turned, dimly aware of the presence at her back.

Bora's white cloak was speckled with blood. Her wrists and hands were slick, glimmering in the firelight. "With me, child."

The booth section was still swarming with chaos. Dogwood soldiers raced down the aisles, barking wasted orders at one another as they tried to stir Nacek's body, Josip's slumping corpse, the—

The tracker was gone.

Teodor was gone.

Pushing through Shem's grip, Anna forced herself to her feet and stared out at the swelling smoke and flames. The fire was a ragged field within the center of the theater, throwing wicked shapes upon the walls and burning white-hot in its core. It ascended the curtains and raced along timber balconies, throwing harsh light on the underside of the smog and billowing clouds above. Everything smelled of scorched metal and charred hair and superheated stone. She saw bodies toppling from the upper tiers, azibahli shearing the limbs from Dogwood men, squads of troops pouring in from every entrance.

Bora's hand clamped onto the back of Anna's neck.

Focus.

Anna locked eyes with Shem and extended her hand to the boy, who still knelt by her feet in a daze. Once his fingers meshed with hers, she wrenched him upright and moved away from the flames and the raining debris. With each *pop* and lightless explosion her hearing dampened once more, leaving her in stunned silence. Her lungs were heavy, pooling with acrid smoke and vapors of burnt flesh.

Bora moved ahead of them both, carving a path through the shadowed side aisle and kicking corpses aside.

Anna glanced back once, and out of the gathering smoke and licking flames and dying men she saw Konrad walking forth, his cuirass blackened and smoldering but still affixed. A skirt of mail hung down to his knees, its lower edge fraught with fused metal.

"He's coming," Anna said.

Bora was quick to spin on her heels and draw her blade, adopting a fighter's stance with bent arms. She circled round Anna and Shem to form a barrier against Konrad, who was slowly picking his way over empty rows of seating and lit braziers.

Most unsettling was the youth that lingered in his face, in his eyes, in his haggard smile. He approached with his blade at his side and shoulders low, ignorant of the blaze and heat welling at his back.

Far behind him, the foreign troops had lost their momentum and now crouched among the rows, exchanging bouts of ruji fire with the Dogwood men between blasts. Most of the azibahli had been cut down or crippled, leaving them writhing as ghoulish, twitching silhouettes within the flames. Patrons continued to scream and shove and collapse under one another. Fire crept along vaulted ceilings and rained burning beams and banners over the crowd. Embers swirled down in fat, darkening motes, fireflies at dusk.

Bora glanced over her shoulder, mouthing her words with stark clarity: "*Go*, child."

Anna lingered, ignoring the tug of Shem's hand and the looming shadow of Konrad. Even as she managed two steps down the aisle, she stared at Bora, wondering how long she could last in a fight against the captain. How long the mind and body could hold out against her ever-bright marks.

Cracking echoed through the theater like thunder. The crooked, glowing spine of a support beam plummeted through the darkness and crashed through the upper balconies, spraying plumes of cinder and ash into the air.

The flames blinded Anna, and as she raised her hand to her eyes and peered through slatted fingers, she saw Konrad close the distance with a running leap and crash into Bora.

They fell to the floor in a tangled mass, rolling and slashing wildly, short blades glinting and sweeping and sparking against stone.

Shem pulled for Anna's attention, and although she followed him blindly, there was no hope of looking away from the struggle. "Shem," Anna said, digging her heels into the floor.

The Huuri's hands eased on hers. He circled to face her. "Come, come!"

Anna dragged him back toward the melee. Toward the flames that consumed her vision, the heat that pressed on her face and hands and threatened to bake her flesh into leather. She dashed up the aisle until she saw the shadows clashing.

Bora was kicking with her back driven into the floor, her blade knocked aside and shimmering. Konrad took blow after blow to his face and wrists, cumbersomely blocking her strikes and edging closer with blade in hand.

"Konrad!" Anna tried to scream, her voice cracking.

Konrad tore his attention from the combat and stared at her. His arms dropped low once again, and his eyes grew quiet and inviting and still, and his lips parted in a gentle gap that might've held soothing words.

Bora's shin crashed into his temple, sent him sprawling to the floor. She threw herself down, rolled, grasped her blade in a tight tumble, shoved off her back leg, diving and thrusting, silent.

Konrad sat up, his head swaying in a concussed daze. But it was too late. Bora's outstretched arm reached him within the space of a breath. She gripped the weapon with her knuckles skyward, the chipped point hammering down and through the graceful curve of Konrad's forehead, a dull clap emanating as the hilt crushed into his skull and pinned him to the timber seating box.

And without words, without a spare glance, without remorse in her eyes, Bora stood and walked toward Anna. She didn't glance at the myriad cuts and welts along her arms and chest, still raw and dribbling bright blood.

"Come, child," Bora managed as she passed Anna. Her only indication of pain was that she fought to show none.

Anna felt for her necklace, tore the links open, and dropped the gemstone on the carpeting.

They descended into the darkness and the hidden egresses Bora seemed to know from prescience alone, but Anna couldn't resist seeing the theater in its death throes. With one glimpse of the flames, she saw Konrad screaming, straining to free himself from the snare; she saw countless bodies smoldering and blackening among the embers; she saw dreams and purpose that was never meant to last.

Luxury and hope and victory, all flaking away.

Some sliver of the thinking mind had always known that it was impermanent. That eventually it would all fail, and she'd be left with nothing. That love and safety and joy would always be passing riders in the night.

But like Julek's freckled face, hopeless dreams kept her alive when the world both despised her and craved her. They were necessary lies in a world of hard truths.

And so she followed Bora and Shem, thinking only of the curtains and stone corridors and partitioned stairwells she passed, begging her feeling mind to hold out for just one day longer. She would break and weep and surrender when the time was right.

But until then, she would survive.

Chapter 29

Eventually the bodies lining the corridors became more than lumps of mangled flesh and silk. Some were children with hands cradled inside oversized sleeves, their eyes glossy and pristine like an artisan's marbles. Others were men with curly, playful hair, or women with hands too delicate to rest upon tiles. They left streaks of blood where they'd tried to crawl, often ending in broken, splotchy nests with interwoven fingers and small, fragile bodies embraced within larger ones. Ribbons and torn scarves and salt pouches formed trails down gilded staircases.

They weren't all wicked. Anna stared at each body as she jogged past, biting hard into her lips to force away the newfound aches of bruises and battered bones.

But pain wasn't enough to ignore perception, nor to fasten her attention on the white blur of Bora's cloak and Shem's frequent backward glances.

They'd been moving for ten minutes, fifteen, perhaps twenty. Time blurred together when the sifting sand rustles of the ruji and the subsonic clap of explosives became constant. Earlier, as they'd woven through passages that bisected the main corridors and pipe dens, Anna had been forced to shoulder her way through the crowds and link hands to avoid being caught in the press. But the crowd had gradually thinned and vanished between Bora's shortcuts. The screeching and gurgled cries always seemed to be elsewhere, far enough to be invisible but near enough to make out final words and gushing liquid.

It crossed her mind that the unknown fighters may not have been Nahoran at all, and were simply a rival cartel; vengeance was a natural motive. But reality defied her hopes.

My consequence.

Ahead, Bora's cloak fell still, remarkably bright in the dimness of the open-sky atrium. Shem stopped in turn.

Usually the rounded space was lit with the pale glow of Dogwood lanterns or shafts of sunlight descending through the open ceiling, but on that evening, clouded starlight guided Anna's steps. Tiers of *nerkoya* dens, steam chambers, and sweet shops once made it more vibrant than the lower market. But that was in a different time. Now there were only shadows and rigid bodies upon tiles.

"Why are we stopping?" Anna asked.

The northerner tilted her head lower, bathing it in moonlight from the soaring gateway ahead. "No matter what you behold when we're outside, child," Bora said, her words resonating in the emptiness, "I expect you to keep moving."

Anna strained to look beyond Bora, to glean some hint as to what awaited them. She saw only ripples of heat and palls of smoke, and beyond it, the menacing and uncertain peaks of Malijad. She heard, faintly, the hissing of ruji and the sobs of dying men, although the noises were so commonplace throughout the *kales* that they hardly alarmed her. "Bora, what's outside?"

"Death," Bora said. She moved forward, her cloak flowing over fragments of setstone and cooled droplets of iron shavings. "Your eyes may be hungry, but don't indulge them. They often wish to gorge."

Anna followed with reservation, taking hold of Shem's wrist and dragging him along like a trinket.

"Anna," Shem said quietly, far more collected than she'd anticipated, "I protect you."

"I know," Anna whispered.

"Through all," he continued, glowing as the moonlight seeped into his skin and bloomed along thick bones. "I protect you through all. Through men with bad hearts like him."

Men like him, Anna pondered. Men she'd trusted and even, in some way, had grown fond of. But such recollection was painful, prodding at the edges of a fresh incision.

They passed through a gateway large enough to accommodate wagons and hundreds of visitors, now so quiet that it reverberated with the thunder of glass shards cracking under Anna's soles. She emerged onto the terrace devoid of flower-peddlers or children running with wind-swept ribbons, and below them, saw the massive sprawl of the courtyard without its giants and incoming merchants and craftsmen huddled within their shacks.

Then she saw fire.

Pools of dark, bubbling liquid covered the courtyard, their surfaces churning with low but bone-white flames. Most of the burning puddles were closer to Anna, gathered along the stretch of the courtyard near the *kales* and the stairwells, but several of the tanning huts were doused in the substance and illuminated the field like wicker effigies.

Anna rushed to the crenellations lining the terrace's wall. She blocked out the lower half of her vision with a flat hand, focusing on the void beyond the inferno. She saw Alakeph streaming in and out of the foundling hall with jars in hand, passing them to waiting brethren who were quick to hurl their payloads toward the *kales* in wild arcs. As the pots impacted and shattered, their contents ignited with a red-purple flash and splashed over packed earth. She saw not only the darting white robes, but the static bodies of fallen Alakeph littering the courtyard, some torn apart or burning within the fires. Many of the warriors crouched behind a wall of sandbags near the hall, their—

Not sandbags, Anna realized. *Bodies.*

Dozens of fallen Alakeph had been woven into the wall, their limp arms draped over crooked legs and white-clad torsos riddled with ruji pellets. Even in death, they offered flesh to the brethren who fought on behind them.

Bouts of river-tongue from below lured Anna's attention. The crystalline grit of Dogwood armor flashed out of the shadows, and entire squads of the attackers pushed across the courtyard, edging back from fresh flames and creeping along the lanes of crafting huts. They were streaming from the market's gates below, sprinting out into the blackness with ruji and blades and thrown explosives.

"Child," Bora snapped. Her shadow edged to Anna's periphery, and she hovered there, waiting. "If we linger, we will lose our breaths. Follow my heels."

"Where are the foundlings?" Anna asked.

Bora turned and ran wordlessly along the terrace's crenellations, her gaze fixed ahead and right, half-bathed in the light of flames. She stole a sharp right down onto the stairwell, disappearing into the masonry, and Anna followed.

"What's wrong, Anna?" Shem asked as they descended the steps.

"Nothing," Anna wheezed, even as the heat of the flames wicked up the narrow stairwell. "Shem, stay by me. Can you promise that?"

"Anything for you," Shem whispered.

Anna staggered out onto the courtyard, nearly at Bora's heels. The flames were relentless, whirling into waves and shedding black smoke, their heat glassing the sand near their base and warming her skin despite the distance. She made out the bulky silhouettes of several dozen Dogwood men against the fire, all struggling to aim their ruji and edge through the burning wall. Some of the braver men—marked captains, no doubt—leapt through the inferno, only to scream and retreat when the agony became too great. Anna watched their blackened, smoking, peeling forms crash to the dirt as she followed Bora to a row of untouched tanning huts.

"*Tem!*" one of the Dogwood shouted, just before Anna reached the safety of the tanner's row.

It was a command she'd heard in years past, when hunters leveled their bows and slings on fleeing stags.

It sounded like a dozen candles being extinguished. Then came the dull *whump* of leather walls being raked, shredded, battered, punctured in the darkness, the screaming of sand as it quenched the iron shrapnel. She ducked lower, plunging into the shade and coolness of the tent wall, listening to the metal whistle past her ears and face.

Something grazed her legs. Pain bolted up her shins and down her ankles, and she pitched forward, slamming into the packed earth with both arms outstretched. Again she was breathless, trembling, clawing her fingers over clay and sand and pulling herself toward Bora's fleeting white fabric.

"Come," Shem said, his boots scraping up behind her. He seized tufts of her dress in his hands and lifted her under the shoulder, pulling her upright despite the deadened nerves along her feet. "We go together. We go slowly."

And Anna pushed herself closer to the Huuri, leaning on his weight and dragging her feet. *One more step*, she thought incessantly. Soon the volleys of ruji fire became constant, and she could feel Shem shifting beside her, angling his body to protect her from the iron. Muffled cracks and the popping of heated flesh were still audible through Shem's cloak.

He never cried out.

The volleys fell still as Anna limped toward the end of the alley, her feet catching on the ground and slowing them. Each time she stumbled, Shem was quick to hoist her back up.

"They'll be coming," she managed with a deep breath, wincing. "Behind us, Shem. They'll be following this way."

"We go," he replied, his pace unfailing. His words were soft ripples in the darkness, soothing her. "We go."

Anna pushed her head up, vaguely discerning Bora's cloak at the mouth of the alley. Other white shapes moved around her like phantoms. "Almost there, Shem."

River-tongue echoed down the alley at her back. Flatspeak leapt at her from ahead. The hurried thumping of boots on soil and the rustle of blades being drawn and readied suddenly flooded the air, and the ground shook with charging.

"I have her." Bora's voice broke through the clamor, and her shadow stalked out of darkness.

Lean, hard arms supported Anna on her left side, and as her own weight fell away, so did the pulsing beneath her knees. Through the pain she considered that they should leave her where she stood. There was nothing dishonorable in girls who went to the Grove at the hands of the enemy, regardless of whether they'd died in a shadowed storeroom or the edges of their keep's field with a dagger in hand. There was only torment in pushing ahead. Bodies had been burned for her; thousands of sigils had been snuffed out in her name; homes and markets had been reduced to ash with her guidance.

Release me, she wanted to say. *Set me down and walk onward.*

But the agony tethered her to the present. Each fleck of skin that burned and bled reminded her that she lived. She held a gift that had been denied to those around her, behind her, in morning bogs and forgotten corners of the city.

And so she walked on.

As she limped from the tanner's row and felt the press of flames at her back once more, the pain swelled and rushed over her. Blackness curled at the fringes of her vision, numbing her lower body and tingling up her spine. Then the darkness rushed in once more, blurring her stretched shadow and the countless Alakeph swarming round.

* * * *

"Look here," Bora commanded. The voice was crisp, pulling her from sleep, and Anna opened her eyes to the northerner's hard stare. The woman knelt to Anna's left. "Focus on me, child."

Despite her efforts, Anna couldn't hold the gaze. Too much had changed; the space was dark, lit by flickering candles, and her legs were pointed out before her like disembodied stumps. Stone cushioned the back of her head, and to her left stood the doorway leading into the courtyard, its frame washed in a hot orange glow. Alakeph men hurried in and out in quick succession, some carrying satchels of ammunition and others bearing wounded men across their backs. Whimpering bled from the deeper recesses of the hall, only to be met by shushing and proverbs in flatspeak.

Still mouths bleed no water.

"Shem," Anna breathed. She tried to turn, but even that induced a feeling of torn guts. She lay back, unbidden tears of pain flowing. "Where is Shem?"

"Be still," Bora said. "He's fetching root pulp for the wound."

The wound.

Anna stole a glance at her shins, now exposed by the hasty removal of her gown's lower pleat. Tattered, bloodied fabric sat to her side in a tangle. All along her legs were patches of charred muscle and dead skin, although their cauterized surface relieved some of her fear. There was no oozing from the burnt gouging, which had cut directly across the legs and grazed bones. A wave of terror came over her as she thought of the armless and legless men of Bylka, forced to walk on crutches after the war.

"I need them," Anna whispered. "I need my legs."

Bora nodded. "They'll remain. The root is for your pain, child." She looked toward the main chamber of the hall. "This is no time to separate flesh."

Anna shuddered. "I can't lose them later, Bora."

"The decision has not arrived," Bora said, "so it does not exist." A series of screams filled the air, followed by another wave of Alakeph dashing outside. "Nothing is worth consideration if we die on this night, child."

Anna kept envisioning the broken men. "Did you see what they did to him?"

Bora squinted.

"Jalwar," Anna said, closing her eyes to the sounds of ruji hissing across the courtyard. "I just watched it happen, you know. They did this."

"They did," Bora said.

A ring of Alakeph congregated near the door to the courtyard, some pressing their backs to the frame and loading ruji. Others milled about with blades against their shoulders or scraping the earth, reserving precious energy. None of them spoke, but they shared a collective patience, and the same dour stare at the melee. The frontline was edging toward them, growing bolder and more fraught with explosions, but they remained.

"Anna," a low and northern voice said. An Alakeph warrior wandered out from behind a column and gave a short bow, wasting no time after his introduction. His robes were a pure white shade, unsullied by the dust and blood. "We stand ready."

Bora eyed the man.

"Ready?" Anna asked. "I don't understand."

"Jalwar, most esteemed and martyred among the hall, gave his last words with clarity." The warrior's eyes were resolute, free of the stain of dusk petals or *nerkoya*. "Follow the words of the prophesied one."

Prophesied. "How did he tell you?"

"Standing before me," the Alakeph replied. "Before he departed to negotiate for you."

Anna's throat tightened. "What?"

"Your commands are our haste," the Alakeph said.

Looking to Bora, Anna found that she was suddenly alone. The Alakeph looked only to her. "Stay with the foundlings," Anna said. "For now, just keep them protected."

The Alakeph inclined his head. "*Uzgun.*" He returned to the shadows with as much expediency as he'd arrived.

Anna pinched her eyes shut. Memories of her morning and the prior night bled together in waves, as vivid in her imagination as they'd been in reality. "He negotiated for me."

Bora hummed. "He did."

"You said you'd be with him. With Jalwar, Bora. You told me that."

"And what did you tell me of the boy?"

"You wanted to bleed him like an animal," Anna said, wrenching her eyes open. "I trusted my mind."

"Suffering is the same for all that breathe," Bora said.

"But I saved him," Anna shot back, unable to push herself up or return an arch to her back. "He isn't suffering anymore. He's alive."

"Eternity holds more suffering than your mind fathoms."

Anna choked back her reply, holding onto the same bitter words she'd once spoken in the markets and the privacy of a ship's quarters. Death truly was an escape; Shem's suffering would extend until stars burnt out and oceans ran dry. "I'm sorry," she whispered.

"Regret fixes nothing." Bora glanced up as Shem hurried out from the main chamber and offered her a bowl. She took it, frowned, and scooped up a lump of pulp with two fingers. "This is all they could offer?"

"More," Shem said. "They use almost all for warriors, but know Anna is here. They give all they have." He smiled, but his brow warped every time he looked helplessly upon Anna's legs. "We fix."

"I know," Anna said softly. She locked her jaws and tensed her forearms as Bora spread pulp over the gashes. Nerve clusters flared, but she kept her legs still, waiting till Bora had applied the bowl's contents before releasing her breath. The numbness was swift and all-consuming; her feet and knees felt linked only by air.

"Shem, we need to raise her," Bora said. She lifted her head toward the doorway as another explosion went off, this one peppering the frame and front stoop with a rain of sparks. "It will not resist the pain for long, child."

Anna bit back a groan as Shem wormed his arm behind her back, gently lifting her to her feet with the wall as support. All feeling had evaporated from her legs, even as she leaned over to test her weight on the damaged ligaments. She looked past Shem and into the darkness of the main chamber, where soft voices formed a chanting chorus. "How many are there?"

Shem blinked at her. "Many foundlings."

"They shouldn't be here," Anna turned to Bora, her hand still braced on the wall. There was no refuge in the northerner's eyes. "They were supposed to leave. Jal—"

"Yes, Jalwar," Bora finished. "They knew everything, child. There are no trails for doomed men."

"They're *children*," Anna said through clenched teeth.

Bora studied the courtyard beyond the atrium, curiously meditative in the midst of rushing and screaming and wheezing around her. "Gates are sealed. The kators are locked. Their men fill every street. What would you wish of me?"

"To try," Anna whispered.

"Do you know how many breaths were lost to bring you to this moment, child?"

Anna bowed her head as the wall rattled, struck by another explosion along its foundation. "Try, or leave without me."

"Without Anna?" Shem tightened his grip beneath her arm. "Not possible."

Bora let the silence hang. "Think, child."

"You don't need me," Anna said.

"I need your light," Bora's glare softened in the flash of an explosion beyond the doors. "Preserve your light. Make your breaths worthwhile."

Anna glanced at Shem, at the collection of wounded Alakeph scattered along the far wall. Bloodstains and smears of soil covered their white robes, but the longer she stared at them and their exposed eyes, the more she saw the reverence in them. "We could mark them."

"They won't accept it," Bora said. "They would shed their breaths before beliefs."

"The foundlings, then."

"You can't solve everything with your cuts, child." It was more of a rebuke than Anna expected. "When the Alakeph fail, they'll be taken. *Think.* Direct my course."

It was strange to hear from Bora's lips, but Anna wasted no time in parsing the situation and working Bora into her plan. In the proper position, she would be worth ten men. "How did you plan to get me out?"

"I didn't," Bora said.

Anna narrowed her eyes. "I don't understand."

"This course is yours, child."

"You led me here," Anna said, her voice rising. "Which way were we going to take?"

The northerner was intent on the three men limping into the darkness. "Tell me your plan."

With the violent pulse of another explosion, Anna centered herself in the chaos. She saw Malijad's streets as a web arcing away from the *kales*, envisioning each junction and towering structure and walkway she'd observed on her walk with Konrad. She recalled the veins of the mule paths, the arteries where worshipers marched in ragged lines, the covered hoods of the water canals, where—

Water.

"Bora," Anna said. "Where are the canals?"

"Near." Her gaze was questioning, thick with doubt. "Speak, child."

"I need a blade." Anna searched the shadows around her legs, thinking. "Shem, could I ask something of you?"

The Huuri nodded excitedly, far removed from the blasts that rained chips of plaster and smoking earth across the floor. "Anything."

"I'd like to give you another mark," she said, trying her hardest to visualize the symbol that she'd once seen in meditation. Its curves and delicate twists were just out of reach, but the mere remembrance of its form was enough to conjure the details. *Water* blossomed in her mind, fracturing the haze of pain and fatigue. "I need something to mark you, Shem."

"Child," Bora said gravely.

That lone word was enough to rekindle every nightmare of the blinded man. Of light pouring from white eyes, of agonizing screams confined in stone walls, of unending torture and the black mask that hid her crime. "I won't force you."

"You give honor," Shem said. "I find a blade."

The boy moved to turn away, but Anna grabbed hold of his collar and fixed him. "You should know what I'll do, Shem."

He gave her a hopeful glance.

"It's water," Anna explained, doing her best to fight for the boy's attention and gravity despite the joy in his stare. "I don't know what it might do. I don't know if you'll be able to control it." Her resolve fell away with every word. "You can't trust me, Shem."

"I trust." He leveled both hands on her arms, drawing her into his grin and the bleeding glow of his rune. His sigils swept beneath the skin in peaceful waves. "This is enough, Anna. Trust."

Bora's wary stance bit into Anna's peripheral vision, but she resisted the urge to meet the woman's eyes. "Find a blade. Be quick, if you can."

"Ask High-Mother Sharel for my pack, Shem," Bora added.

With a reassuring squeeze against Anna's upper arms and a nod to Bora, Shem whirled away and sprinted into the shadows.

Anna gazed into the darkness. "Say it."

"What words should I speak, child?" Bora's voice was soft, but no more compassionate than ever before. "Your reality is not mine. Our truths are not the same."

"So go," Anna whispered. She lowered her eyes to the floor, then glanced up cautiously, edging toward the hard lines of Bora's face.

"I'll remain until the end," Bora said. "Our paths are stitched together by thorns, child."

Somewhere within her voice was trust, or loyalty, or any number of heart-rending things that Bora could never express with sweet and empty words. Things that broke Anna because she believed them but didn't deserve them.

"I'm glad," Anna said.

Two Alakeph made their way into the hall, a third man hoisted between them with his innards spilling from his belly. They walked in eerie silence, as though oblivious to the wet, slippery coils dragging along the floor.

"They are brave," Bora said, "but they can't win, child. What's your course?"

"The canals." Anna worked out their path in a slow trickle of analysis. "If we can lead them to the canals near the gardens, we'll be able to make it out of the district." She took a deep breath to repel the throbbing across her skin. "I can see the marking, Bora, but I don't know if it's enough." Rather, she didn't know if it was *too much*. If it could maim him.

"If we move with haste, we can reach them," Bora said.

"Was that your plan, too?"

"No."

Anna glared. "You told me you knew a way out, Bora."

"A cornered hound will do anything to run free."

A gust of anger built in Anna, but it was quick to dissipate against the pop of explosions and barks of flatspeak. For once she understood the cold detachment in Bora's eyes, the measured cruelty that she used to twist minds and hearts alike. Piece by piece, the shadowed edges of *water* sharpened in Anna's mind, leaving behind a perfect memory where there had only been glimmers of recollection.

What Anna knew as the fear of death fractured.

When she locked eyes with Bora she saw an equal in her impassionate stare. There was nothing to fear about wicked men, or the tracker, or the shrapnel from lobbed bombs in the darkness. There was only fear of failing those around her.

She heard Bora's words like the singsong call of birds in spring, echoing. *Life escapes us all. In time, it will outrun the fastest among us.*

"Gather the Alakeph," Anna said. She pushed away from the wall with numbed legs. "Half should hold a line, and you should take the other half down one of the alleyways. Whichever path will get us to the gardens soonest." Anna glanced outside, noting the ragged band of warriors and their ever-mounting barricade of flesh. "We can start sending the foundlings in your direction once it's safe enough, and from there—"

"Mark him well, child," Bora spoke out.

"Do you know what it will do?"

Shadows gathered beneath Bora's brow. "Our outcomes are simple. They shouldn't be feared."

Anna watched the Alakeph loading, aiming, firing in their ranks. "What are they?"

"Finding refuge among the sands," Bora said, "or bleeding to our ends." A rare grin distorted her lips, tilting one corner up like a bent candle wick. "You've meditated upon the end before, child. If we lose our breaths beneath the stars, you'll know if my ways held any truth at all. Perhaps they were all sweet untruths to busy you."

Old ligaments shifted along Anna's jaw. It began as an impulse rather than a reaction, and it wasn't until she focused on the northerner's words that she realized she'd heard something akin to a joke. She smiled.

They were still standing in silence, sharing feelings long thought abandoned and thoughts of the end, when Shem returned with a scalpel.

Chapter 30

"Just stay still," Anna told Shem, the scalpel's polished edge suspended a hair's width from his rune and the pulsing veins beneath the skin. There was no way to block out the gathering press of hall sisters and Alakeph on the far side of the atrium; their collective intentness was far more unnerving than the fighting outside. "It might hurt."

"I trust," Shem said. The vibrant edge of his smile did little to ease Anna's fears.

She glanced at the courtyard and its wash of fire-lit soil, unable to make out Bora's cloak from those around her, before pressing the blade to Shem's flesh. *Guide me,* she prayed to whatever force might help. To the hayat swirling somewhere in her veins, waiting for a taste of liberation before it surged forth.

The first cut was effortless, slipping into the skin and bypassing so many crisscrossed veins that it was nearly bloodless. Until she made the incision, it hadn't occurred to her if the marks could even be applied. With each gentle curve of the blade's path, she expected the skin to heal itself and reject the metal, molding back together as it did on marked ones.

But the hayat knew its own.

Deep in her bones, she felt its ways and fears and boundaries. Its sweet scent begged her hand to press the blade deeper, to leave traces so indelible that the hayat could burn indefinitely.

Little by little she branched away from his rune with the fresh cuts, trailing the hayat's template and working in quick strokes. She'd garnered so much practice in meditation and actual cutting that the mystique had evaporated. Now she made her cuts like the woodmen of Bylka, each tree felled and corded and hauled away without ceremony.

Water.

She saw its unusual curves and impossible geometry coming together as her hand neared the end of its work. Panicked thoughts of the outcome rose in her mind, but the hayat twisted them away and lured her, pulling her fingers to arc the blade in faster, certain strokes. Blood coated her hands in a sticky film, but it felt as natural as the hayat's beckoning. As natural as Shem's heartbeat, hastening within his neck.

The lines curved together and joined in a pointed angle.

Hayat seeped through the folds in a wispy string.

With the horrid sound of ripping linen came the regeneration, pinching the split skin folds together and wicking the blood back into its crevices. Flesh crawled over the gaps and the hayat burned bright and beautiful behind the markings, swelling and filling.

Candlelight refracted through droplets along Shem's hands.

Anna stared down at the boy's palms before she moved the blade away, watching the dots bleed through his skin and pool together into rivulets along the creases of his hands and the joints of his fingers, dribbling down and pattering against the stone floor in a rhythm that was inexplicably deafening.

Gasps and mutterings of prayer broke out behind Shem. Trickling built to splashing, then rose to a constant stream.

Anna met Shem's eyes and lost herself in their brightness, hoping that the boy could focus himself in the same fashion. She sensed mounting panic in his stare, which was warranted, given the rate of the water's shedding. Her hands were gentle but firm upon the sides of his neck, reading every nervous twitch along his jaw.

"Look at me." Anna ignored the water pooling around her feet, soaking through to the torn flesh of her heels. She ignored the boy's eyes darting wildly beneath him, his arms shaking from the torrents, his hayat-infused droplets raining down in a puddle and spattering her ankles. Firelight danced into the atrium, painting the ceiling as water flooded toward the door and over the steps. "Shem, look only at me."

Light grew and diminished within his stare as they locked eyes. His brow worked in sporadic folds.

It's not fear, Anna realized. *It's pain.*

His hands trembled and the water fell away from him in rapid bursts, ceasing when he managed to hold Anna's gaze. Behind him the crowds were stricken by the spectacle, kneeling or chanting in forgotten tongues as the water dribbled onto the soil outside. Explosions tore through the night. Everything worked against his focus, against his caution and concentration.

It all faded when their eyes met.

"That's it," she said. The cascading water slowed and weakened around her ankles. "It's only us, Shem. Just look at me. Listen to me."

"I listen." Beads of crystalline sweat working down his face. "I listen, Anna."

"You can control it," she said in a soothing tone. It was the hayat that assured her, of course. There was no guarantee of control for the boy and his fresh mark. "Keep looking at me."

Little by little the light returned to his stare. Tremors worked their way through his arms and hands, but the flow of water soon fell away to dripping, then an occasional drop, and finally silence. *Water* pulsed with latent energy before burning with a steady glow.

"Good," Anna whispered. "How do you feel?"

Shem looked down at his hands, turning them over and flexing his fingers to make sense of their power. He swept his feet through the pool of water around him, entirely bemused. "Wet."

Anna smiled and cupped her hands along the curve of his jaw, just as her mother had done in warmer days. And just like her mother, Anna leaned forward and kissed the boy's forehead. His skin was smooth and burning hot.

"Do I save us?" he asked.

Anna nodded. "You will."

I hope.

Most of the hall sisters, wounded Alakeph, and even foundlings had wandered into the atrium by then. They formed a loose crescent around the scene, some with both knees to the floor and others touching the pool of water with hesitant fingers. Prayers were a low droning behind the clamor of violence.

Anna thought of the stories they'd been told about the hayajara, about the fated one to enter their hall and cure their sickness. Surely they'd never been able to prophesize a hayajara with her powers. With her marks, for that matter.

She wondered who they prayed to.

"Child." Bora appeared in the doorway with a ruj in hand, her face and torso awash in blood. She looked down at the water descending the steps. "We should depart."

"Is it clear?" Anna asked, nearly overpowered by another cluster of explosions.

"For an instant," Bora said. She nodded toward something just behind Anna. "Take it with you, child." As Anna turned and noticed the burlap sack leaning against the wall, she heard Bora calling out commands in flatspeak: "Form with me! Forward striking!"

The Alakeph were the first to move, rising on broken and bleeding limbs without even a groan. They wandered toward the foundlings at the back of the hall and spoke to them in hushed tones, some picking up the sickest or frailest children and cradling them in their arms. Next came the hall sisters, demure and whispering assurances, who rushed to gather the foundlings.

"What I do?" Shem asked. He gazed at Anna as she unfolded the pack's flap and rifled through its contents.

"I'll tell you when we need your help, Shem." She dug through the top layer of wrapped bread and fresh linen to find the heaviest, and most concealed, element of the pack. Moving aside a leather flask, she uncovered the shortened barrel and wrapped iron pouches of a ruj. "Stay close to me." Anna jarred the ruj free and set the pack down by her ankles. She fished out the iron shavings, unscrewed the bulb at the rear of the weapon, filled it with a handful of the coarse powder, then threaded the bulb back onto the ruj as the hall sisters gathered their ranks of foundlings near the doors. At one time, she'd worried about wringing the necks of pigeons and quails. Staring down at the ruj, she realized she no longer considered the Dogwood living. It would be simple to take a life. "Are you ready?"

Shem examined the ruj warily. "I keep you safe, Anna."

"Keep yourself safe," Anna said. "Come on."

Most of the fires were dying down on the far side of the courtyard, plunging the area around the foundling hall into near-blackness. Splotches of white along the ground indicated where Alakeph had fallen, and those maintaining the frontline worked with grim efficiency to stack their comrades into a wall two corpses wide and fifteen in length, its height overshadowing Anna's shoulders.

Yet beyond the barricade she saw the extent of the Alakeph ferocity. Bodies of the Dogwood carpeted the courtyard, some of them scorched beyond recognition, and others pinned to the soil with spears and daggers, screaming into the night for mercy. Craters and gouges from their bombs were everywhere, leaving mangled limbs and flesh strewn about. Flames peeled back into their shrinking cores as they consumed the last of their fuel, turning the earth from shades of ochre to ashen black.

Both the looming *kales* and the stars were blotted out by a veil of smoke.

This is war, Anna told herself. She searched for glory among the devastation to no avail.

"This way," Bora called from Anna's far left, waiting at the entrance of an alley with six Alakeph. Even with her white cloak, she was nearly invisible due to the soot and crimson smears. "*Shar'oz!*" she yelled to the column of hall sisters and foundlings. Even her command wasn't enough to distract the children from the carnage laid before them.

Anna proceeded into the alley behind Bora and the warriors, struggling to walk on legs that felt more fluid than flesh. Every so often her steps faltered, and Shem was quick to grasp her arm and keep her upright.

"Bora," Anna said. Her throat burned from the pall of smog and scorched oil. "Are they gone now?"

"Who, child?"

Anna frowned. "The Dogwood."

"They retreated to reform," Bora said. "That was their scouting group. The Alakeph say that they used mirror signals to call for the main force."

"How many is it?"

"I don't know. It's best not to think of such things, child. Whether they bring a hundred or a thousand, it is immutable."

"I'd like to know our chances," Anna said. "We can't have more than fifty Alakeph."

"Forty-one."

Anna's heart sank as she glanced over her shoulder, staring at the procession of foundlings and hall sisters in the shadows of the alleyway. She listened to their murmurs and quiet sobs. "We'll never make it, Bora."

"Do you see the enemy?"

Anna's eyes snapped back to the black ahead, but there was only the distant glow of Malijad's neighboring districts and the pastel light of a brazier. "No."

"Then they do not exist," Bora said. "It's a fool's habit to fear the unreal."

Each shadow held the promise of a Dogwood soldier or a Nahoran agent with a curved blade, but Anna held her tongue. Real or unreal, Bora was right: Their fate was sealed.

It comforted her.

They exited the lane and crept through a series of smaller courtyards before reaching the garden complex, which seemed wild and dangerous in the shadows of night. Everything about the *kales*—indeed, about Hazan—was flat and plain and dead. Yet the saplings and rows of plants growing beneath the blackened skies were alive, swaying in the breeze and glistening with remnants of moisture from their dusk watering. The Alakeph moved gracefully through the rows, although they maintained formation and swiveled their ruji to detect the slightest omen of violence.

"This may be the time to share your vision, child," Bora said as they walked behind the Alakeph, scanning the hedges and canvas coverings.

Anna tried to condense the idea mentally, only to find that she'd never truly considered it herself. More than anything, it was a spark from the hayat, no more realized or sensible than a lifelike dream. "The water flows downward to reach the *kales*," Anna said. "We'll follow the canals moving upward. Well, a bit upward."

"If they follow us, they'll be at a lower level." Anna struggled to relay the plan as it came to her. "We'll be higher than them."

"Elevation is advantageous," Bora said. "Is that all?"

Water. "We can drown them," she said in a low voice.

Bora cast a dark look at Anna. "You assume Shem is ready."

"Ready?" Shem asked.

"He is," Anna said, hardly sparing a glance at the Huuri. "You said it yourself. When we're cornered, he'll fight."

"Anything for Anna." Shem grinned. "What you require?"

"Water, Shem," Anna said. "If they follow, I need your hands to work. To make water."

The Huuri turned his hands over for inspection, offering a satisfied smile as he did so. "Simple. Much water?"

"As much as you can," Anna said. "I need you to drown them, or push them away."

"Drown?" Shem was silent for a moment. "You want to kill."

Anna nodded. "I want you to kill all of them."

A deeper silence fell over the three of them, and as they wandered through the gardens with smoke above and blossoming plants to their sides, Anna felt a brief peace. It was a fragile peace that wouldn't survive even the cracking of a branch in a forest clearing, but it was peace all the same.

Shem gazed skyward and smiled. "You ask, and I do."

"Welcome to your new life, child," Bora said. It was simple enough to pass over Shem as idle chatter, but it conjured up the life Anna had feared since childhood.

A set of vine-choked arches crowded the rear of the complex, and beyond it was an enclosed square framed with high stone walls. The advance unit of Alakeph stood ready in the space, huddled around a well's circular stump and a metal grate over its top. A thick sheet of linen was draped over the square as shade, and only the light of a rusted lantern illuminated the space.

Anna watched the Alakeph work in tandem to free the metal grate from its hinges using hammers, timing each strike of metal against metal to the footsteps of the foundlings and hall sisters at their back. Their entire procession was crowding into the archways, murmuring and straining to peer at the odd noises ahead.

Hall sisters hushed the children, but it did little to dampen their voices. The largest continent of Alakeph warriors guarded the column's rear, trailing at a comfortable distance to ensure that they hadn't been followed. Or, in the most cynical sense, to ensure that stray ruji blasts would take their lives rather than the foundlings'.

Metal squealed and cracked.

Anna edged closer to the canal's rounded entrance as the Alakeph lifted the metal grate and set it aside. The lantern light was meager at best, but it framed the haggard lines of the warriors' faces and the bright red stains across their robes. She stared down into the covered portion of the canal, hoping that she'd be able to make their pain worthwhile. Or, at the very least, say she'd tried.

Aside from a shallow pool at the bottom of the canal, where water tended to accumulate between flooding cycles, the basin was empty. It was a short drop to the bottom, and walking only a few paces up the canal's path led to the exposed section of the track, where the canvas covering allowed some of the city's ambient lights to seep into the crevice. Utilizing shadows would be essential, Anna reasoned, which removed the possibility of bringing lanterns with them. And it required some degree of stealth.

She thought of the children and their sobbing, wondering how far they could go before the Dogwood realized their ploy.

"A few of them should take the foundlings and the sisters," Anna said, leaning back from the opening and meeting Bora's eyes. "Tell them not to make any noise, and to stay close to one another. They can move slowly, if it helps."

Bora gave an obedient tilt of the head and approached the crowd of foundlings, delivering the commands in a soft whisper.

"When we go, Anna?" Shem asked.

"At the very end," Anna said. "When everybody else has gone."

"Why?"

"Because." Anna watched Bora speaking to the group, wondering how Bora had looked or behaved when she was just a child. When she couldn't control her terror, and expected others to provide answers and hush her tears. "If they follow us, you'll need to be at the back so you can stop them. And I don't want to leave you alone."

"I have mark," Shem said. "Nothing harms me."

"Even so," Anna said, unwilling to imagine his torture and the depths of Dogwood hatred. "Just stay by me, Shem. We'll go together."

She pulled Shem aside as the first Alakeph clambered over the side of the stone ring and dropped into the basin with a solid clap. Without intending it, she imagined each of the Alakeph as children during their descent, wondering if they'd been so nimble and stoic before they'd learned to keep quiet during pain. She wondered what led them to this life, and if any of them would change anything now.

She found no answers.

When all of the Alakeph in the advance group had reached the bottom, those remaining above picked up the foundlings and lowered them into the darkness. The hall sisters went with them, offering gentle shushes if the children cried out or whimpered.

Anna took hold of Shem's waiting hand, slick with sweat or perhaps the last traces of the hayat's water, and squeezed.

"What's wrong?" he asked.

"Nothing," Anna lied with a weak smile. "Nothing at all, Shem."

When all the foundlings and hall sisters had been lowered into the basin, the pattering of furtive steps echoed from below. Anna examined the faces of the Alakeph, of Bora, of Shem, enduring the silence while they waited for the procession to forge ahead.

"*Shara,*" Bora said at last. She tucked her blade into her waistband and swung herself down into the basin. There was no preamble, and none of the dread that festered in Anna's stomach.

When it was Anna's turn to descend, assisted by the callused hands of the Alakeph and listening to her breaths reverberating in the stone chamber, she closed her eyes. She begged reality to reverse its course and grant her the freedom she deserved.

But that was unreal, and she pushed it away. Reality was only the darkness below her, the trembling muscles in the forearms of the Alakeph, and Bora's discolored cloak.

It was screams of river-tongue in the gardens.

Chapter 31

The canal was darkness and rot and footsteps louder than hammers upon anvils. Above were the parallel tracks of the canal's lip and the hooded canvas, and in their empty space, the metal grating that choked out everything but the harshest starlight in the eastern skies.

Anna refused to cry out, even as the foundlings ahead screamed in flatspeak. Pain tore through her legs as the pulp's effects lessened, and each step, uphill and against the slick paste of filth and mold underfoot, threatened to send her crashing to her knees. Everything around her was swift and formless in the shadows, and the boots clapped and crushed past her, the hands of the Alakeph occasionally working to support her and hasten her steps.

Violence roared behind her. The Dogwood had lobbed their bombs down into the basin and torn apart the last Alakeph to descend, and two more had been killed trying to drag his body from the mire.

Bora's words flooded Anna's ears as she ran:

Faster.

Hasten yourself, child.

Shara, shara.

Shem's flesh was the guiding light at Anna's side, refracting starlight and scattered braziers aboveground as he ran. Yet he pulled ahead as Anna faltered, her lungs burning and tendons seizing along the backs of her legs. She gripped the ruj tighter, resolute to keep herself armed and ready if she ever fell. Not that her odds of survival would change.

Again she was in the woods at sunrise, and Julek's weight pressed down upon her back.

Hold on, little bear.

She'd failed then, and she'd fail now.

"Anna," Shem managed, raising his voice above the striking of boot soles against wet stone. "I kill?"

"Wait," Anna said, the words burning her throat. "Soon."

Hayat spoke to her with its will, with its design for murder. She saw their numbers swelling behind them in the canal, overflowing like vermin before the waters reached them. Before air drained from their lungs and bones shattered in the darkness.

Footsteps pounded from the recesses of the basin, and the screeches grew. Hatred flared up the canal. "*Sukra!*"

Laughter met the screams of the foundlings.

Ruji whistled from behind, followed by the shearing of raw flesh and sparks in the shadows. Bodies collapsed with hollow thuds as the Alakeph at Anna's back absorbed the fire. A flatspeak command for *churning winds* raced down the tunnel, and in the same breath, the Alakeph and their joint footsteps slowed, fell away, drummed in the opposite direction.

Anna spun and watched their white mass descending, accelerating, crashing into the mass of Dogwood men with the force a horseman's charge. Bora seized Anna's shoulder and pulled her along, forcing her legs to work through the agony. Her ears were full of the ringing from the blasts, the shrill clanging of metal on metal, the screeches of men's final moments.

"Don't squander their breaths, child," Bora said. She tugged harder on Anna's arm. "There are only the steps beyond you."

Pain came in harsh waves, distorting Anna's vision. Each step was a tremor up her legs and into her hips, amplifying with the jumble of luminous sigils hovering before her in the darkness, a reminder of every life she wouldn't be able to save.

Two more concussive blasts broke out. Sound vanished.

"Now," Anna said, seizing Shem's wrist and repeating the word despite the silence of her own voice.

Shem obeyed.

The Huuri braced himself against the canal's wall, both hands held downward. His eyes lit up the stone around him as his hands bled water, the droplets surging through his skin and trickling to join the stream beneath his boots. They congealed into unbroken rivulets, then into spouting that drained through his fingers, then into a rush that frothed with white and ran down the canal in a dark, snaking river.

It wasn't enough.

"More, Shem," Anna called. She saw the dark forms of the Dogwood crawling over the dead, their sigils streaking in wild arcs. Water splashed up and against her legs, but it was still too mild, too thin to slow their advance. "Shem!"

The Huuri's fingers widened with a snapping motion, and water roared forth. Geysers pulsed free and tore down the canal, riding up its walls and curling over on themselves in grayish peaks, bubbling and roiling and breaking in waves.

Yet the Dogwood pushed through the torrent.

"Don't think, Shem!" Anna barked in his ear. "Kill them."

That was all he needed.

His hands snapped upward, and at once the water was a wall rather than a push, exploding from his palms and overtaking the entirety of the darkness in a single swell. Through the shifting wall, some of the Dogwood seemed to endure. Yet as the torrent bellowed and crashed to the basin below, leaving behind a slick afterglow on the walls, it became clear that the canal's track was purged of life. There was only a hollow dripping, and the bobbing of broken corpses in the pool far beneath them.

There was only death.

Shem slumped down against the wall. His hands fell away to a trickle once more. Nothing about his body seemed taxed, save his eyes. He gazed at the devastation with a quiet sense of pride, gripping his kneecaps with still-dribbling palms and squinting to discern the full scene before him. Light grew in his eyes as he watched, taking in the slow rise and swirl of the bodies, the gurgling water draining into overflow pipes, the—

"Shem?" Anna laid a hand on his shoulder and set the ruj down. She shuddered as she glanced down at the crowded basin, its bobbing ceramic, its mass of crippled flesh. "Shem, we need to go."

"Did you see?" Shem asked. He grinned up at her.

"I did." Anna forced her own smile, then took hold of his wrist. "Come with me."

As Anna pulled up on Shem's wrist and whirled to face the canal's ascent, she brushed against Bora. The northerner stared down at her with dark eyes, shoulders low and resigned. Behind her the masses of foundlings, hall sisters, and Alakeph alike had fallen silent. They stood and stared at the black waters, at the bodies, at the marked boy sitting and marveling at his work.

"Shem," Anna whispered, pulling harder. "Let's go."

Bora said nothing as Anna picked up the ruj and pulled Shem past her. For the first time in several cycles, she couldn't envision an inkling of what the northerner might say. She wasn't sure she wanted Bora's counsel either.

They trudged up the canal quietly, threading through the press of foundlings, hall sisters, and remaining Alakeph like animals in a traveler's menagerie. Anna fastened her eyes to the dark strip of runoff below and walked with a mindless gait. Her sensitive hearing restored, she detected every instrument being played in the streets above, every midnight call to prayer for the astral worshipers, every creak of every wagon wheel that passed through Malijad.

We're free, Anna told herself, if only to fight the nausea in her guts. *We can go anywhere.*

Yet as they moved in a wordless procession, accompanied only by boots on tile and their raw breaths and coughing, Anna wasn't sure if there was a place for her on the surface.

For her, or for her creation.

Chapter 32

Before Julek had even been born, a rider in Radzym's service had arrived in Bylka and demanded the arrest of a sow thief. His words to the angry crowd had never left Anna:

There is no justice in the world's womb. Justice is forged by men.

Both the world and men had failed, Anna supposed. As she wandered up the canal with the first stains of pale orange light breaking across the sky, she tried to imagine what horrors she'd find. She'd been walking for hours, or so it seemed, and it was impossible to resist the flood of memories that she'd become so adept at blocking out. Thoughts of an old home, of dusty towns where the wicked resided, of childhood dreams involving living somewhere lush and peaceful. Physical sensations barely registered with her anymore, having congealed into a wash of pain and dying nerves. Several times her legs had failed entirely, and Shem lifted her beneath her shoulder and returned her to her feet.

Light beamed down from a grated opening in the distance. It had come into view after turning a rare corner in the canal, but there was no celebration at the sight. Even the children held back most of their elation and conversed in tired mumbles; the hall sisters had abandoned quieting the children long ago. In fact, the din of the streets above, which was curiously absent of river-tongue or commands, drowned out any hope of steady conversation in the shadows.

Nothing about their march was inspiring, let alone victorious.

A hushed exchange of flatspeak echoed at Anna's back, and soon Bora appeared at the girl's side. Her eyes were glassy but present, betraying the exhaustion that was surely taking its toll. "You can leave the ruj, child."

Anna had almost forgotten she was carrying it. The weight was a constant presence in her hand, pulling her down as much as her pack and the burning in her legs. "I'll hold onto it," she said, her voice scratchy. "I don't know what we'll find when we emerge."

It seemed surreal to discuss the surface. It was just above them, but the horrors that had transpired near the basin kept Anna's mind tethered to the depths. It wasn't pity for the Dogwood, but fear of the unknown. Fear of worse things to come. "Do you think we killed them all?"

Bora raised her head to the grate. "No. But they lack the gift of true seeing and prediction. They may believe you dead."

"Then I don't know what we'll do," Anna said. She was stunned by the honesty in her words. "We can't stay in the city."

"A kator's rail sits above us," Bora explained. "They ferry the water to this place, child."

A kator. After so many hours of terror and fleeing, hearing the word lifted her heart and mind. They could go anywhere. They could leave Malijad and never look back, and—

And Anna didn't know where to go.

Even in the sands of Hazan they wouldn't survive more than a week. Shem could provide water, but there was no promise of it being drinkable, or even infinite. There was nothing to hunt, nothing to farm, and nothing resembling safety until they reached the plains, which were just as foreign but hardly as sun-scorched. Better than anything else, however. Especially if they could find the Halshaf monasteries.

"Bora," Anna said, working past the dried saliva along her tongue, "how much do you know of the plains?"

"War will come to them, in time."

Anna's chest tightened. "So where will we go?"

"Your mind will guide you."

"I don't want my mind," Anna hissed. She fought to conceal her bitterness from the foundlings, who could no doubt read her tone better than her tongue. "I want your guidance, Bora. We're not cornered anymore. Don't make me fight my way out."

"You assume I have a path to follow," Bora spat back.

"You always did."

"And now her breaths are gone. At one time, I told you that we were beholden to masters, child. But perhaps there is greater enslavement to be found in total release."

"I don't understand," Anna said.

"Exactly." Motes of daylight shimmered in Bora's eyes. "You'll be a slave to the end so long as you exist without a calling, child. Leave your marks while you still can."

Anna drew in a long breath. "Then we'll go to the Halshaf. Wherever we can find them, I mean. They're already expecting the foundlings."

"So we will."

"But not me," Anna said. "Nobody was ever expecting me, were they?" Bora shot her an inquisitive glance.

"The tome-men," Anna explained.

"What of them?"

"They don't exist, do they?"

"No."

It was a question that had crept into Anna's mind during meditation, but fear of the answer always drove her thoughts away. Hearing Bora confirm her nightmares did little to calm her.

"I've taught you as much as I could."

"I don't have any answers," Anna whispered.

"Nobody does, child. But you have the clearest concept of the void. In time, you might master the markings."

I won't master anything without masters.

They trudged closer to the grate in silence, though Anna's unspoken words burned on her tongue. It was futile to ask further questions about hayat, but there was so much to ask, so much to discuss. "Bora," she said grimly. "What do you mean about war?"

Bora took the ruj without contest from Anna's hands and moved to the ladder before staring up into the grate's latticework. Wreathed in day's nascent light, and in spite of the bloodstains and soot and mud, she was radiant. "It's best not to think of such things, child." Then she clambered up the ladder, as lithe as ever, and unlatched the bolt on the grate's underside. "*Shar'oz.*"

Shem lumbered back to Anna's side after having walked with some of the hall sisters for the final leg of the journey. His rune staved off the need for sleep, but his stubborn insistence on appearing strong for Anna made him smile. "I help you up," he said. He moved toward the ladder and up the first two rungs, then held out a vein-wrapped hand. "Come, come."

Bora had already ascended. She now loomed over the opening like a watchful raven, squatting down to make eye contact with Anna.

The procession was eerily quiet at Anna's back. She wanted to turn and command them to speak, to move past her, to look anywhere but upon her. *I'm like you,* she wanted to yell, but reality disputed the words. Instead she approached the ladder, straining to lift her leg onto the slick metal. She winced away from the blackened, fraying flesh along her shins. Reaching upward, she locked hands with Shem and let him draw her up easily. The pressure and pain fell away, and she climbed toward orange tendrils in the sky, toward Shem's unbroken gaze.

Bora and Shem pulled Anna through the opening when she reached the final rung. Her eyes were shut against the light and the throbbing in her legs, but she felt the warm winds rushing over her, brushing hairs past her face and dancing through the folds of her ruined dress. Through a bleary gaze she saw the black forms of setstone rising to the morning clouds and beyond. She saw passersby glancing at her and stalking past in clumps, too absorbed in their own chatter to take note of a pale-skinned, broken girl.

As she glanced sidelong, she realized she wasn't lying on the packed street at all, but was cradled in Shem's arms. His knees supported her back, and he tilted her upward to look at the streets that reached in all directions, at the low arches and swooping canvas of bazaar stalls near the markets, at the nearby kator at its docking platform. Soft sunlight played over its surface in orange bands, and Anna couldn't imagine anything more enchanting.

"Help her to her feet," Bora said, pacing in tight circles around the grate's opening. "*Shara*, Shem."

Anna's eyes drifted shut as she listened to the drumming of tiny hands and feet ascending the ladder rungs.

Every time she plunged toward sleep, shocks ripped through her spine. Her eyes remained still and sealed, dimly aware of Shem's prodding to keep her up. She pressed herself against him and trusted him to guide her up, leaning upon his shoulders and arms, confusing his movements and strength with the way her mother had carried her to bed on long summer nights.

"Child." Bora's voice cut through memories of auburn hair and sap-smelling hearth fires, forcing Anna's eyes open. The northerner stood midway down the street amid a stream of passing merchants and laborers, beckoning her and Shem toward the kator.

"That's strange, Shem," Anna whispered, wiping at her eyes to clear the blurriness.

A pace away, his hands still wrapped around her shoulders, Shem cocked his head to the side. "How you are feeling?"

Ignoring the Huuri's question, Anna continued to stare at the kator beyond Bora. She tried to parse its sedentary quality, how it dominated the entire street without any trace of watermen or Dogwood or the scavengers that pilfered shipments. "It shouldn't be here, should it? It's empty."

"Come," Shem said. "We go to Bora."

To Bora, Anna weighed in her head. She latched onto the idea and its safety, and set out with awkward steps across packed earth. At her side, the foundlings and hall sisters formed loose rows flowing in the same direction, making no attempt to hide their curiosity about the city. Those in the streets were even more mystified. Some collected in crowds or halted their wagons, perhaps due to the remaining Alakeph and their bloodstained vestments. The procession lumbered past as though trapped in the eye of a storm, slowing the gusts around them and draining noise from the air itself. They were an anomaly, an omen beyond explanation. Muttering and shouting and whispering fell away as they walked forth.

Anna lifted her head and focused on Bora's sigils through the press of bodies, trying to predict their movements and failing as the sun crept from beneath cloud cover and blinded her. There was something erratic in the northerner's blood, something guarded against the moment.

Bora lifted her head to the muddied skies, the loaded ruj resting harmlessly against her thigh. "They've come."

Stillness fell over the streets in a manner more suited to a startled herd than crowds of onlookers. It was sensory overload, and those lining the roads simply shied away or shrank back from the soldiers, as though they might be trampled or beaten for standing anywhere near the targets. There were hundreds of the Dogwood, it seemed, all swelling forth through the civilian ranks like blood squeezed from a pricked fingertip. They bore helmets and shoulder plates and fastened cuirasses with films of heated sand, and their ruji jutted out to form an all-encompassing firing ring. Shadowed warriors materialized on the balconies and terraces above, and more shooters burst from nearby doorways and storeroom stairwells, deploying behind stacked crates on the street's western approach. Their mass blocked off the frontal approach to the kator as well as the path back to the grate, though their weapons were enough to dissuade flight. When the clapping of boots and the rustle of metal against leather faded, the crowds resumed their murmuring.

Bora was motionless at the head of the procession, showing no alarm. The dullness in her gaze suggested she was counting granules of sand along the road.

Shem curled his fingers around the back of Anna's arm.

"Don't," Anna whispered. "Be still, Shem."

His grip loosened.

In the calmness, Anna met the hooded eyes of the Dogwood men and wondered which would be her killer. It seemed incredible that they'd even reached the kator, let alone nearly fled. But perhaps that illusion had been their intent all along. For wicked men there was nothing sweeter than the death of hope.

"*Pohamov!*" The command was grating within the silence, and some of the ruji wavered as their bearers flinched.

But something grew more familiar about the voice as it folded again and again through Anna's mind, circling closer with each pass to the truth.

The tracker shouldered his way through the press and stood against the kator's darkened chrome. The corners of his burlap stirred in the breeze like cropped horns. "Anna," he called, free of scorn.

She shivered with her eyes cast low. She avoided Shem's eyes and shifted her arm out of his grip, then gently shouldered her way through the crowd. Despite the gnawing aches down her shins, she forced herself to walk with Bora's grace.

Beneath fetid burlap folds, the tracker's rune bled its light as brightly as it had the day it was carved into his flesh. Its stare was more intense than any of the soldiers crowding her periphery, more unreadable than the black slits of its owner's mask.

"You're alive and well." The tracker's chest fell in a rush. To the uninformed, it could've been mistaken as relief. "Most of you."

Anna edged past Bora and glared at the tracker.

"All good things have their end." The tracker edged forward with a hollow laugh. "By the Grove. You ought to see the fucker's face, Anna. It'll take the herbmen a cycle before he can open both—"

"I hate you," Anna said.

The wind shifted. He tipped his head lower and darkness creased his mask. "Come back with me. We'll drown out the bad blood in arak and roasts, eh?"

Silence.

"No more orza to bitch, and moan, and bitch," the tracker groaned. "Nahoran fucks left a small mess, but it'll be swept away by dusk. Just means more casks for the rest of us. Almost too much to go around. Almost."

"I'm done with you."

"Done with *me?*" the tracker asked. "Without me you'd be minced somewhere down in those canals. Who do you think called off Teodor's hounds?"

Anna's haggard eyes were slate.

"Oh, don't tell me the *sukra* got to you that deeply." He shook his head, his voice like the scratching of frayed bowstring. "I see your wit, Anna. You can see a fair peace offering when it's dangling in front of you."

"There is no peace," Anna said. "You killed them."

The tracker leaned around Anna to inspect the mass of foundlings, hall sisters, and Alakeph, offering only a weary huff in response. "You must mean the shepherd for this tired lot, right? You can pin that to Teodor."

"You knew."

"Huh." The tracker crossed his arms. "Must've lost my ability to hear thoughts, then."

"That must be what Teodor did," Anna hissed. "That must be how he knew what happened."

The tracker remained quiet, but slowly the realization flickered in his eyes, biting through the dusk petals and bloodshot tendrils. "In the forest."

"In the forest." Anna clenched her jaw. "You're not a friend."

"Partners. I never said friends."

"Then I'm walking away," Anna whispered. "You'll need to kill me."

His shoulders hunched in an anxious curve, and his eyes widened to fill the mask's slits. "He's a sadistic breed. I never surrendered your secrets. Not the ones you'd cry about."

Anna's face flushed. "You told them everything."

"Didn't think they'd corrupt the report like that." For better or worse, a note of earnestness had crept into his voice. "We can rein him in. Now that he's seen the shit that he slops in from the pens."

"There's no change for wicked men."

The tracker gazed skyward. "Might be."

"And no forgiveness," she finished.

"But you'll plant your boots and stand by them," the tracker said. "Forget every trace of Rzolka, Anna. Forget your blood and your home. Just like she taught you."

Anna's lips shook. "I'll save it myself."

"She *wants* you to think you can." The tracker moved closer, but Anna shied away. "Do you remember the tomesroom, girl? How that iron slipped across your neck? Warm blood all over you?"

Anna glowered.

"Lost causes come and go. That's the fucking flow of war, really." He sighed. "I saw something in you, Anna. Something you can't toss onto a pyre like any other mound of flesh. We were fated to be partners, you and I. Kindred souls, bound for glory or the Grove, eh? There's a will to fight in you, and gifts, and if you—"

"I," Anna said softly, her brittle words enough to silence the tracker, "hate you."

"You need me."

"Kill me."

The tracker folded his arms, scoffing. His laughter started out gently, tucked away beneath his burlap, before he raised his voice. "Ever lie awake and dream about those green fucking fields?" He leaned in with a monstrous shadow. "Peace can be sweet, Anna. It can be warm beds and warmer tits. Pipes so full that they overflow. Might even be young blood in your family, and little girls running round the house, calling you mum and clinging to your skirts." He stepped back. "But peace isn't bought with salt, girl. It's won with blood. We've reddened these fields enough."

Anna blinked back burning tears. "And there's still no peace. There never will be."

"Not if you walk away," the tracker said. "Teodor has the blood of wolves. Once he has a scent, he'll hunt you endlessly."

"And you can't stop him," Anna spat, "because you have a coward's blood."

"Because we bled together," the tracker said. "Because we made oaths. I always keep my promises, girl. Always."

"You can't promise me peace."

"If you come now, I might. A touch of groveling to Teodor, some alone time to wash the blood from your pretty little hairs, few runes here and there . . ."

Anna took in a measured breath. "Death is easier."

"Back to this, are we?"

"I won't go with you."

"And them?" The tracker gestured over Anna's shoulder at Bora, at Shem, at the masses of nameless and innocent followers held at the barrels of ruji. "Teodor wants your fucking scalp for what you did. Imagine what he'd do to them." The tracker's eyes lingered on Shem and his fresh runes. "Oh, the fun he'd have with the Huuri *korpa.*" When he noticed the twitch in Anna's brow he laughed. "Ah. Taken back, girl. Your friend."

The streets were entirely silent, the crowd likely only able to understand flecks of the river-tongue, if anything. Yet the gravity of the exchange muted them.

Anna looked upon the kator with a blank mind, caught between what could've been and what was. "We'll make a deal, then."

It caught the tracker off-guard. "Deal?"

"My word and yours."

"Go on," he said.

"Let them leave." Anna nodded toward the kator. "They leave and you don't hunt them, and I'll return with you."

"That simple?"

"I suppose."

The tracker's head lulled to one side. "Could be that you turn on us as soon as you get back, no?"

"Then you'll kill me."

"Hardly. Teodor'll have his way before he kills you."

"Even if I help you, it could happen."

"I wouldn't let it," the tracker said. "Consider it part of the deal, Anna."

Anna met the tracker's clouded eyes and weighed the truth of his words. Compared to the wicked men in the *kales*, she believed him. There was grief that had neither reason nor any attempt at concealment.

"You have to swear that you'll leave them alone," Anna said.

The tracker's nod was a solemn thing. "On my word."

"And you can't send these warriors after them."

"Pedantic." The tracker chuckled. "Fine. It's agreed, girl. Send them off, and let's be quick of it."

Anna turned away from the tracker and felt a thousand stares wash over her. Their sigils were a nebula woven together by hayat and countless essences, distilling down from noble bloodlines and bastards and the wickedest seeds born of violence until they congealed into an ocean of colliding symbols. They swam before her and coalesced and diverged as though speaking, more connected than Anna could ever be to another person, even to her own kin. It was beautiful, striking, transient. It simply *was*.

Orders for movement in flatspeak echoed down the lines, and the long march to the kator began with the foundlings and the hall sisters in a tired, beaten slog, staring at Anna with faint understanding as they passed her and brushed her hands with their own. Their sigils drifted past like the first snowfall of autumn, dancing down and reveling in their beauty before they faded among the leaves. The Alakeph passed her with bowed heads.

One by one they followed the Dogwood's paths and vanished, trickling away until only Shem and Bora remained in the street. Shem, as always, wore a look of perpetual bemusement, and the brightness in his eyes suggested that he hadn't deciphered Anna's decision. Bora, by contrast, wore a look Anna had never seen—resignation.

There was a relaxed curve in the northerner's back that would've been normal for anybody else, but Bora looked broken without her tension. Only the hard amber of her eyes preserved her identity.

I'm so sorry, Anna wanted to say. But to whom?

She wondered, as Bora pressed Shem's back and urged the boy forward, if the apology was meant for herself. If Shem could even survive in the sands without her affection, without her touch.

"We go," Shem said as he approached Anna, the skin around his teeth stretching back to expose his smile. He took her hand and waited. "We go?" The words stalled in Anna's throat, yet she held his gaze. "Of course," she managed at last, almost too quiet to hear. "I'll meet you on the kator." For all of Shem's skill in reading her and drawing out her fears, he failed in that moment. He gave her hands a last squeeze and began his patient march to the kator, his shoulders drawn back in triumph.

Finally came Bora. She stood before Anna with the ruj clutched in her hands and angled toward the dirt, her face caked in grime and torso splotched with blood. New hairs sprouted along her scalp like the bristles of a boar, and for reasons Anna couldn't understand, she wanted to touch the northerner's head and trace the sigils along her skull. She wanted to draw out the concentrated knowledge that she hadn't been wise enough to glean during her training.

"We always have a choice," Bora said.

"I know." She admired the way Bora seemed to already know when her words weren't finished. "You heard what I told them, didn't you?"

"I did," Bora said. "It is admirable, child."

"Sooner, please," the tracker called from the kator's platform, evidently having been midway through scolding Shem with pointed fingers. "Vital things to be done, Anna."

Bora paid it no mind. "Someday, I may have to kill you."

"You won't need to," Anna whispered. She glanced down at the ruj. "Could I have it, Bora?"

Bora realized the implication. The hard edge in her stare bit into Anna. "Press it beneath your chin, child," Bora said. "Be sure that you're committed when you do so, and maintain your aim. Otherwise, the end will come slowly."

Anna swallowed the knot forming in the back of her throat. She lowered her hand to Bora's and felt the cold metal of the ruj barrel. She glanced back at the tracker, who had torn his gaze from Shem to watch the exchange, and detected no alarm in his movements. To the contrary, he seemed relieved by the northerner's disarming.

Considering the number of ruji and blades encircling the street and surrounding square, there was little risk in an armed child.

Or so Anna assumed.

She grasped the upper portion of the barrel, and the underside of her fist brushed the top of Bora's. She felt the woman's warmth and leathery skin and tactile bones in one feeling, and in the—

A lone ruj hissed among the Dogwood ranks.

In one instant Bora stood before Anna, a placid smile on her face. Her tarnished cloak hung in pleats about her, swirling in the breeze and twisting over the dirt near Anna's heels. She was not a warrior, but a child who'd wandered the world and tucked away her loves and fears where nobody could find and break them.

In the next, she was not there.

There was only a torso shorn of its neck and head and shoulders and half of a ribcage. Bits of fractured bone, like those of a sow in a dusty market so long ago, protruded from the mess, and everywhere was bright and dark red liquid, bits of torn flesh that could not have belonged to a living creature, curving up and out of disembodied legs that—

Ringing. Screaming deep in her skull. Heartbeats. Her face stung from chips of bone and cartilage, but the pain was not real, and neither was the red, dripping pulp across her chest, or the ruptured coils of intestines spilling to her feet, or—

The body that could not be Bora toppled to one side and twitched, gushed, then fell still, the packed soil brightening and spreading its stain as it sopped up her life.

Without the sound of footsteps, Shem appeared at Anna's side and was screaming something to her, shaking her shoulders.

The street receded in her mind like the tide, rolling back and shrinking until it was only a keyhole of reality, and around that sliver of perception spun blackness and fog. In the haze, Anna walked and freed her legs from the pain, and she rebuilt the broken bodies she'd seen strewn across sand and bogs and cobblestones. Black reeds sprouted up among the mists, but she pushed through them and peeled off her shoes when the ground became too damp. Ahead was a monolith, the shape she'd seen in dreams and meditation. Its perfect sides called out to her, no longer taunting but inviting, and she approached the obsidian angles as a child approaches a fawn. Again, it was wreathed in the smog that distorted its shapes and formed impossible geometry, so far beyond the mind's capacity that it could only be parsed in divided units.

But this time, the monolith welcomed her.

Hayat curled over the mist and peeled it away, unveiling the shape Anna had waited so long to embrace. Each segment fed her insight of its brilliance and its power, and her eyes chased the revelations as they tore over the surface, faster and faster—

She saw *death*.

Before the world reassembled itself, Anna's limbs moved of their own accord. Their actions were veiled behind the mist, but slowly Anna's vision cleared and the dusty street refocused, and she saw her hands gripping Shem's collarbones. Dimly aware of the tracker as he struck the guilty Dogwood man and threw him to the dirt, she stared at the unmarked flesh below Shem's rune. With the hayat's strength and the burning shape of *death* fresh in her vision, she dug the nail of her index finger into Shem's throat.

All else faded as the translucent skin bled and split apart, gushing hayat in primordial tufts. She dragged her nail downward then bisected the incision near its origin, curving the second line and arcing it toward his jugular vein. The blood slowed, retreated, and crystallized into mottled scar tissue over the mark.

Hayat smoldered in its new vessel.

While the world was still silent and Shem's eyes wrenched open in terror, Anna leaned forward, took hold of the boy's shoulders, and brushed her lips past his ear.

"Kill them," she whispered.

It may have been devotion, or panic, or the decisive thinking of the Huuri mind. It may have been the whispers of hayat, just as irresistible to the boy as to Anna or any other scribe who knew its tongue.

Whatever compelled Shem to follow her order was potent enough.

Shem gazed past Anna and adopted the long stare of a broken man, but Anna saw the hayat boiling from his eyes, radiating so quickly that it thickened the air with hues of cobalt and azure. He was staring at the Dogwood with equanimity, as though they were nothing more than passing clouds or gentle swirls on a pond's surface.

Anna turned to see the first man writhing. His ruj fell to the dirt as he clawed at himself, desperately peeling at the gaps in his armor, contorting his limbs and neck. Blood seeped between the armor in slow trickles before it began to gush. Then came spatters of pink mist and micronized gristle.

The Dogwood man sank onto bowed legs, and collapsed.

Those flanking the warrior, bearing armor with dappled crimson sand, had barely enough time to step back before they were stricken in turn. It was a slow wave across the streets, ruji twisting and clattering and rolling, armor crunching and reddening and clashing, a thousand screams distantly flowing to Anna's ears like a field of crickets.

You earned it.

Anna marveled in their agony, their painful ends that bloodied the streets and their comrades and the air alike. In every direction the Dogwood let out their murderous screeches and thrashed until they were lifeless, piling atop one another, crawling over the packed earth and whimpering, praying to gods who could not save them.

You all earned this.

Again came the stillness. It crawled from the last clinking of armor plates and the final gurgles of fluid-choked throats. Shem wavered in place for a moment, his face speckled with innocent wonder, before leaning against Anna and slinking down against her hip.

She stood in the center of the devastation, ignoring the bodies and their red presses that formed a halo within the firing ring. She looked down at Shem and into the translucent shine of his skull, her hand resting on the back of his neck.

"It's okay now," she whispered. "It's all over."

But Shem did not speak. His breaths were slow and shallow.

"Shem," she whispered. Anna squeezed the boy to rouse him, but then a dark shape appeared at the edge of her vision. She glanced up at the tracker, whose burlap mask and tunic were bathed in blood but still intact. Deep beneath the stained fabric she saw the rune's persistent glow.

"By the fucking Grove," the tracker said. "How wrong I was about you."

"Get back."

The tracker laughed, the sound dampened by the wetness of his mask. He raised his arms in mock surrender. Footsteps drummed from out of sight, and soon the Alakeph rushed past Anna in an off-white tide, their blades and ruji poised for combat. Their half-circle forced the tracker away, though he took his steps with great deliberation.

"Simple cuts," the tracker sniffed. "Do you remember when I called them that?"

Anna held Shem closer, squeezing at his neck to wake him. She felt for his heartbeat, wondering if even a rune could be broken.

"Remember Rzolka, Anna."

"Leave," Anna said.

The tracker's voice grew deeper. "We could change everything. You and I, partners."

"Leave now." Her arms tensed as she held Shem, waiting.

"Or what, Anna?" the tracker asked. "You'll have me strung up by these *korpy*, tortured until I can't tell black from white? Think about it. You wouldn't do it to your kind. I know you far too well."

Her hands gripped Shem's neck. "You know *nothing* about me."

"Know enough," the tracker said. "Know that you wouldn't put a blade to my throat."

Something faint stirred beneath Anna's touch. Her own heart surged when she felt Shem's pulse, no matter that it was weak and fleeting. "No, I wouldn't." She raised a hand for one of the Alakeph, drawing his attention out of the corner of his eye. "Take him, please." She kept Shem upright until the Alakeph moved to her side and lifted the boy over one shoulder. "Put him someplace safe."

"It's almost touching." The tracker's eyes trailed the Alakeph warrior as he hurried to the kator. "Sweet enough to scar the tongue."

Anna straightened up. "We're leaving."

"We?"

"Go back to him," Anna said. "Tell him not to pursue us. Tell him to disappear. Tell him to break up his warriors."

"You know he won't," the tracker replied. "Not after what you did here." He clicked his tongue, gazing at the array of corpses. "He'll want your flesh as a hanging. Believe me, Anna, he has the blades to do it."

Anna held his gaze. "Tell him what I told you here."

"Best tell it to your own blades too," the tracker said, nodding at each of the Alakeph in the crescent formation. "Gifts like you have, Anna. . . . It's only a matter of time. You're wild, untamable." He laughed. "Wild things are born to be bled. And when it happens, some *sukra* will line their pouch with salt for it. Maybe even the Huuri."

The words meant nothing to Anna; they crossed over Bora's once-body, which now whispered its truth in Anna's ear:

In time, it will outrun the fastest among us.

"Tell him." Anna turned away, gazing at the kator and the silhouettes of its foundlings along the outer rails. She glanced back over her shoulder. "If you follow us, just remember what you saw here. I'll do this to everything you ever loved. Anybody you ever trusted."

Something in the tracker's broken stance told her that it was an empty threat.

Somehow, at some time, such horrors had come to fruition.

Anna started toward the kator. "Tell him," she repeated as the Alakeph's footsteps drummed in tow. Her voice was fractured, worn down by days without rest and the scars upon her cords, but it didn't matter.

No matter how loudly she spoke, wicked men would never hear her.

Chapter 33

The jinn returned that night. They were streaks of color and life upon the black crests of dunes and rocky steppes, and at times they drifted so close to the kator's rails that Anna wanted to reach out and touch them. Even with their motes of neon and pastel and hazy tints, she resisted the urge. She admired them at a distance, concentrating on the glowing pools they shed beneath their forms to brighten the sand and grit and cracked earth, unwilling to break their illusions.

It was exactly what Bora would've wanted, but there was no clever loophole of the mind to distract her from the last glimpse of Bora's eyes. To lure her thoughts from the way she'd told the Alakeph to leave Bora's remains behind, since it was merely a body and would be a nuisance to burn. It was what the northerner would've wanted, surely.

Maybe someday Anna could leave bodies behind without remorse. She could master more than hayat in herself.

She'd retreated to an empty capsule not long after they departed, delaying sleep only long enough to check on Shem and ensure that he was breathing. She'd rested for countless hours, occasionally waking to her own screams within the lightless chamber. She didn't eat, didn't drink, didn't peer outside. Instead she cycled between sleep and wakefulness in her black, thinly blanketed space, unaware of time as she meditated upon her breathing to sidestep memories of canals and theaters.

At times the pain had also woken her, and she'd been forced to douse her shins with the nearby liquor and sap mixture. Between some bouts of consciousness she fell into fever dreams of crawling around the chamber on stumped limbs. Most comforting were her dreams of Shem, of lying beside him and hearing his stories and drinking his bowl of broth on stairwells.

When the chamber had grown cold she'd opened the doors and met the waiting stares of two Alakeph warriors, who were quick to clean out her resting space and bring even more untouched rations and drinks.

Anna had merely sat down and clung to the railing, watching.

Her eyes were still latched onto a sprinting jinn when a familiar voice, both calming and Orsas-tinged, cracked her focus. "Anna?"

She turned to find Shem and an Alakeph escort just five paces away. Moonlight and starlight sank deep into the boy's skin, making his bones lustrous and his veins crystalline. He was more beautiful than anything she'd ever seen.

"Shem." She struggled to whisper, to pull herself up on the railing. Soon she felt the Huuri's hands on her arm and back, and she was upright, glancing down at the rainbow spectrum along his wrists. "Thank you."

Creases of skin around his eyes gave him a hollow, battle-fatigued stare. After the day he'd endured, it was an expected trait in any other man. But his rune should've given him a surplus of energy. "You sleep?"

Anna nodded and looked over the boy's body, searching for wounds that couldn't possibly exist. Not on the surface, anyway. "Did you?"

"Some." He struggled to focus on Anna, his attention falling away and grazing the sands. "They wait a long time to let me go. I always ask to see you." An ember of his normal self flickered in his stare, and he smiled at Anna. "You are living."

"Of course," Anna said. The low whispers of Hazani winds passed over the kator and crackled in her ears. She imagined that the Alakeph pacing the walkways heard the same sounds, but could somehow glean secrets and tales from their gusts. Old lands couldn't keep their sins buried forever. "I was worried for you, Shem."

He blinked at her. "For me?"

"I did things to you," Anna said, wondering if her words seeped into the breeze and found their way to the corners of Hazan. "What I did to you could have killed you."

"I'm protected," Shem said, touching his neck. "You see?"

"It's not about that."

"Don't fear." He grinned, but the fatigue was thick and draining in his stare. "You save us, Anna. Such blessings could not be given to me. Perhaps this is all dreaming."

Beneath his fatigue there was a thread of fanaticism that Anna could never truly unravel. After all they'd been through, his appreciation should've meant so much more than it did. She'd seen fever dreams of Shem glaring at her, crying out for the way she'd experimented on him, but neither of those came to fruition. She didn't know whether she expected his mistrust, or desired it.

"You must know you bring goodness," Shem said, drawing Anna out of her thoughts. "I protect always."

"I know," Anna whispered. "You did the right thing, Shem."

"Right?"

"To the soldiers." She gazed out at the jinn as they raced one another and plunged through dunes. "You had to kill them, I think."

"You ask, so I do."

Anna met Shem's eyes, but there was nothing to dissect. Obedience smothered what had once been innocence. "Do you feel anything for them?"

"I kill them," he said proudly.

"But did you *feel* anything?"

"Confusion," he said with a distorted brow. "I was confused because they want to hurt you. But I protect." His smile widened until it filled with curving bands of starlight. "I always protect."

She sat with Shem by the railing for some time, studying the silvery wash of moonlight as it crested the basins and carved notches out of rock stacks. Her mind juggled visions of burning cities, Galipa's weathered face, the nameless wicked men of her homeland, soldiers strung up at the gallows, fields wreathed with the black cotton over Malijad—

Her only conscious thoughts concerned the innocents aboard the kator, and what she had to do to ensure their survival.

Including her own.

Some hours later the clouds grew thick overhead, and the night became a chilling black expanse. It was silent for a time, devoid of whipping winds and Shem's tales, until a set of clanging footsteps approached from further down the walkway.

Anna jerked her head up to a blur of white fabric. Deep in her mind, somewhere juvenile and desperate, she expected Bora.

"Forgive my presence," the figure said, standing between a pair of his brethren and offering a shallow bow. It was the commander Anna had seen in the foundling hall, his voice sounding no worse for wear. "Some of the foundlings grow restless, as do our sisters."

Anna looked him over sadly. "I'm not sure what I can do."

Shem tugged at her sleeve. "See them!"

"The High-Mother does not breathe," the man said after a time. "There is a lack of guidance."

"I'm not sure I could help," Anna said. Being a leader had never been comfortable to her, much less in her current state. "I don't speak their tongue."

"We will transform your words to the most accurate flatspeak," the man said. "Nothing shall be lost."

She was certain that language was far from the largest barrier between herself and the foundlings. What could she say to those who had lost everything? She'd lived for seemingly endless cycles with the very same question for herself, and even then she'd never found true answers. Only platitudes and tricks to gaze ahead.

Maybe that was all they needed.

"I could try," Anna said.

"If you wish," the man said, "you need not use words. It is certain that your presence will be sufficient."

It chilled Anna. Nevertheless she stood with Shem's aid and made her way down the walkway, one hand gripping the cool metal of the railing and the other tucked around the small of Shem's back. She focused through her pain by staring at the Alakeph commander's bright blur in the night, burrowing into its faded whiteness and pushing on.

"Here," the man said at last, pausing at a capsule with no markings or special distinctions beyond a pair of Alakeph guardsmen. Its reflective sides receded into the dark, offering a limited suggestion of its true extent. "Low suns be upon you, Kuzashur."

She was sure her birthday had come and gone, but couldn't recall when.

Metal crunched along its rails as the Alakeph guardsmen hauled the door open, painting a square of the walkway in soft yellow light. Swells of warmth, wafting free with lavender and rosewater, bled into the night as Anna wandered closer. Scattered cries and hushes overtook the whistle of the winds.

She stepped into the capsule on her own, having released Shem and concentrating her efforts on dousing the pain. There was no strength to be found in a girl who walked on the legs of another.

They were huddled in circles around small oil lamps and candles, their faces scarred and rosy-cheeked and etched with lines far deeper than their youth deserved. Blankets bundled them together, and the hall sisters wrapped their wide arms around the outside of the clusters, whispering assurances in flatspeak. The more she stared at them, meeting the eyes of boys and girls—some a bright Hazani gold, others pale blue or green—the more she realized that their ages were of no import. They were all bound by suffering. They all breathed.

And as the attention of the chamber rolled toward her, an unstoppable force that demanded silence with each set of new and reverent eyes, Anna realized that the commander was correct: She wouldn't need any words.

And yet she opened her mouth to speak, to offer whatever comfort could be derived from one sufferer to another.

At the back of the chamber, almost dwarfed by her lone candle and the shawl draped over her head and shoulders, was a Hazani girl. Unlike those around her, her skin was dark and featureless. She had no sigils.

No essence.

And as Anna's eyes lingered upon her, the gesture returned with a burnished stare, they looked upon one another as kin.

Schisms

If you enjoyed *Scribes,* be sure not to miss the second book in James Wolanyk's Scribe Cycle.

Keep reading for an early look!

A Rebel Base e-book on sale July 2018.

Chapter 1

When Anna donned the wool shawl of a goat herder, she'd thought nothing of murder. There had been only wind skittering over the lip of the rock overhang, the dry shuffling of boots and cloth wraps, the creaking of trigger mechanisms being locked in place. Four hours of collective meditation had settled her mind and made violence foreign to the core of her being. Of *their* being, she supposed. They'd stared at one another, *through* each other, so inwardly naked and still that anything beyond compassion was unthinkable.

But violence was a language imposed from birth to death.

"Where's the fifth pebble?" Anna asked the Hazani girl as they knelt in shadow.

Ramyi gave a petulant sigh. "Five paces behind me, on the third ledge."

"Second."

By the time the girl had memorized their shelter the skies were endless mica and tufts of violet. Anna led the herders-who-were-not-herders and their goats down hills threaded by narrow switchbacks. They were a ragged procession of silhouettes and bleats and tin bells, bronze skin and threadbare coverings, a stream mingling with the wagons and traders flooding the valley's night markets. It was jarring to see how many travelers had resorted to using century-old footpaths to reach a city's outlying districts. But with the region's kator networks torn up or taxed to the point of bankruptcy, a return to the old ways was inevitable.

Some of the foundlings jogged after her and called out and rattled handfuls of beads. Years ago the children of Leejadal had been charming, practiced sellers, but eagerness had soured to hurried barks at her back. "Five stalks, five stalks only. Just for you, morza." Old men with milk-white eyes and mouthfuls of khat swiveled their heads as she passed.

They were strangers, outsiders in the most dangerous sense of the word, but not unwelcome: The market's usual well of flesh-peddlers and spicemen had dried up over the past two cycles, and only the foreign caravans—those from Malijad or Qar Annah—brought any hope of profit.

A sea of lanterns lay below her, giving shape to curtains of shifting sand, the hard edges of mud storehouses and ramshackle fencing, brick walls marred with soot stains. A black expanse of stars framed the curvature of the hills and the towers of Leejadal, which now stood high and unlit against the moon.

"Was it always like this?" Ramyi asked in flatspeak, surely knowing the answer already. She was young, but she knew better.

Anna glared at her, but the girl missed it. She missed many things.

Once they'd crossed a dry gully and its tariff checkpoint, Yatrin's broad silhouette angled back toward Ramyi. His eyes were weary yet alert, sapphire in the light of hanging lanterns. Sapphire in a damning, eastern way. He must've felt it too, as he glanced away immediately; that sort of instinct couldn't always be trained into operatives. "It's no better." He clicked at Ramyi through his teeth. "Watch the goats. They like to wander."

"Yes, of course," Ramyi said. "The *goats*." She moved on the outside of their column, using her walking stick to herd the goats back into a tight cluster. The indolence in her walk said it all: She was too blunt to respect a plan's subtlety. "What will we even do with them?"

"Sell them," Anna hissed, and that was it.

But Anna had the walk of a goat herder, the strong yet labored gait of those who'd had their legs broken and mended countless times. Woven cotton strips concealed shins laced with pink and white scars. It was systemic, really: Her body throbbed incessantly, seemingly protesting against its own existence, crying out for relief she'd stopped seeking long ago.

She watched Ramyi's steps, the way they shifted on loose patches of sand and clay and rock. The way they squandered youth and being unbroken. Granted, Anna wasn't a foundling, nor had she been born into—and lived through—constant war, but they shared gifts that came with the price of duty. Duty that Ramyi shirked at every turn. During most operations her eyes were skyward rather than sweeping, more invested in memorizing lunar patterns than surveying the essences of passersby.

Anna's blades walked like beaten dogs around Ramyi, but she couldn't cow Anna so easily.

Just shy of the market's entrance, where peddlers' booths and alcoves sat nestled between narrow brick walls, bathing in the light of eerie red lamps, the contact waited. He was shorter than she'd remembered, bundled up in mustard-shaded robes and hunched over a gnarled walking stick. His *fatiyen* trinkets—shriveled red berries, packed into hive-like clumps by dark resin—hung along his belt as usual. And she couldn't forget the essence lurking beneath his skin: a ten-pronged oval, its spindles extending through one another like tree branches. Shadows pooled beneath his hood, concealing deep folds of sun-beaten skin and a patchy white beard. Old Tensic, always milling about. Always, by some miracle, finding lodging for the herders that passed through Nur Ales-Leejadal.

"Low suns," Anna said, joining Tensic as he leaned against a dust-laden setstone well. She waited for Yatrin and the others to guide their herd off the main path, which was growing busier by the moment, then unfurled the fingers of her right hand. Her palm held a bruised flower petal, once rich saffron as it had bloomed in the meadows of the plains.

It caught the old man's eye. "You need bedding," he croaked. "The beasts?"

"Hold them in the pens," Baqir said in perfect flatspeak. "We'll let them feed and sell them tomorrow morning, if we don't take a carving knife to them for our last meal." He grinned, as did they. Especially Ramyi. It was hard to ignore his singsong voice, his slender yet graceful face that reflected little of what he'd done during his seven cycles under Anna's command.

But it crept into everybody eventually, Anna supposed.

Khara moved past them. "I'll take them in." She led the goats with her pack shifted high across her shoulders, weaving between fires in stone-lined pits and lanterns swaying in the breeze. Her frame was broader than it had been just a year before, her waist and legs corded with dense muscle. When she'd been initiated with Baqir, Anna wondered how long her honesty and humility would last. But nothing had shifted in her, warped her like Anna had seen in others. She was good for Baqir, truthfully. Ten years Anna's senior, but carrying the sense of a beloved daughter nonetheless.

They trailed Khara into the dry heat of the settlement, basking in its candles and guttering flames after the chill of windswept darkness. Tensic's lodging wasn't far, but shuffling past crowds of ink-faced workmen and shivering *nerkoya* addicts made the trip harrowing. Even the air warned them, somehow—echoes of snarling hounds, stinging smoke, the shrill cries of whores parading on the settlement's eastern terraces.

It felt wrong to Anna, but then again, everything had since Malijad.

When they reached the lodge Khara was already working to seal the paddock, her gaze sweeping up and down the nearby road and its lanes of caravans. The goats were bleating madly, stomping across the hard soil and clacking their horns together, putting a wrinkle of doubt in Tensic's thick brow.

"Come," Tensic said. He gestured to the mud building's low doorway and hanging tapestry. The lodge's five floors tapered inward as they ascended, suggesting a scarcity of engineers. "Apple or ginger tea?"

"We won't need tea," Anna said. "Which room?"

"You've come a long way. You ought to warm your blood, you know. This is our way."

"And this is ours," Yatrin cut in.

Anna stared so intently into the blackness of the old man's pupils that she forgot what she was searching for. "We'd like to rest first."

"Ah." Tensic's attention shifted to Ramyi. "Perhaps the sixth room will suit you."

The lodge's main hall was quiet and hazy with a pall of pipe smoke. Most of those lying on the earthen floor were Hazani, their tunics and wraps hanging from the rafters to dry the day's sweat. A pair of Huuri, gleaming translucently in candlelight, lay huddled together near the door with their packs clutched to their chests. But the stillness was deeper than an absence of guests; the lodge's ornate silk carpets and silver kettle sets were gone, likely converted to a few stalks or iron bars by a crafty peddler.

Déjà vu crept over Anna, thick and threatening.

Yatrin and Baqir headed for the latrine dugout behind a partition, while Khara slumped down beside the door. The woman fished a cylinder of aspen and a blade from her pack, whittling with rhythmic scrapes, eyeing Ramyi as she wandered aimlessly between cushions and hookahs. When Anna was certain of everybody's routines, she jogged up the spiral stairwell in darkness.

The muffled cries of babes leaked through locked doors on the second and third levels, but the fourth was silent. Anna wondered if that was conspicuous, or if it might lure unwanted attention from those who searched for that kind of thing, but she trusted in Tensic's judgment: Many of the veterans in Anna's company, living or dead, had arranged things through him. Sharp minds and tight lips were rare things in the north.

Anna crossed the corridor and its patches of moonlight, halting at the sixth door. She gave a soft tap with her knuckles and waited.

Silence.

She recalled her infiltrator's instructions, the exact exchange of one knock for one cough. If she hadn't been so headstrong, she might've fetched Yatrin. But she was. With heartbeats trickling through her core, Anna reached into the folds of her shawl, unlatched a shortened ruj from the clasp on a ceramic-plated vest, and cradled it against her hip.

It was the length of her forearm, strangely cumbersome despite her having trained with it nearly as long as it had existed as a prototype among Hazani cartels. Two stubby barrels housed in a cedar frame, a fully-wound cog on its side, payload sacs of iron shavings waiting beside spring plungers. Most of her fighters had taken to calling it by northern name: *yuzel*, thorn. Crude, inaccurate, unpredictable—but that had become the nature of this war.

Anna pressed her back to the wall and took hold of the door handle. Cycles of training coalesced in her stilled lungs, in the hare-twitch muscles of her wrists, inviting peace in the face of unease. Clarity gave form to violence, after all. In a single breath she shoved the door inward, dropped to one knee, swept her *yuzel's* dual barrels across the room.

The mirrorman's body was sprawled out in a wash of candlelight and ceramic fragments, flesh glimmering with slick red. Stale air and sweat wafted out to meet her.

"*Shes'tir.*" Her curse was a whisper, a surge of hot blood.

Anna stood, keeping the *yuzel* aimed at the shadows around the corpse. Piece by piece, the room revealed the scope of their work, starting with blood-spattered mud-and-straw walls. A dented copper kettle, an overturned table, a tapestry shredded by errant blade slashes. Then she saw it, gleaming like a spider web or silk strand: A tripwire was suspended across the doorway, just above ankle-level, set with enough precision to rival some of Malijad's best killers.

But subtlety had never been the way of southerners.

After edging to the left and right, examining the chamber's hidden corners for assailants she suspected were long gone, Anna stepped over the tripwire and approached the body carefully.

His face was distorted, bulging out and cracked inward with oozing welts, both eyes swollen shut. A garrote's deep purple traces ringed his neck. With some difficulty, Anna discerned that he'd also been a southerner, not a local conscript or hired hand from Hazan—he'd had naturally pale skin, now darkened by years beneath a withering sun. A mercenary. But his role—passing information through a mirror's glints—had made him their best chance for information on the tracker's whereabouts.

Their only chance, after three years of frayed leads and compromised operations.

Anna bent down and turned the man's head from side to side, noting its coldness, its turgid and leathery texture as a result of beatings. His lips were dark, and—

Ink.

A dark, narrow stripe of ink ended at the crest of his lower lip, originating somewhere far deeper in his mouth. The application had been hasty, forceful even. Using her middle finger Anna peeled the mirrorman's lip forward. A triangular pattern had been needled into the soft tissue, still inflamed with networks of red capillaries but recognizable all the same: It was an old Nahoran system, more a product of surveyors than soldiers, aiming to meld coordinates with time.

Here, now, her only chance.

Anna reattached her *yuzel* to its hook, slipped her pack off, fished out a brass scroll tube and charcoal stick. With a moment of silence to listen, to observe the empty doorway and the night market's routine din, she copied the symbol onto the blank scroll. She then furled the parchment and slipped it back into its tube.

Its weight was eerie in her pack, crushing with importance she understood both intensely yet not at all.

She hurried out of the chamber and toward the stairwell, but before she'd cleared the corridor she glanced outside, where she noticed a dark yellow cloth waving atop a post near the paddock. It hadn't been there when they arrived. Her breaths seized in the back of her mouth, and—

A door squealed on its hinges.

Anna pivoted, *yuzel* unclasped and drawn in both hands, eyes focused to the slender ruj barrel emerging from the seventh doorway. A dark hand followed, swathed in leather strips far too thick for northern fighters. She slid to the left and squeezed the trigger.

It was a hollow whisper in the corridor, perhaps a handful of sand pelting mud, a rattle down her wrists. Iron shavings collided as the magnetic coils accelerated them, sparking in brilliant whites and blues and oranges. The wall behind the shooter exploded in a burst of dust and dried grass, sending metal shards ricocheting and skittering across the floor. A scream ceased in a single gust, as bone and cloth and flesh scattered just as quickly. The shooter staggered forward in the haze, howling as he stared at the stump of his wrist.

Anna fired again.

When the dark cloud vanished the shooter's upper half was strewn down the corridor and dripping from the ceiling.

She spun away, sensing the tremors in her hands and the hard knot in her throat, and started down the stairwell. Three years of violence hadn't made killing any more pleasurable, nor even easier, but decidedly more common. In fact, time had only made her more aware of how warriors were shaped: The nausea and terror remained, but everything was so perfunctory, done as habitually as breathing or chewing. Not that she had the luxury of being revolted by that fact. As she descended she unscrewed the weapon's empty shaving pouches and replaced them with fresh bulbs.

Footsteps echoed up from the staircase's depths. Yatrin appeared a moment later, his face a mass of tension and pockmarks in the light of an alcove's candle. He had a black beard, dense, verging on wild, that nearly hid the tight line of his mouth. It wasn't that Anna forgot his youth at times; to the contrary, she often remembered it. Especially when he was afraid.

"Did I hear it?" he whispered in river-tongue.

Anna nodded. "We'll go in pairs."

Yatrin glared at her. "They could've had you, you know."

"But they didn't." Anna stepped past him, lingering in his shadow. "Dragging him out is too much of a risk."

"You didn't even tell me."

"We have our tasks," she hissed. "Listen to what I'm telling you now."

Yatrin seemed to be looking within himself, searching for some mote of calmness in the eye of the storm, as Anna had taught him so long ago. His brow relaxed. "Kill, then?"

She held Tensic's face in her mind, envisioning the creases set by a long and cruel life, the distance in his eyes that was surely born from stillborn babes and dead lovers. "Kill."

Anna picked her way through the hall and its huddled travelers, flashing hard stares at Khara and Baqir as they carved wood by the doorway. She rarely had to say more to them. As the pair stood and slipped out into the darkness, two bulky shawls among many, Anna searched the room: blankets, ceramic cups, pipes, rolled burlap covers, dark and clear bodies—

Ramyi.

The girl was a thin, motionless shape in the corner of the room, a purple silk cushion tucked under her head and black hair pooling at her back. Her shawl rose and fell with the rhythm of a dreamer's breaths.

Anna stalked toward her as Yatrin did his work behind the partition— the soft opening of skin, the gurgling of open veins, the muted final words buried behind a killer's hand. She stood over the girl and prodded her with a mud-spattered boot. "Get up," she hissed in flatspeak.

Ramyi stirred and rolled over with a scowl. "What is it?"

"Come outside." Anna glanced sidelong at Yatrin, who'd emerged from behind the curtain, wiping a short blade with the inner fold of his shawl. "I said get up."

"I'm not some hound," Ramyi whispered. She lay still, staring up at Anna with clenched hands, but finally shifted to stand.

"You need to listen," Anna said, leading the girl to the door and holding it open as a gust of cool wind rolled down from the hills. She waited till Yatrin and Ramyi had both passed, then closed it gently. Sound carried easily in the valley. "I address you as you behave, you know. Some things have to be earned."

Ramyi's jaw tightened, ready to spill all the bitter words she'd learned in the streets of Nur Kalimed, but the anger drained from her eyes at once. She was staring past Anna, more curious than concerned.

That was a warning in itself.

Anna whirled, catching a fleeting glimpse of the shadows darting between market lanes. She spotted Khara and Baqir near the road, their shawls lit by firelight and dancing in the breeze, walking with the gait of soldiers who mistook silence for safety.

"Call," Anna said to Ramyi. "Call!"

"What?" Ramyi whispered.

"*Am'dras!*" Yatrin shouted. Heads swiveled toward them from all corners of the artisan flats, drinking up the eastern tongue with a mix of fear and awe, but secrecy was now a wasted effort.

The two soldiers dropped to their stomachs.

The blast was transient, little more than a flash amid fire pits and a blossom of dark smoke. The air itself burst, fanning dust up and out in a tight wave, scattering caravan attendants, sending screams into the night. Shrapnel whistled overhead and smoldered in pockets of sand.

Ramyi stared at the wisps of smoke, huffing, fumbling for words. "So close."

Anna's hearing trickled back as Yatrin rushed past her. She seized Ramyi by the arm, pulled her into a low run toward Khara and Baqir. "That was their first strike."

More *pops* sounded, muffled but prominent, no longer frightening her as they had years before. She watched the bakers and clothiers and spicemen scrambling from the market, awash in dust and soot, and beyond them, killers flooding out of walled compounds and the cover of awnings. Six, perhaps seven, all bearing *ruji* and blades.

Anna froze, fixing Ramyi in place at the edge of the haze. She'd expected more.

A moment later, she found it.

Black shapes squirmed on the crest of the surrounding hills. Rusted plates reflected moonlight in jagged stains, gave shape to dozens of churning cogs and cylinders and an enormous firing tube. Even the southern nebulae were soon blotted out, smothered by the fumes bleeding from smokestacks and iron grates. Twitching, awkward legs, strung together with iron cables to resemble a puppeteer's monstrous spider, rose out of nothingness and crashed down on the nearby hillside, drilling through a granite outcropping, fountaining dirt over a terraced opium sprawl.

The machine's cannon wobbled on its suspension cables, coming to rest as a *ruj's* payload bit into the low wall near Ramyi. More blasts tore through the sand around Khara's head.

Ramyi gazed wide-eyed at the machine. "It's going to fire."

"Keep moving." Anna pulled her along, even as she stared at the cannon herself. "Yatrin, Khara, Baqir. Do you understand?" The order was practical, not personal. "Do you?"

"Yes!"

"Calm down," Anna said. "You need to still your hands."

Yatrin cut to the right, dashing past a dying peddler and into the cover of a tailor's shop. It was a low, sturdy box, their best hope of surviving the machine's volley. He called to Khara and Baqir, but the blasts were constant now, drowning out his words.

Another curtain of smoke and sand brushed past the flats, and when it cleared Anna saw the two fighters kneeling by a ruined brick wall, their ruji assembled and loaded. She pulled Ramyi toward the tailor's shop, whistling as she ran. Before she trained with Nahoran fighters, she hadn't known the force of proper whistling. It was loud enough to pierce nearly chaos.

Khara lifted her head to the sound. She slapped Baqir on the arm, pointing.

Anna sprinted into the shop's cover, which was cool and dark and deafening with the sound of boots scraping over packed earth. She spotted Yatrin by the slit of the far window, peering out with his yuzel in hand, calmly selecting his target in that haunting eastern way. Another blast thudded against Yatrin's cover, flooding the room with a flash of white light and sparks.

Ramyi was hunkering down behind a crooked wooden table, digging through her pack for supplies she'd memorized a thousand times in training. She fumbled and spilled a set of vials into the shadows around her knees.

Anna knelt beside Ramyi as the other two fighters dashed through the door, ruji smoking and ripped shawls exposing ceramic panels. "Be still, or we'll die." Glancing at the window slit's firing position, she saw Baqir changing places with Yatrin.

"I can't help it," Ramyi said.

"Focus on me." Anna waited for Yatrin to scramble behind the table before taking the girl's hand. It had gone cold with panic. "Remember the moment before your birth." It was an old Kojadi meditation, a paradoxical challenge to conjure vapidness, but it worked. She watched Ramyi's irises settle back into the notch of her lids.

Yatrin angled toward Ramyi, unwound his neck scarf, and lifted his chin, exposing a smooth canvas. It had been marked countless times, but Ramyi's cuts were accurate: She hadn't marred a single fighter's throat, and her runes faded as delicately as tracks in the southern woods. When she was calm.

"There are too many," Khara called out from the firing position near Baqir's. Her voice was as measured as ever, but the urgency of her shots— rapid, snapping between targets as she leaned in and out of iron-flecked cover—betrayed her concerns.

"Focus on the essence," Anna said. Ramyi's blade lingered over Yatrin's throat with a wavering edge. Two volleys clipped the edge of Baqir's cover, showering them with plumes of pulverized clay and mud, filling the room with the odor of scorched dust. "Nothing but the essence, Ramyi. Become it." While counseling the girl, Anna slid her own pack off her shoulders and slid the two ruj halves from their webbing. One trigger mechanism, locked in place for sixteen clicks of a cog's teeth, and one barrel, heat-tempered with webweave. "Don't be afraid." She slotted the barrel in its housing, threaded the components together, and slid the sixteen-pouch cartridge into the central chamber. An explosive burst near the door as Anna disengaged the bolt lock and shouldered the weapon, training her eyes on the blast zone and its gray wisps. "We'll make it out of here."

Ramyi's first cut was uncertain yet manageable. Anna could feel it in the hayat's bleed-off, the way Yatrin's crescent configuration swarmed toward the open wound with hungry curiosity. In her periphery she watched the girl's hands sweep with increasing confidence, arcing over the windpipe and past the major arteries, sweeping up to join the lines at their apex. Beyond the doorway shadows flitted past her ruj's barrel and Anna fired once, twice, three times, raking a still-smoldering brick oven and patches of blackened sand with her shots but failing to connect.

Yatrin's neck gleamed with hayat's pale luminescence.

"It's done." Ramyi's smiling lips were an icy blue shimmer in its light.

"You're not finished," Anna said, firing once more as a fighter dashed from wall to wall. "Add the bridge." Every second of pride gritted her teeth further. For all of Anna's meditation and prolific rune revelations, she hadn't been able to mimic—or merely parse—some of the designs Ramyi had gained while simply *toying* with awareness. It was a skillful waste. "Add it now!"

That startled the girl to action. Her blade slid back into the fresh protection rune, channeling hayat down parallel tracks to form a branching addition. As she carved the third line a pair of fighters burst out of a nearby compound's entryway and unleashed a coordinated volley, their shots chipping away the doorframe and drilling into Yatrin's back. Plates across his ceramic vest exploded in white puffs.

Yatrin's cry was low, buried. His flesh sizzled as it ejected the iron shavings, reformed, and grew glossy with a sheen of sweat.

Rage flickered through Anna. It was a shadow of her former self, of the days before she'd tamed her mind, but forceful nonetheless. She let off three shots and eviscerated one shooter's knees, forearm and skull, picking apart his body before putting a fourth payload squarely into his partner's jaw. The dust ceded to a sprawl of stringy limbs and blood. Khara's desperation was resonating in her, fed by the fact that Ramyi's best markings endured for an hour. Terror and haste would only bleed their efficiency.

"There!" Ramyi jerked her blade away. revealing the bridging rune: long, intricate rows, bisecting sweeps, clusters of dotted gouges, and an alien labyrinth encircling the entire design. It was beyond comprehension, stranger than anything Anna had ever glimpsed, and beyond memorization. Every bridge was unique and folded space itself, requiring meditation so thorough that there could be no divide between Ramyi and the tethering site. Not if they wanted to emerge intact.

Anna whistled again, this time competing with a tortured, rumbling scream from the market. *Giants,* she realized, wondering just how far they'd go to destroy her. She heard timber cracking and clay panels shattering and duzen-swollen feet stomping closer as Baqir slid behind the table.

Khara joined them when the air grew hot and charged, heralding the first volley from the hilltop's machine. Both of the Nahorans' faces were streaked with blood, dotted with wasp-bites of shrapnel and scalding grit. She and Baqir knelt with their hands on Yatrin's shoulders, shutting their eyes to the shop's smoke-laden dust and shouts in river-tongue.

When Yatrin's runes began to pulse, oscillating between cobalt and ivory, Anna gripped Khara and Ramyi's shoulders. She glared at Ramyi, who then held them to join the circle in tandem with the cannon's tinny howl.

Everything crystallized for an instant. Anna had no body, no singular mind, no presence beyond mere awareness of the shop as it imploded and vaporized in a hail of liquefied iron pellets.

She was there and not there. She was *everywhere.*

An unbroken ring consumed her awareness.

In the darkness of the overhang, which materialized as though she'd been plucked from a nightmare and thrust back into the world, frigid wind kissed her face. Her fingers vibrated as they vented the energy that had, in some sense, killed her.

Baqir was lying on his side and coughing up bile. Khara knelt by his side, gently caressing his back and its chipped ceramic covering. Yatrin's rune had taken most of the load, it seemed, judging by the stillness with which he gazed at Anna, and the delicate folding of his hands across his lap. Ramyi's breaths echoed through the chamber, raspy and broken. Bits of the shop's debris—mostly wool scraps and measuring string—were swept away on the breeze.

Rising from her knee, Anna slid off her pack and retrieved the scroll case. There was no guarantee it was worth anything, much less reliable in her hunt, but it was her only chance for progress amid ruins. A seed of sorts.

"Just breathe." Khara was still touching Baqir, but she'd shifted her attention to the mirage-like flickering of the rear wall's basalt. "Anna, it's open again."

Far in the distance, beyond an expanse of rock and silver dunes, the valley twinkled with blossoms of white light. Distorted aftershocks arrived with groans and playful flurries of sand.

She turned away and stared at the Nest's warped opening. There was no salvation for those trapped in a war they hadn't engineered nor fed—only sacrifice.

Anna gripped the scroll case till her knuckles ached. *You have to sprout, little seed.*

Meet the Author

Credit: Nelly Aleksanyan

James Wolanyk is both a writer and teacher from Boston. He holds a B.A. in Creative Writing from the University of Massachusetts, where his writing has appeared in its quarterly publication and *The Electric Pulp*. After studying fiction, he pursued educational work in the Czech Republic, Taiwan, and Latvia. Outside of writing, he enjoys history, philosophy, and boxing. His post-apocalyptic novel, *Grid*, was released in 2015. He currently resides in Riga, Latvia as an English teacher.

Visit him online at jameswolanykfiction.wordpress.com.